My Little Pony
Friendship is Magic

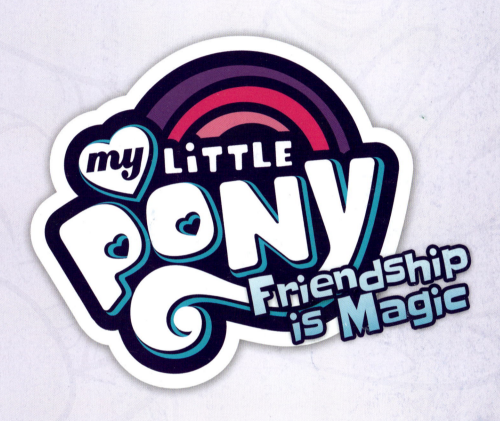

My Little Pony: Friendship is Magic

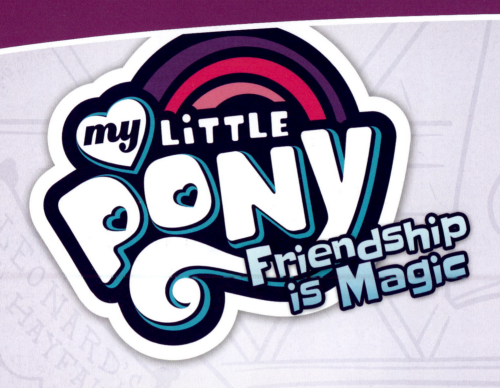

COVER BY
Andy Price

SERIES EDITS BY
Megan Brown and Bobby Curnow

COLLECTION EDITS BY
Justin Eisinger and Alonzo Simon

COLLECTION DESIGN BY
Clyde Grapa

Special thanks to Tayla Reo, Ed Lane, Beth Artale, and Michael Kelly.

For international rights, contact **licensing@idwpublishing.com**

ISBN: 978-1-68405-526-5

22 21 20 19 1 2 3 4

IDW®
Licensed By: Hasbro

www.IDWPUBLISHING.com

Chris Ryall, President, Publisher, & CCO • **John Barber**, Editor-In-Chief • **Cara Morrison**, Chief Financial Officer • **Matt Ruzicka**, Chief Accounting Officer **David Hedgecock**, Associate Publisher • **Jerry Bennington**, VP of New Product Development • **Lorelei Bunjes**, VP of Digital Services • **Justin Eisinger**, Editorial Director, Graphic Novels & Collections • **Eric Moss**, Senior Director, Licensing and Business Development

Ted Adams and **Robbie Robbins**, IDW Founders

Facebook: **facebook.com/idwpublishing** • Twitter: **@idwpublishing** • YouTube: **youtube.com/idwpublishing**
Tumblr: **tumblr.idwpublishing.com** • Instagram: **instagram.com/idwpublishing**

Originally published as MY LITTLE PONY: FRIENDSHIP IS MAGIC issues #74–78.

Coiffure Confidence

WRITTEN BY
Ted Anderson

ART BY
Kate Sherron

Cosmos

WRITTEN BY
Katie Cook
& Andy Price

ART BY
Andy Price

COLORS BY
Heather Breckel

LETTERS BY
Neil Uyetake

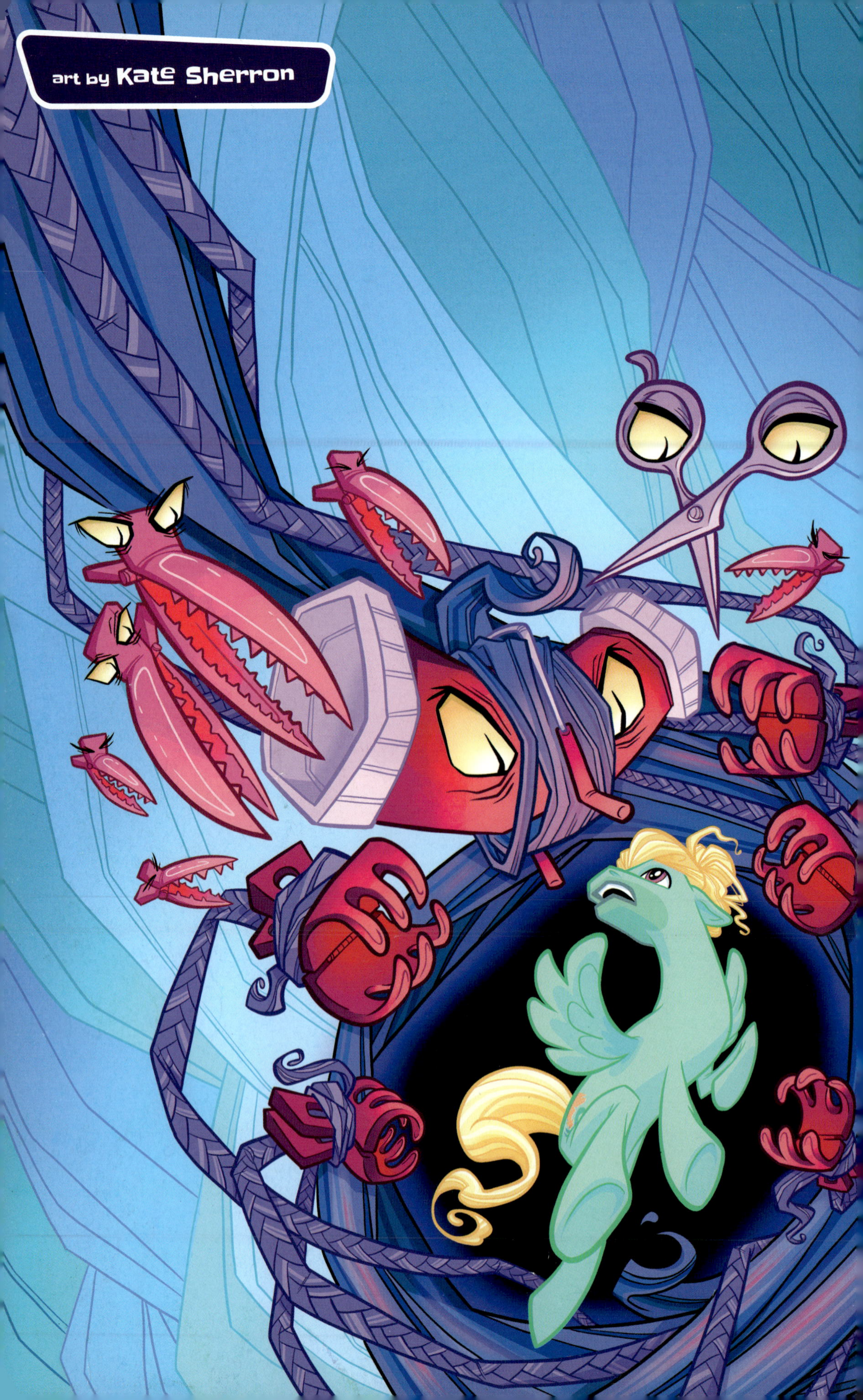
art by Kate Sherron

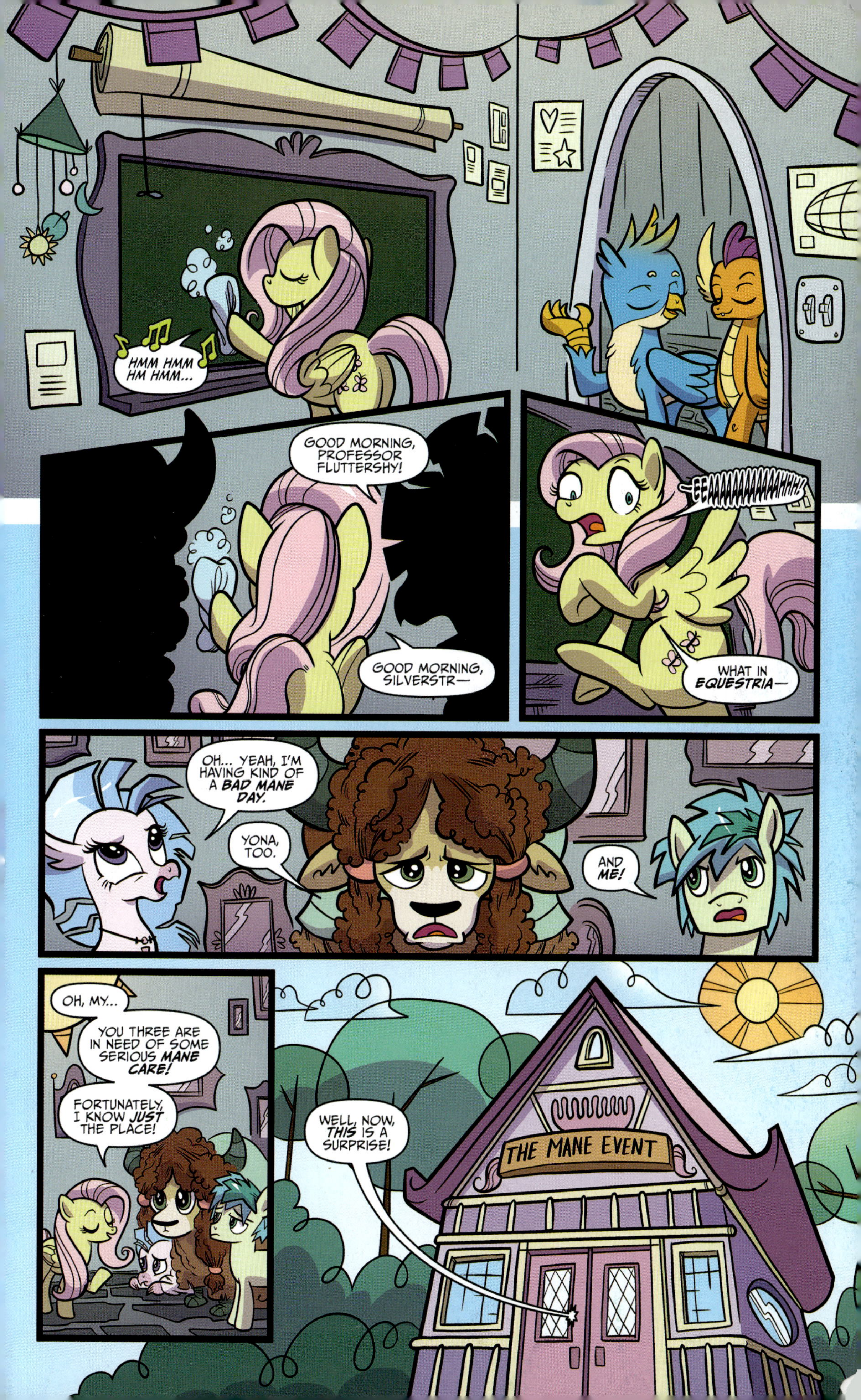
HMM HMM HM HMM...
GOOD MORNING, PROFESSOR FLUTTERSHY!
GOOD MORNING, SILVERSTR—
EEAAAAAAAAAAAAHHH!
WHAT IN EQUESTRIA—
OH... YEAH, I'M HAVING KIND OF A BAD MANE DAY.
YONA, TOO.
AND ME!
OH, MY...
YOU THREE ARE IN NEED OF SOME SERIOUS MANE CARE!
FORTUNATELY, I KNOW JUST THE PLACE!
WELL, NOW, THIS IS A SURPRISE!
THE MANE EVENT

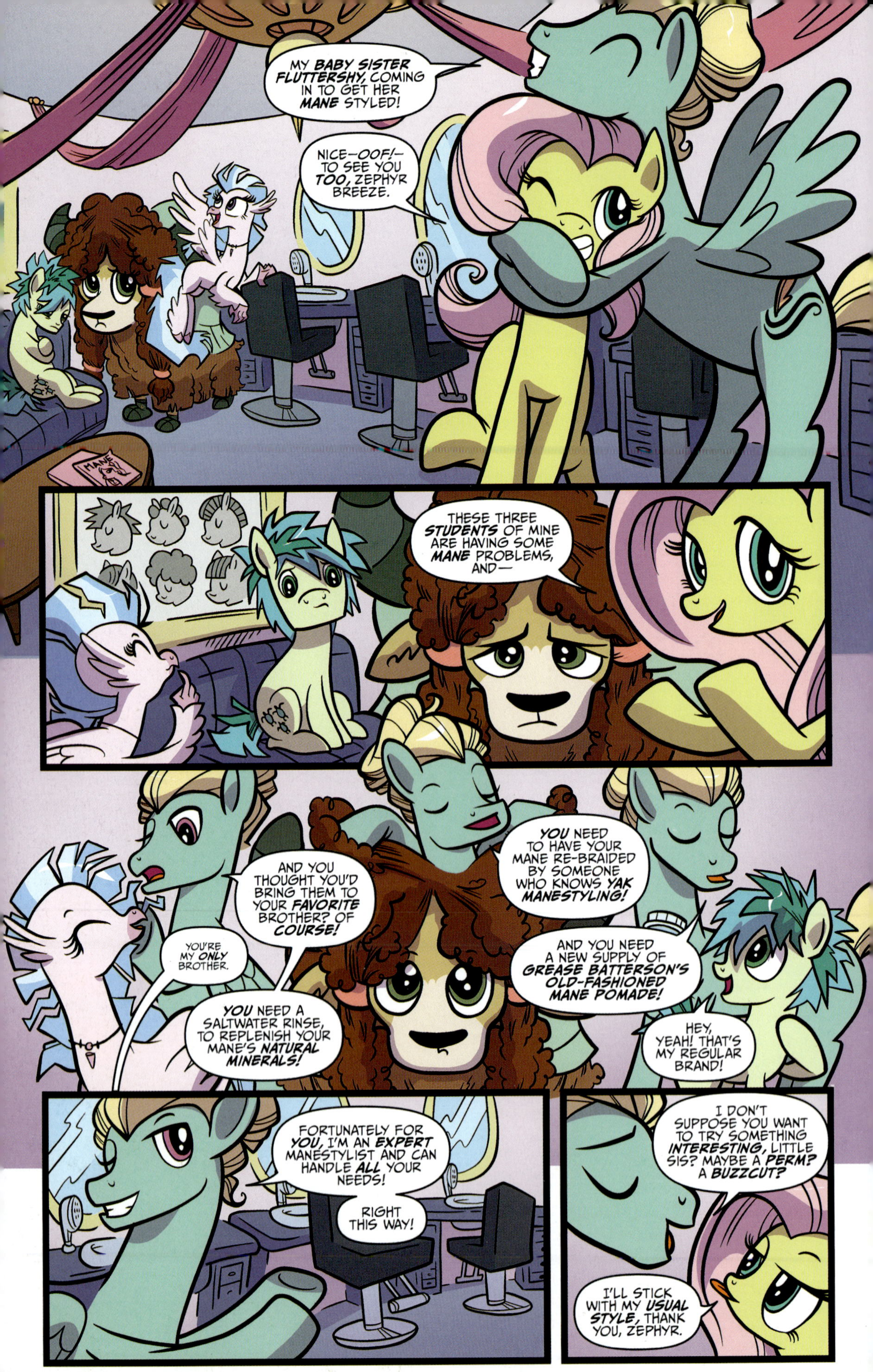

MY BABY SISTER FLUTTERSHY, COMING IN TO GET HER MANE STYLED!
NICE—OOF!—TO SEE YOU TOO, ZEPHYR BREEZE.
MANE
THESE THREE STUDENTS OF MINE ARE HAVING SOME MANE PROBLEMS, AND—
AND YOU THOUGHT YOU'D BRING THEM TO YOUR FAVORITE BROTHER? OF COURSE!
YOU'RE MY ONLY BROTHER.
YOU NEED A SALTWATER RINSE, TO REPLENISH YOUR MANE'S NATURAL MINERALS!
YOU NEED TO HAVE YOUR MANE RE-BRAIDED BY SOMEONE WHO KNOWS YAK MANESTYLING!
AND YOU NEED A NEW SUPPLY OF GREASE BATTERSON'S OLD-FASHIONED MANE POMADE!
HEY, YEAH! THAT'S MY REGULAR BRAND!
FORTUNATELY FOR YOU, I'M AN EXPERT MANESTYLIST AND CAN HANDLE ALL YOUR NEEDS!
RIGHT THIS WAY!
I DON'T SUPPOSE YOU WANT TO TRY SOMETHING INTERESTING, LITTLE SIS? MAYBE A PERM? A BUZZCUT?
I'LL STICK WITH MY USUAL STYLE, THANK YOU, ZEPHYR.

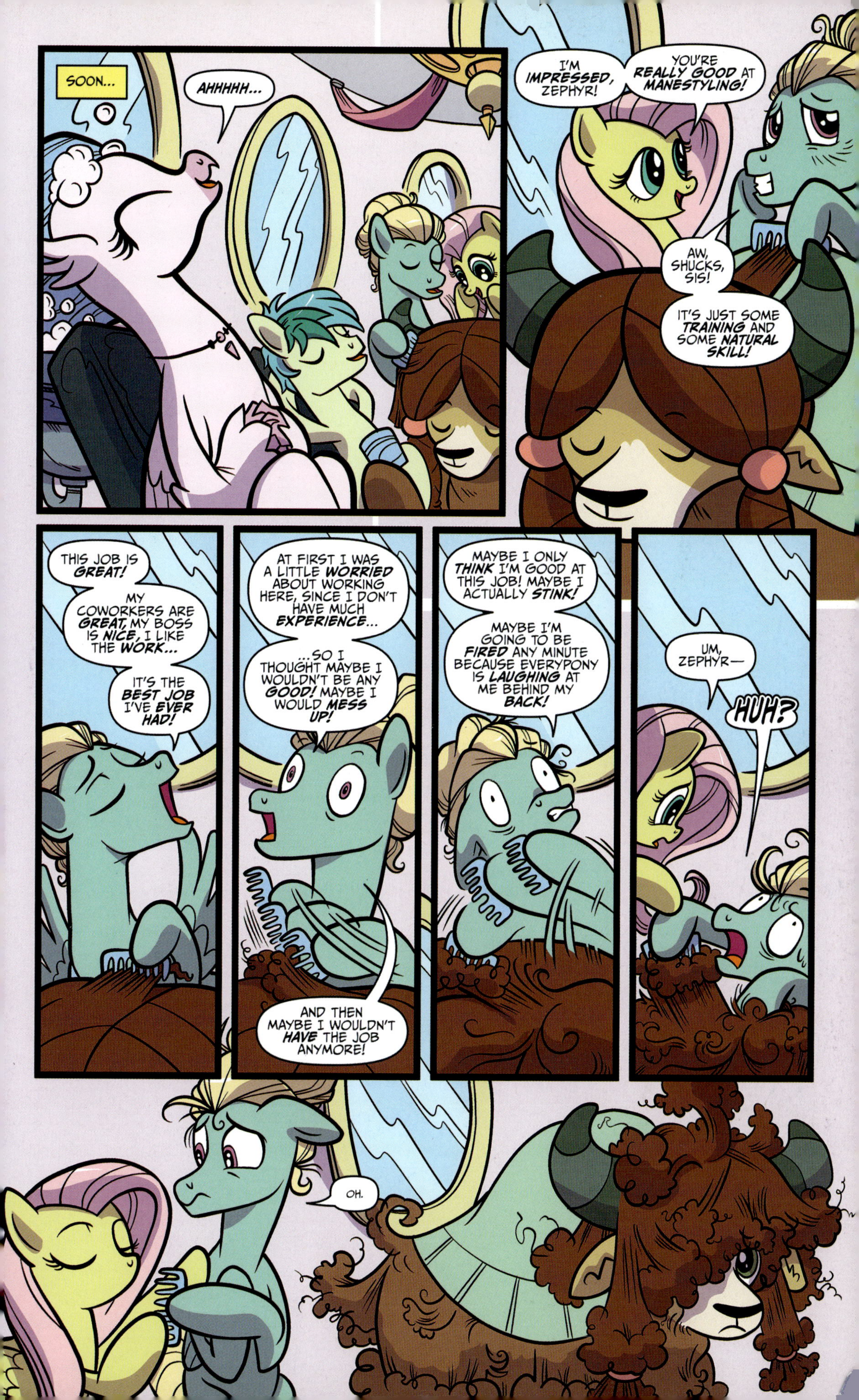
SOON...
AHHHHHH...
I'M *IMPRESSED,* ZEPHYR!
YOU'RE *REALLY GOOD* AT *MANESTYLING!*
AW, SHUCKS, SIS!
IT'S JUST SOME *TRAINING* AND SOME *NATURAL SKILL!*
THIS JOB IS *GREAT!*
MY COWORKERS ARE *GREAT,* MY BOSS IS *NICE,* I LIKE THE *WORK*...
IT'S THE *BEST JOB* I'VE *EVER* HAD!
AT FIRST I WAS A LITTLE *WORRIED* ABOUT WORKING HERE, SINCE I DON'T HAVE MUCH *EXPERIENCE*...
...SO I THOUGHT MAYBE I WOULDN'T BE ANY *GOOD!* MAYBE I WOULD *MESS UP!*
AND THEN MAYBE I WOULDN'T *HAVE* THE JOB ANYMORE!
MAYBE I ONLY *THINK* I'M GOOD AT THIS JOB! MAYBE I ACTUALLY *STINK!*
MAYBE I'M GOING TO BE *FIRED* ANY MINUTE BECAUSE EVERYPONY IS *LAUGHING* AT ME BEHIND MY *BACK!*
UM, ZEPHYR—
HUH?
OH.

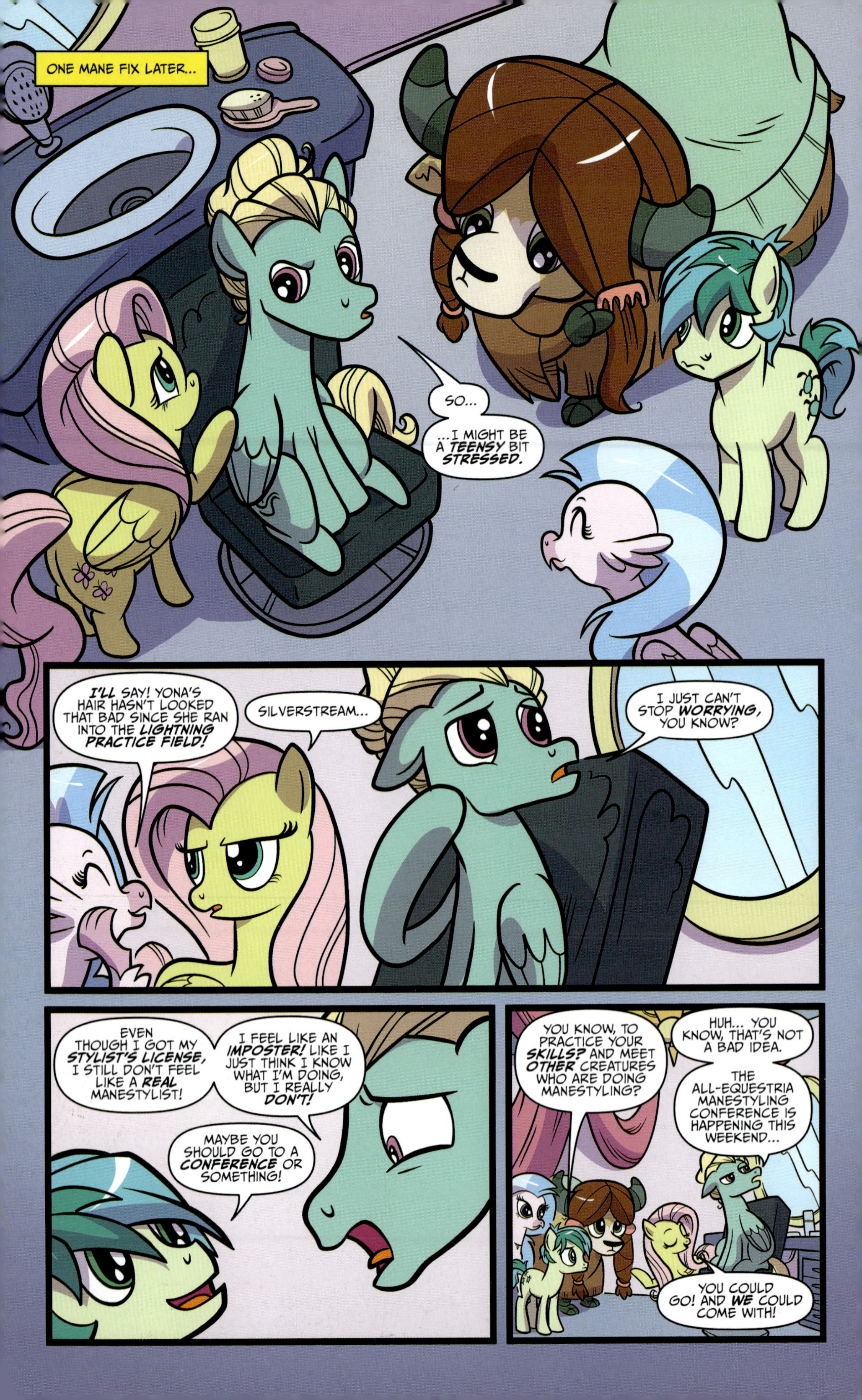
ONE MANE FIX LATER...
SO...
...I MIGHT BE A *TEENSY* BIT *STRESSED.*
I'LL SAY! YONA'S HAIR HASN'T LOOKED THAT BAD SINCE SHE RAN INTO THE *LIGHTNING PRACTICE FIELD!*
SILVERSTREAM...
I JUST CAN'T STOP *WORRYING,* YOU KNOW?
EVEN THOUGH I GOT MY *STYLIST'S LICENSE,* I STILL DON'T FEEL LIKE A *REAL* MANESTYLIST!
I FEEL LIKE AN *IMPOSTER!* LIKE I JUST THINK I KNOW WHAT I'M DOING, BUT I REALLY *DON'T!*
MAYBE YOU SHOULD GO TO A *CONFERENCE* OR SOMETHING!
YOU KNOW, TO PRACTICE YOUR *SKILLS?* AND MEET *OTHER* CREATURES WHO ARE DOING MANESTYLING?
HUH... YOU KNOW, THAT'S NOT A BAD IDEA.
THE ALL-EQUESTRIA MANESTYLING CONFERENCE IS HAPPENING THIS WEEKEND...
YOU COULD GO! AND *WE* COULD COME WITH!

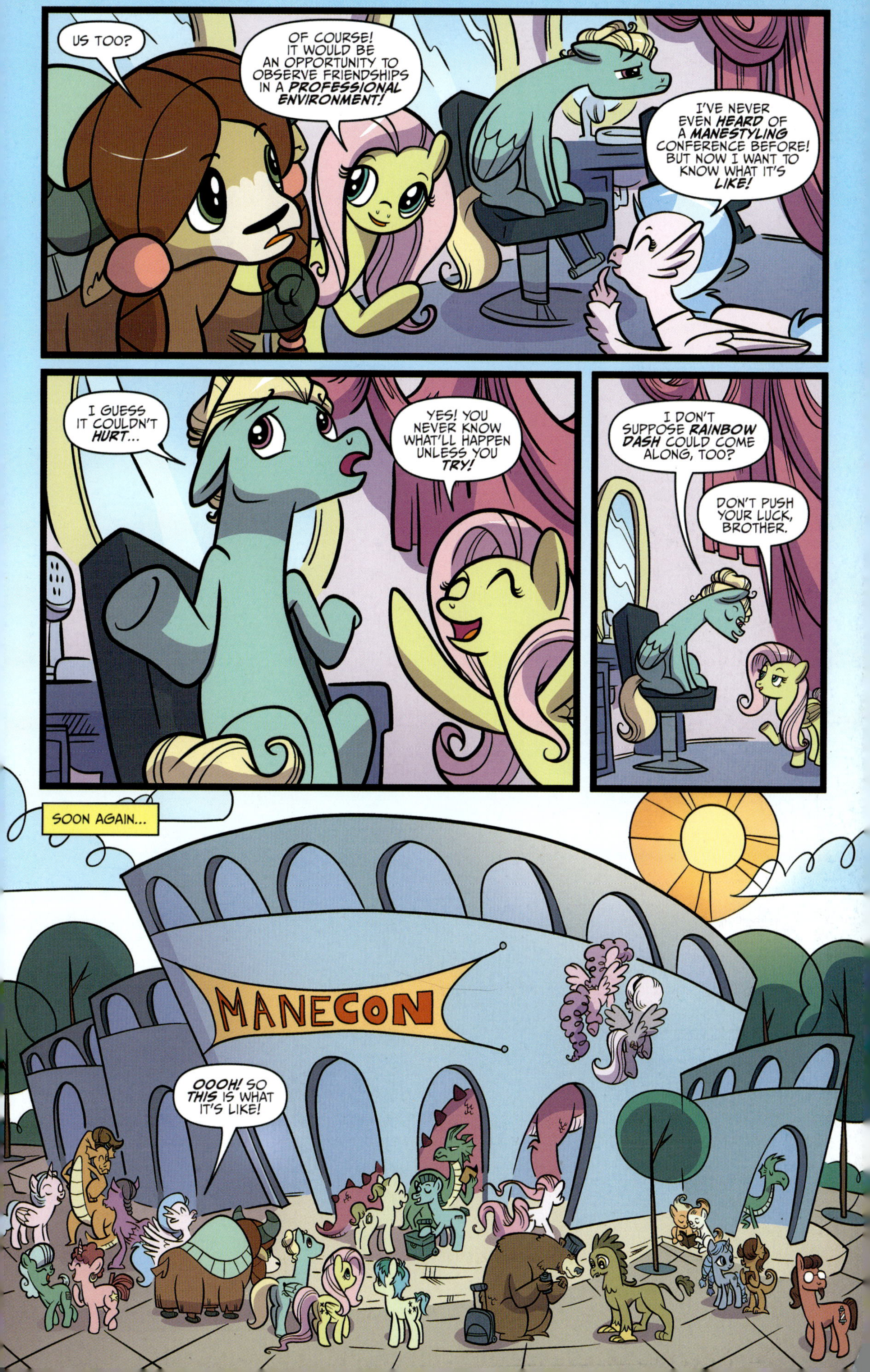
US TOO?
OF COURSE! IT WOULD BE AN OPPORTUNITY TO OBSERVE FRIENDSHIPS IN A PROFESSIONAL ENVIRONMENT!
I'VE NEVER EVEN HEARD OF A MANESTYLING CONFERENCE BEFORE! BUT NOW I WANT TO KNOW WHAT IT'S LIKE!
I GUESS IT COULDN'T HURT...
YES! YOU NEVER KNOW WHAT'LL HAPPEN UNLESS YOU TRY!
I DON'T SUPPOSE RAINBOW DASH COULD COME ALONG, TOO?
DON'T PUSH YOUR LUCK, BROTHER.
SOON AGAIN...
MANECON
OOOH! SO THIS IS WHAT IT'S LIKE!

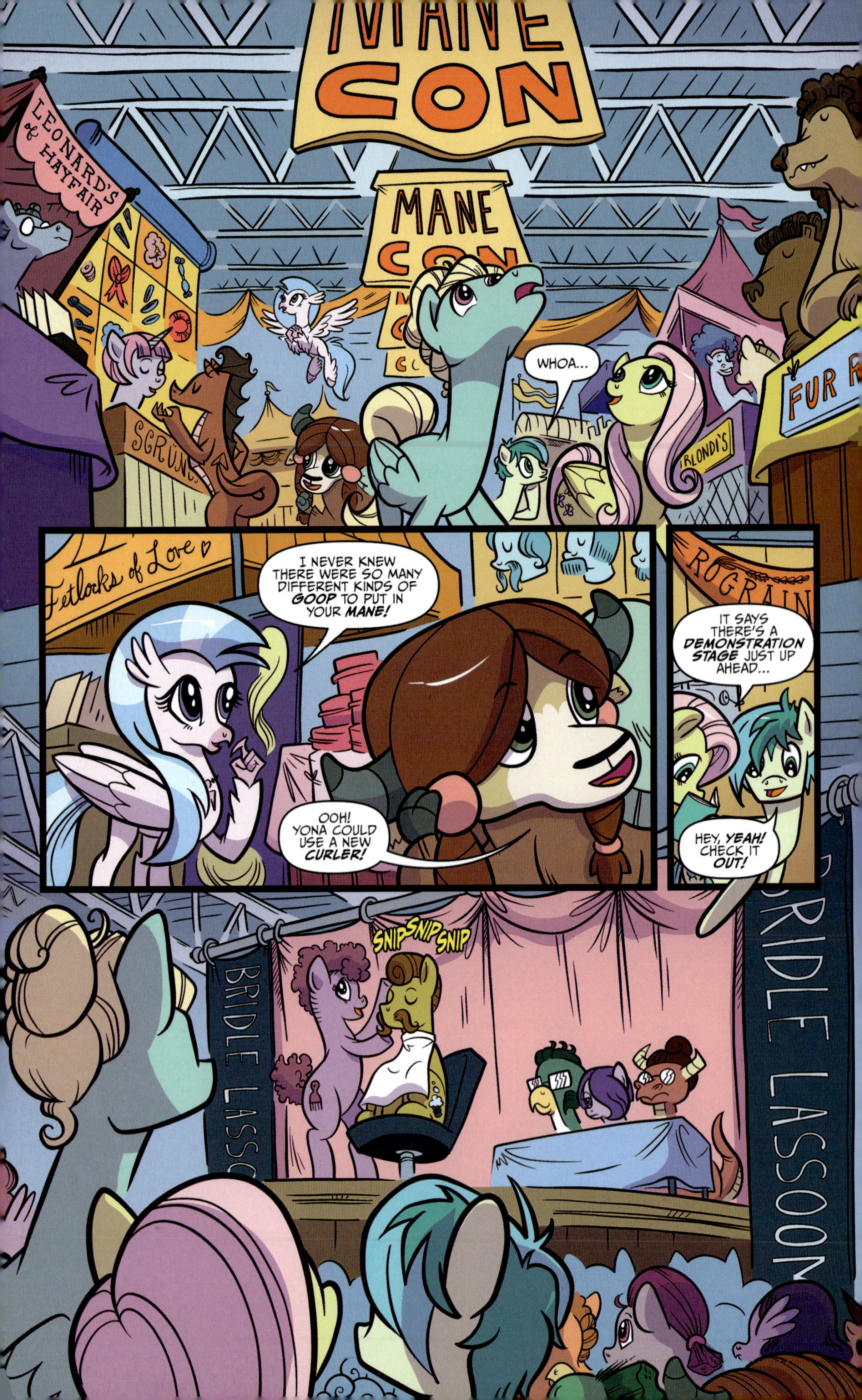

MANE CON
LEONARD'S & HAYFAIR
MANE CON
SCRÜNS
WHOA...
BLONDI'S
FUR R
Fetlocks of Love
I NEVER KNEW THERE WERE SO MANY DIFFERENT KINDS OF *GOOP* TO PUT IN YOUR *MANE!*
OOH! YONA COULD USE A NEW *CURLER!*
ROGRAIN
IT SAYS THERE'S A *DEMONSTRATION STAGE* JUST UP AHEAD...
HEY, *YEAH!* CHECK IT *OUT!*
SNIP SNIP SNIP
BRIDLE LASSO
BRIDLE LASSOON

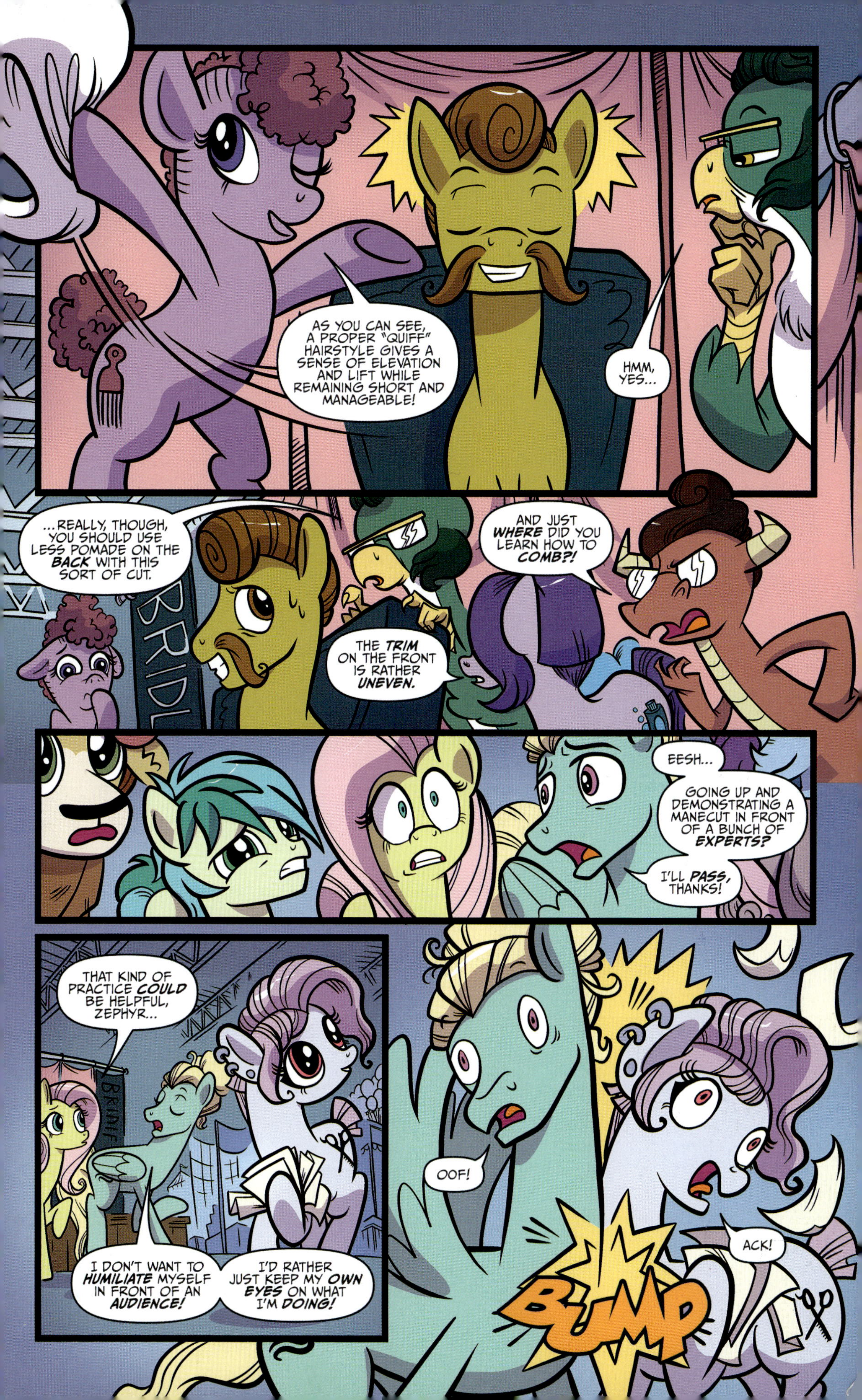
AS YOU CAN SEE, A PROPER "QUIFF" HAIRSTYLE GIVES A SENSE OF ELEVATION AND LIFT WHILE REMAINING SHORT AND MANAGEABLE!
HMM, YES...
...REALLY, THOUGH, YOU SHOULD USE LESS POMADE ON THE BACK WITH THIS SORT OF CUT.
AND JUST WHERE DID YOU LEARN HOW TO COMB?!
THE TRIM ON THE FRONT IS RATHER UNEVEN.
BRIDL
EESH...
GOING UP AND DEMONSTRATING A MANECUT IN FRONT OF A BUNCH OF EXPERTS?
I'LL PASS, THANKS!
THAT KIND OF PRACTICE COULD BE HELPFUL, ZEPHYR...
I DON'T WANT TO HUMILIATE MYSELF IN FRONT OF AN AUDIENCE!
I'D RATHER JUST KEEP MY OWN EYES ON WHAT I'M DOING!
OOF!
ACK!
BUMP

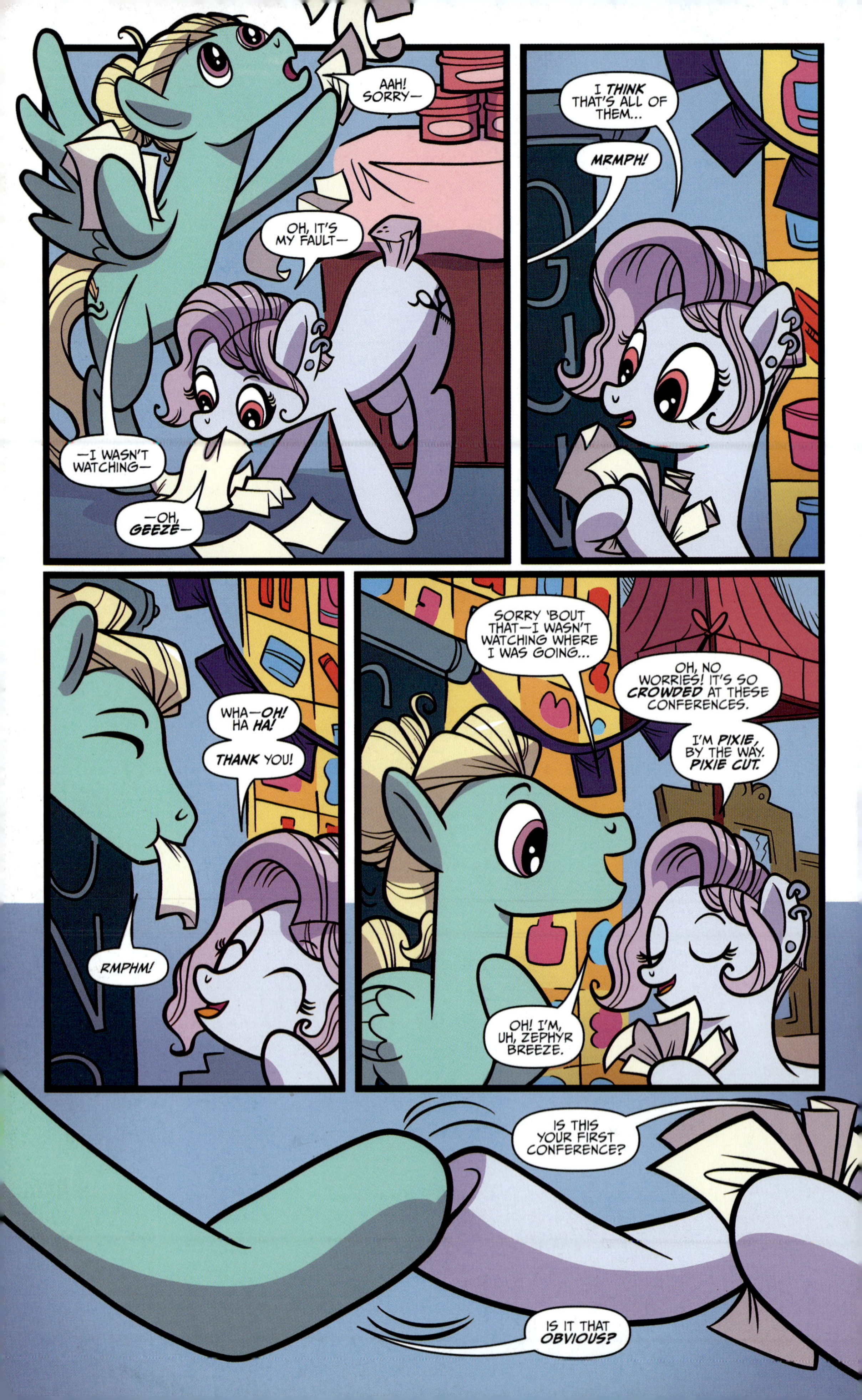
AAH! SORRY—
OH, IT'S MY FAULT—
—I WASN'T WATCHING—
—OH, GEEZE—
I THINK THAT'S ALL OF THEM...
MRMPH!
WHA—OH! HA HA!
THANK YOU!
RMPHM!
SORRY 'BOUT THAT—I WASN'T WATCHING WHERE I WAS GOING...
OH, NO WORRIES! IT'S SO CROWDED AT THESE CONFERENCES.
I'M PIXIE, BY THE WAY. PIXIE CUT.
OH! I'M, UH, ZEPHYR BREEZE.
IS THIS YOUR FIRST CONFERENCE?
IS IT THAT OBVIOUS?

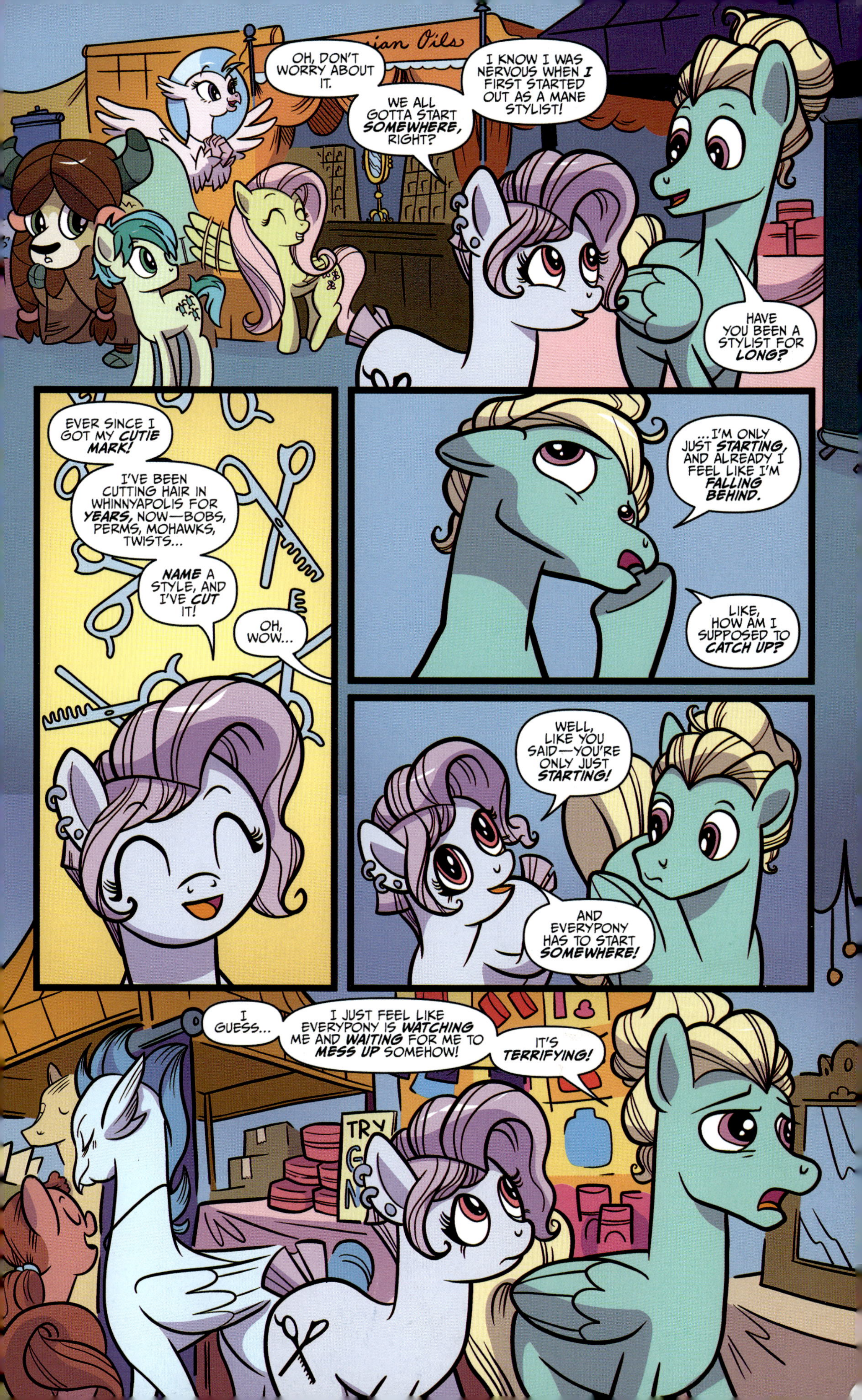
OH, DON'T WORRY ABOUT IT.
WE ALL GOTTA START *SOMEWHERE,* RIGHT?
I KNOW I WAS NERVOUS WHEN *I* FIRST STARTED OUT AS A MANE STYLIST!
HAVE YOU BEEN A STYLIST FOR *LONG?*
EVER SINCE I GOT MY *CUTIE MARK!*
I'VE BEEN CUTTING HAIR IN WHINNYAPOLIS FOR *YEARS,* NOW—BOBS, PERMS, MOHAWKS, TWISTS...
NAME A STYLE, AND I'VE *CUT* IT!
OH, WOW...
...I'M ONLY JUST *STARTING,* AND ALREADY I FEEL LIKE I'M *FALLING BEHIND.*
LIKE, HOW AM I SUPPOSED TO *CATCH UP?*
WELL, LIKE YOU SAID—YOU'RE ONLY JUST *STARTING!*
AND EVERYPONY HAS TO START *SOMEWHERE!*
I GUESS...
I JUST FEEL LIKE EVERYPONY IS *WATCHING* ME AND *WAITING* FOR ME TO *MESS UP* SOMEHOW!
IT'S *TERRIFYING!*

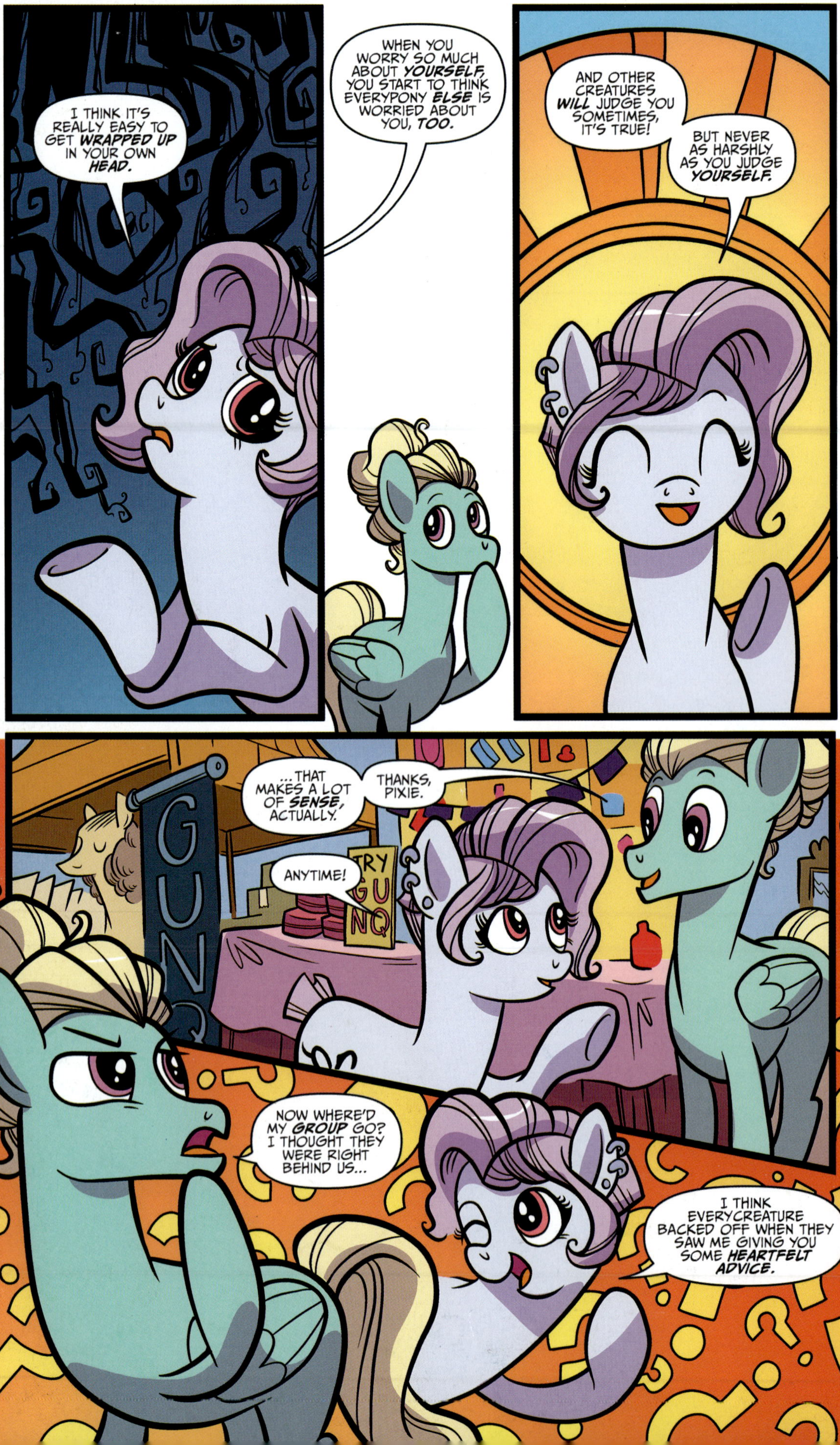
I THINK IT'S REALLY EASY TO GET WRAPPED UP IN YOUR OWN HEAD.
WHEN YOU WORRY SO MUCH ABOUT YOURSELF, YOU START TO THINK EVERYPONY ELSE IS WORRIED ABOUT YOU, TOO.
AND OTHER CREATURES WILL JUDGE YOU SOMETIMES, IT'S TRUE!
BUT NEVER AS HARSHLY AS YOU JUDGE YOURSELF.
...THAT MAKES A LOT OF SENSE, ACTUALLY.
THANKS, PIXIE.
ANYTIME!
TRY GUNQ
GUNQ
NOW WHERE'D MY GROUP GO? I THOUGHT THEY WERE RIGHT BEHIND US...
I THINK EVERYCREATURE BACKED OFF WHEN THEY SAW ME GIVING YOU SOME HEARTFELT ADVICE.

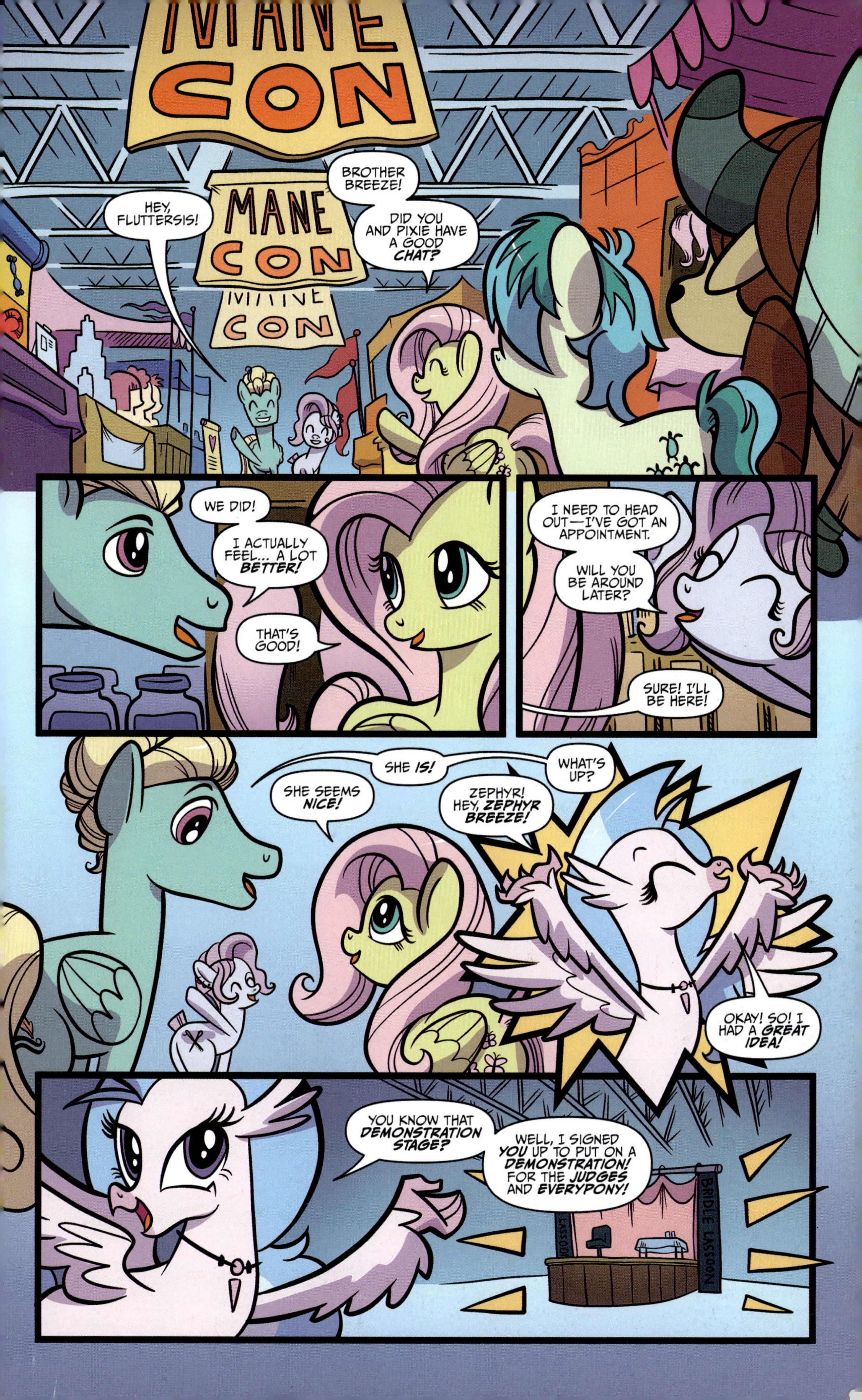
MANE CON
MANE CON
MANE CON
HEY, FLUTTERSIS!
BROTHER BREEZE!
DID YOU AND PIXIE HAVE A GOOD CHAT?
WE DID!
I ACTUALLY FEEL... A LOT BETTER!
THAT'S GOOD!
I NEED TO HEAD OUT—I'VE GOT AN APPOINTMENT.
WILL YOU BE AROUND LATER?
SURE! I'LL BE HERE!
SHE SEEMS NICE!
SHE IS!
WHAT'S UP?
ZEPHYR! HEY, ZEPHYR BREEZE!
OKAY! SO! I HAD A GREAT IDEA!
YOU KNOW THAT DEMONSTRATION STAGE?
WELL, I SIGNED YOU UP TO PUT ON A DEMONSTRATION! FOR THE JUDGES AND EVERYPONY!
BRIDLE LASSOON
LASSOON

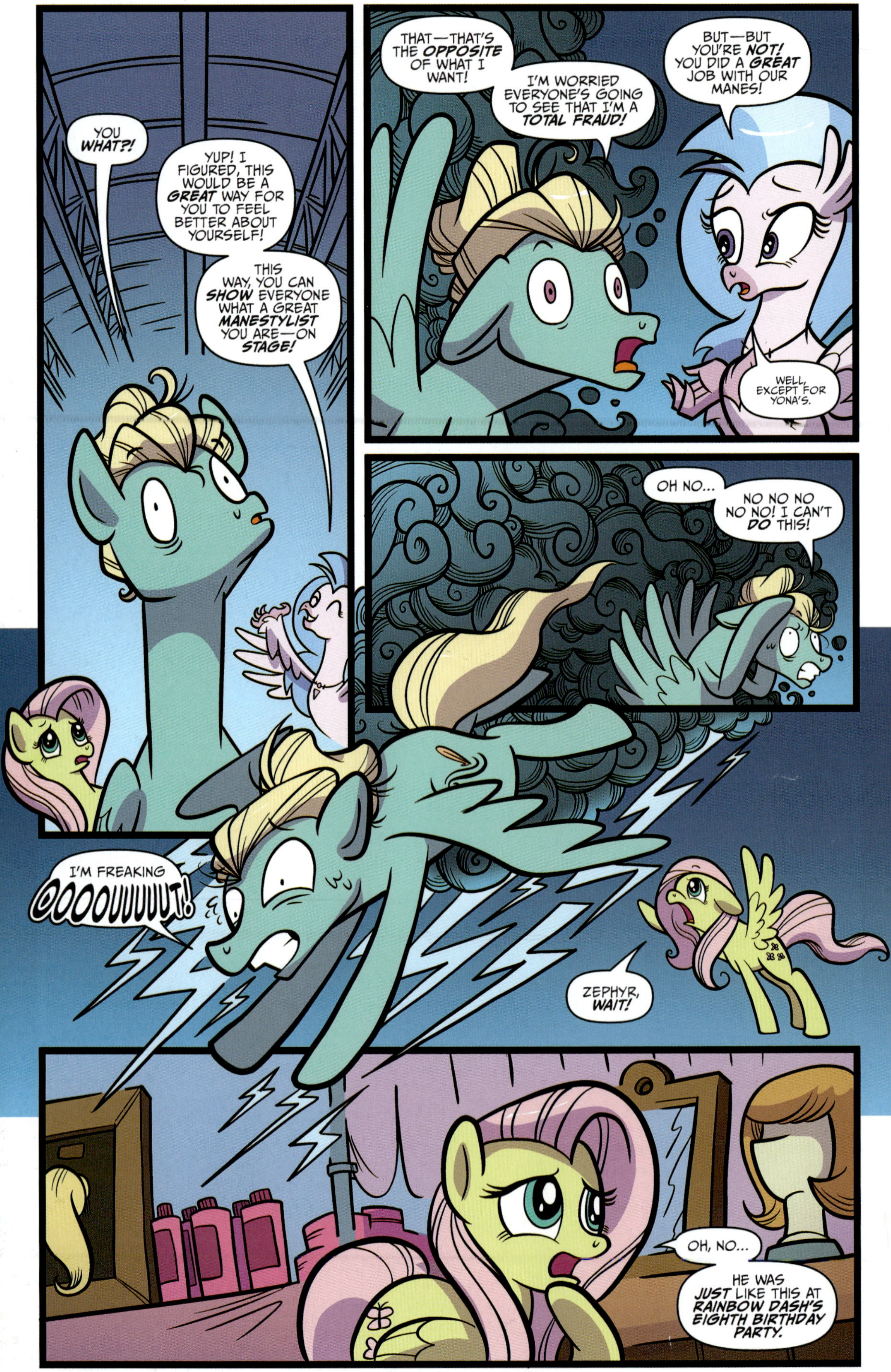
YOU WHAT?!
YUP! I FIGURED, THIS WOULD BE A GREAT WAY FOR YOU TO FEEL BETTER ABOUT YOURSELF!
THIS WAY, YOU CAN SHOW EVERYONE WHAT A GREAT MANESTYLIST YOU ARE—ON STAGE!
THAT—THAT'S THE OPPOSITE OF WHAT I WANT!
I'M WORRIED EVERYONE'S GOING TO SEE THAT I'M A TOTAL FRAUD!
BUT—BUT YOU'RE NOT! YOU DID A GREAT JOB WITH OUR MANES!
WELL, EXCEPT FOR YONA'S.
OH NO...
NO NO NO NO NO! I CAN'T DO THIS!
I'M FREAKING OOOOUUUUUT!
ZEPHYR, WAIT!
OH, NO...
HE WAS JUST LIKE THIS AT RAINBOW DASH'S EIGHTH BIRTHDAY PARTY.

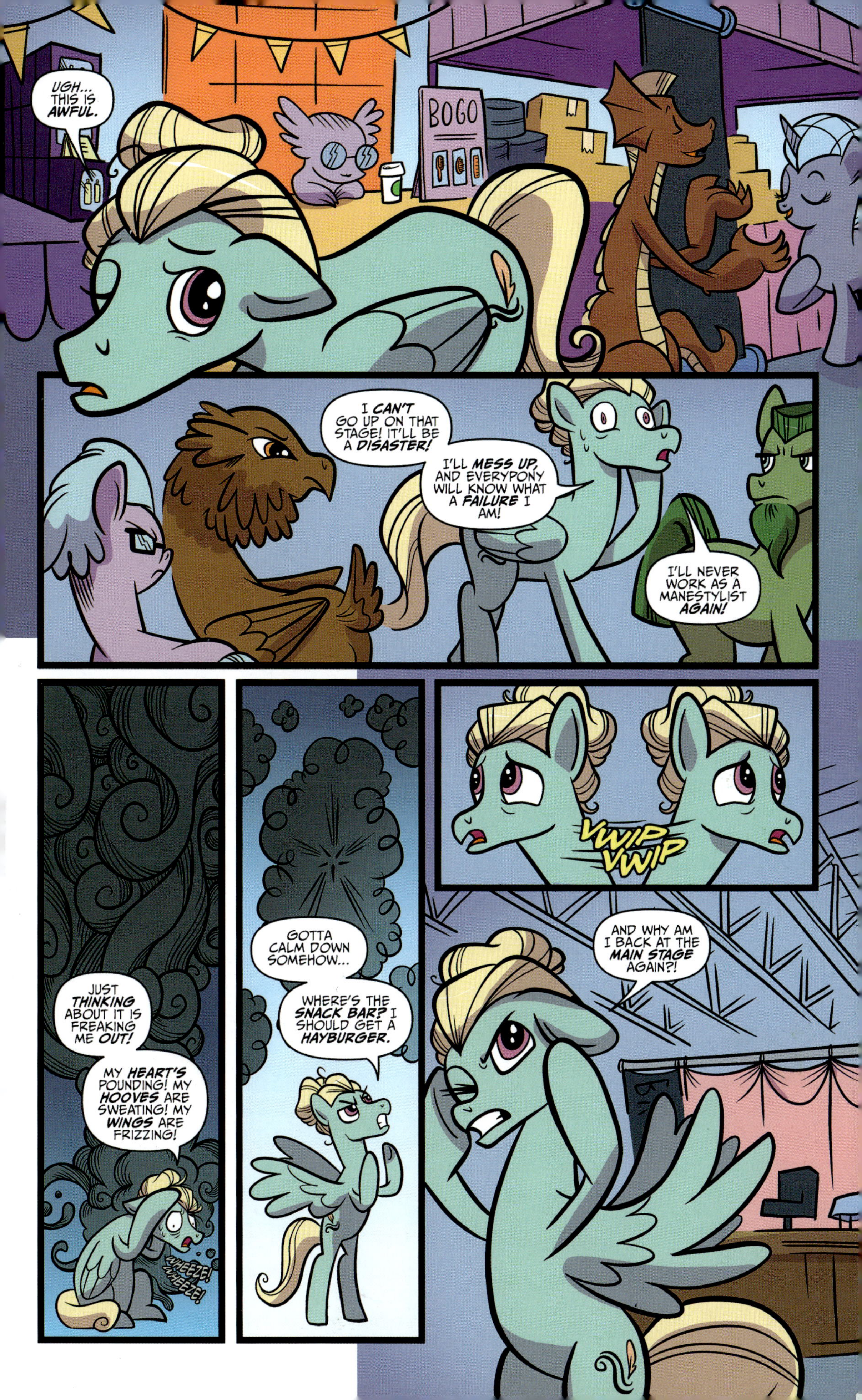

UGH... THIS IS AWFUL.
BOGO
I CAN'T GO UP ON THAT STAGE! IT'LL BE A DISASTER!
I'LL MESS UP, AND EVERYPONY WILL KNOW WHAT A FAILURE I AM!
I'LL NEVER WORK AS A MANESTYLIST AGAIN!
JUST THINKING ABOUT IT IS FREAKING ME OUT!
MY HEART'S POUNDING! MY HOOVES ARE SWEATING! MY WINGS ARE FRIZZING!
WHEEZE! WHEEZE!
GOTTA CALM DOWN SOMEHOW...
WHERE'S THE SNACK BAR? I SHOULD GET A HAYBURGER.
VWIP VWIP
AND WHY AM I BACK AT THE MAIN STAGE AGAIN?!

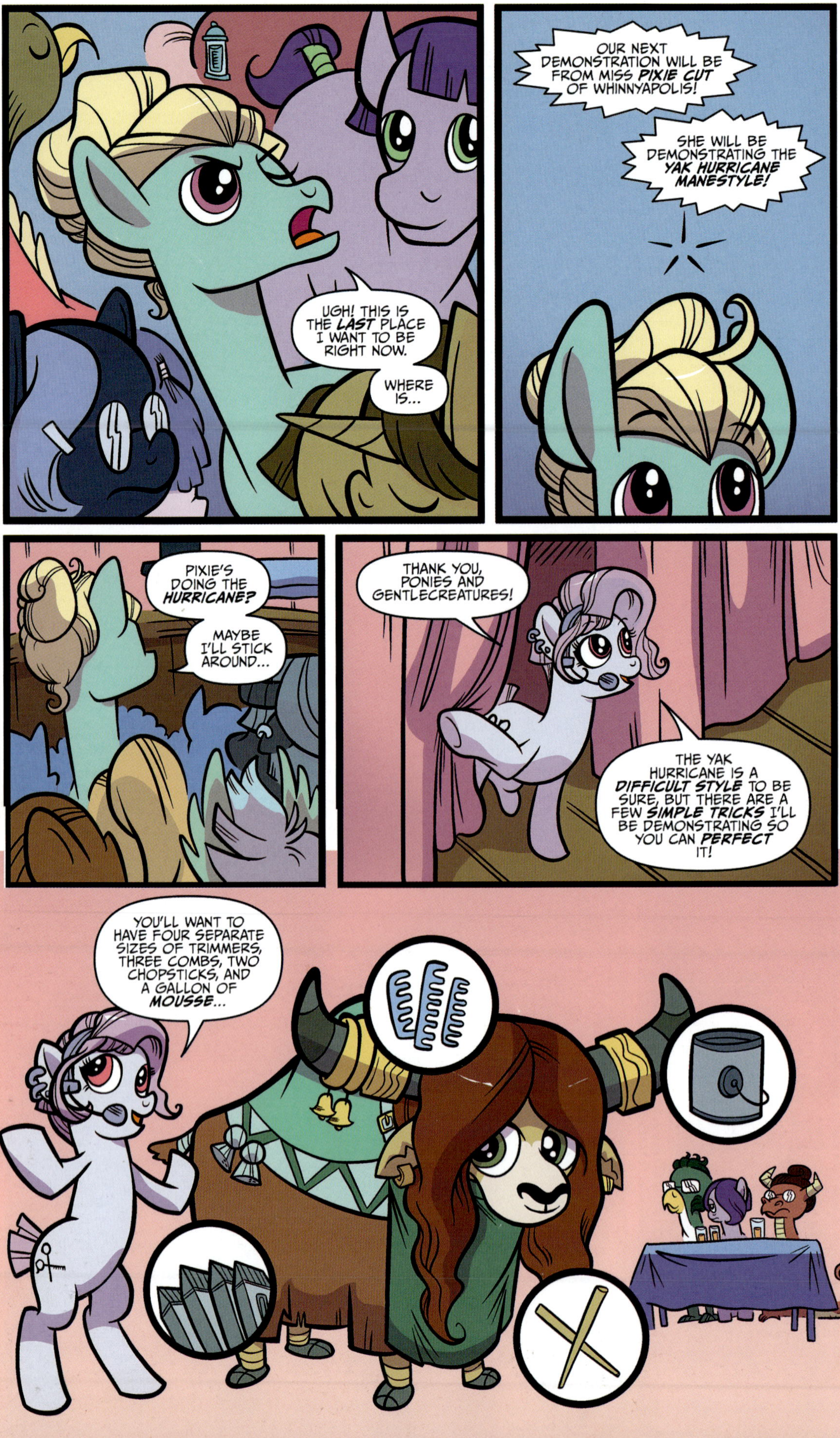
UGH! THIS IS THE *LAST* PLACE I WANT TO BE RIGHT NOW.
WHERE IS...
OUR NEXT DEMONSTRATION WILL BE FROM MISS *PIXIE CUT* OF WHINNYAPOLIS!
SHE WILL BE DEMONSTRATING THE *YAK HURRICANE MANESTYLE!*
PIXIE'S DOING THE *HURRICANE?*
MAYBE I'LL STICK AROUND...
THANK YOU, PONIES AND GENTLECREATURES!
THE YAK HURRICANE IS A *DIFFICULT STYLE* TO BE SURE, BUT THERE ARE A FEW *SIMPLE TRICKS* I'LL BE DEMONSTRATING SO YOU CAN *PERFECT* IT!
YOU'LL WANT TO HAVE FOUR SEPARATE SIZES OF TRIMMERS, THREE COMBS, TWO CHOPSTICKS, AND A GALLON OF *MOUSSE*...

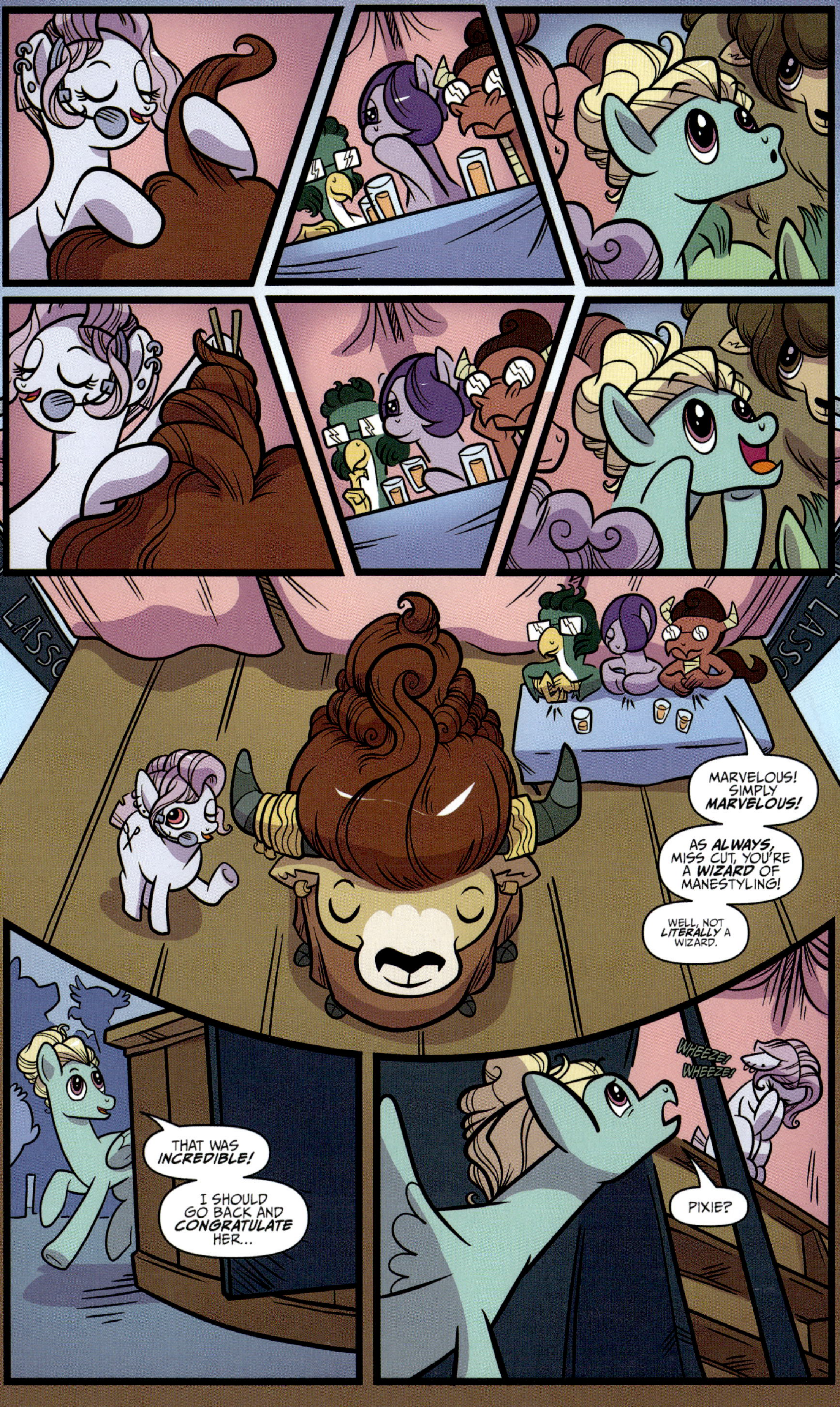
MARVELOUS! SIMPLY MARVELOUS!
AS ALWAYS, MISS CUT, YOU'RE A WIZARD OF MANESTYLING!
WELL, NOT LITERALLY A WIZARD.
THAT WAS INCREDIBLE!
I SHOULD GO BACK AND CONGRATULATE HER...
WHEEZE! WHEEZE!
PIXIE?

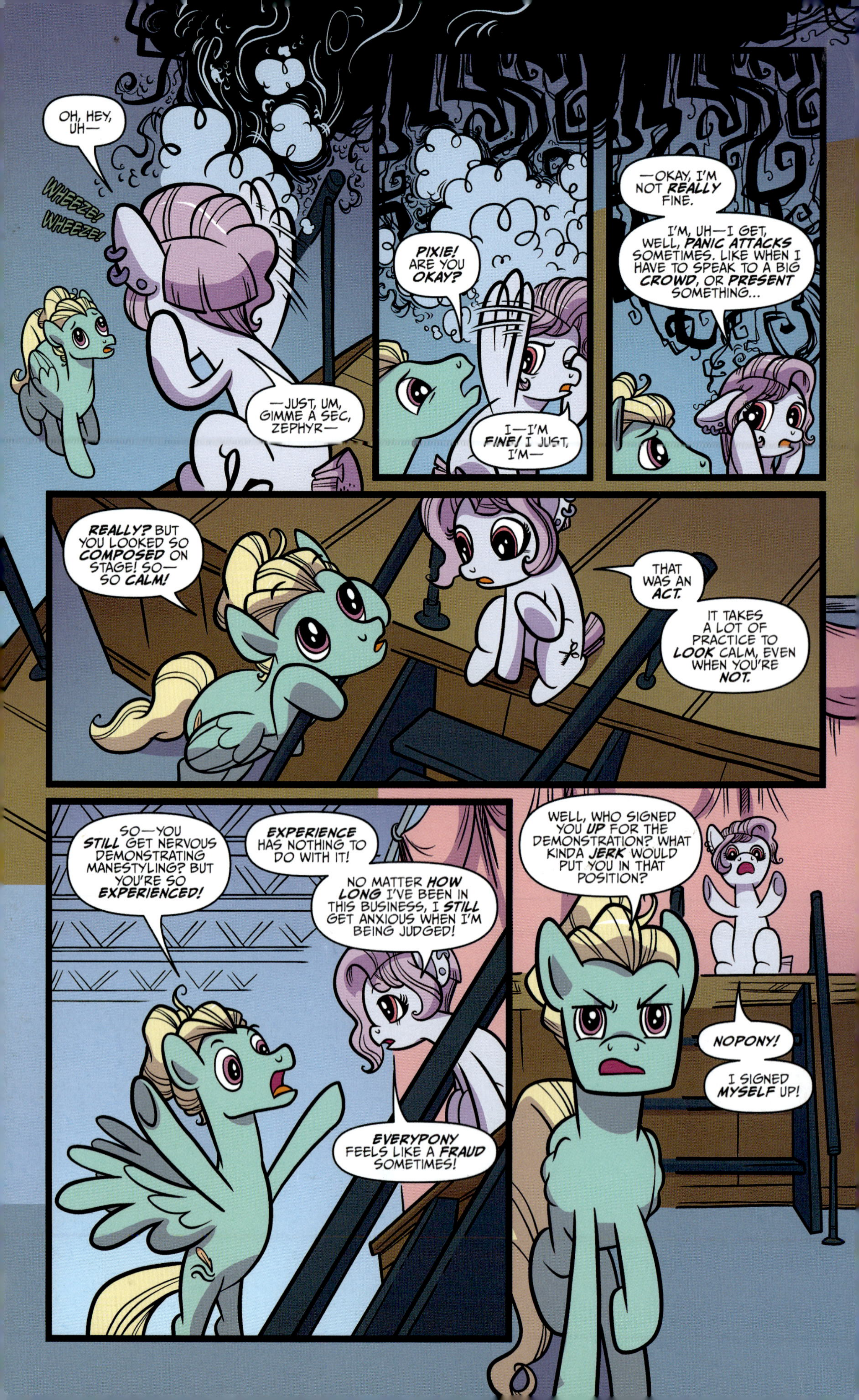
OH, HEY, UH—
WHEEZE! WHEEZE!
—JUST, UM, GIMME A SEC, ZEPHYR—
PIXIE! ARE YOU OKAY?
I—I'M FINE! I JUST, I'M—
—OKAY, I'M NOT REALLY FINE.
I'M, UH—I GET, WELL, PANIC ATTACKS SOMETIMES. LIKE WHEN I HAVE TO SPEAK TO A BIG CROWD, OR PRESENT SOMETHING...
REALLY? BUT YOU LOOKED SO COMPOSED ON STAGE! SO— SO CALM!
THAT WAS AN ACT.
IT TAKES A LOT OF PRACTICE TO LOOK CALM, EVEN WHEN YOU'RE NOT.
SO—YOU STILL GET NERVOUS DEMONSTRATING MANESTYLING? BUT YOU'RE SO EXPERIENCED!
EXPERIENCE HAS NOTHING TO DO WITH IT!
NO MATTER HOW LONG I'VE BEEN IN THIS BUSINESS, I STILL GET ANXIOUS WHEN I'M BEING JUDGED!
EVERYPONY FEELS LIKE A FRAUD SOMETIMES!
WELL, WHO SIGNED YOU UP FOR THE DEMONSTRATION? WHAT KINDA JERK WOULD PUT YOU IN THAT POSITION?
NOPONY!
I SIGNED MYSELF UP!

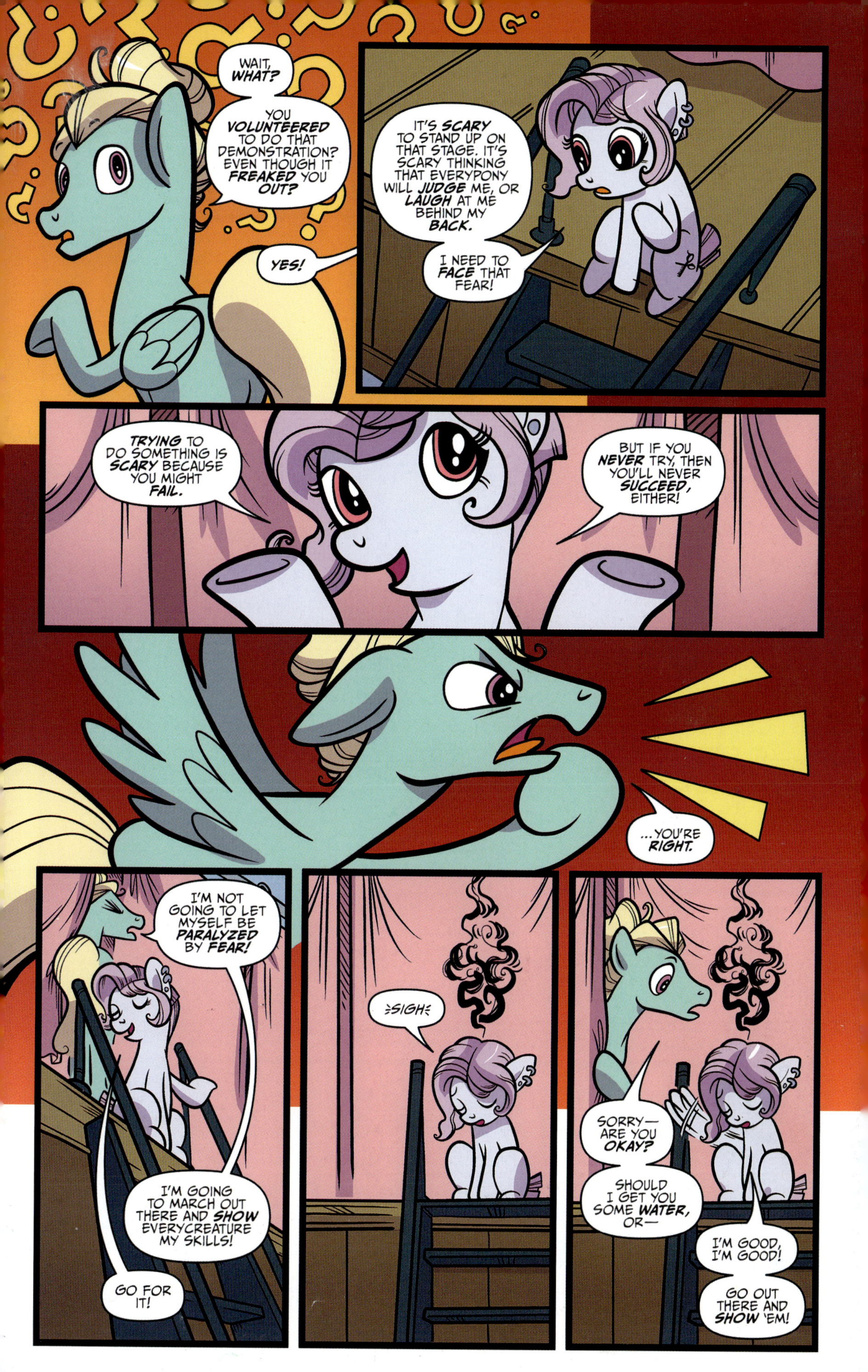
WAIT, WHAT?
YOU VOLUNTEERED TO DO THAT DEMONSTRATION? EVEN THOUGH IT FREAKED YOU OUT?
YES!
IT'S SCARY TO STAND UP ON THAT STAGE. IT'S SCARY THINKING THAT EVERYPONY WILL JUDGE ME, OR LAUGH AT ME BEHIND MY BACK.
I NEED TO FACE THAT FEAR!
TRYING TO DO SOMETHING IS SCARY BECAUSE YOU MIGHT FAIL.
BUT IF YOU NEVER TRY, THEN YOU'LL NEVER SUCCEED, EITHER!
...YOU'RE RIGHT.
I'M NOT GOING TO LET MYSELF BE PARALYZED BY FEAR!
I'M GOING TO MARCH OUT THERE AND SHOW EVERYCREATURE MY SKILLS!
GO FOR IT!
SIGH
SORRY— ARE YOU OKAY?
SHOULD I GET YOU SOME WATER, OR—
I'M GOOD, I'M GOOD!
GO OUT THERE AND SHOW 'EM!

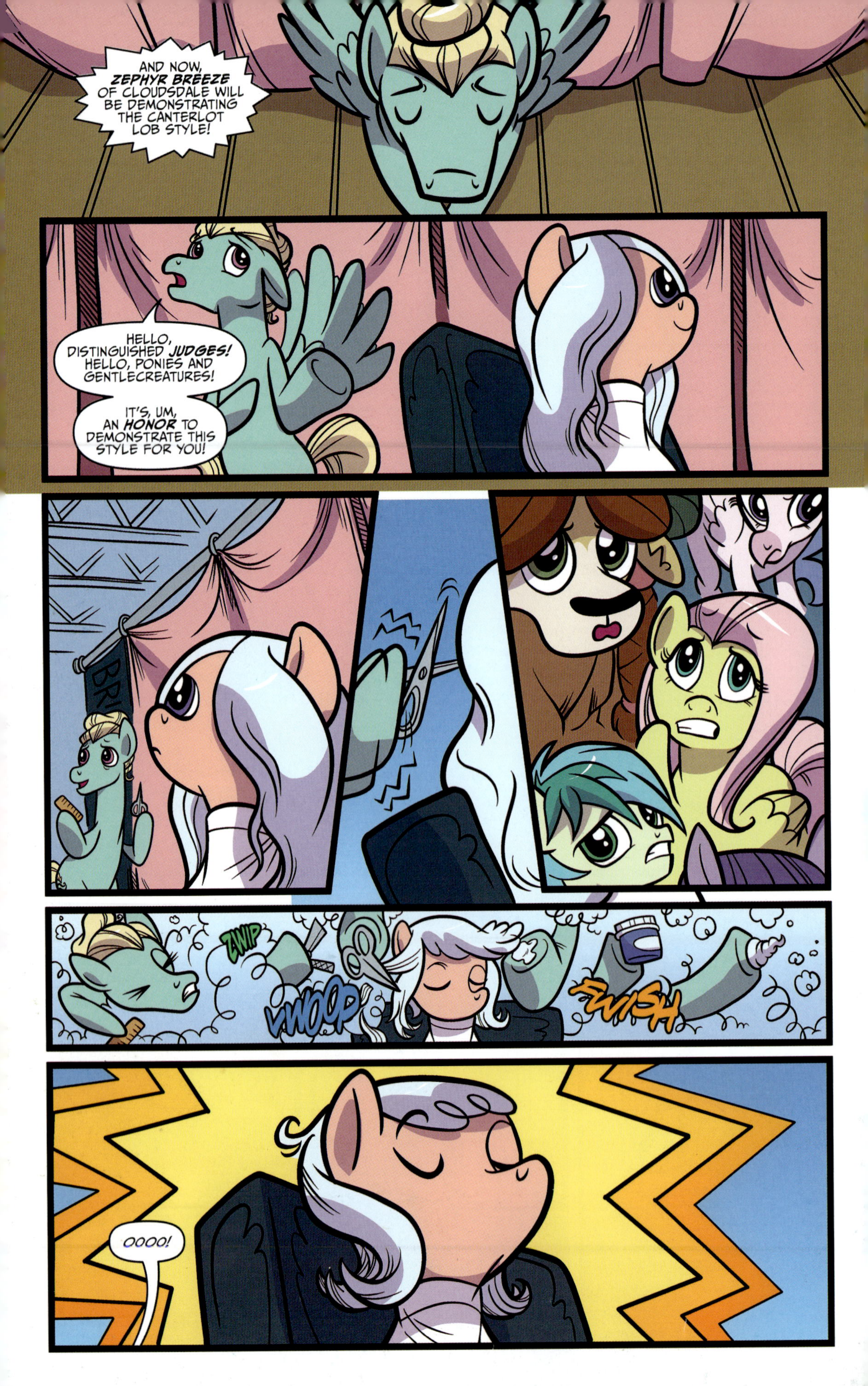
AND NOW, ZEPHYR BREEZE OF CLOUDSDALE WILL BE DEMONSTRATING THE CANTERLOT LOB STYLE!
HELLO, DISTINGUISHED JUDGES! HELLO, PONIES AND GENTLECREATURES!
IT'S, UM, AN HONOR TO DEMONSTRATE THIS STYLE FOR YOU!
ZWIP
VWOOP
FWISH
OOOO!

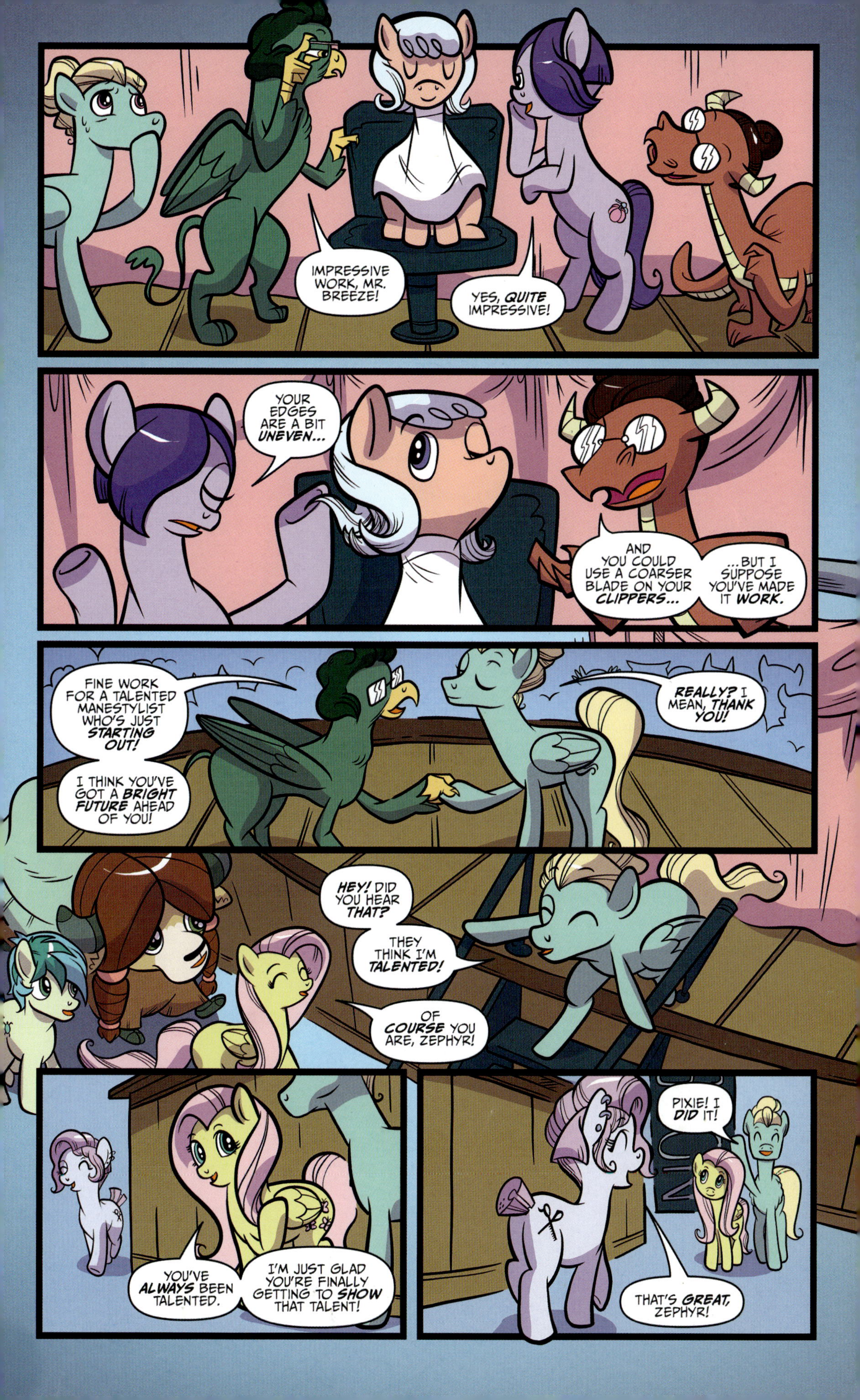

IMPRESSIVE WORK, MR. BREEZE!
YES, *QUITE* IMPRESSIVE!
YOUR EDGES ARE A BIT *UNEVEN...*
AND YOU COULD USE A COARSER BLADE ON YOUR *CLIPPERS...*
...BUT I SUPPOSE YOU'VE MADE IT *WORK.*
FINE WORK FOR A TALENTED MANESTYLIST WHO'S JUST *STARTING OUT!*
I THINK YOU'VE GOT A *BRIGHT FUTURE* AHEAD OF YOU!
REALLY? I MEAN, *THANK YOU!*
HEY! DID YOU HEAR *THAT?*
THEY THINK I'M *TALENTED!*
OF *COURSE* YOU ARE, ZEPHYR!
YOU'VE *ALWAYS* BEEN TALENTED.
I'M JUST GLAD YOU'RE FINALLY GETTING TO *SHOW* THAT TALENT!
PIXIE! I *DID* IT!
THAT'S *GREAT,* ZEPHYR!

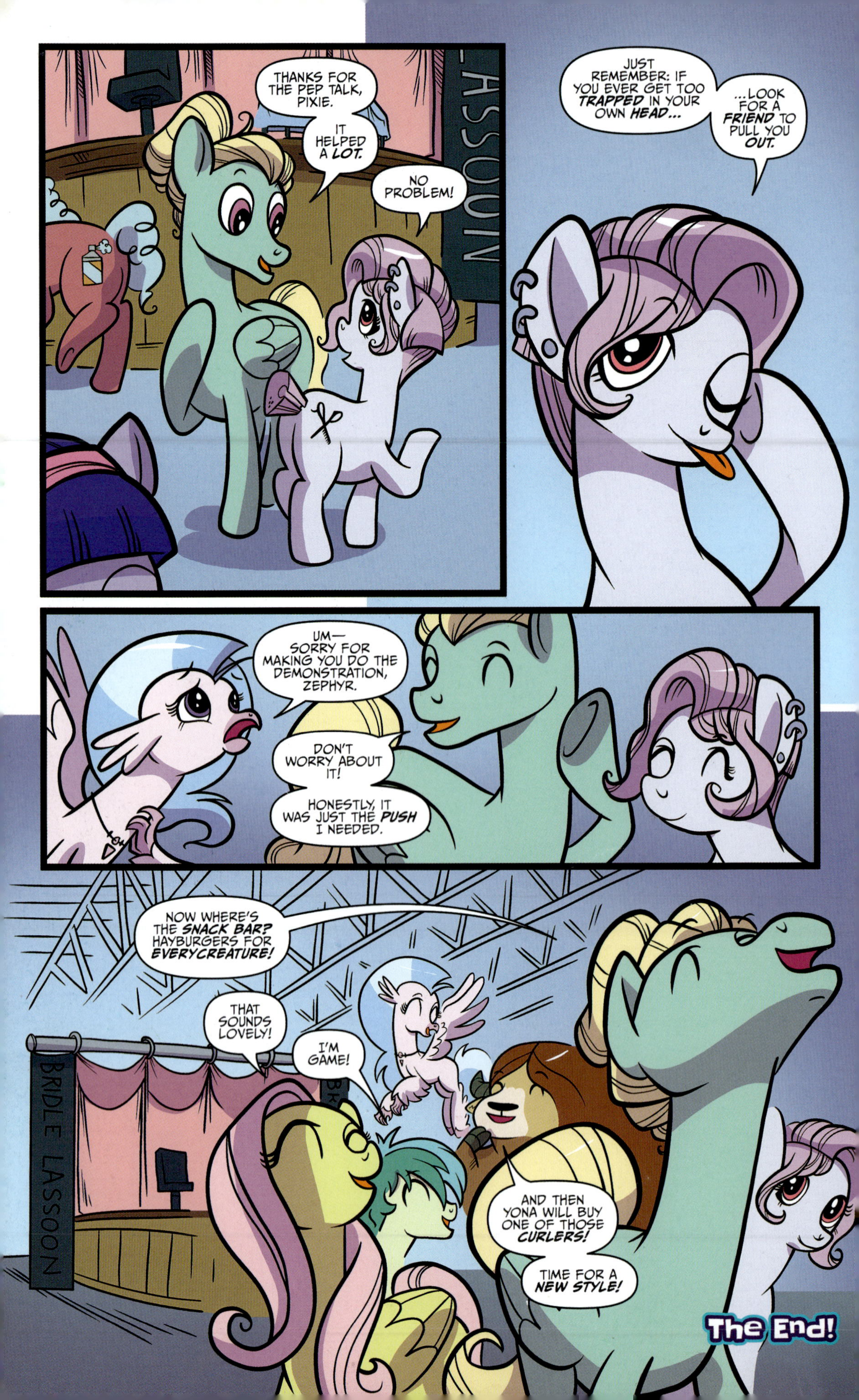
LASSOON
THANKS FOR THE PEP TALK, PIXIE.
IT HELPED A LOT.
NO PROBLEM!
JUST REMEMBER: IF YOU EVER GET TOO TRAPPED IN YOUR OWN HEAD...
...LOOK FOR A FRIEND TO PULL YOU OUT.
UM— SORRY FOR MAKING YOU DO THE DEMONSTRATION, ZEPHYR.
DON'T WORRY ABOUT IT!
HONESTLY, IT WAS JUST THE PUSH I NEEDED.
NOW WHERE'S THE SNACK BAR? HAYBURGERS FOR EVERYCREATURE!
THAT SOUNDS LOVELY!
I'M GAME!
BRIDLE LASSOON
AND THEN YONA WILL BUY ONE OF THOSE CURLERS!
TIME FOR A NEW STYLE!
The End!

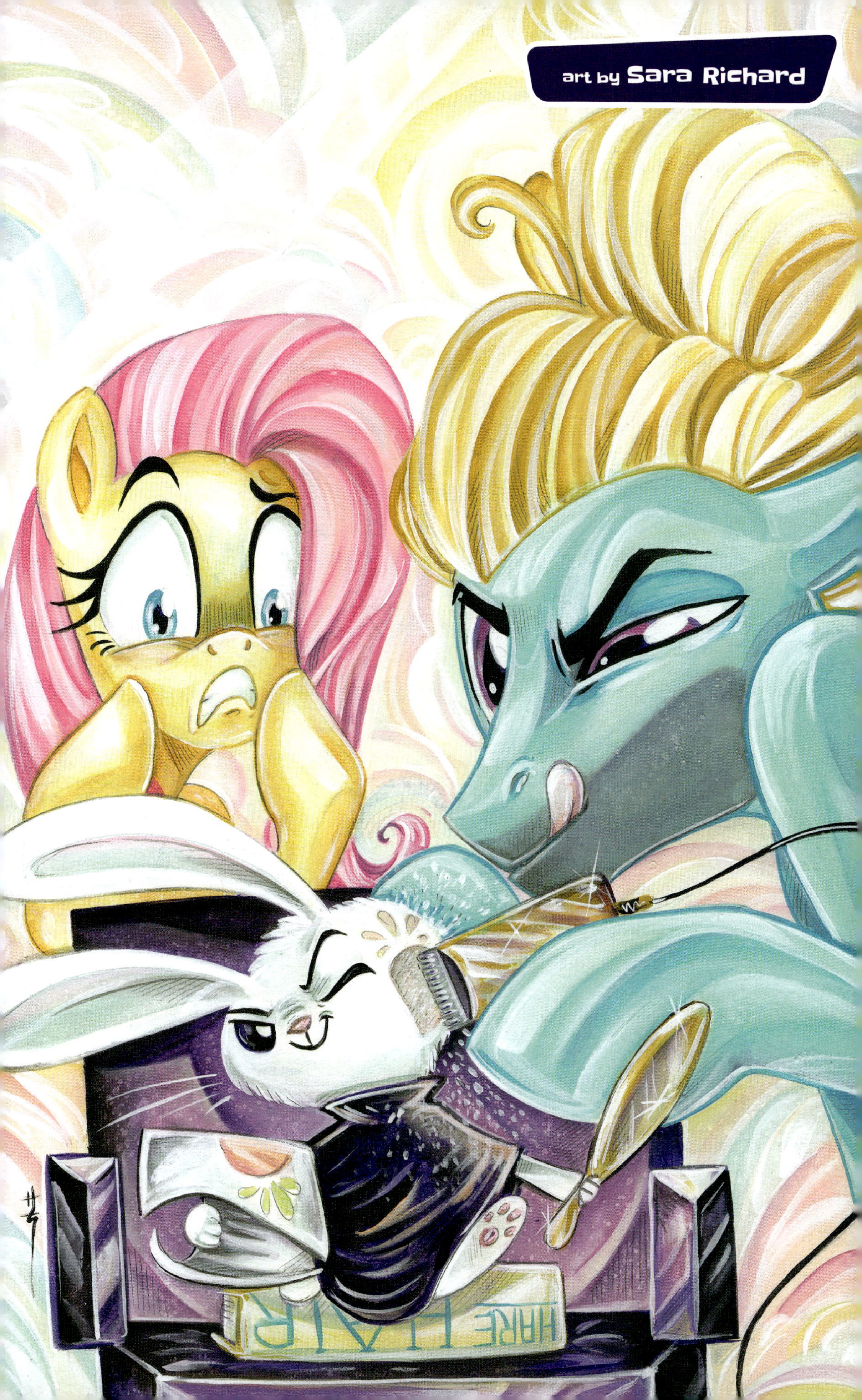
HARE HAIR

art by Sara Richard

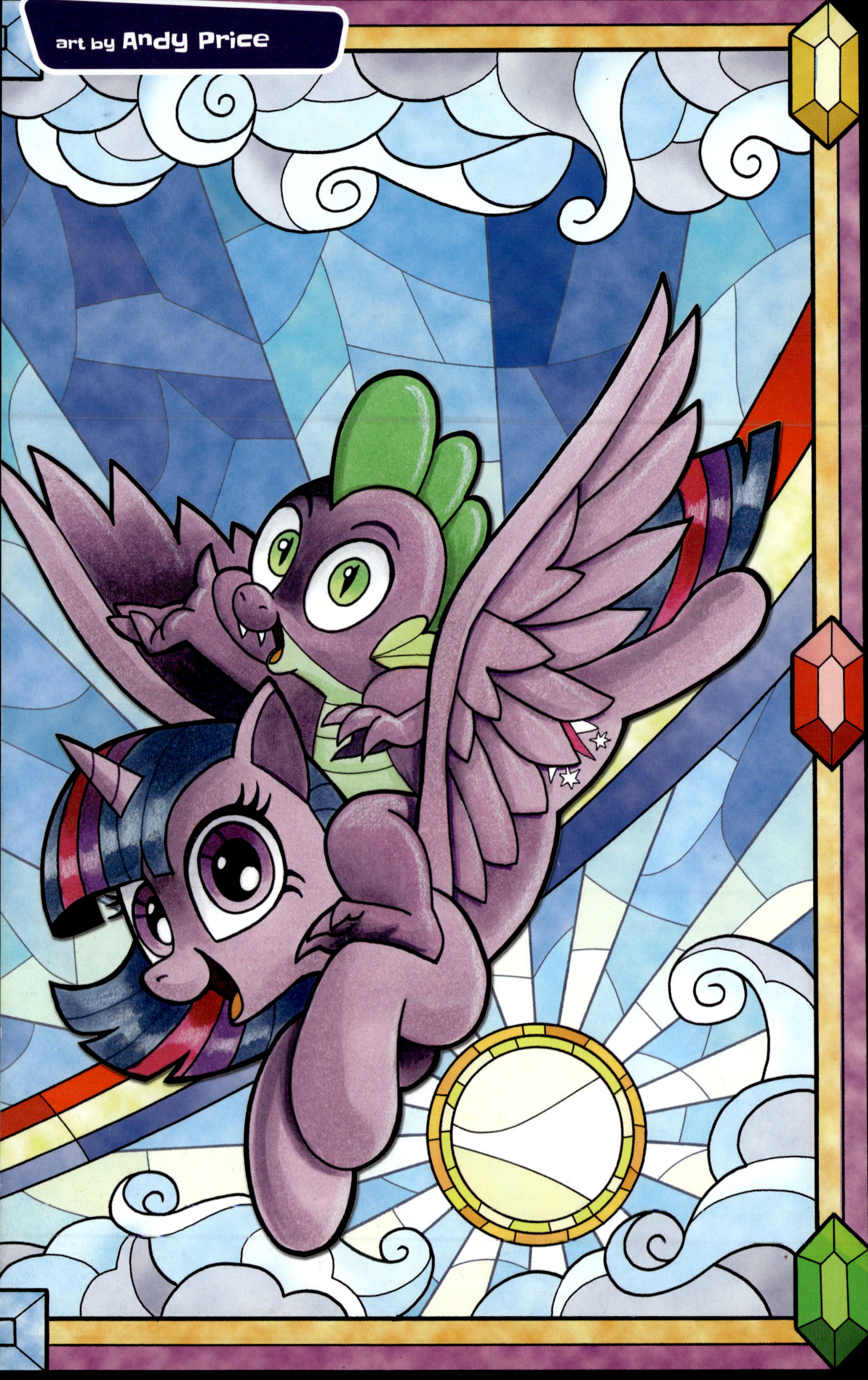
art by Andy Price

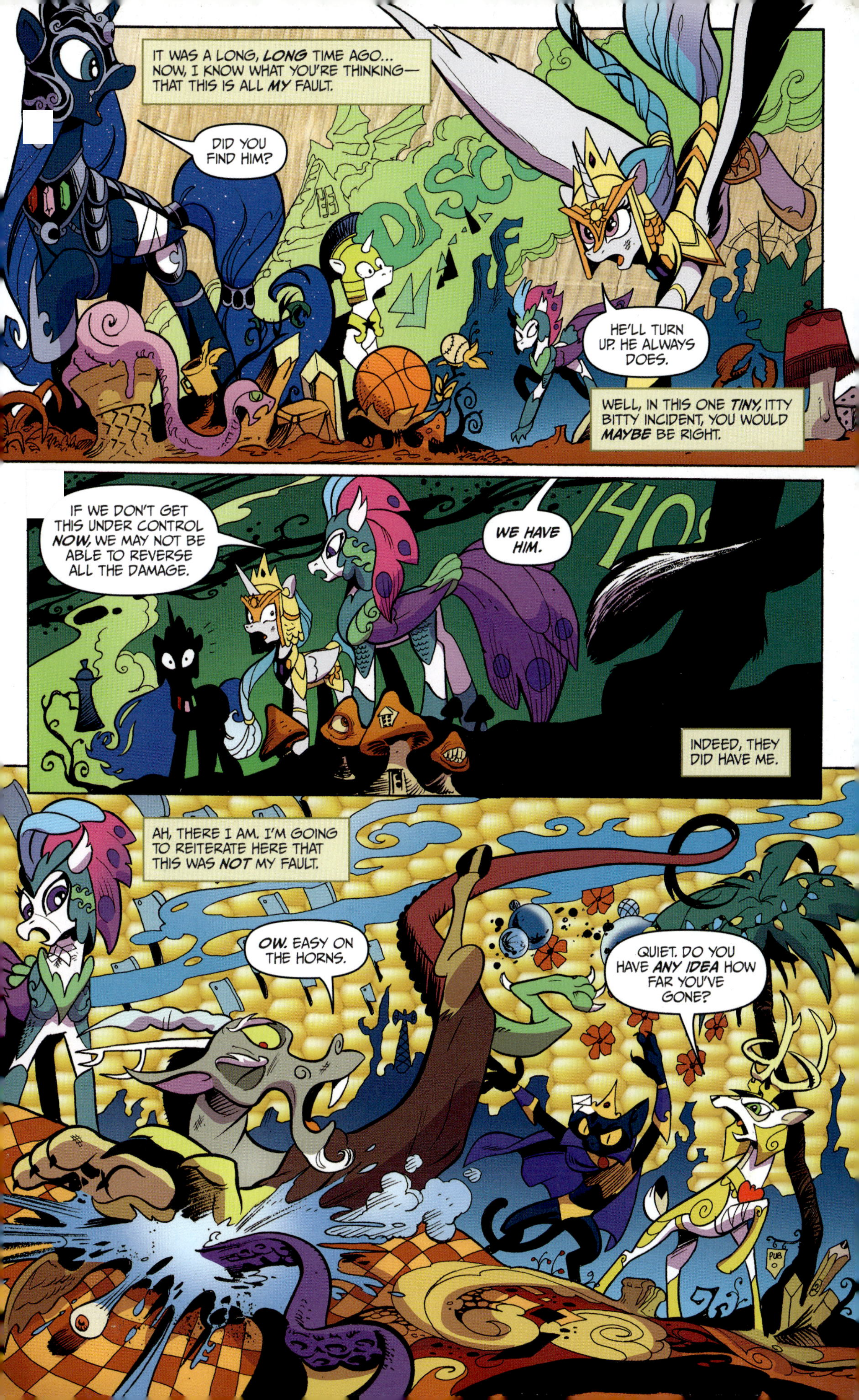
IT WAS A LONG, LONG TIME AGO... NOW, I KNOW WHAT YOU'RE THINKING— THAT THIS IS ALL MY FAULT.
DID YOU FIND HIM?
HE'LL TURN UP. HE ALWAYS DOES.
WELL, IN THIS ONE TINY, ITTY BITTY INCIDENT, YOU WOULD MAYBE BE RIGHT.
IF WE DON'T GET THIS UNDER CONTROL NOW, WE MAY NOT BE ABLE TO REVERSE ALL THE DAMAGE.
WE HAVE HIM.
INDEED, THEY DID HAVE ME.
AH, THERE I AM. I'M GOING TO REITERATE HERE THAT THIS WAS NOT MY FAULT.
OW. EASY ON THE HORNS.
QUIET. DO YOU HAVE ANY IDEA HOW FAR YOU'VE GONE?

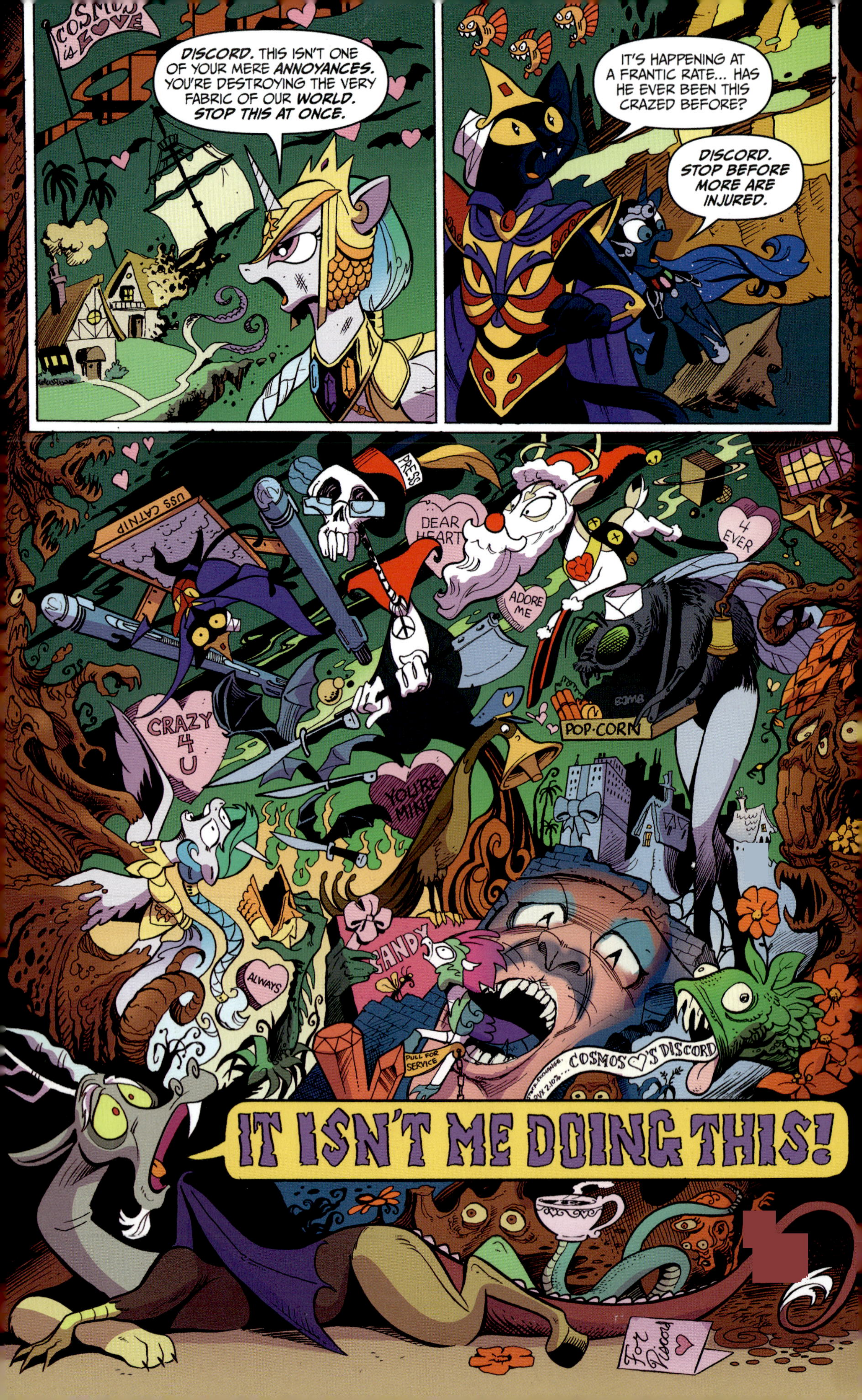
COSMOS is LOVE
DISCORD. THIS ISN'T ONE OF YOUR MERE ANNOYANCES. YOU'RE DESTROYING THE VERY FABRIC OF OUR WORLD. STOP THIS AT ONCE.
IT'S HAPPENING AT A FRANTIC RATE... HAS HE EVER BEEN THIS CRAZED BEFORE?
DISCORD. STOP BEFORE MORE ARE INJURED.
USS CATNIP
PRESS
DEAR HEART
4 EVER
ADORE ME
CRAZY 4 U
YOU'RE MINE
POP-CORN
ALWAYS
PULL FOR SERVICE
COSMOS ♡'S DISCORD
IT ISN'T ME DOING THIS!
For Discord

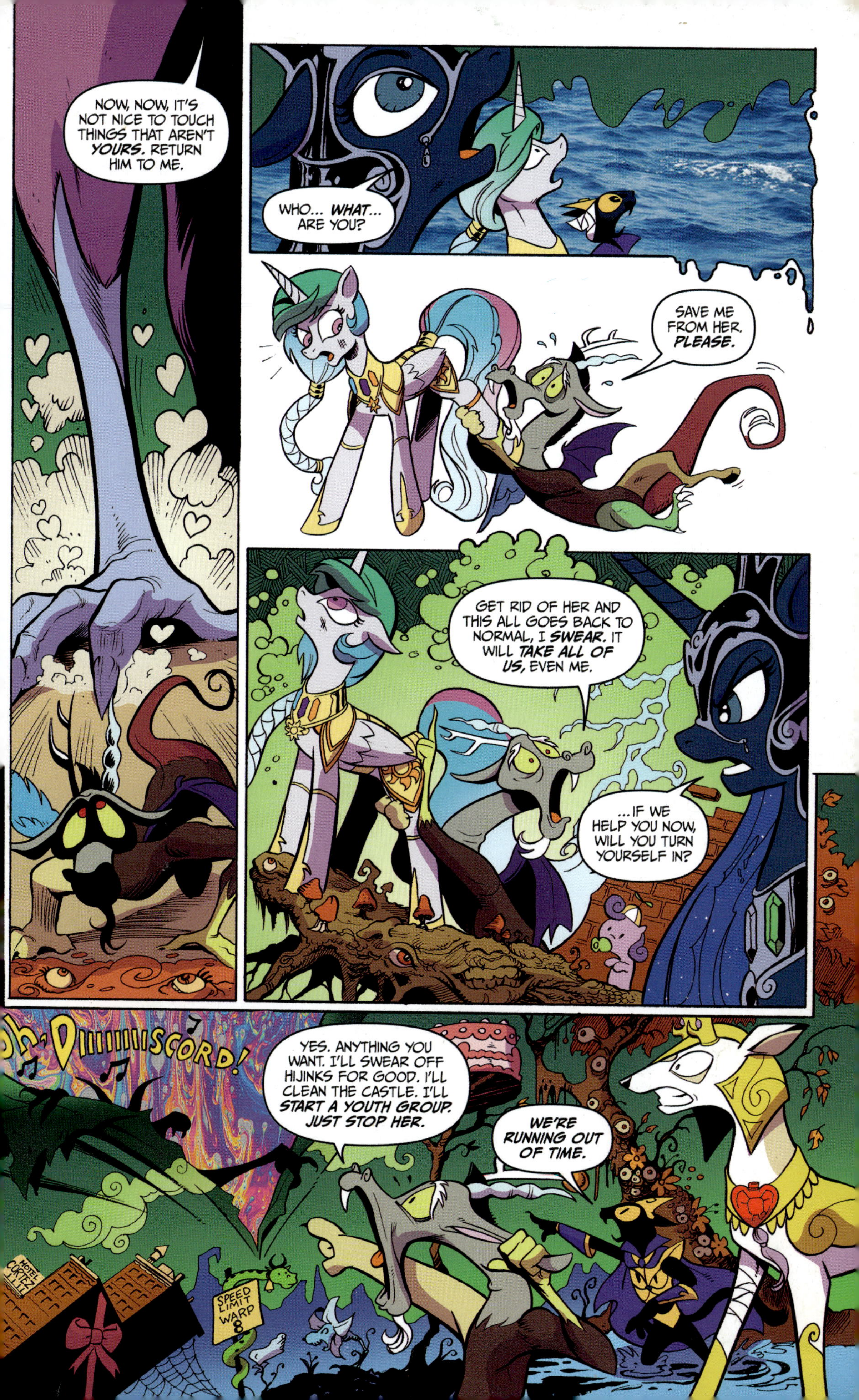
NOW, NOW, IT'S NOT NICE TO TOUCH THINGS THAT AREN'T *YOURS.* RETURN HIM TO ME.
WHO... *WHAT...* ARE YOU?
SAVE ME FROM HER. *PLEASE.*
GET RID OF HER AND THIS ALL GOES BACK TO NORMAL, I *SWEAR.* IT WILL *TAKE ALL OF US,* EVEN ME.
...IF WE HELP YOU NOW, WILL YOU TURN YOURSELF IN?
OH-DIIIIIIISCORD!
YES. ANYTHING YOU WANT. I'LL SWEAR OFF HIJINKS FOR GOOD. I'LL CLEAN THE CASTLE. I'LL *START A YOUTH GROUP. JUST STOP HER.*
WE'RE RUNNING OUT OF TIME.
SPEED LIMIT WARP 8

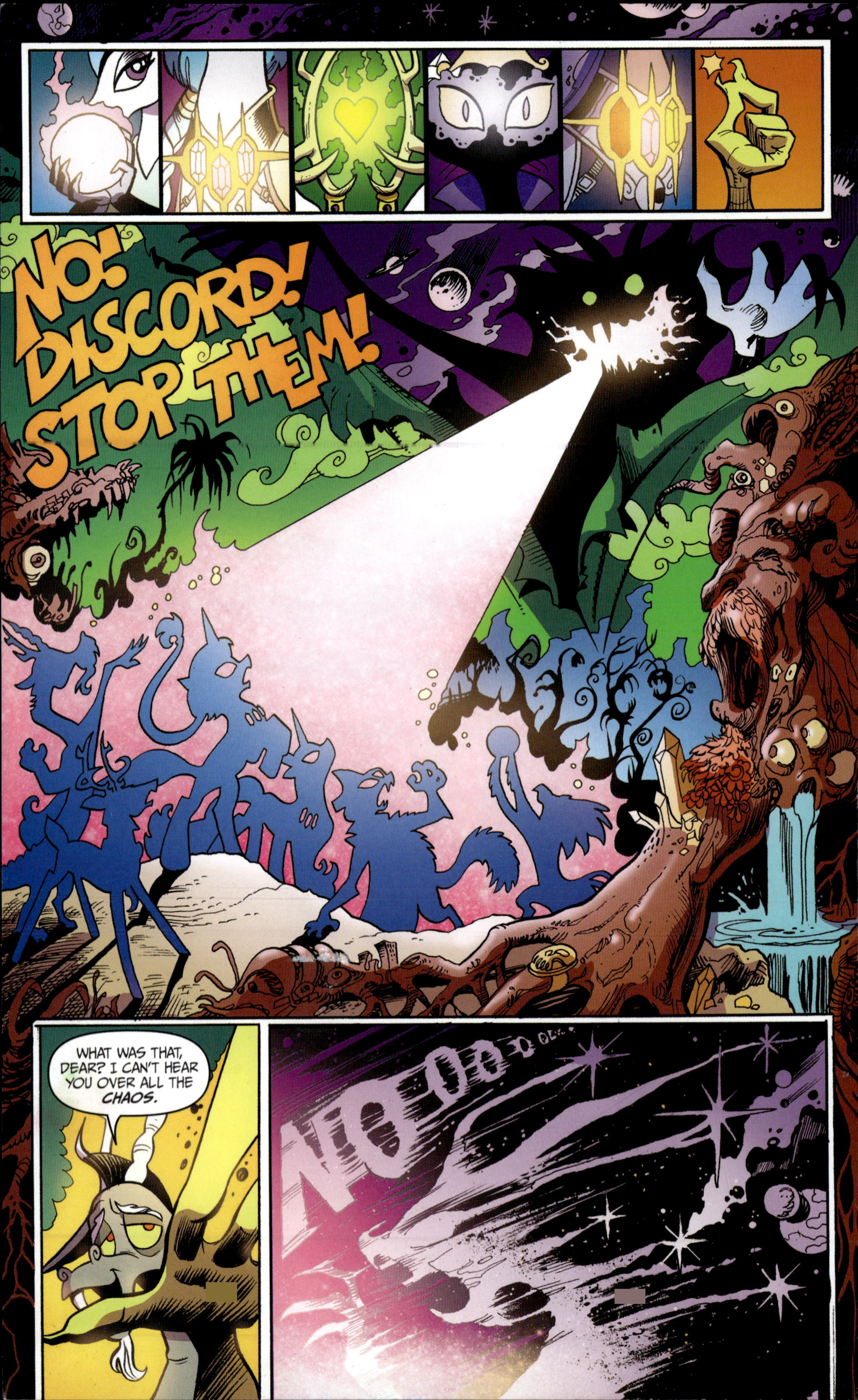

NO! DISCORD! STOP THEM!
WHAT WAS THAT, DEAR? I CAN'T HEAR YOU OVER ALL THE *CHAOS*.
NOOOOOOO

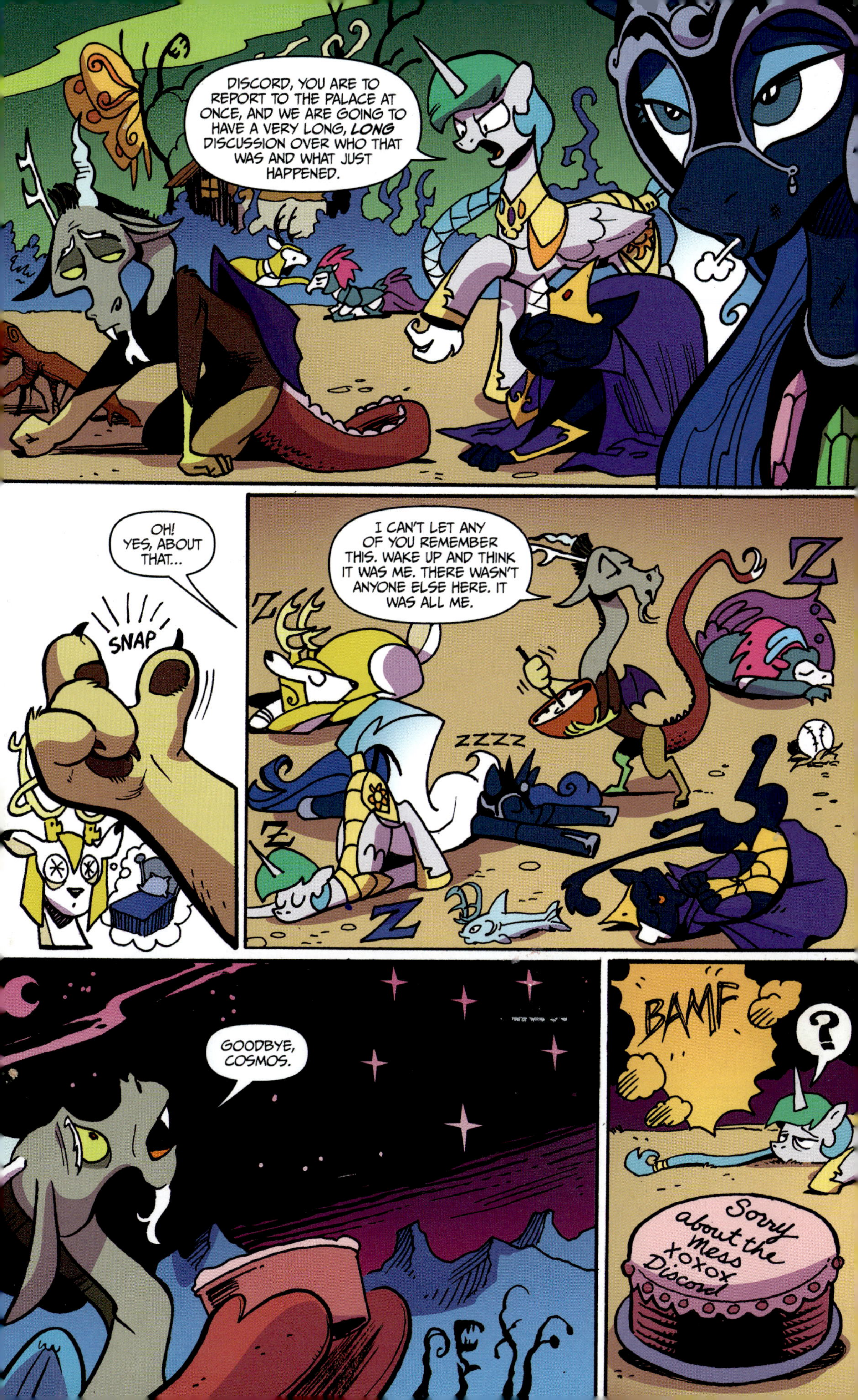
DISCORD, YOU ARE TO REPORT TO THE PALACE AT ONCE, AND WE ARE GOING TO HAVE A VERY LONG, LONG DISCUSSION OVER WHO THAT WAS AND WHAT JUST HAPPENED.
OH! YES, ABOUT THAT...
SNAP
I CAN'T LET ANY OF YOU REMEMBER THIS. WAKE UP AND THINK IT WAS ME. THERE WASN'T ANYONE ELSE HERE. IT WAS ALL ME.
Z
ZZZZ
Z
Z
Z
GOODBYE, COSMOS.
BAMF
?
Sorry about the mess
XOXOX
Discord

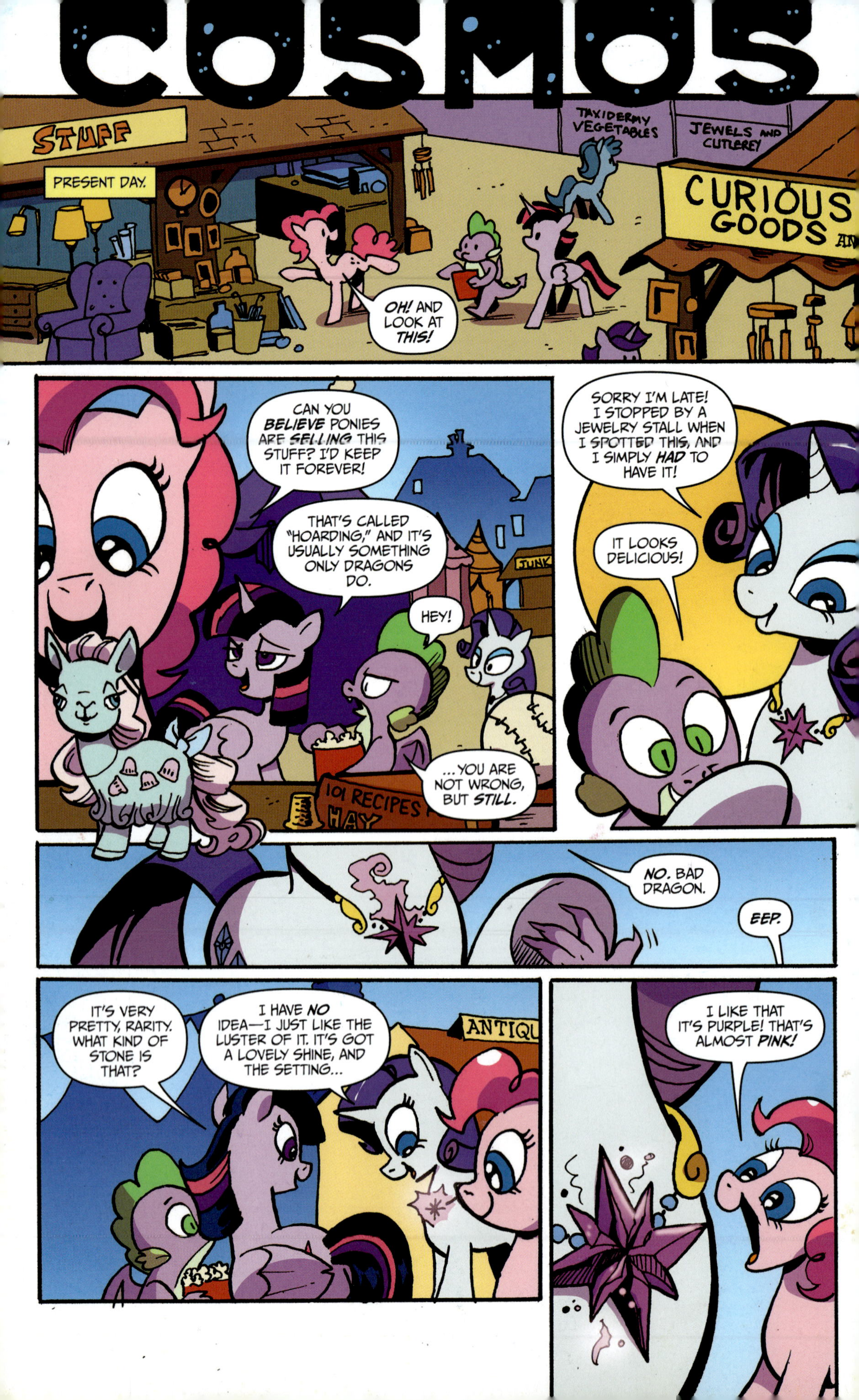
COSMOS
STUFF
PRESENT DAY.
TAXIDERMY VEGETABLES
JEWELS AND CUTLERY
CURIOUS GOODS
OH! AND LOOK AT THIS!
CAN YOU BELIEVE PONIES ARE SELLING THIS STUFF? I'D KEEP IT FOREVER!
THAT'S CALLED "HOARDING," AND IT'S USUALLY SOMETHING ONLY DRAGONS DO.
HEY!
JUNK
...YOU ARE NOT WRONG, BUT STILL.
101 RECIPES HAY
SORRY I'M LATE! I STOPPED BY A JEWELRY STALL WHEN I SPOTTED THIS, AND I SIMPLY HAD TO HAVE IT!
IT LOOKS DELICIOUS!
NO. BAD DRAGON.
EEP.
IT'S VERY PRETTY, RARITY. WHAT KIND OF STONE IS THAT?
I HAVE NO IDEA—I JUST LIKE THE LUSTER OF IT. IT'S GOT A LOVELY SHINE, AND THE SETTING...
ANTIQU
I LIKE THAT IT'S PURPLE! THAT'S ALMOST PINK!

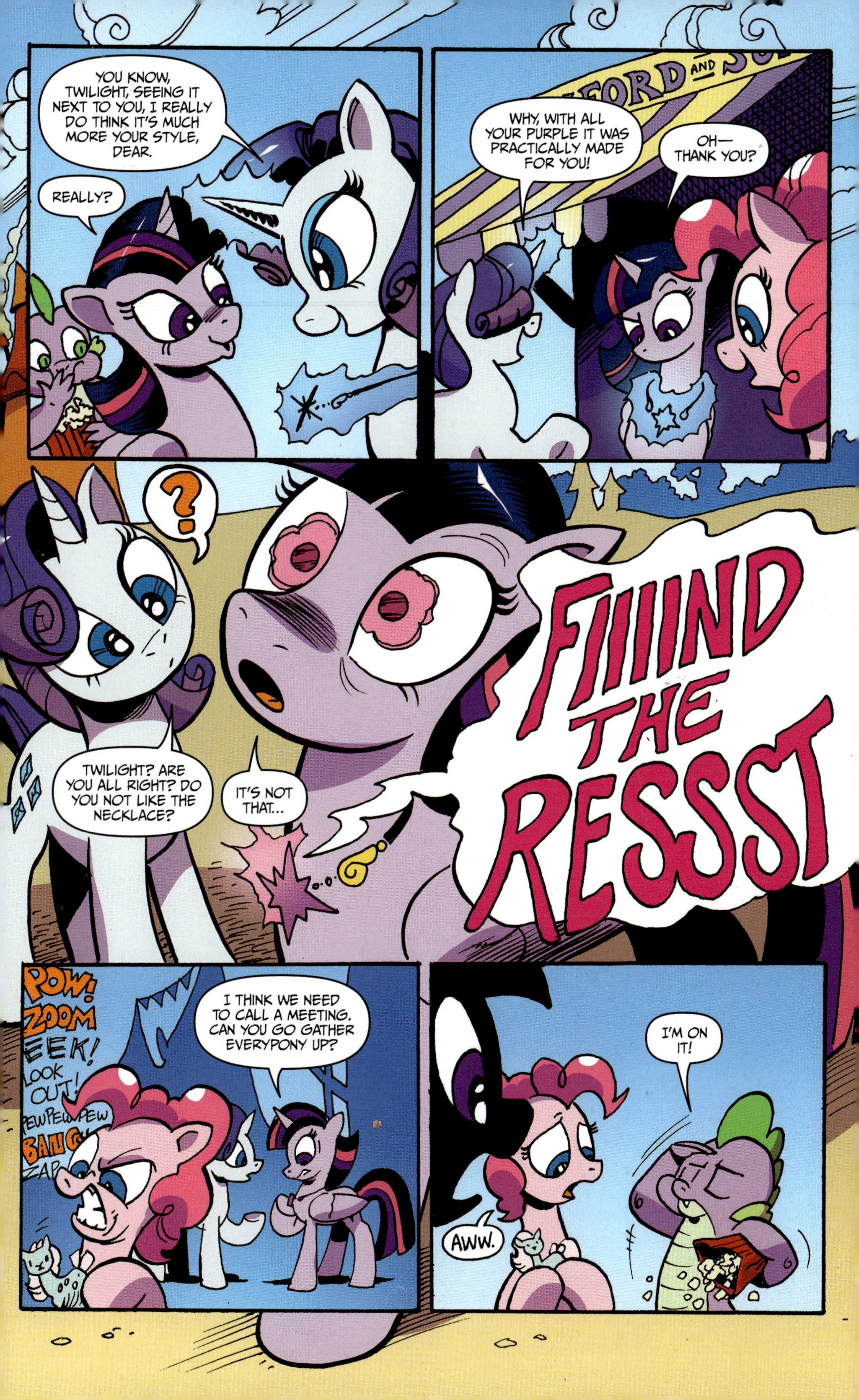
YOU KNOW, TWILIGHT, SEEING IT NEXT TO YOU, I REALLY DO THINK IT'S MUCH MORE YOUR STYLE, DEAR.
REALLY?
WHY, WITH ALL YOUR PURPLE IT WAS PRACTICALLY MADE FOR YOU!
OH— THANK YOU?
?
TWILIGHT? ARE YOU ALL RIGHT? DO YOU NOT LIKE THE NECKLACE?
IT'S NOT THAT...
FIIIND THE RESSST
POW!
ZOOM
EEK!
LOOK OUT!
PEWPEWPEW
BANG
ZAP
I THINK WE NEED TO CALL A MEETING. CAN YOU GO GATHER EVERYPONY UP?
I'M ON IT!
AWW.

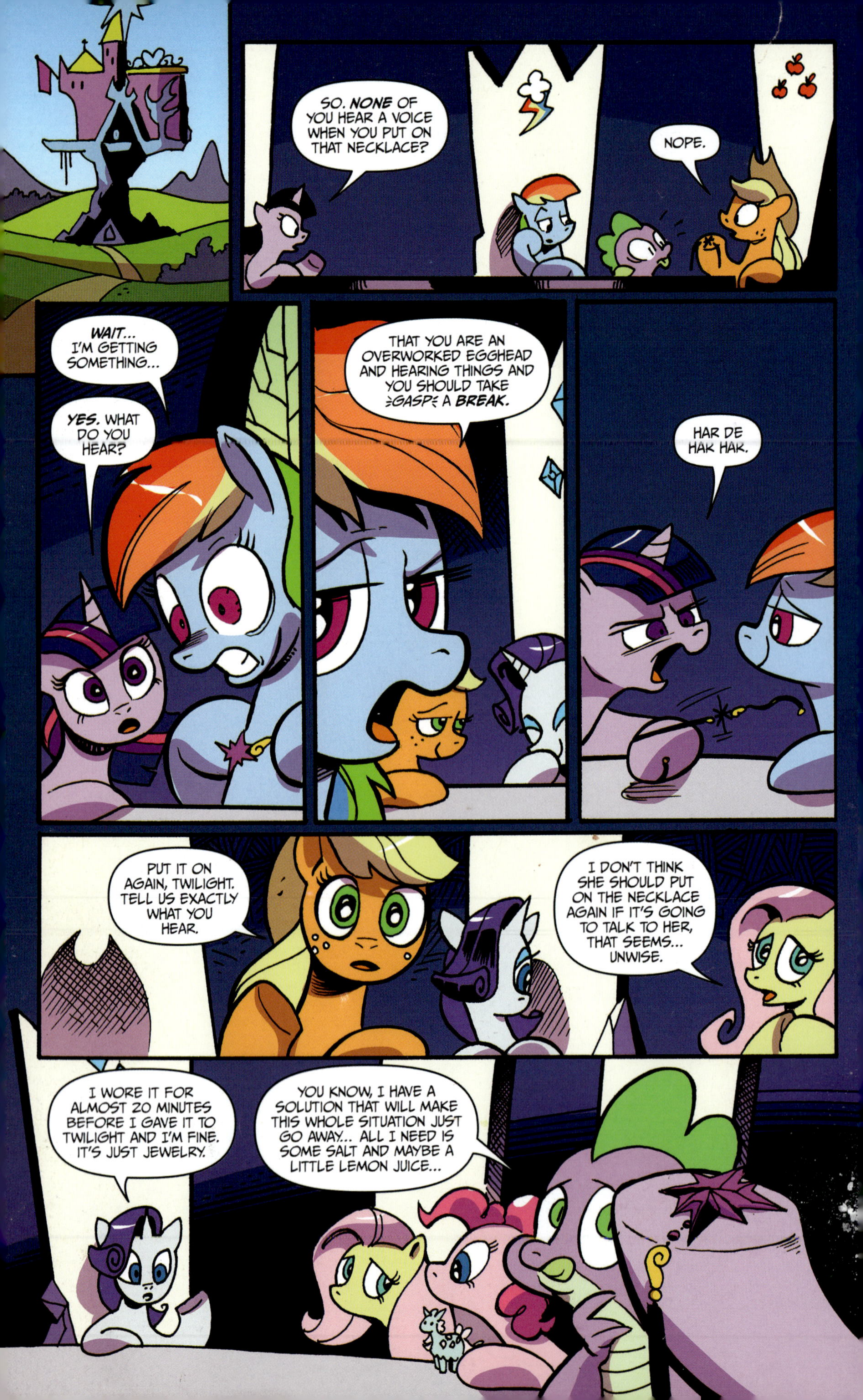
SO. NONE OF YOU HEAR A VOICE WHEN YOU PUT ON THAT NECKLACE?
NOPE.
WAIT... I'M GETTING SOMETHING...
YES. WHAT DO YOU HEAR?
THAT YOU ARE AN OVERWORKED EGGHEAD AND HEARING THINGS AND YOU SHOULD TAKE GASP A BREAK.
HAR DE HAK HAK.
PUT IT ON AGAIN, TWILIGHT. TELL US EXACTLY WHAT YOU HEAR.
I DON'T THINK SHE SHOULD PUT ON THE NECKLACE AGAIN IF IT'S GOING TO TALK TO HER, THAT SEEMS... UNWISE.
I WORE IT FOR ALMOST 20 MINUTES BEFORE I GAVE IT TO TWILIGHT AND I'M FINE. IT'S JUST JEWELRY.
YOU KNOW, I HAVE A SOLUTION THAT WILL MAKE THIS WHOLE SITUATION JUST GO AWAY... ALL I NEED IS SOME SALT AND MAYBE A LITTLE LEMON JUICE...

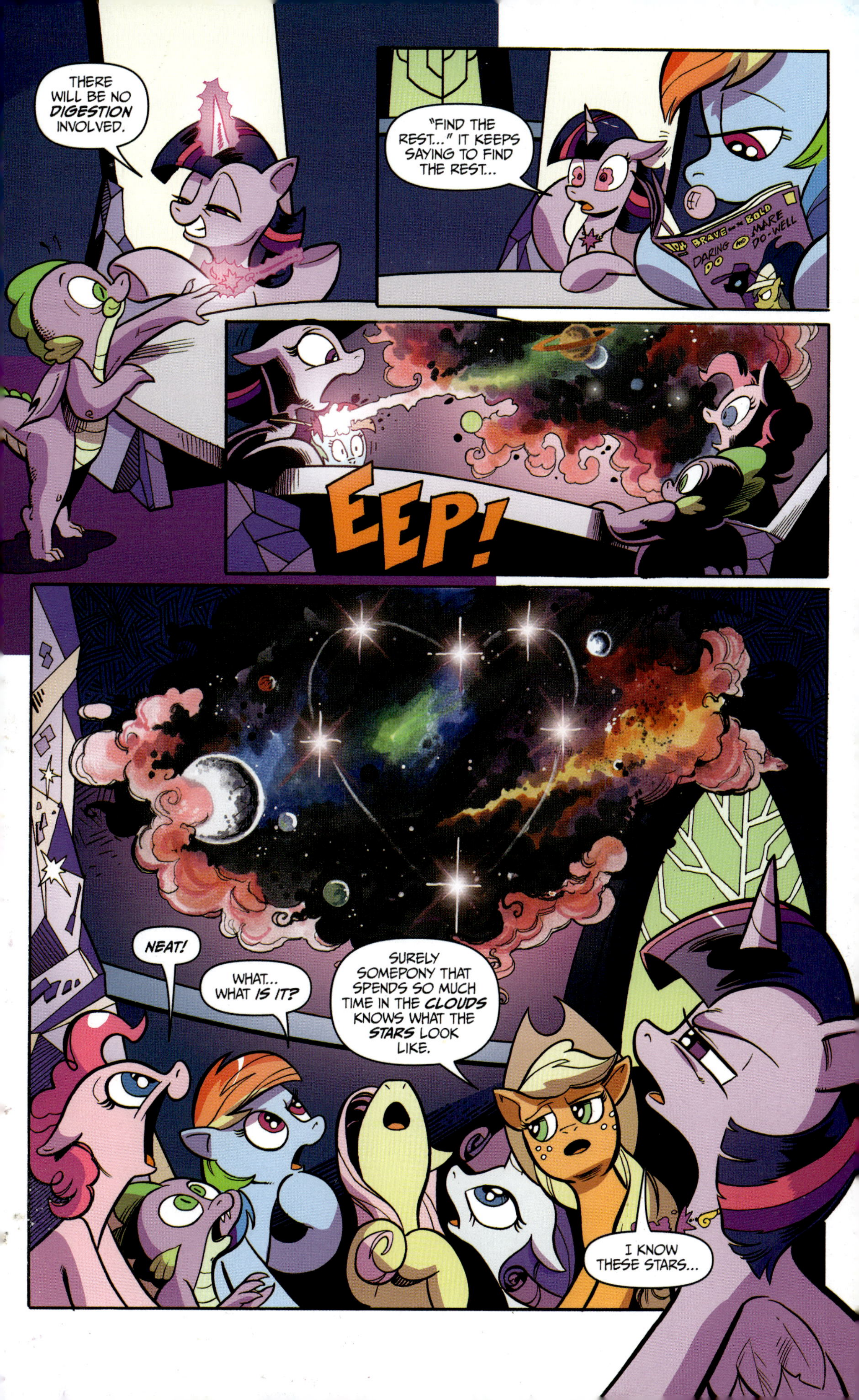

THERE WILL BE NO DIGESTION INVOLVED.
"FIND THE REST..." IT KEEPS SAYING TO FIND THE REST...
BRAVE AND THE BOLD DARING DO AND MARE DO-WELL
EEP!
NEAT!
WHAT... WHAT IS IT?
SURELY SOMEPONY THAT SPENDS SO MUCH TIME IN THE CLOUDS KNOWS WHAT THE STARS LOOK LIKE.
I KNOW THESE STARS...

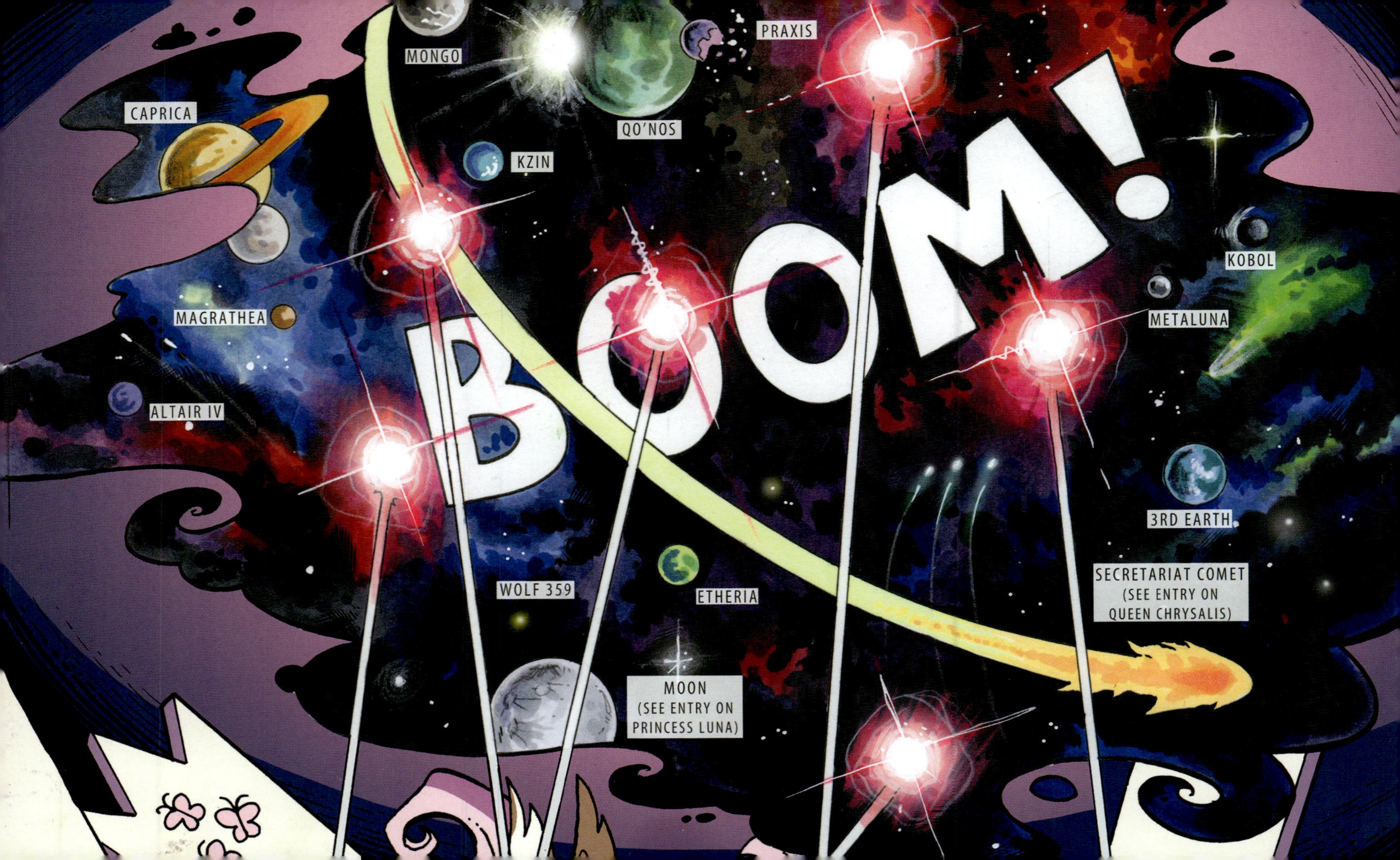
BOOM!
CAPRICA
MONGO
KZIN
QO'NOS
PRAXIS
MAGRATHEA
ALTAIR IV
WOLF 359
ETHERIA
MOON
(SEE ENTRY ON
PRINCESS LUNA)
KOBOL
METALUNA
3RD EARTH
SECRETARIAT COMET
(SEE ENTRY ON
QUEEN CHRYSALIS)

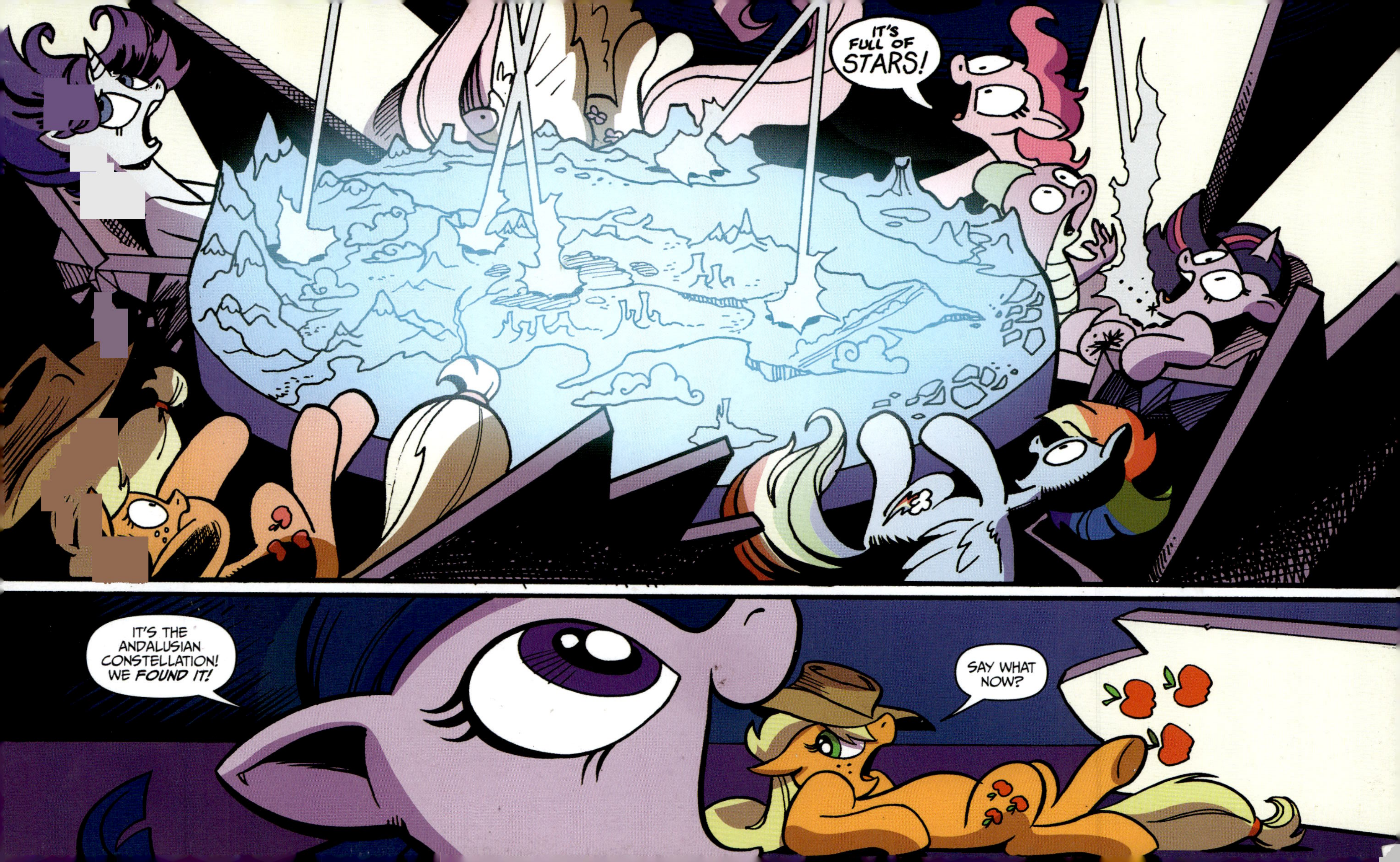
IT'S FULL OF STARS!
IT'S THE ANDALUSIAN CONSTELLATION! WE FOUND IT!
SAY WHAT NOW?

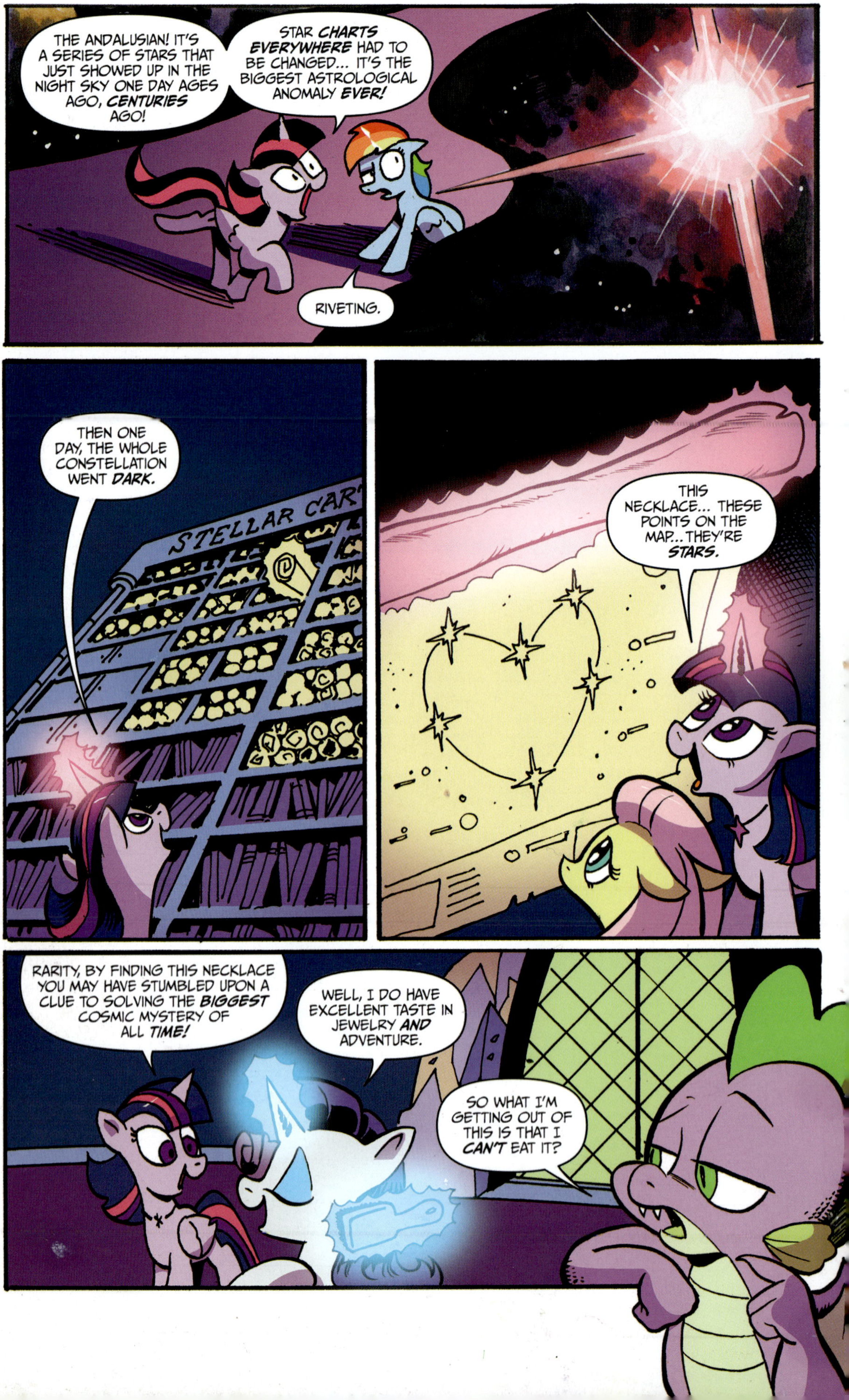
THE ANDALUSIAN! IT'S A SERIES OF STARS THAT JUST SHOWED UP IN THE NIGHT SKY ONE DAY AGES AGO, CENTURIES AGO!
STAR CHARTS EVERYWHERE HAD TO BE CHANGED... IT'S THE BIGGEST ASTROLOGICAL ANOMALY EVER!
RIVETING.
THEN ONE DAY, THE WHOLE CONSTELLATION WENT DARK.
STELLAR CART
THIS NECKLACE... THESE POINTS ON THE MAP...THEY'RE STARS.
RARITY, BY FINDING THIS NECKLACE YOU MAY HAVE STUMBLED UPON A CLUE TO SOLVING THE BIGGEST COSMIC MYSTERY OF ALL TIME!
WELL, I DO HAVE EXCELLENT TASTE IN JEWELRY AND ADVENTURE.
SO WHAT I'M GETTING OUT OF THIS IS THAT I CAN'T EAT IT?

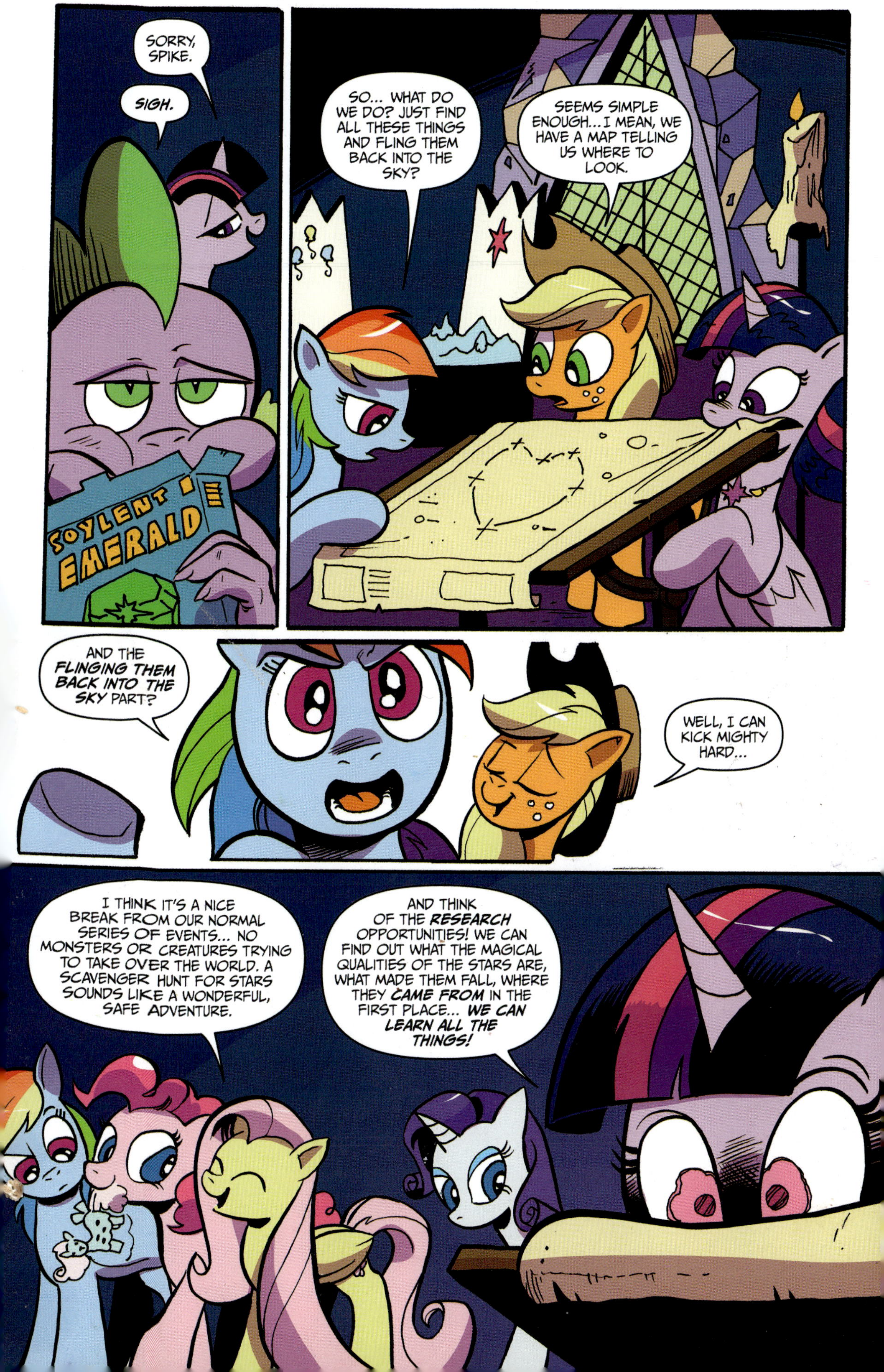
SORRY, SPIKE.
SIGH.
SOYLENT EMERALD
SO... WHAT DO WE DO? JUST FIND ALL THESE THINGS AND FLING THEM BACK INTO THE SKY?
SEEMS SIMPLE ENOUGH... I MEAN, WE HAVE A MAP TELLING US WHERE TO LOOK.
AND THE FLINGING THEM BACK INTO THE SKY PART?
WELL, I CAN KICK MIGHTY HARD...
I THINK IT'S A NICE BREAK FROM OUR NORMAL SERIES OF EVENTS... NO MONSTERS OR CREATURES TRYING TO TAKE OVER THE WORLD. A SCAVENGER HUNT FOR STARS SOUNDS LIKE A WONDERFUL, SAFE ADVENTURE.
AND THINK OF THE RESEARCH OPPORTUNITIES! WE CAN FIND OUT WHAT THE MAGICAL QUALITIES OF THE STARS ARE, WHAT MADE THEM FALL, WHERE THEY CAME FROM IN THE FIRST PLACE... WE CAN LEARN ALL THE THINGS!

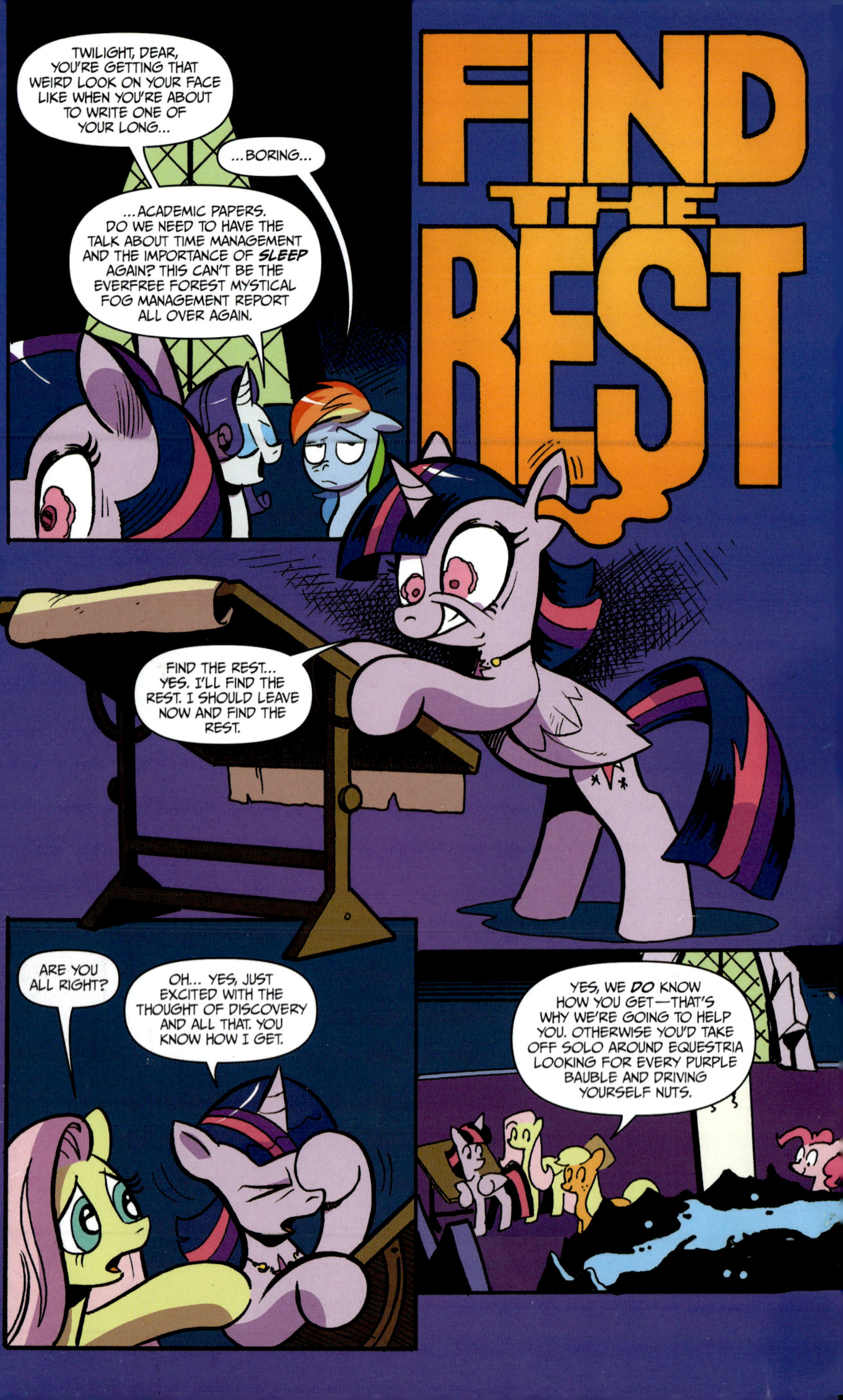
TWILIGHT, DEAR, YOU'RE GETTING THAT WEIRD LOOK ON YOUR FACE LIKE WHEN YOU'RE ABOUT TO WRITE ONE OF YOUR LONG...
...BORING...
...ACADEMIC PAPERS. DO WE NEED TO HAVE THE TALK ABOUT TIME MANAGEMENT AND THE IMPORTANCE OF *SLEEP* AGAIN? THIS CAN'T BE THE EVERFREE FOREST MYSTICAL FOG MANAGEMENT REPORT ALL OVER AGAIN.
FIND THE REST
FIND THE REST... YES. I'LL FIND THE REST. I SHOULD LEAVE NOW AND FIND THE REST.
ARE YOU ALL RIGHT?
OH... YES, JUST EXCITED WITH THE THOUGHT OF DISCOVERY AND ALL THAT. YOU KNOW HOW I GET.
YES, WE *DO* KNOW HOW YOU GET—THAT'S WHY WE'RE GOING TO HELP YOU. OTHERWISE YOU'D TAKE OFF SOLO AROUND EQUESTRIA LOOKING FOR EVERY PURPLE BAUBLE AND DRIVING YOURSELF NUTS.

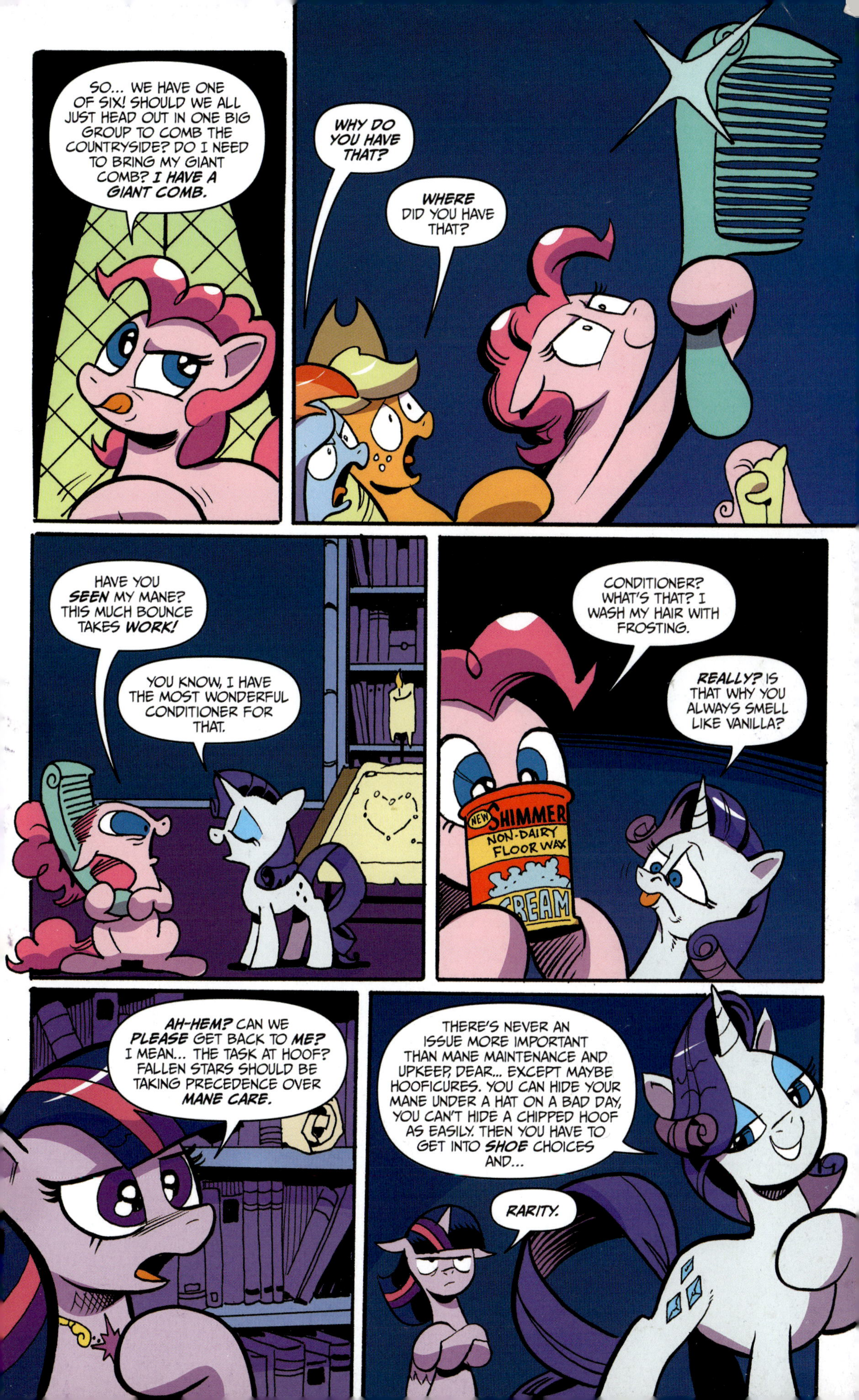

SO... WE HAVE ONE OF SIX! SHOULD WE ALL JUST HEAD OUT IN ONE BIG GROUP TO COMB THE COUNTRYSIDE? DO I NEED TO BRING MY GIANT COMB? I HAVE A GIANT COMB.
WHY DO YOU HAVE THAT?
WHERE DID YOU HAVE THAT?
HAVE YOU SEEN MY MANE? THIS MUCH BOUNCE TAKES WORK!
YOU KNOW, I HAVE THE MOST WONDERFUL CONDITIONER FOR THAT.
CONDITIONER? WHAT'S THAT? I WASH MY HAIR WITH FROSTING.
NEW SHIMMER NON-DAIRY FLOOR WAX CREAM
REALLY? IS THAT WHY YOU ALWAYS SMELL LIKE VANILLA?
AH-HEM? CAN WE PLEASE GET BACK TO ME? I MEAN... THE TASK AT HOOF? FALLEN STARS SHOULD BE TAKING PRECEDENCE OVER MANE CARE.
THERE'S NEVER AN ISSUE MORE IMPORTANT THAN MANE MAINTENANCE AND UPKEEP, DEAR... EXCEPT MAYBE HOOFICURES. YOU CAN HIDE YOUR MANE UNDER A HAT ON A BAD DAY, YOU CAN'T HIDE A CHIPPED HOOF AS EASILY. THEN YOU HAVE TO GET INTO SHOE CHOICES AND...
RARITY.

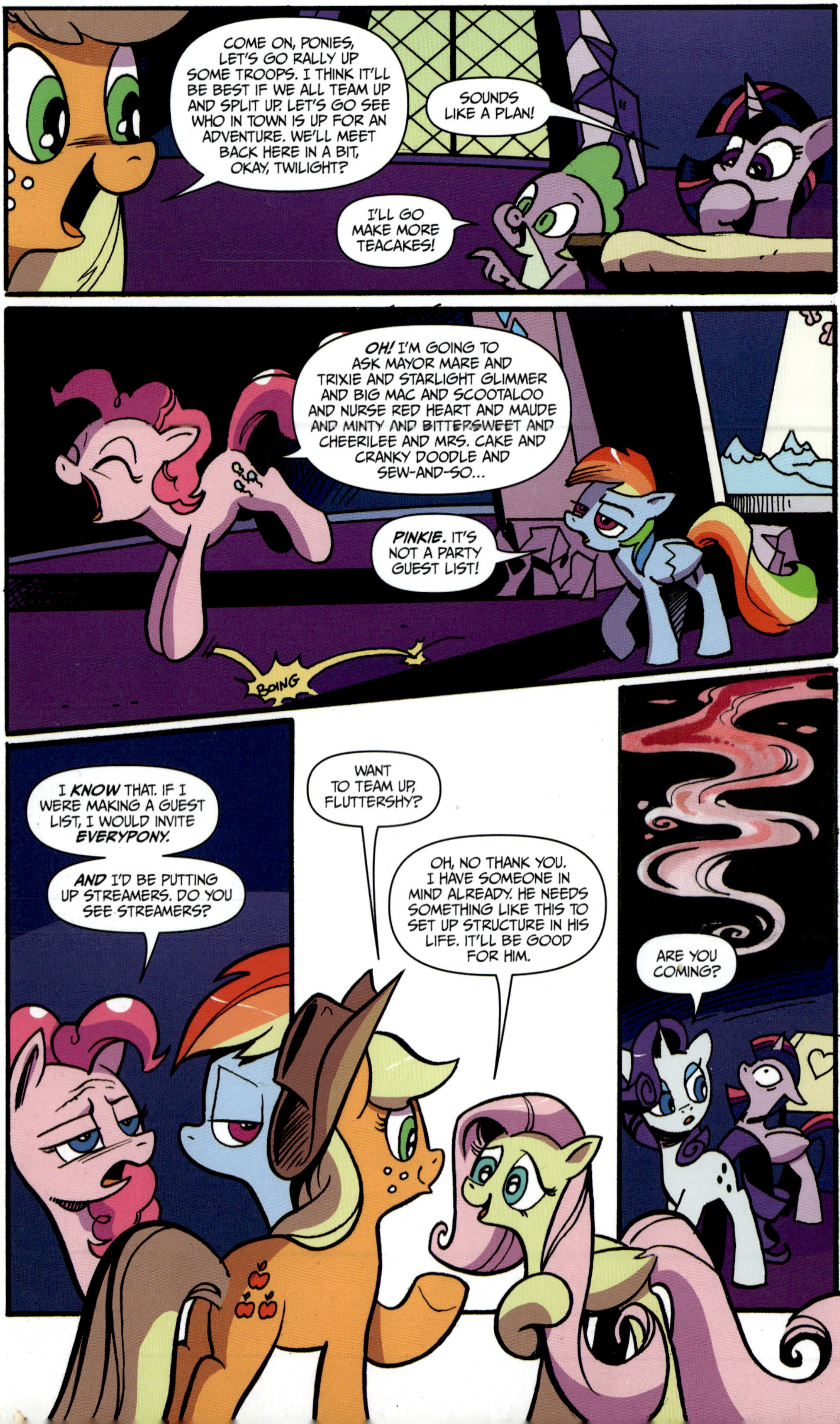
COME ON, PONIES, LET'S GO RALLY UP SOME TROOPS. I THINK IT'LL BE BEST IF WE ALL TEAM UP AND SPLIT UP. LET'S GO SEE WHO IN TOWN IS UP FOR AN ADVENTURE. WE'LL MEET BACK HERE IN A BIT, OKAY, TWILIGHT?
SOUNDS LIKE A PLAN!
I'LL GO MAKE MORE TEACAKES!
OH! I'M GOING TO ASK MAYOR MARE AND TRIXIE AND STARLIGHT GLIMMER AND BIG MAC AND SCOOTALOO AND NURSE RED HEART AND MAUDE AND MINTY AND BITTERSWEET AND CHEERILEE AND MRS. CAKE AND CRANKY DOODLE AND SEW-AND-SO...
PINKIE. IT'S NOT A PARTY GUEST LIST!
BOING
I KNOW THAT. IF I WERE MAKING A GUEST LIST, I WOULD INVITE EVERYPONY.
AND I'D BE PUTTING UP STREAMERS. DO YOU SEE STREAMERS?
WANT TO TEAM UP, FLUTTERSHY?
OH, NO THANK YOU. I HAVE SOMEONE IN MIND ALREADY. HE NEEDS SOMETHING LIKE THIS TO SET UP STRUCTURE IN HIS LIFE. IT'LL BE GOOD FOR HIM.
ARE YOU COMING?

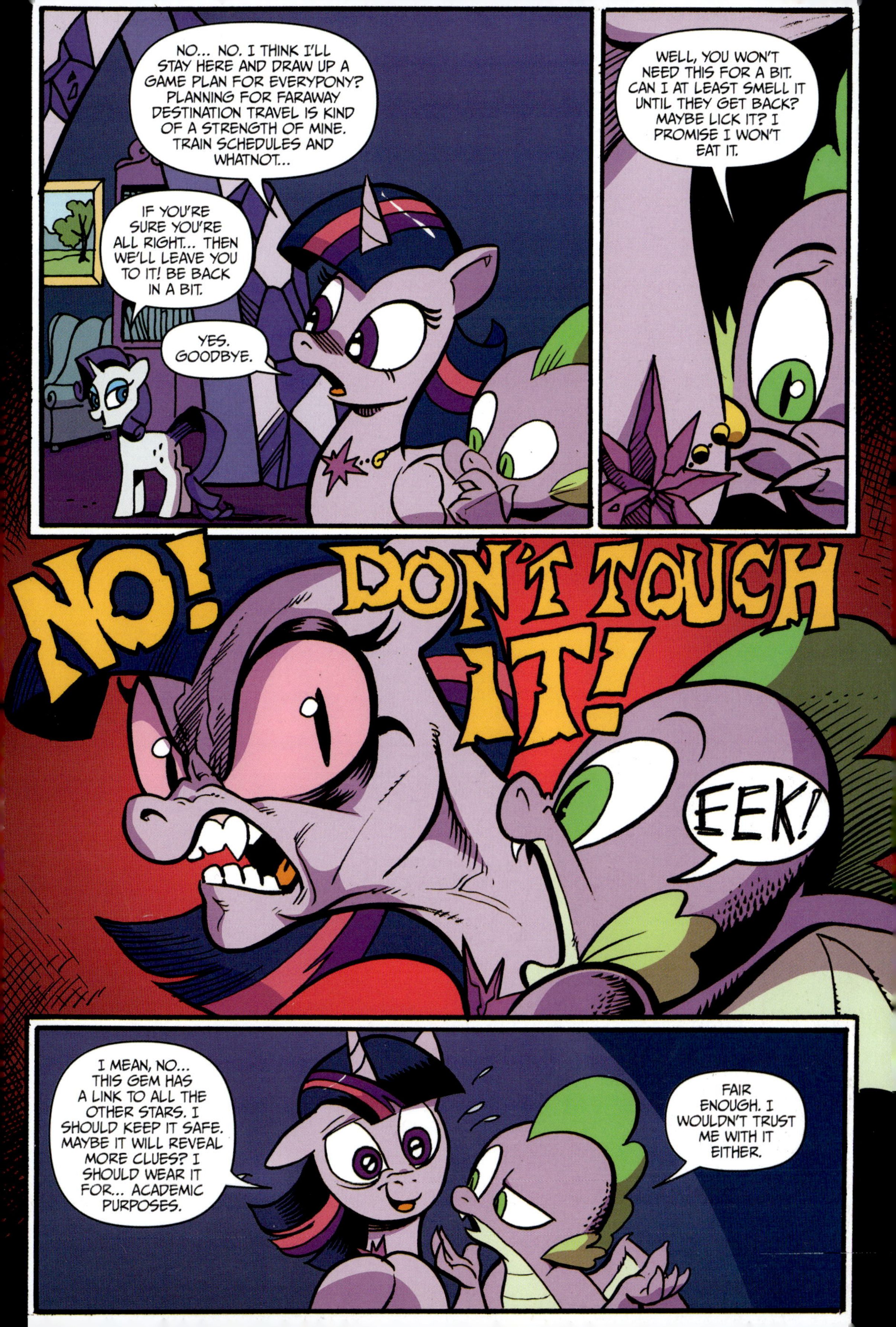
NO... NO. I THINK I'LL STAY HERE AND DRAW UP A GAME PLAN FOR EVERYPONY? PLANNING FOR FARAWAY DESTINATION TRAVEL IS KIND OF A STRENGTH OF MINE. TRAIN SCHEDULES AND WHATNOT...
IF YOU'RE SURE YOU'RE ALL RIGHT... THEN WE'LL LEAVE YOU TO IT! BE BACK IN A BIT.
YES. GOODBYE.
WELL, YOU WON'T NEED THIS FOR A BIT. CAN I AT LEAST SMELL IT UNTIL THEY GET BACK? MAYBE LICK IT? I PROMISE I WON'T EAT IT.
NO! DON'T TOUCH IT!
EEK!
I MEAN, NO... THIS GEM HAS A LINK TO ALL THE OTHER STARS. I SHOULD KEEP IT SAFE. MAYBE IT WILL REVEAL MORE CLUES? I SHOULD WEAR IT FOR... ACADEMIC PURPOSES.
FAIR ENOUGH. I WOULDN'T TRUST ME WITH IT EITHER.

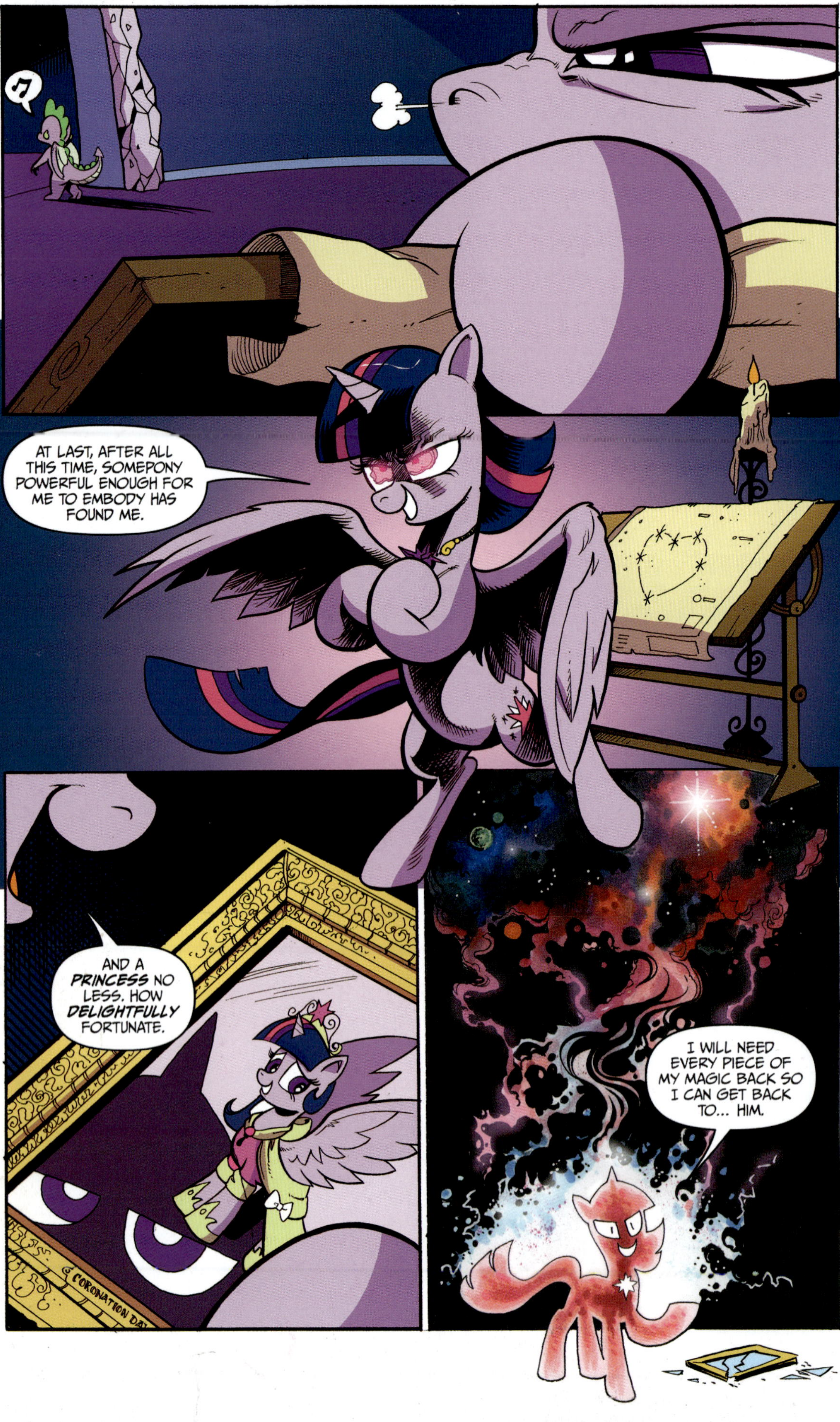
AT LAST, AFTER ALL THIS TIME, SOMEPONY POWERFUL ENOUGH FOR ME TO EMBODY HAS FOUND ME.
AND A PRINCESS NO LESS. HOW DELIGHTFULLY FORTUNATE.
CORONATION DAY
I WILL NEED EVERY PIECE OF MY MAGIC BACK SO I CAN GET BACK TO... HIM.

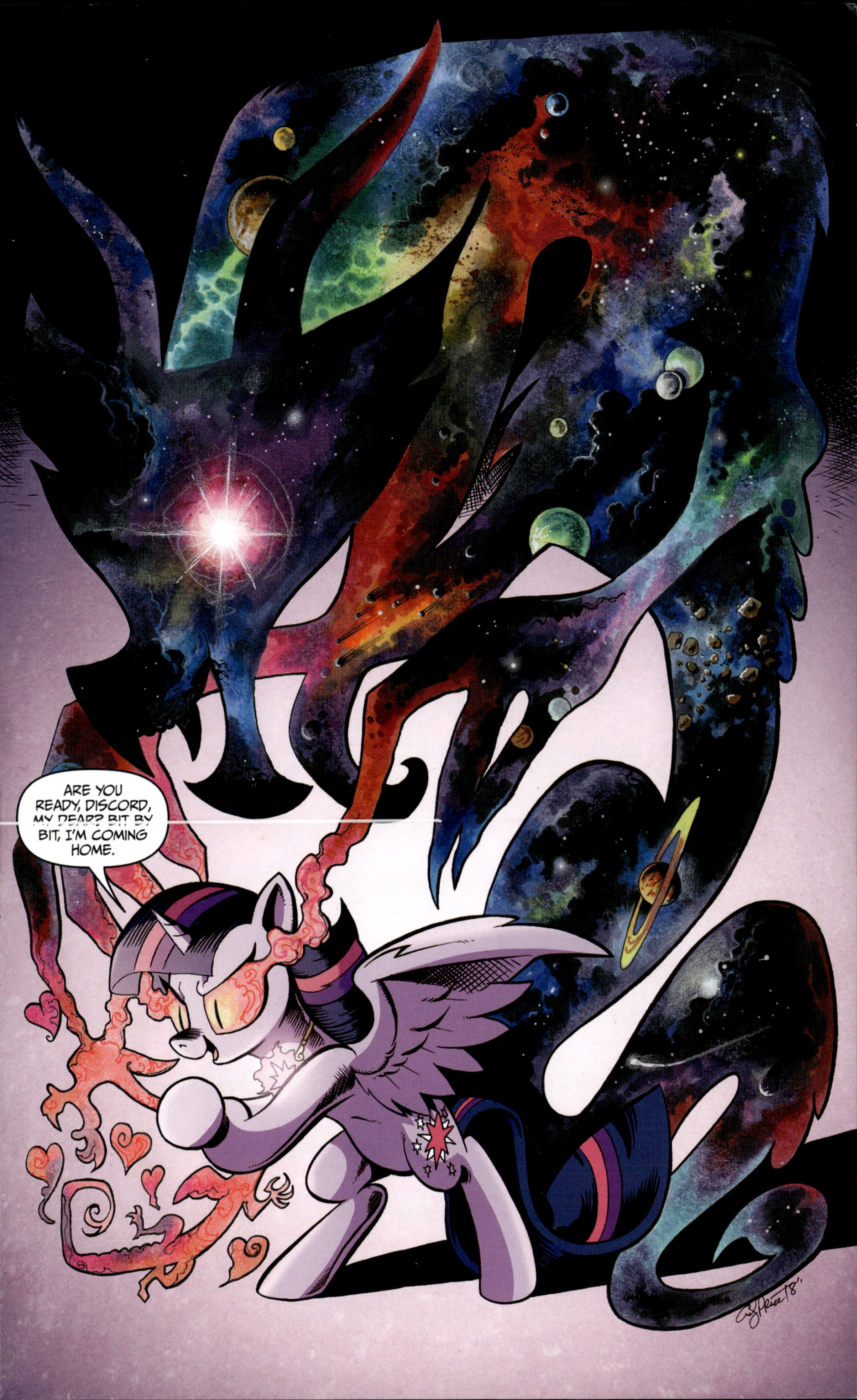
ARE YOU READY, DISCORD, MY DEAR? BIT BY BIT, I'M COMING HOME.

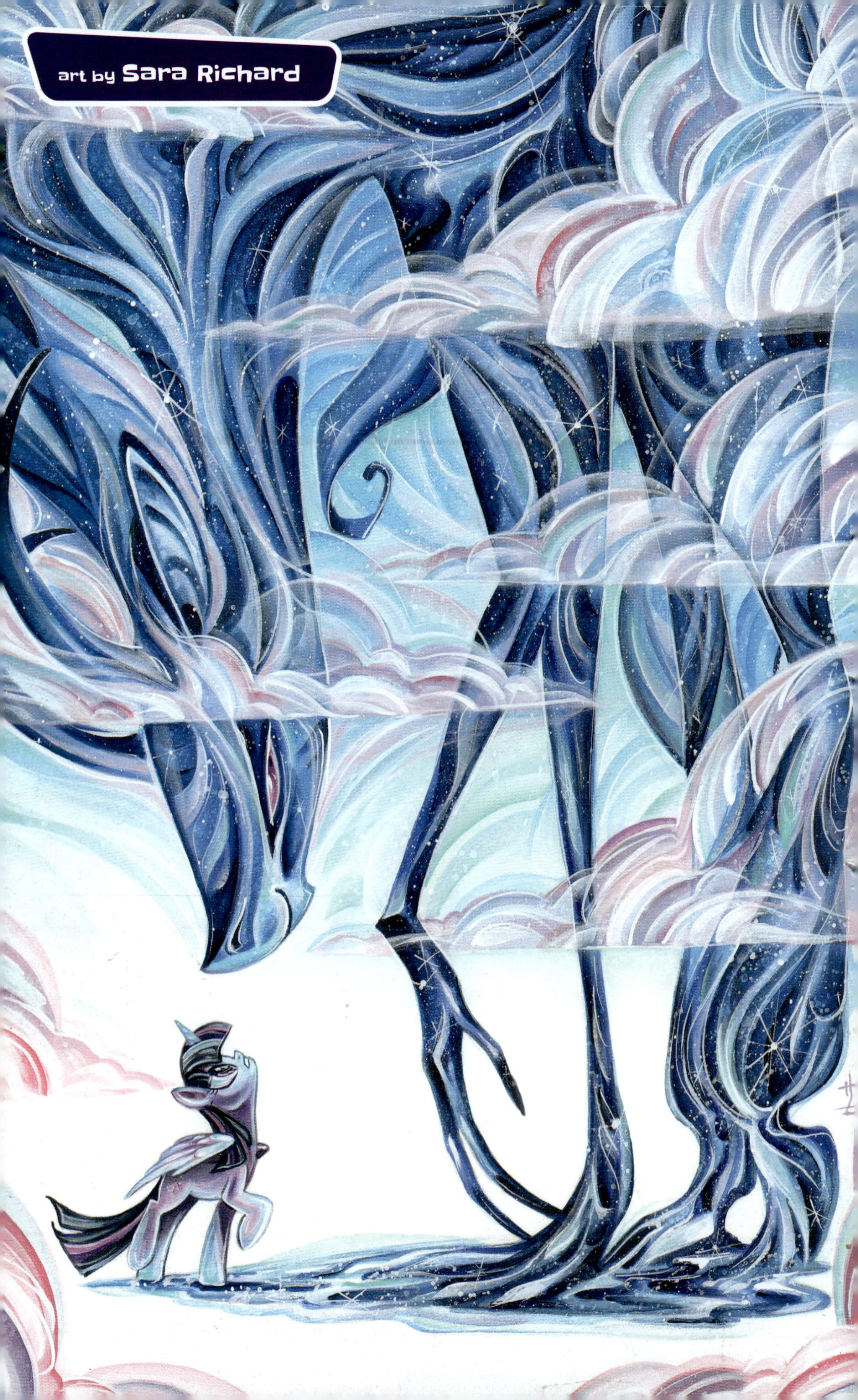

art by Sara Richard

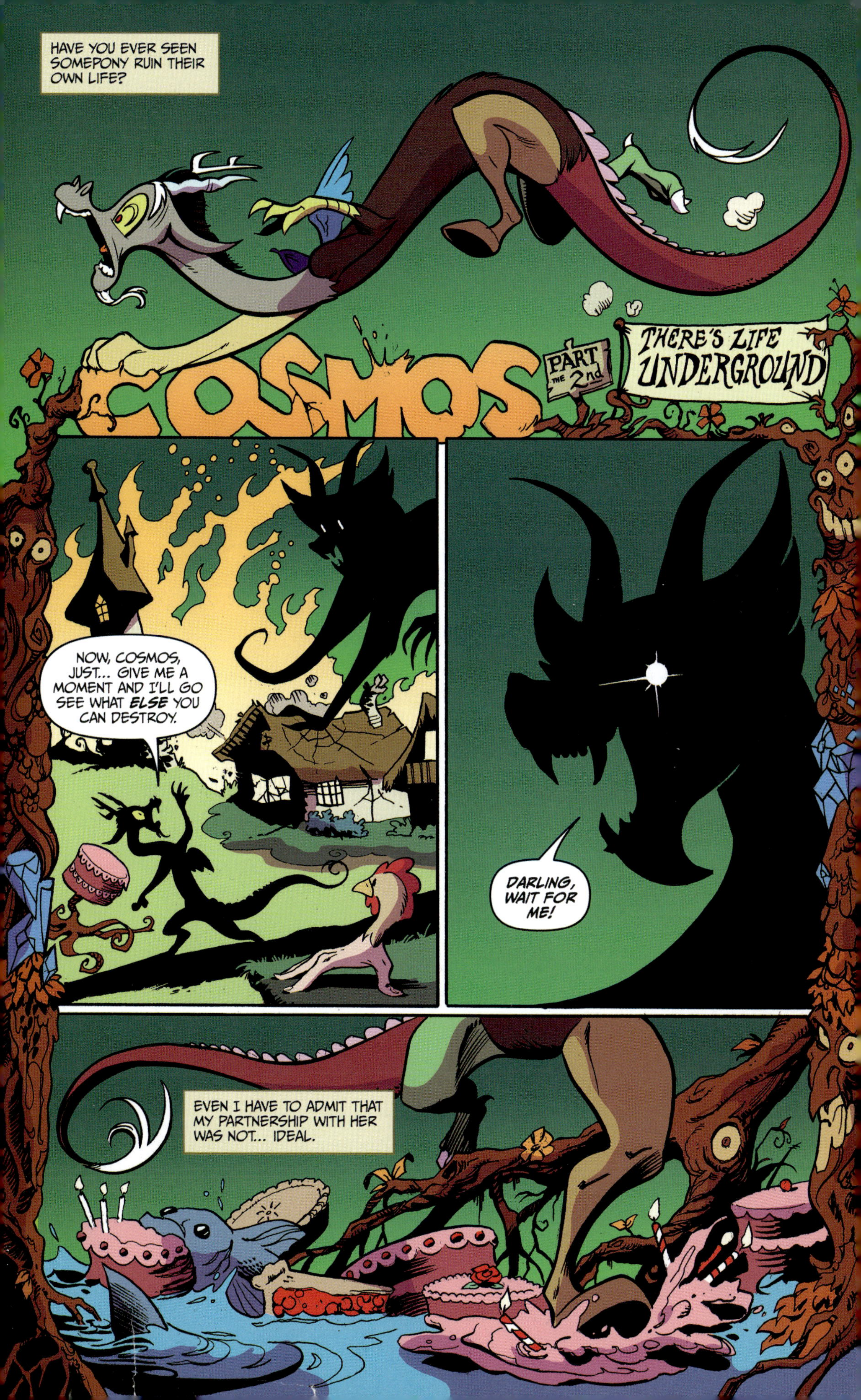
HAVE YOU EVER SEEN SOMEPONY RUIN THEIR OWN LIFE?
COSMOS
PART THE 2nd
THERE'S LIFE UNDERGROUND
NOW, COSMOS, JUST... GIVE ME A MOMENT AND I'LL GO SEE WHAT *ELSE* YOU CAN DESTROY.
DARLING, WAIT FOR ME!
EVEN I HAVE TO ADMIT THAT MY PARTNERSHIP WITH HER WAS NOT... IDEAL.

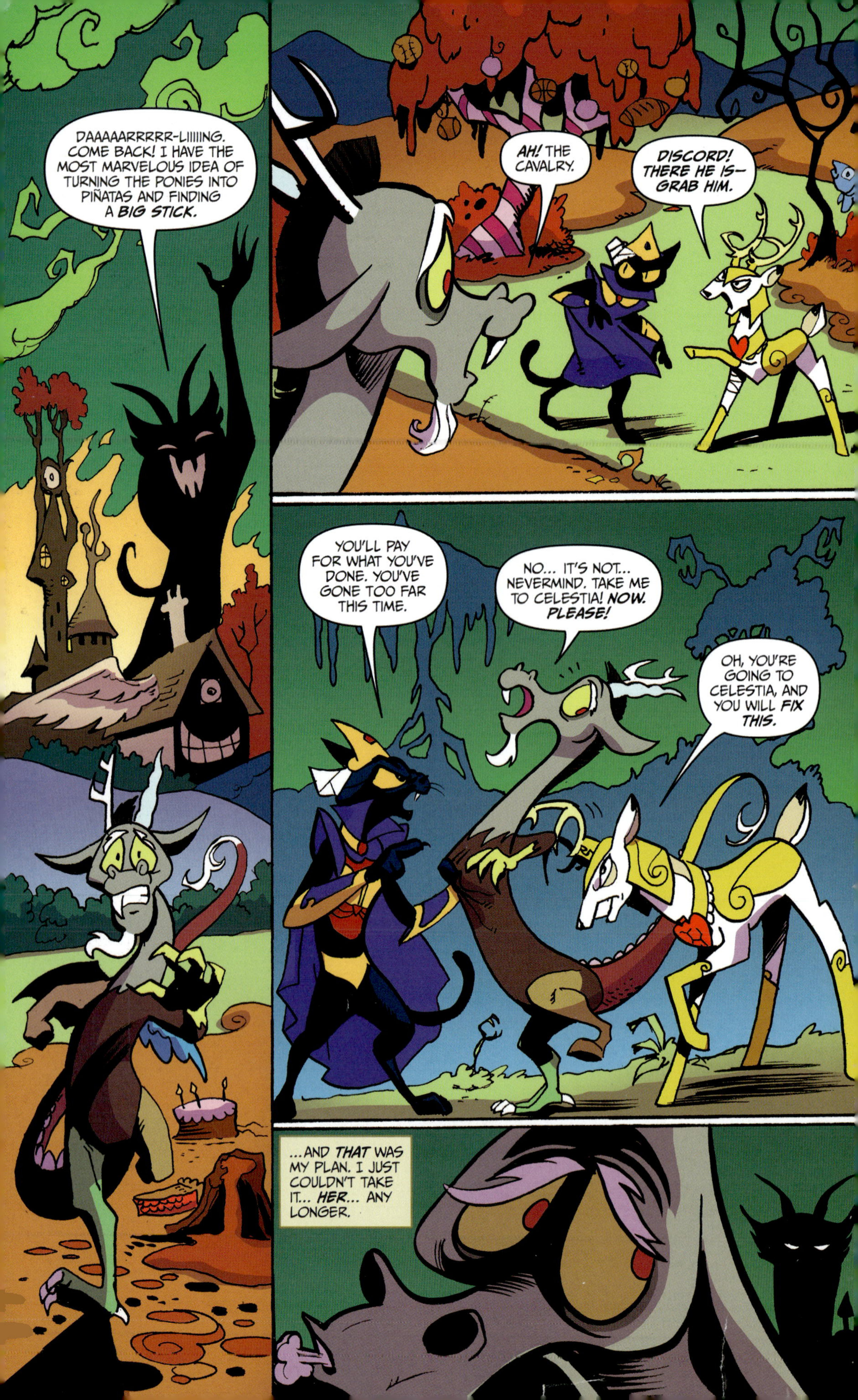
DAAAAARRRRR-LIIIIING. COME BACK! I HAVE THE MOST MARVELOUS IDEA OF TURNING THE PONIES INTO PIÑATAS AND FINDING A BIG STICK.
AH! THE CAVALRY.
DISCORD! THERE HE IS-GRAB HIM.
YOU'LL PAY FOR WHAT YOU'VE DONE. YOU'VE GONE TOO FAR THIS TIME.
NO... IT'S NOT... NEVERMIND. TAKE ME TO CELESTIA! NOW. PLEASE!
OH, YOU'RE GOING TO CELESTIA, AND YOU WILL FIX THIS.
...AND THAT WAS MY PLAN. I JUST COULDN'T TAKE IT... HER... ANY LONGER.

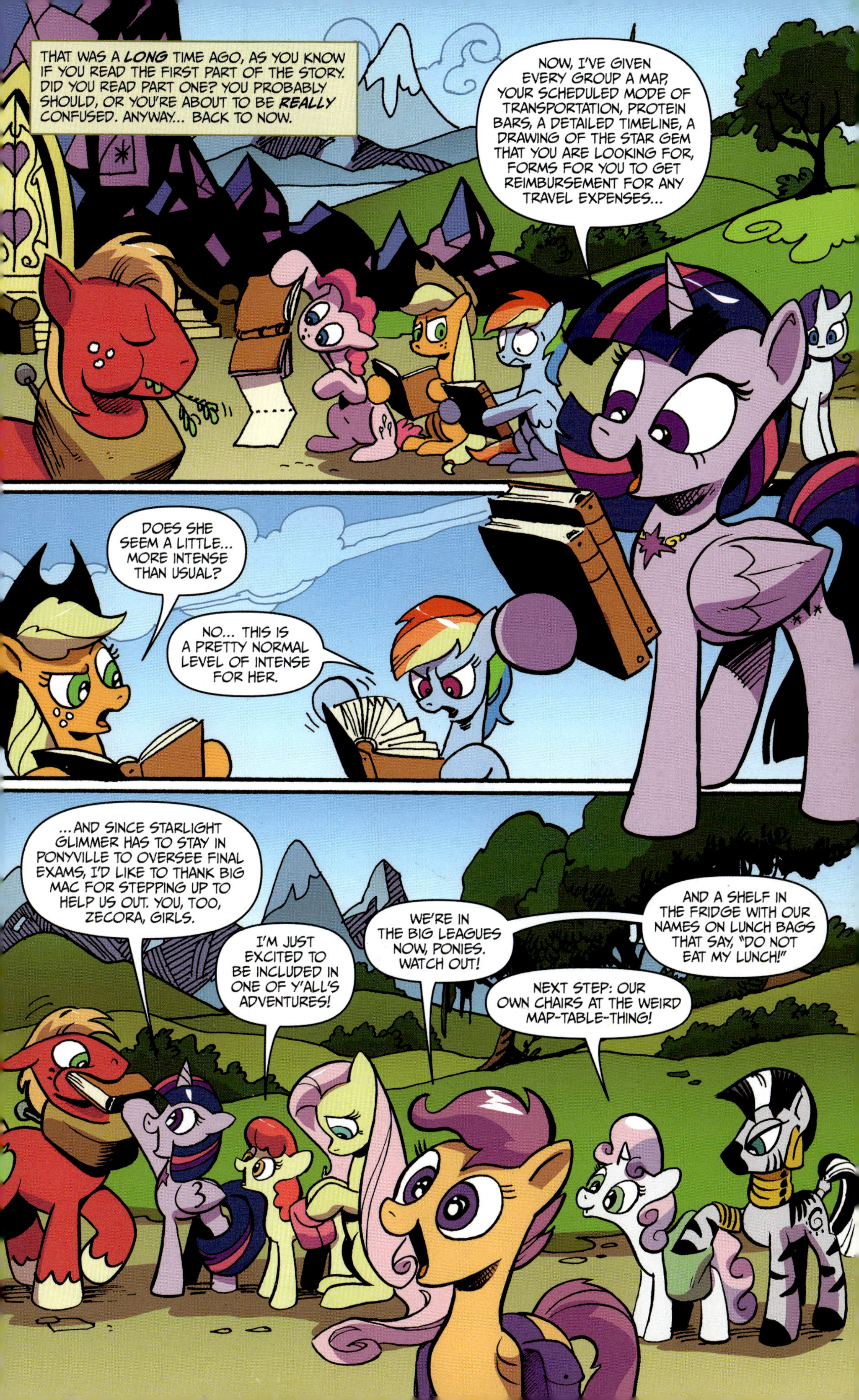
THAT WAS A LONG TIME AGO, AS YOU KNOW IF YOU READ THE FIRST PART OF THE STORY. DID YOU READ PART ONE? YOU PROBABLY SHOULD, OR YOU'RE ABOUT TO BE REALLY CONFUSED. ANYWAY... BACK TO NOW.
NOW, I'VE GIVEN EVERY GROUP A MAP, YOUR SCHEDULED MODE OF TRANSPORTATION, PROTEIN BARS, A DETAILED TIMELINE, A DRAWING OF THE STAR GEM THAT YOU ARE LOOKING FOR, FORMS FOR YOU TO GET REIMBURSEMENT FOR ANY TRAVEL EXPENSES...
DOES SHE SEEM A LITTLE... MORE INTENSE THAN USUAL?
NO... THIS IS A PRETTY NORMAL LEVEL OF INTENSE FOR HER.
...AND SINCE STARLIGHT GLIMMER HAS TO STAY IN PONYVILLE TO OVERSEE FINAL EXAMS, I'D LIKE TO THANK BIG MAC FOR STEPPING UP TO HELP US OUT. YOU, TOO, ZECORA, GIRLS.
I'M JUST EXCITED TO BE INCLUDED IN ONE OF Y'ALL'S ADVENTURES!
WE'RE IN THE BIG LEAGUES NOW, PONIES. WATCH OUT!
AND A SHELF IN THE FRIDGE WITH OUR NAMES ON LUNCH BAGS THAT SAY, "DO NOT EAT MY LUNCH!"
NEXT STEP: OUR OWN CHAIRS AT THE WEIRD MAP-TABLE-THING!

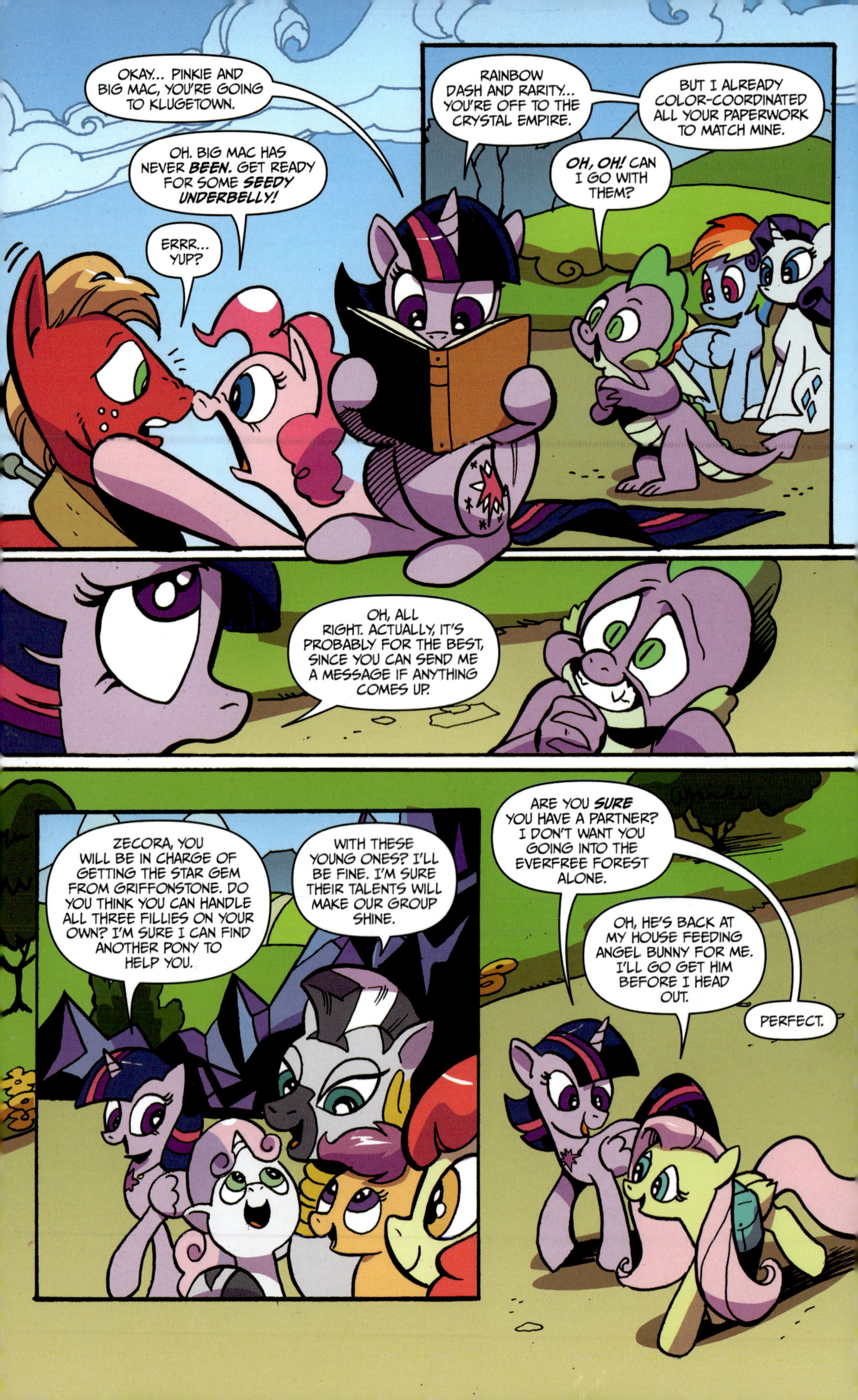
OKAY... PINKIE AND BIG MAC, YOU'RE GOING TO KLUGETOWN.
OH. BIG MAC HAS NEVER **BEEN.** GET READY FOR SOME ***SEEDY UNDERBELLY!***
ERRR... YUP?
RAINBOW DASH AND RARITY... YOU'RE OFF TO THE CRYSTAL EMPIRE.
BUT I ALREADY COLOR-COORDINATED ALL YOUR PAPERWORK TO MATCH MINE.
OH, OH! CAN I GO WITH THEM?
OH, ALL RIGHT. ACTUALLY, IT'S PROBABLY FOR THE BEST, SINCE YOU CAN SEND ME A MESSAGE IF ANYTHING COMES UP.
ZECORA, YOU WILL BE IN CHARGE OF GETTING THE STAR GEM FROM GRIFFONSTONE. DO YOU THINK YOU CAN HANDLE ALL THREE FILLIES ON YOUR OWN? I'M SURE I CAN FIND ANOTHER PONY TO HELP YOU.
WITH THESE YOUNG ONES? I'LL BE FINE. I'M SURE THEIR TALENTS WILL MAKE OUR GROUP SHINE.
ARE YOU ***SURE*** YOU HAVE A PARTNER? I DON'T WANT YOU GOING INTO THE EVERFREE FOREST ALONE.
OH, HE'S BACK AT MY HOUSE FEEDING ANGEL BUNNY FOR ME. I'LL GO GET HIM BEFORE I HEAD OUT.
PERFECT.

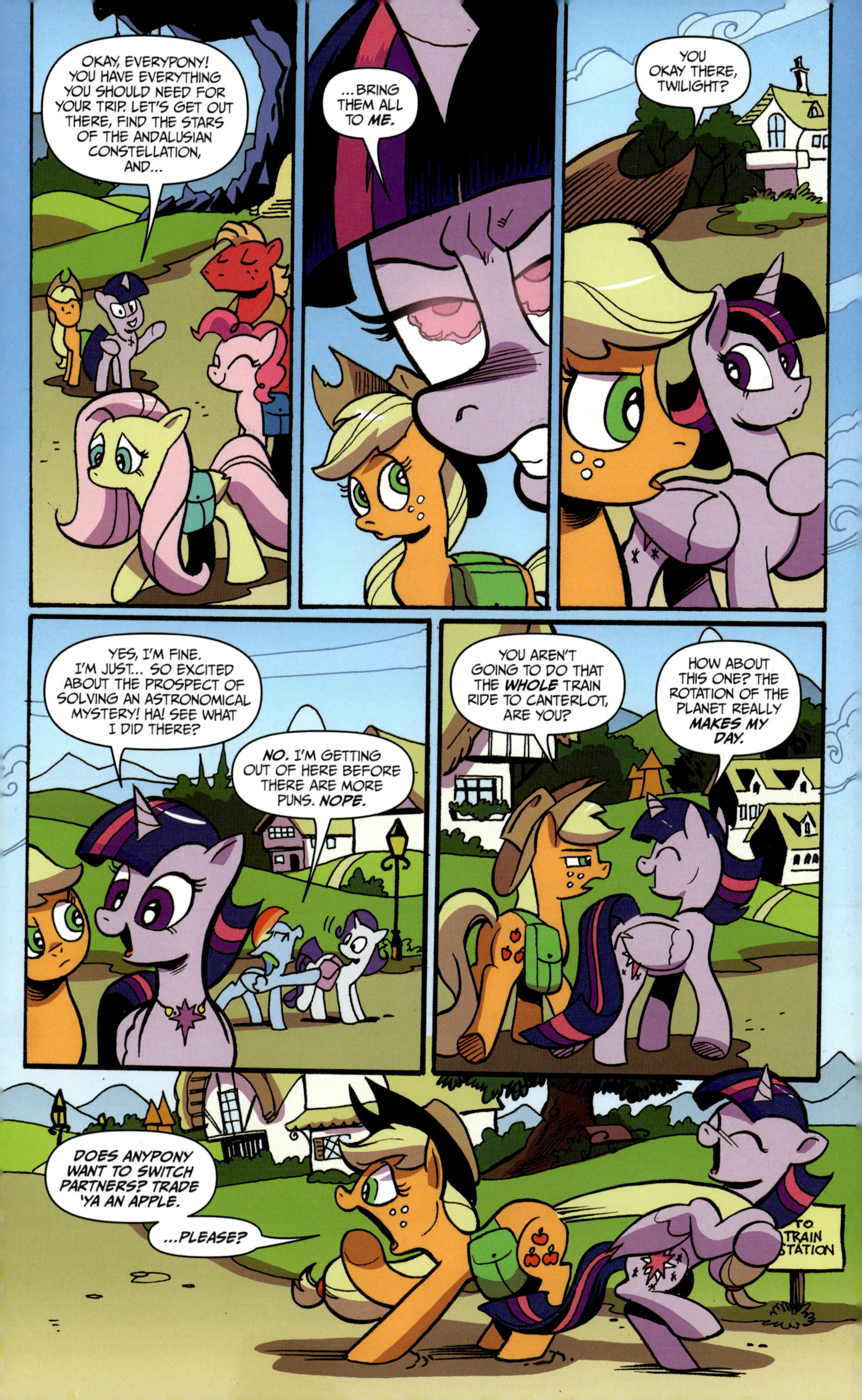
OKAY, EVERYPONY! YOU HAVE EVERYTHING YOU SHOULD NEED FOR YOUR TRIP. LET'S GET OUT THERE, FIND THE STARS OF THE ANDALUSIAN CONSTELLATION, AND...
...BRING THEM ALL TO ME.
YOU OKAY THERE, TWILIGHT?
YES, I'M FINE. I'M JUST... SO EXCITED ABOUT THE PROSPECT OF SOLVING AN ASTRONOMICAL MYSTERY! HA! SEE WHAT I DID THERE?
NO. I'M GETTING OUT OF HERE BEFORE THERE ARE MORE PUNS. NOPE.
YOU AREN'T GOING TO DO THAT THE WHOLE TRAIN RIDE TO CANTERLOT, ARE YOU?
HOW ABOUT THIS ONE? THE ROTATION OF THE PLANET REALLY MAKES MY DAY.
DOES ANYPONY WANT TO SWITCH PARTNERS? TRADE 'YA AN APPLE.
...PLEASE?
TO TRAIN STATION

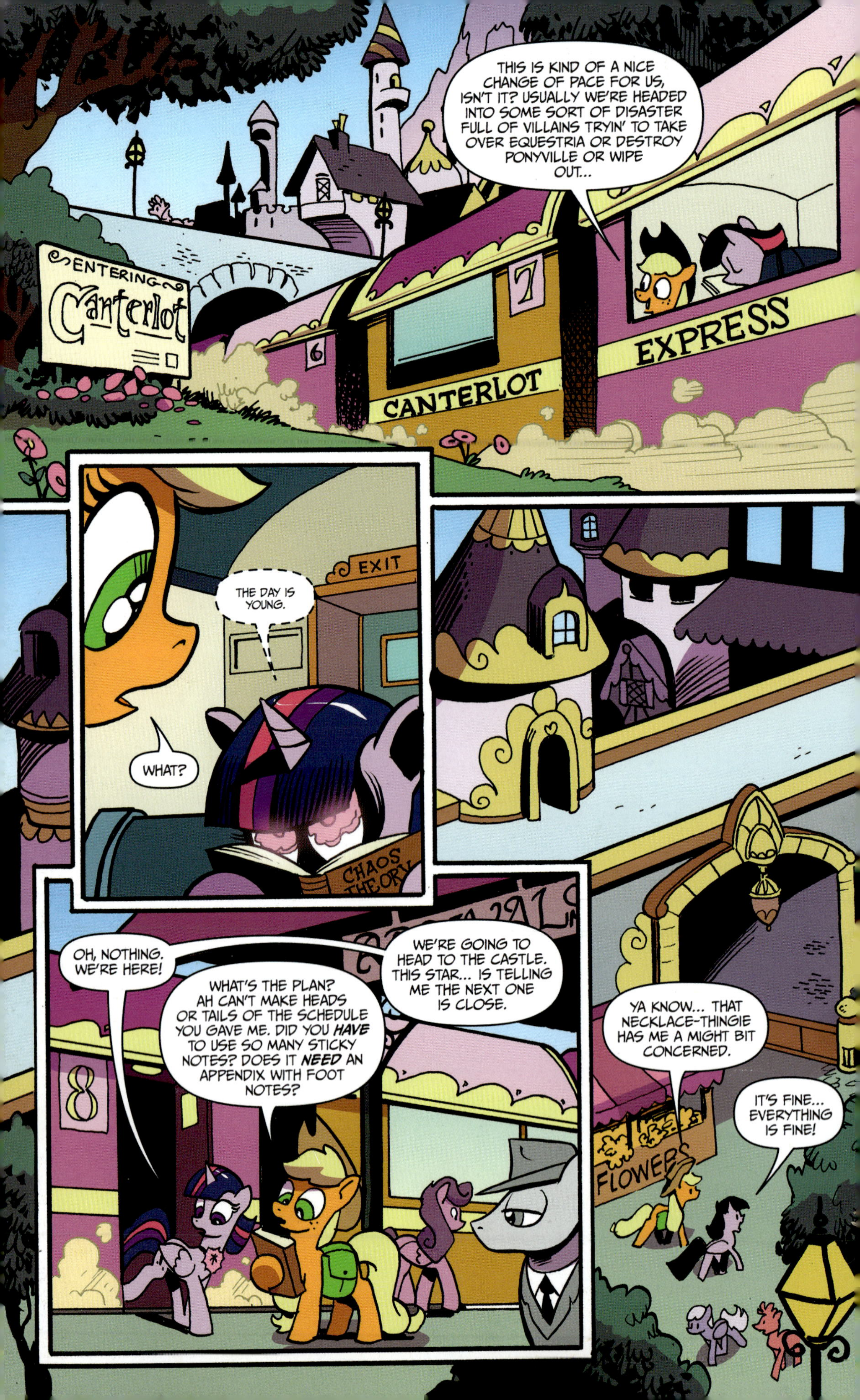
ENTERING Canterlot
THIS IS KIND OF A NICE CHANGE OF PACE FOR US, ISN'T IT? USUALLY WE'RE HEADED INTO SOME SORT OF DISASTER FULL OF VILLAINS TRYIN' TO TAKE OVER EQUESTRIA OR DESTROY PONYVILLE OR WIPE OUT...
CANTERLOT EXPRESS
THE DAY IS YOUNG.
EXIT
WHAT?
CHAOS THEORY
OH, NOTHING. WE'RE HERE!
WHAT'S THE PLAN? AH CAN'T MAKE HEADS OR TAILS OF THE SCHEDULE YOU GAVE ME. DID YOU *HAVE* TO USE SO MANY STICKY NOTES? DOES IT *NEED* AN APPENDIX WITH FOOT NOTES?
WE'RE GOING TO HEAD TO THE CASTLE. THIS STAR... IS TELLING ME THE NEXT ONE IS CLOSE.
YA KNOW... THAT NECKLACE-THINGIE HAS ME A MIGHT BIT CONCERNED.
IT'S FINE... EVERYTHING IS FINE!
FLOWERS

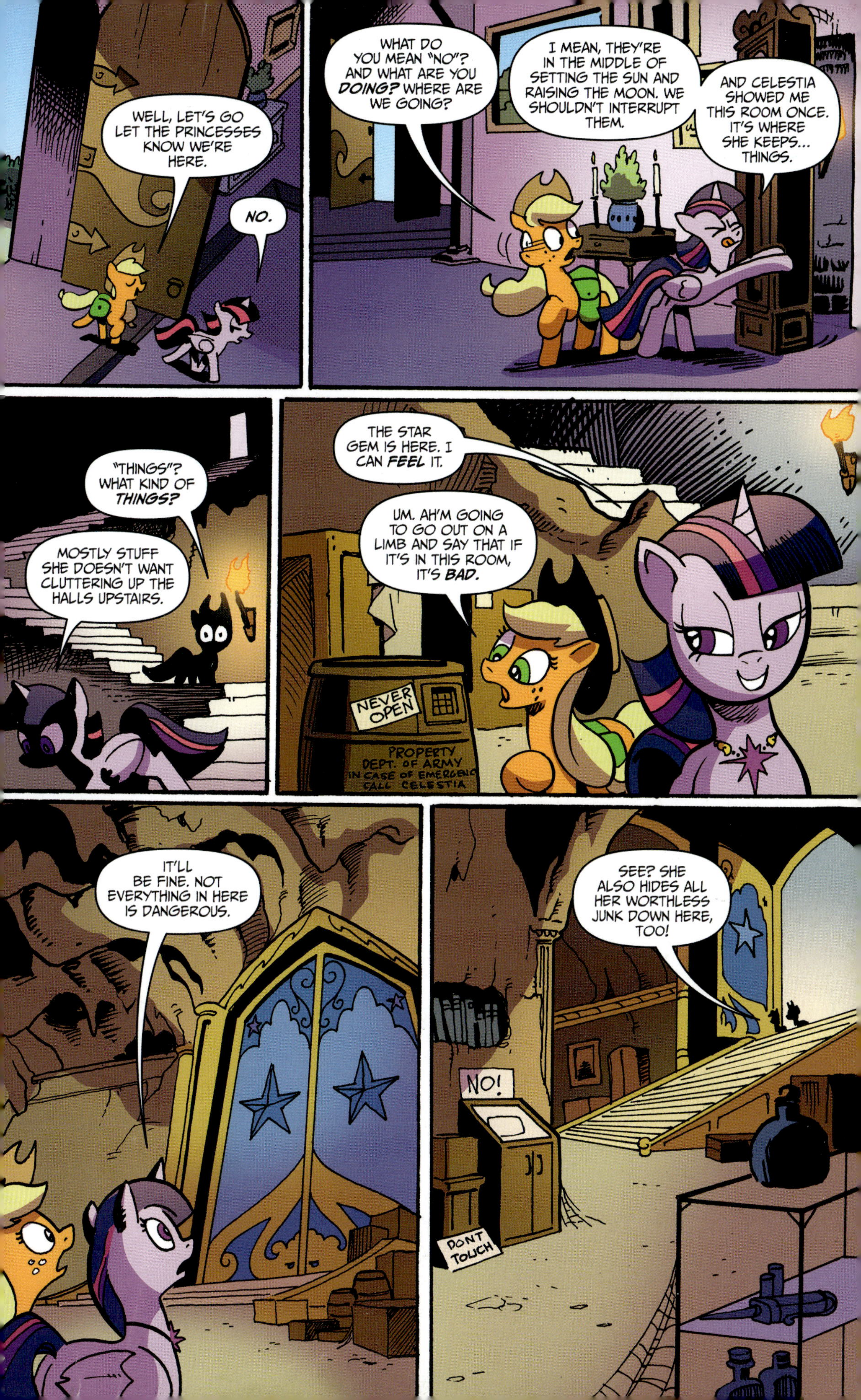
WELL, LET'S GO LET THE PRINCESSES KNOW WE'RE HERE.
NO.
WHAT DO YOU MEAN "NO"? AND WHAT ARE YOU DOING? WHERE ARE WE GOING?
I MEAN, THEY'RE IN THE MIDDLE OF SETTING THE SUN AND RAISING THE MOON. WE SHOULDN'T INTERRUPT THEM.
AND CELESTIA SHOWED ME THIS ROOM ONCE. IT'S WHERE SHE KEEPS... THINGS.
"THINGS"? WHAT KIND OF THINGS?
MOSTLY STUFF SHE DOESN'T WANT CLUTTERING UP THE HALLS UPSTAIRS.
THE STAR GEM IS HERE. I CAN FEEL IT.
UM. AH'M GOING TO GO OUT ON A LIMB AND SAY THAT IF IT'S IN THIS ROOM, IT'S BAD.
NEVER OPEN
PROPERTY DEPT. OF ARMY IN CASE OF EMERGENC CALL CELESTIA
IT'LL BE FINE. NOT EVERYTHING IN HERE IS DANGEROUS.
SEE? SHE ALSO HIDES ALL HER WORTHLESS JUNK DOWN HERE, TOO!
NO!
DONT TOUCH

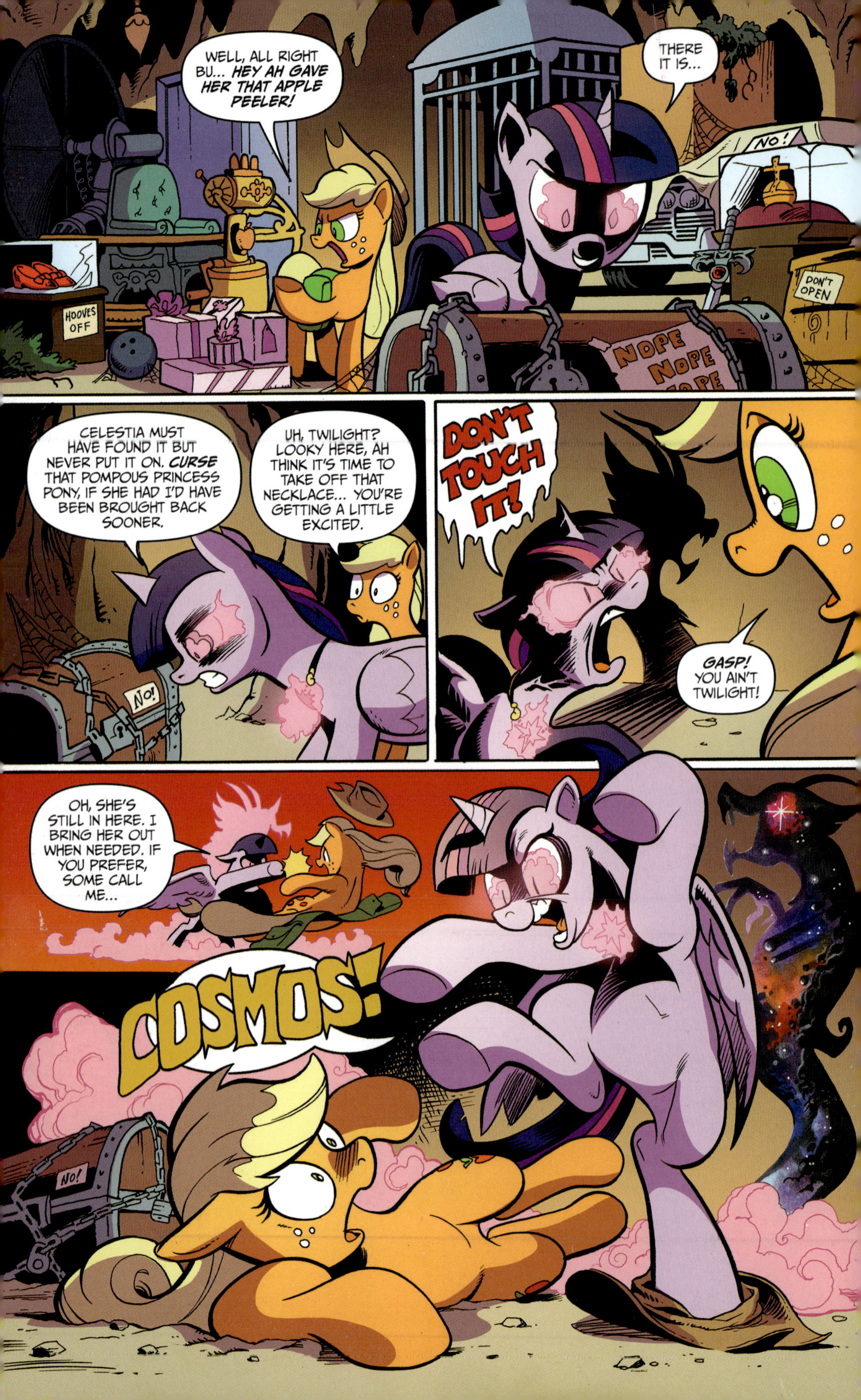
WELL, ALL RIGHT BU... HEY AH GAVE HER THAT APPLE PEELER!
THERE IT IS...
NO!
HOOVES OFF
DON'T OPEN
NOPE NOPE
CELESTIA MUST HAVE FOUND IT BUT NEVER PUT IT ON. CURSE THAT POMPOUS PRINCESS PONY, IF SHE HAD I'D HAVE BEEN BROUGHT BACK SOONER.
UH, TWILIGHT? LOOKY HERE, AH THINK IT'S TIME TO TAKE OFF THAT NECKLACE... YOU'RE GETTING A LITTLE EXCITED.
NO!
DON'T TOUCH IT!
GASP! YOU AIN'T TWILIGHT!
OH, SHE'S STILL IN HERE. I BRING HER OUT WHEN NEEDED. IF YOU PREFER, SOME CALL ME...
COSMOS!
NO!

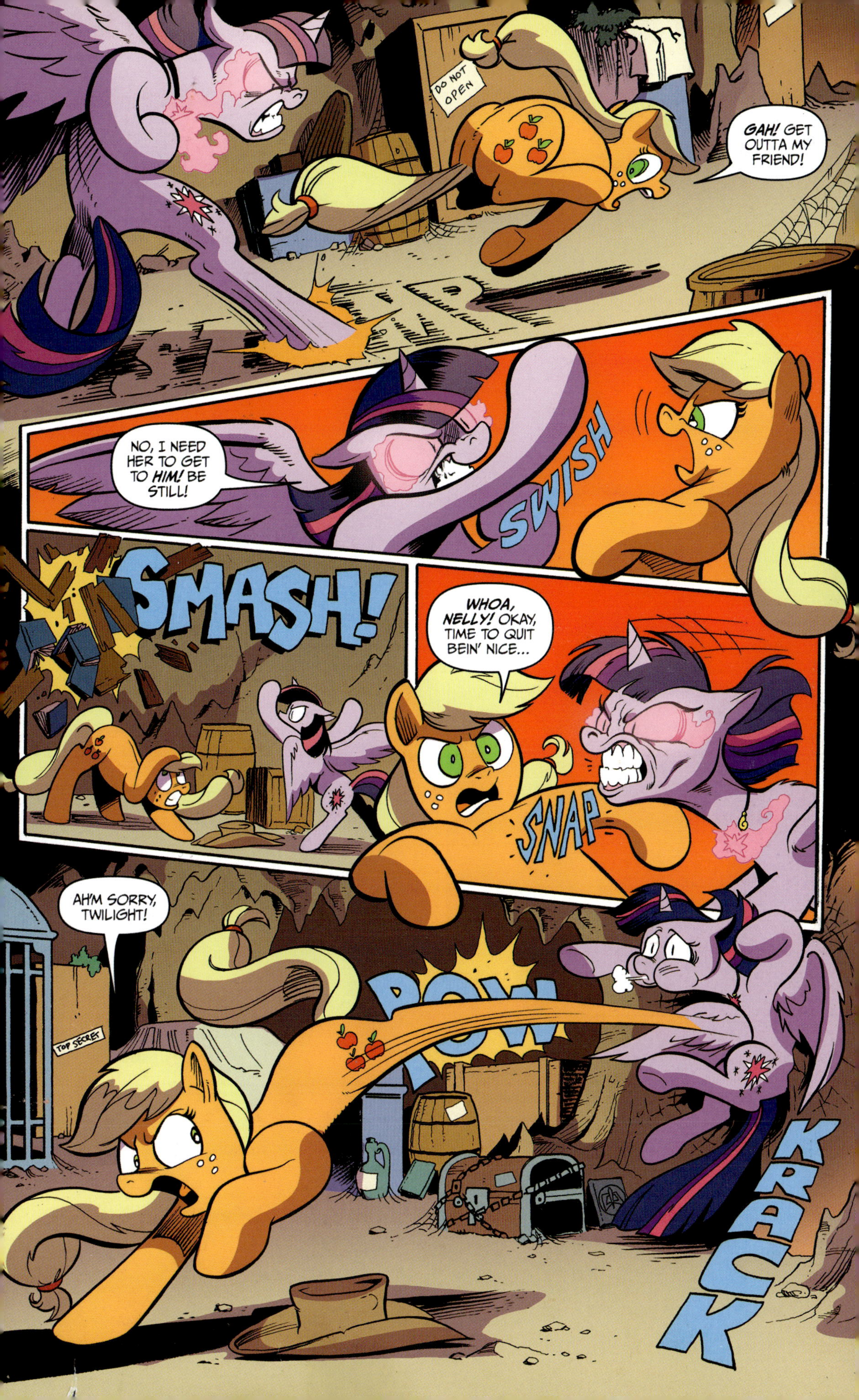
DO NOT OPEN
GAH! GET OUTTA MY FRIEND!
NO, I NEED HER TO GET TO HIM! BE STILL!
SWISH
SMASH!
WHOA, NELLY! OKAY, TIME TO QUIT BEIN' NICE...
SNAP
AH'M SORRY, TWILIGHT!
TOP SECRET
POW
KRACK

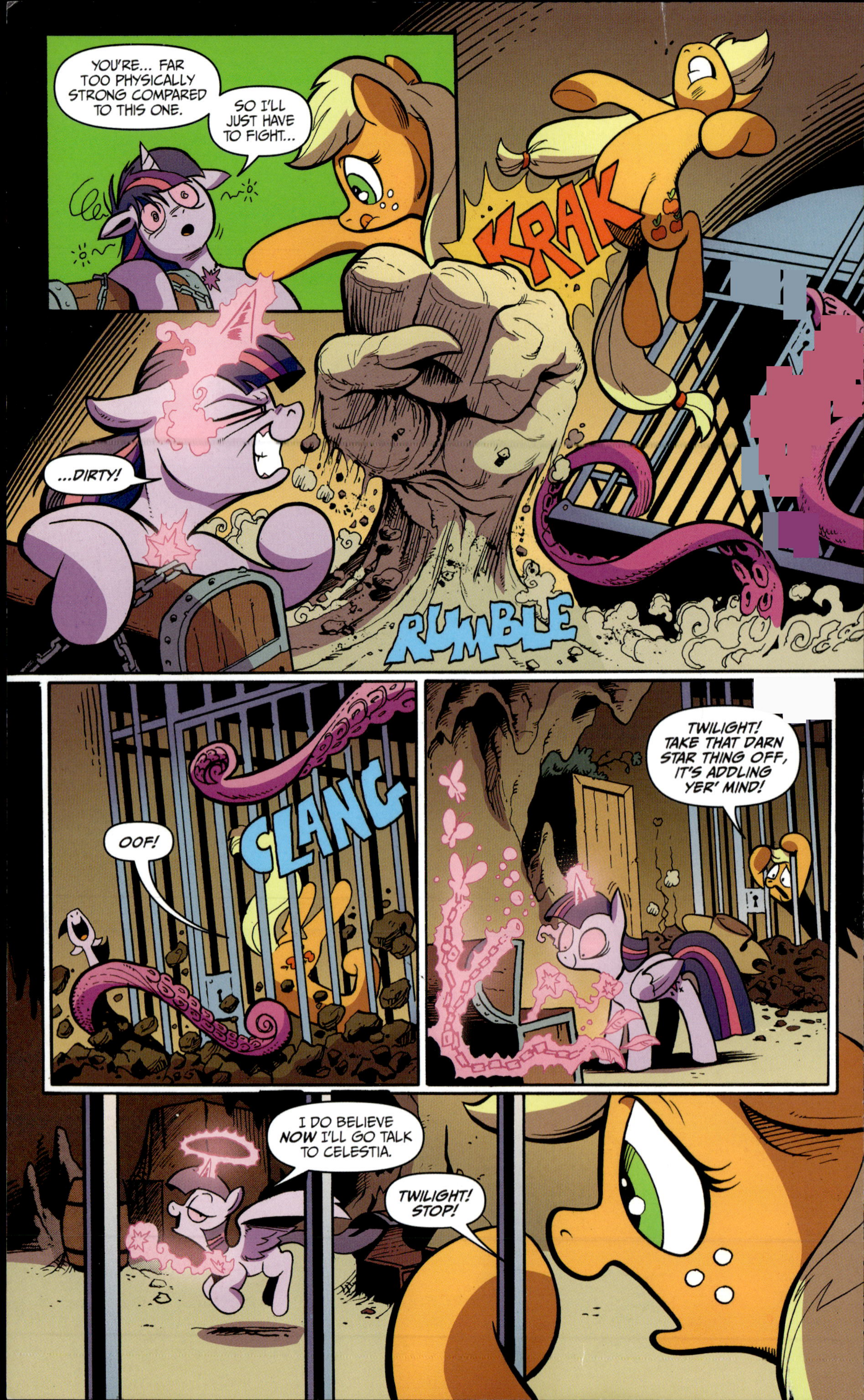
YOU'RE... FAR TOO PHYSICALLY STRONG COMPARED TO THIS ONE.
SO I'LL JUST HAVE TO FIGHT...
KRAK
...DIRTY!
RUMBLE
OOF!
CLANG
TWILIGHT! TAKE THAT DARN STAR THING OFF, IT'S ADDLING YER' MIND!
I DO BELIEVE *NOW* I'LL GO TALK TO CELESTIA.
TWILIGHT! STOP!

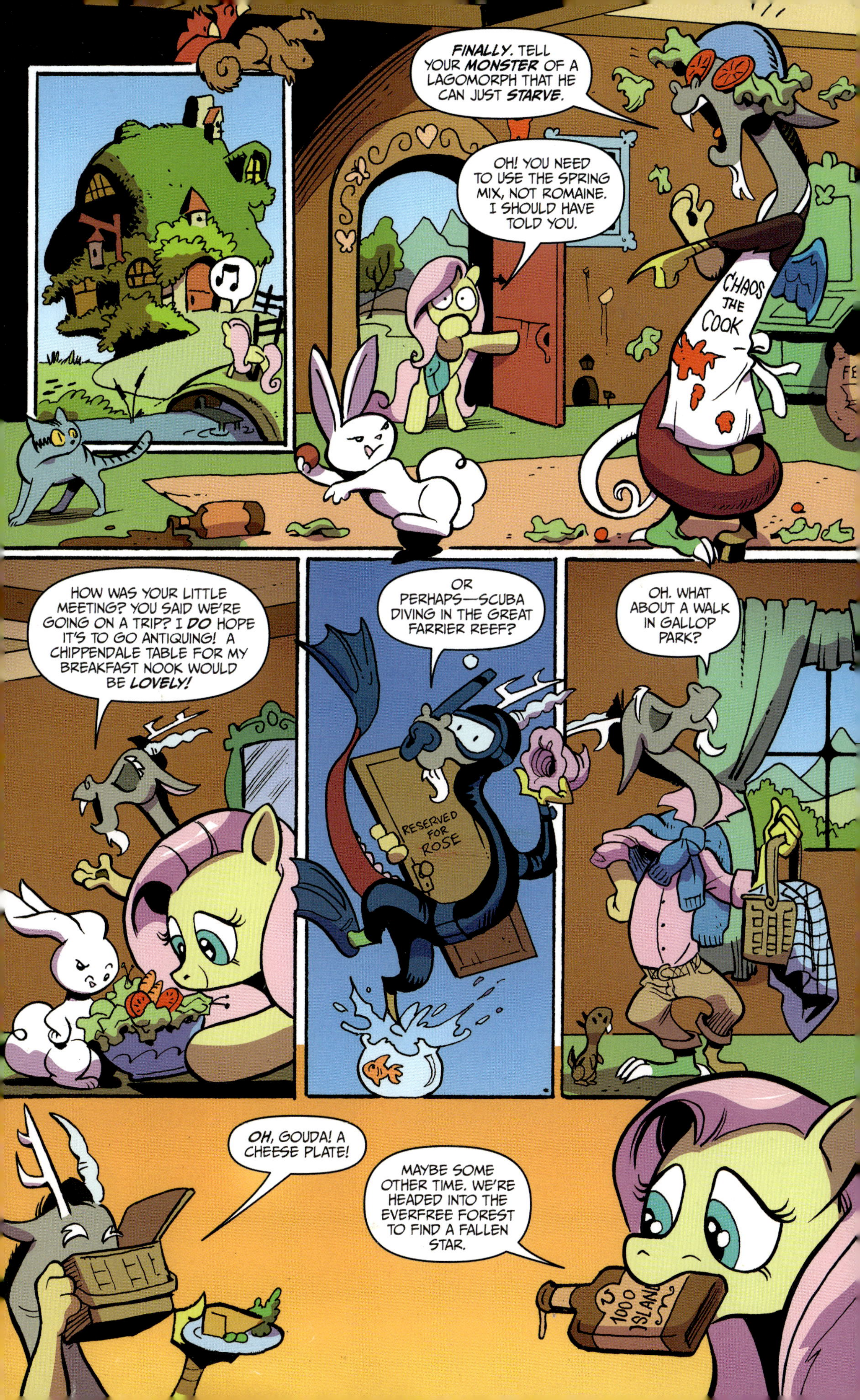

FINALLY. TELL YOUR MONSTER OF A LAGOMORPH THAT HE CAN JUST STARVE.
OH! YOU NEED TO USE THE SPRING MIX, NOT ROMAINE. I SHOULD HAVE TOLD YOU.
CHAOS THE COOK
HOW WAS YOUR LITTLE MEETING? YOU SAID WE'RE GOING ON A TRIP? I DO HOPE IT'S TO GO ANTIQUING! A CHIPPENDALE TABLE FOR MY BREAKFAST NOOK WOULD BE LOVELY!
OR PERHAPS—SCUBA DIVING IN THE GREAT FARRIER REEF?
RESERVED FOR ROSE
OH. WHAT ABOUT A WALK IN GALLOP PARK?
OH, GOUDA! A CHEESE PLATE!
MAYBE SOME OTHER TIME. WE'RE HEADED INTO THE EVERFREE FOREST TO FIND A FALLEN STAR.
1000 ISLAND

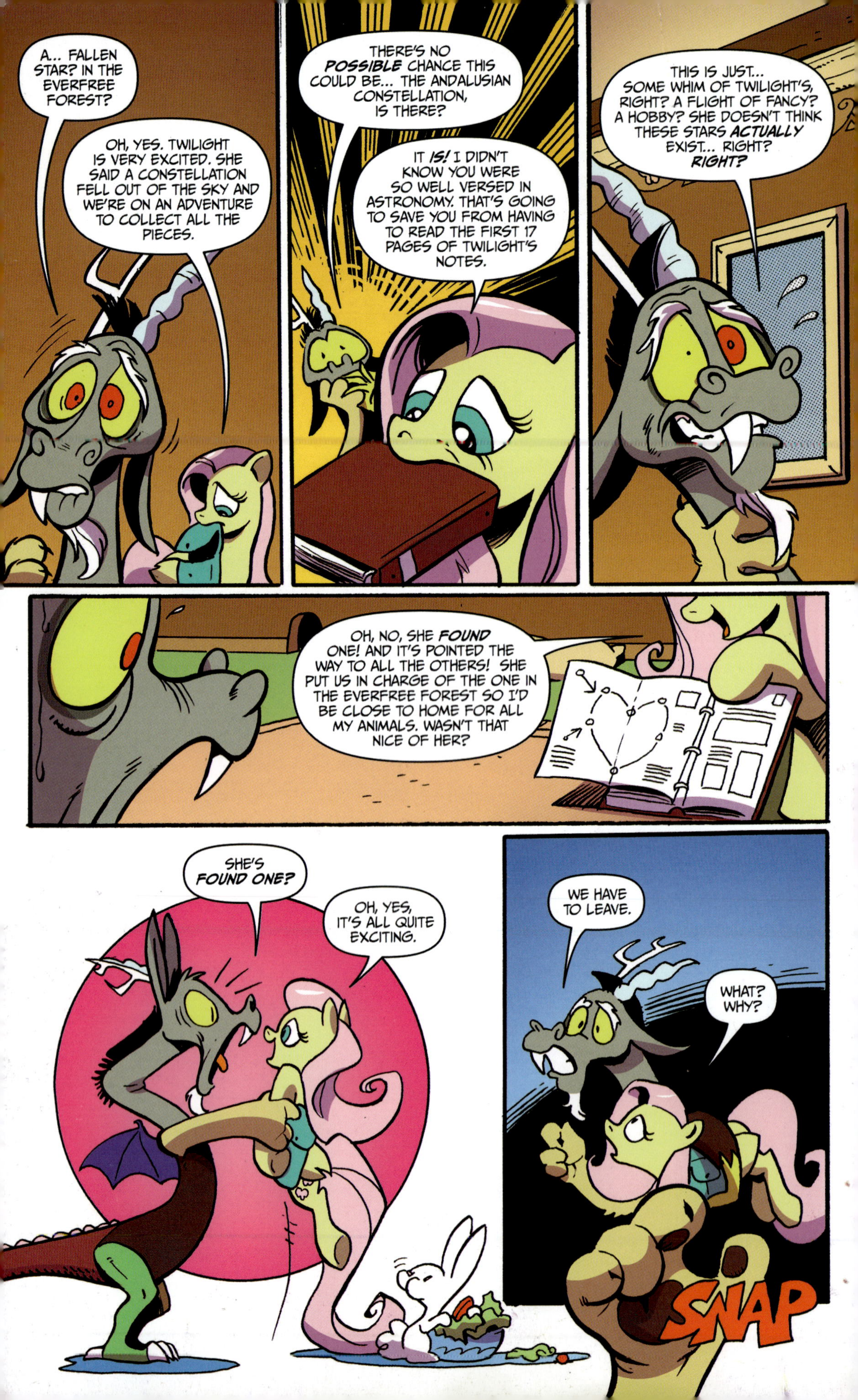
A... FALLEN STAR? IN THE EVERFREE FOREST?
OH, YES. TWILIGHT IS VERY EXCITED. SHE SAID A CONSTELLATION FELL OUT OF THE SKY AND WE'RE ON AN ADVENTURE TO COLLECT ALL THE PIECES.
THERE'S NO POSSIBLE CHANCE THIS COULD BE... THE ANDALUSIAN CONSTELLATION, IS THERE?
IT IS! I DIDN'T KNOW YOU WERE SO WELL VERSED IN ASTRONOMY. THAT'S GOING TO SAVE YOU FROM HAVING TO READ THE FIRST 17 PAGES OF TWILIGHT'S NOTES.
THIS IS JUST... SOME WHIM OF TWILIGHT'S, RIGHT? A FLIGHT OF FANCY? A HOBBY? SHE DOESN'T THINK THESE STARS ACTUALLY EXIST... RIGHT? RIGHT?
OH, NO, SHE FOUND ONE! AND IT'S POINTED THE WAY TO ALL THE OTHERS! SHE PUT US IN CHARGE OF THE ONE IN THE EVERFREE FOREST SO I'D BE CLOSE TO HOME FOR ALL MY ANIMALS. WASN'T THAT NICE OF HER?
SHE'S FOUND ONE?
OH, YES, IT'S ALL QUITE EXCITING.
WE HAVE TO LEAVE.
WHAT? WHY?
SNAP

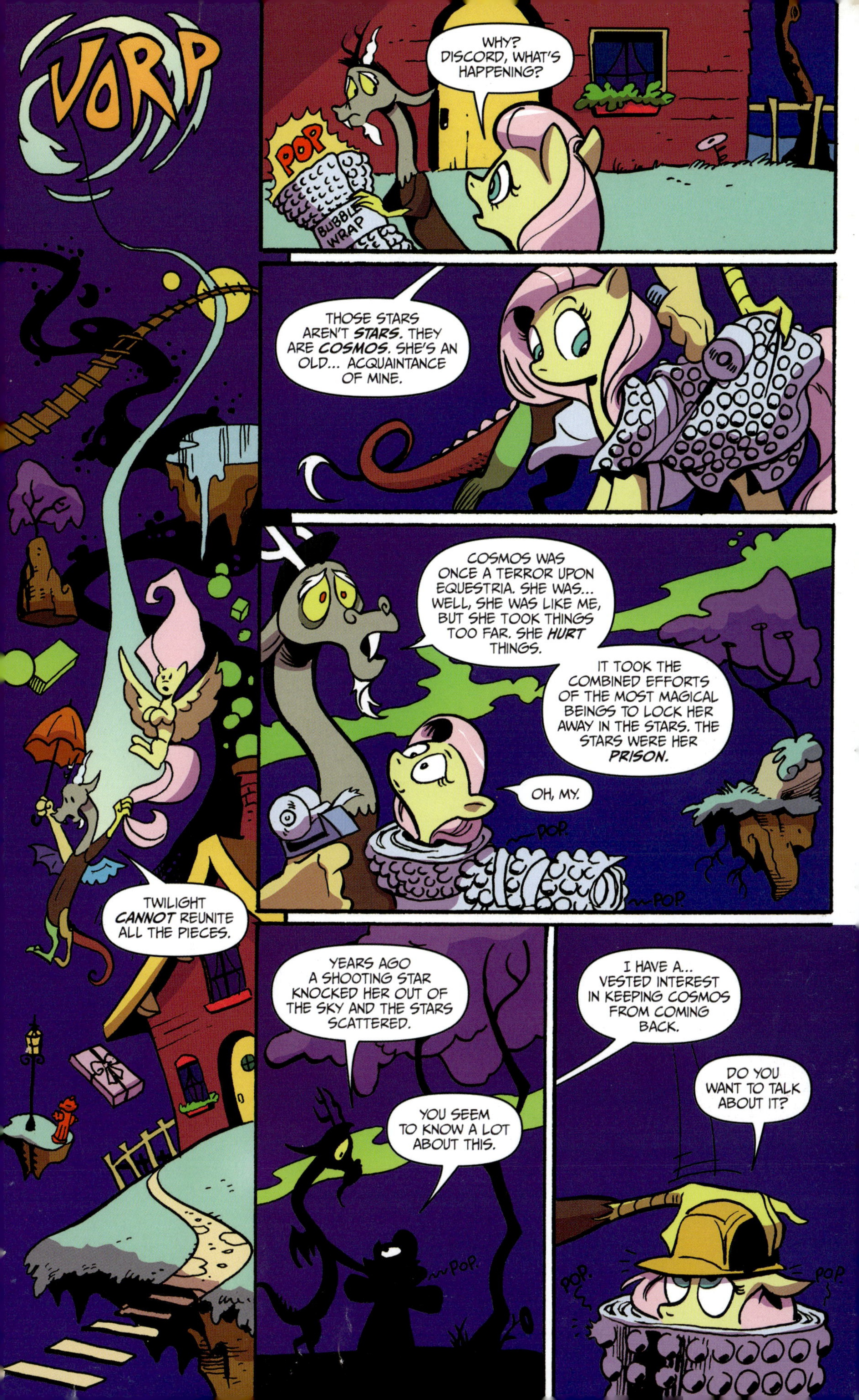
VORP
POP
BUBBLE WRAP
WHY? DISCORD, WHAT'S HAPPENING?
THOSE STARS AREN'T *STARS.* THEY ARE *COSMOS.* SHE'S AN OLD... ACQUAINTANCE OF MINE.
COSMOS WAS ONCE A TERROR UPON EQUESTRIA. SHE WAS... WELL, SHE WAS LIKE ME, BUT SHE TOOK THINGS TOO FAR. SHE *HURT* THINGS.
IT TOOK THE COMBINED EFFORTS OF THE MOST MAGICAL BEINGS TO LOCK HER AWAY IN THE STARS. THE STARS WERE HER *PRISON.*
OH, MY.
POP.
POP.
TWILIGHT *CANNOT* REUNITE ALL THE PIECES.
YEARS AGO A SHOOTING STAR KNOCKED HER OUT OF THE SKY AND THE STARS SCATTERED.
YOU SEEM TO KNOW A LOT ABOUT THIS.
POP.
I HAVE A... VESTED INTEREST IN KEEPING COSMOS FROM COMING BACK.
DO YOU WANT TO TALK ABOUT IT?
POP.
POP.

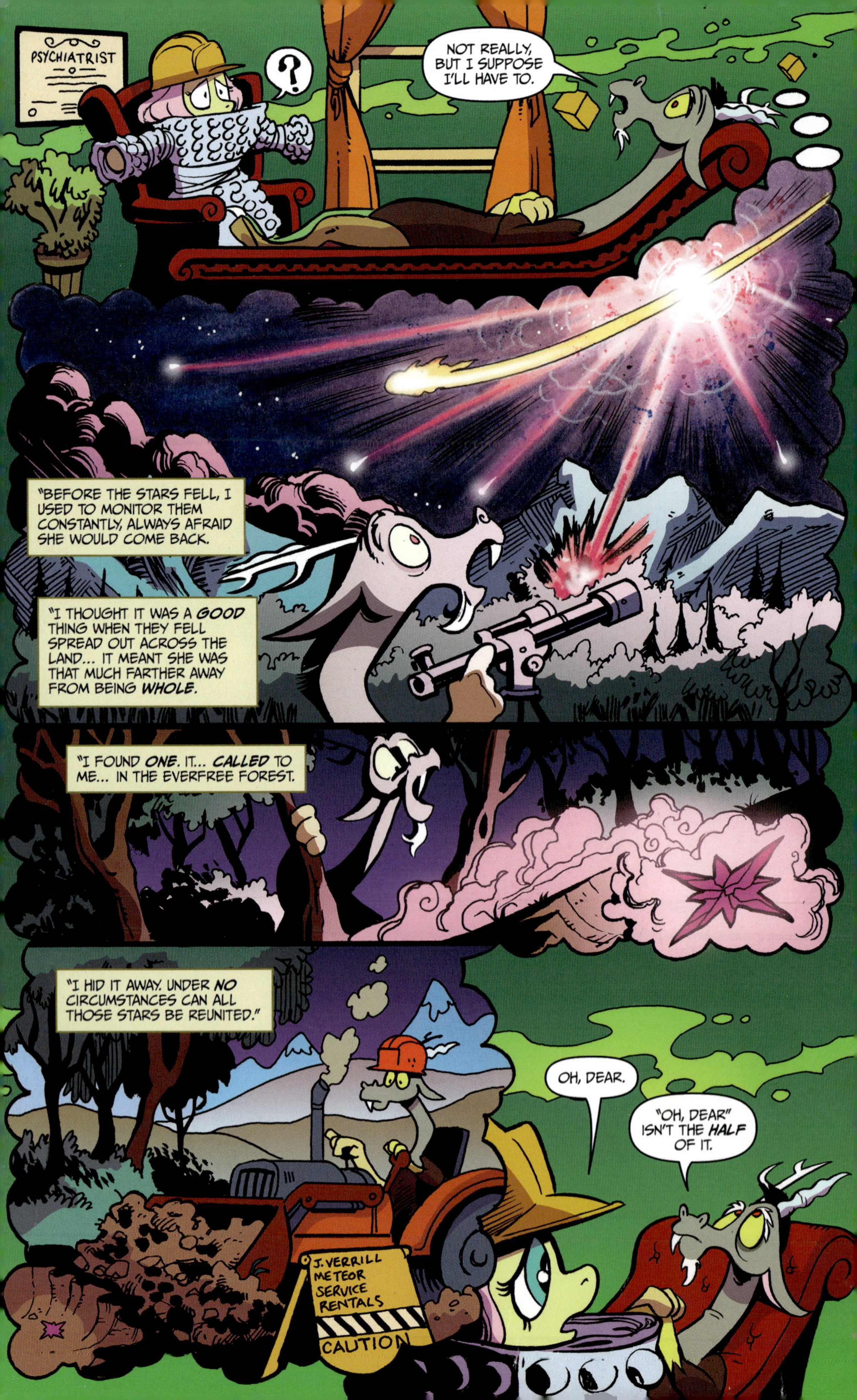
PSYCHIATRIST
?
NOT REALLY, BUT I SUPPOSE I'LL HAVE TO.
"BEFORE THE STARS FELL, I USED TO MONITOR THEM CONSTANTLY, ALWAYS AFRAID SHE WOULD COME BACK.
"I THOUGHT IT WAS A *GOOD* THING WHEN THEY FELL SPREAD OUT ACROSS THE LAND... IT MEANT SHE WAS THAT MUCH FARTHER AWAY FROM BEING *WHOLE*.
"I FOUND *ONE*. IT... *CALLED* TO ME... IN THE EVERFREE FOREST.
"I HID IT AWAY. UNDER *NO* CIRCUMSTANCES CAN ALL THOSE STARS BE REUNITED."
J. VERRILL METEOR SERVICE RENTALS
CAUTION
OH, DEAR.
"OH, DEAR" ISN'T THE *HALF* OF IT.

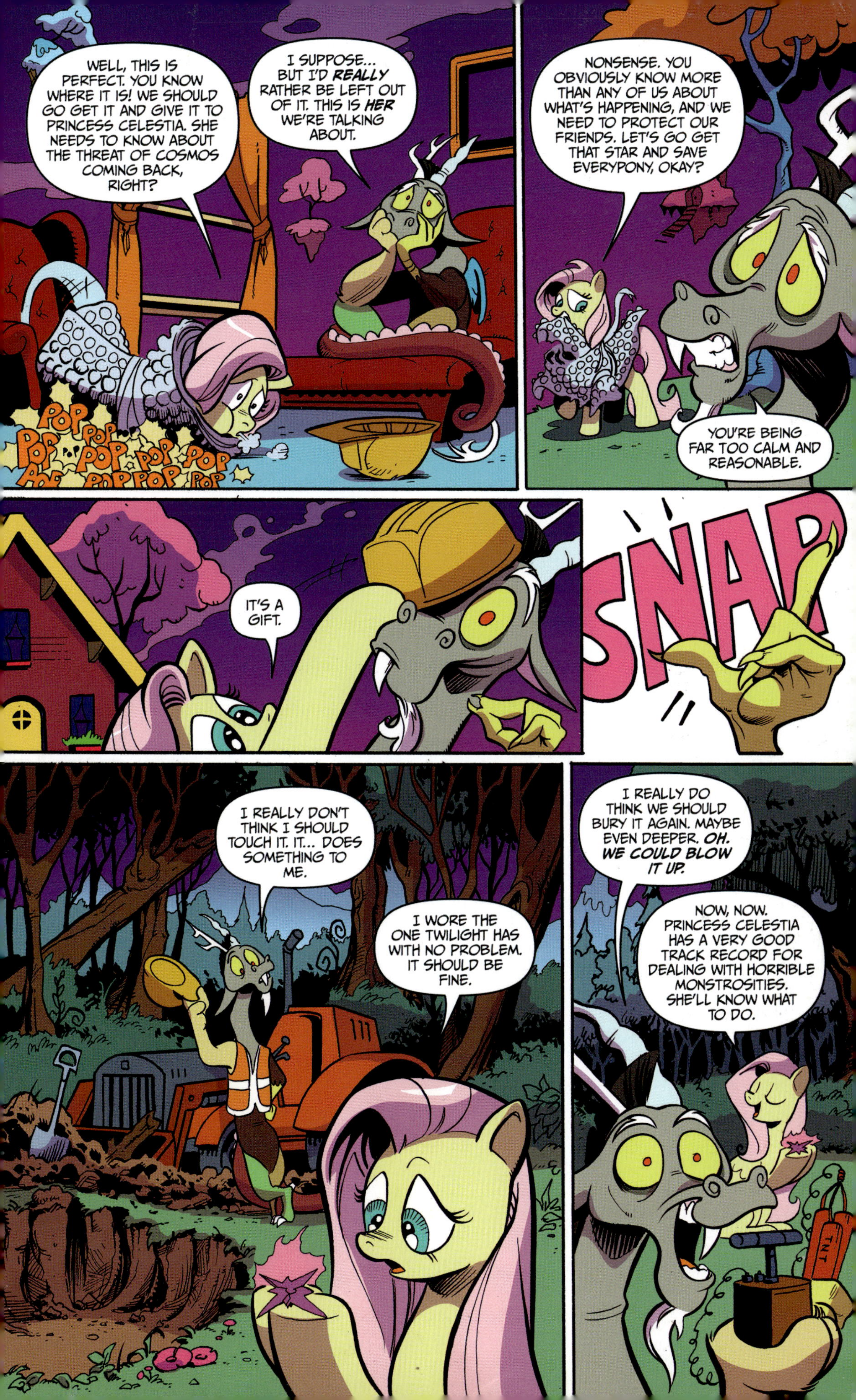
WELL, THIS IS PERFECT. YOU KNOW WHERE IT IS! WE SHOULD GO GET IT AND GIVE IT TO PRINCESS CELESTIA. SHE NEEDS TO KNOW ABOUT THE THREAT OF COSMOS COMING BACK, RIGHT?
I SUPPOSE... BUT I'D **REALLY** RATHER BE LEFT OUT OF IT. THIS IS **HER** WE'RE TALKING ABOUT.
POP POP POP POP POP POP POP POP POP POP
NONSENSE. YOU OBVIOUSLY KNOW MORE THAN ANY OF US ABOUT WHAT'S HAPPENING, AND WE NEED TO PROTECT OUR FRIENDS. LET'S GO GET THAT STAR AND SAVE EVERYPONY, OKAY?
YOU'RE BEING FAR TOO CALM AND REASONABLE.
IT'S A GIFT.
SNAP
I REALLY DON'T THINK I SHOULD TOUCH IT. IT... DOES SOMETHING TO ME.
I WORE THE ONE TWILIGHT HAS WITH NO PROBLEM. IT SHOULD BE FINE.
I REALLY DO THINK WE SHOULD BURY IT AGAIN. MAYBE EVEN DEEPER. ***OH. WE COULD BLOW IT UP.***
NOW, NOW. PRINCESS CELESTIA HAS A VERY GOOD TRACK RECORD FOR DEALING WITH HORRIBLE MONSTROSITIES. SHE'LL KNOW WHAT TO DO.
TNT

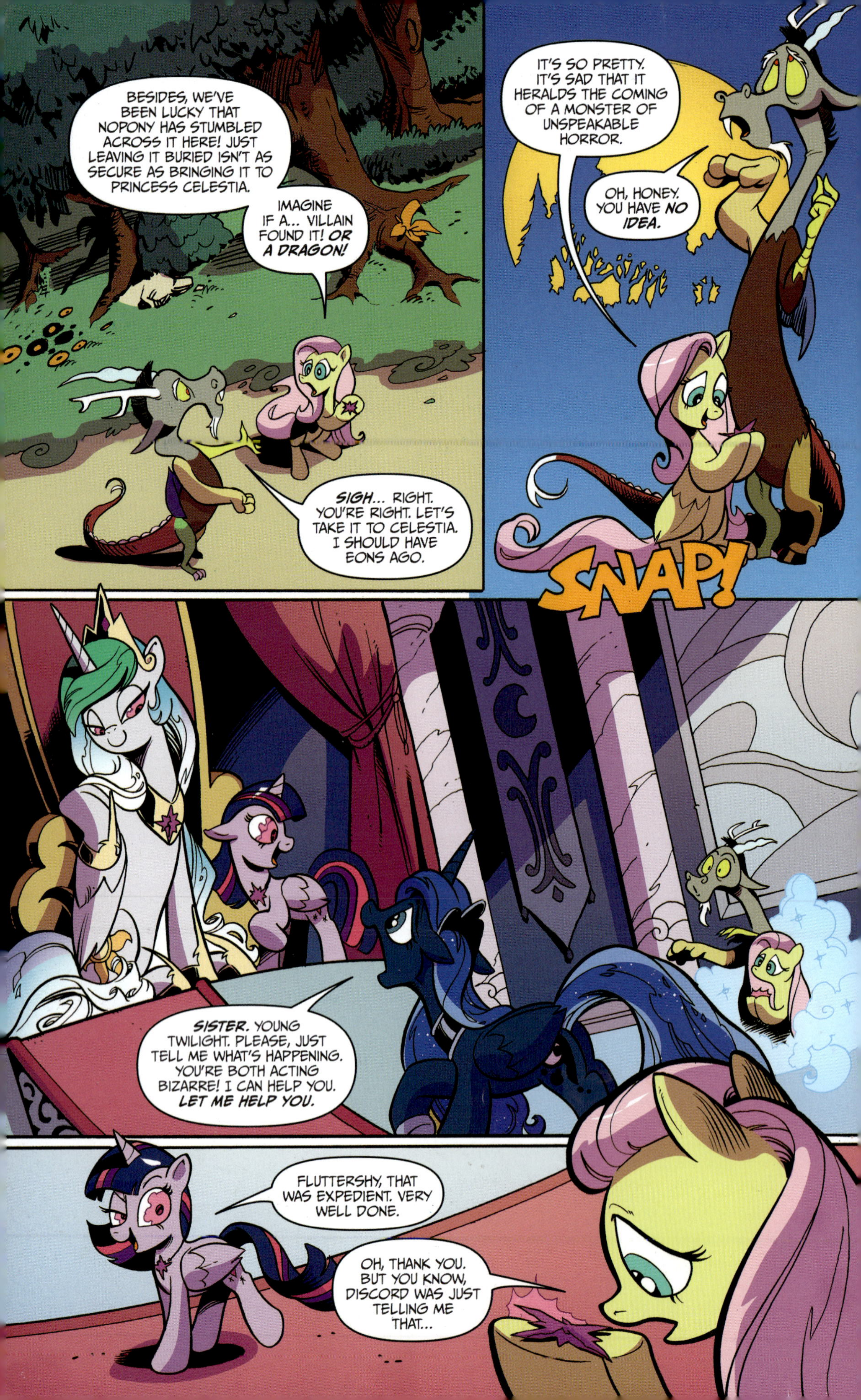
BESIDES, WE'VE BEEN LUCKY THAT NOPONY HAS STUMBLED ACROSS IT HERE! JUST LEAVING IT BURIED ISN'T AS SECURE AS BRINGING IT TO PRINCESS CELESTIA.
IMAGINE IF A... VILLAIN FOUND IT! OR A DRAGON!
SIGH... RIGHT. YOU'RE RIGHT. LET'S TAKE IT TO CELESTIA. I SHOULD HAVE EONS AGO.
IT'S SO PRETTY. IT'S SAD THAT IT HERALDS THE COMING OF A MONSTER OF UNSPEAKABLE HORROR.
OH, HONEY. YOU HAVE NO IDEA.
SNAP!
SISTER. YOUNG TWILIGHT. PLEASE, JUST TELL ME WHAT'S HAPPENING. YOU'RE BOTH ACTING BIZARRE! I CAN HELP YOU. LET ME HELP YOU.
FLUTTERSHY, THAT WAS EXPEDIENT. VERY WELL DONE.
OH, THANK YOU. BUT YOU KNOW, DISCORD WAS JUST TELLING ME THAT...

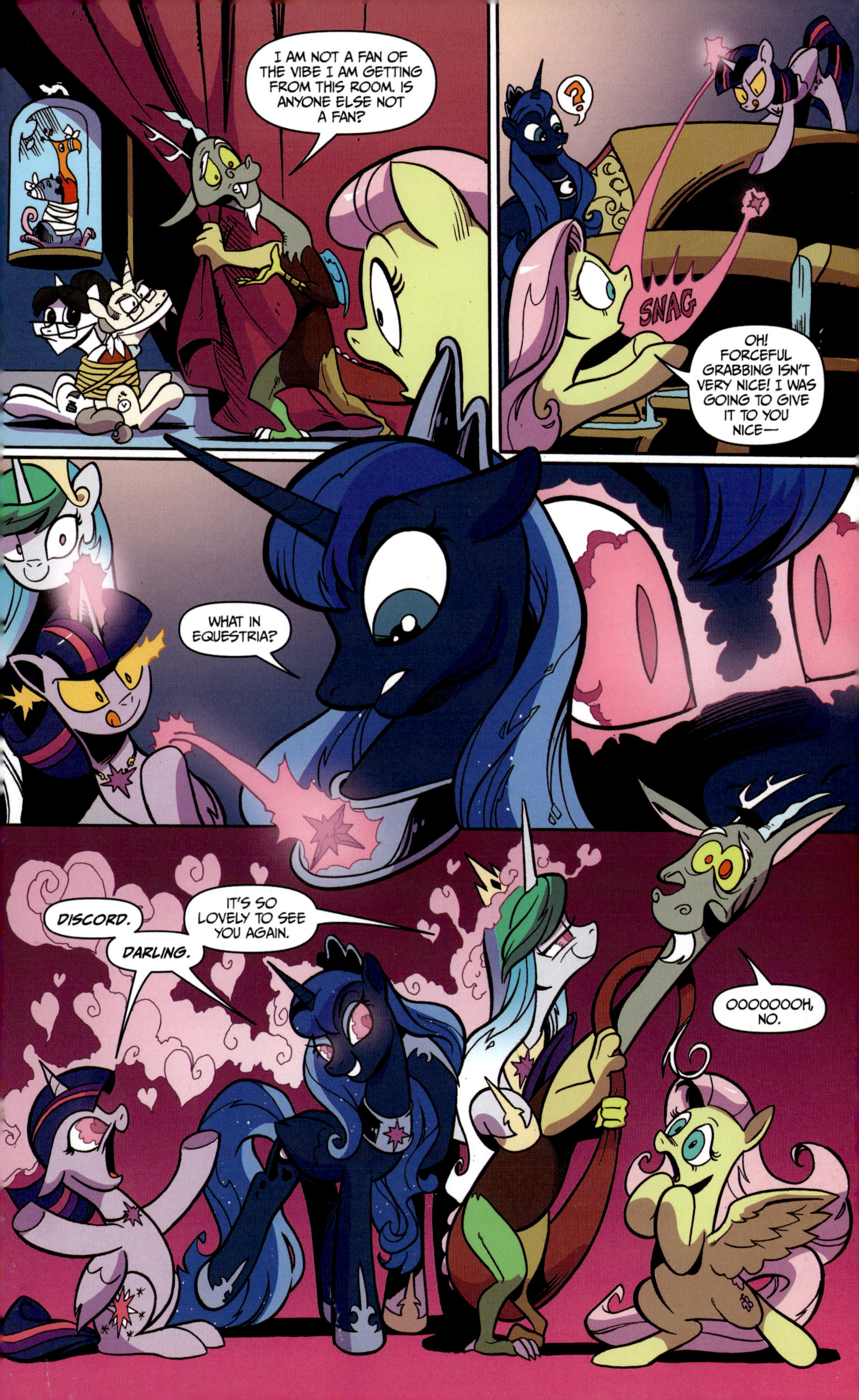
I AM NOT A FAN OF THE VIBE I AM GETTING FROM THIS ROOM. IS ANYONE ELSE NOT A FAN?
?
SNAG
OH! FORCEFUL GRABBING ISN'T VERY NICE! I WAS GOING TO GIVE IT TO YOU NICE—
WHAT IN EQUESTRIA?
DISCORD.
DARLING.
IT'S SO LOVELY TO SEE YOU AGAIN.
OOOOOOOH, NO.

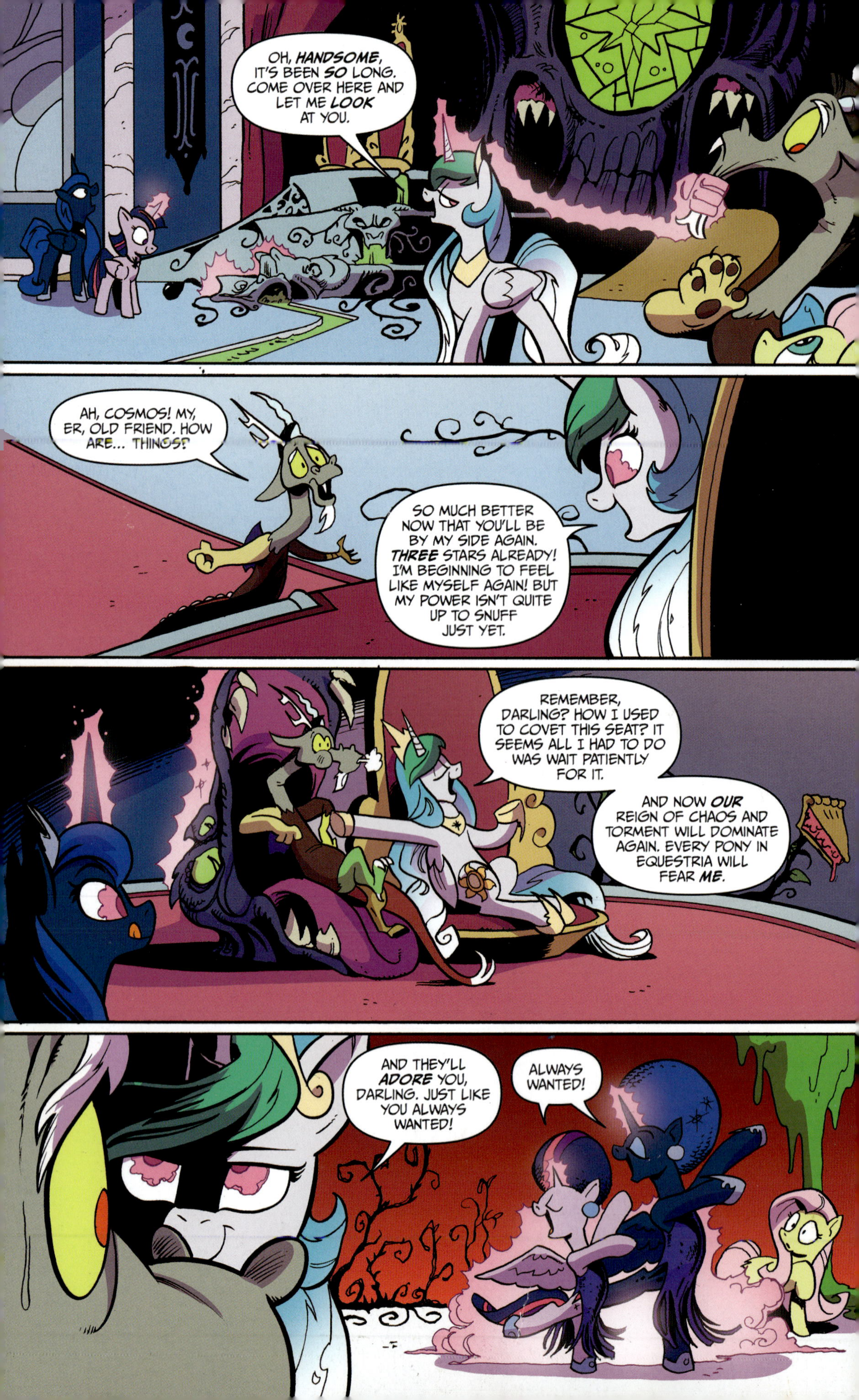
OH, *HANDSOME*, IT'S BEEN *SO* LONG. COME OVER HERE AND LET ME *LOOK* AT YOU.
AH, COSMOS! MY, ER, OLD FRIEND. HOW ARE... THINGS?
SO MUCH BETTER NOW THAT YOU'LL BE BY MY SIDE AGAIN. *THREE* STARS ALREADY! I'M BEGINNING TO FEEL LIKE MYSELF AGAIN! BUT MY POWER ISN'T QUITE UP TO SNUFF JUST YET.
REMEMBER, DARLING? HOW I USED TO COVET THIS SEAT? IT SEEMS ALL I HAD TO DO WAS WAIT PATIENTLY FOR IT.
AND NOW *OUR* REIGN OF CHAOS AND TORMENT WILL DOMINATE AGAIN. EVERY PONY IN EQUESTRIA WILL FEAR *ME*.
AND THEY'LL *ADORE* YOU, DARLING. JUST LIKE YOU ALWAYS WANTED!
ALWAYS WANTED!

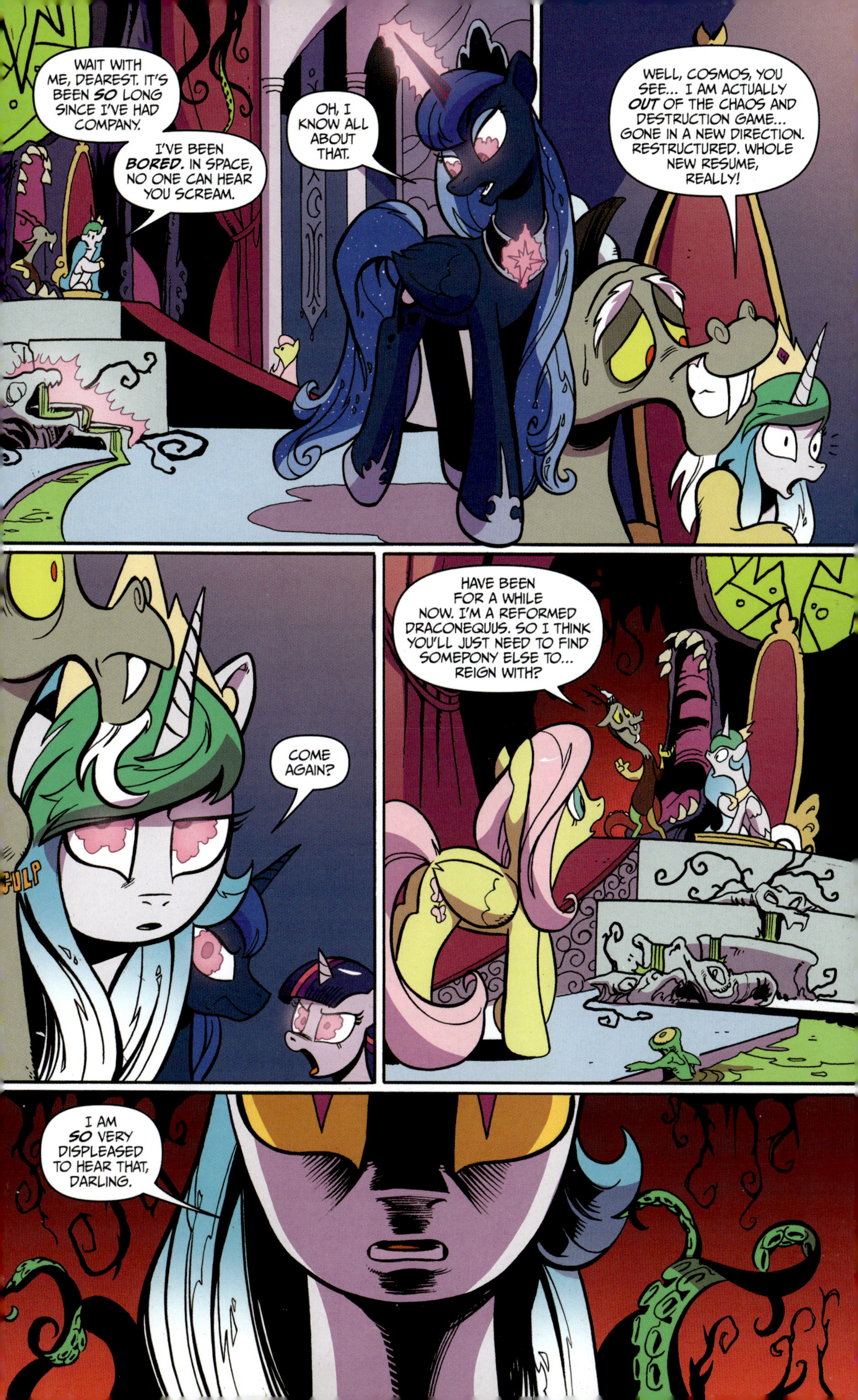
WAIT WITH ME, DEAREST. IT'S BEEN SO LONG SINCE I'VE HAD COMPANY.
I'VE BEEN BORED. IN SPACE, NO ONE CAN HEAR YOU SCREAM.
OH, I KNOW ALL ABOUT THAT.
WELL, COSMOS, YOU SEE... I AM ACTUALLY OUT OF THE CHAOS AND DESTRUCTION GAME... GONE IN A NEW DIRECTION. RESTRUCTURED. WHOLE NEW RESUME, REALLY!
GULP
COME AGAIN?
HAVE BEEN FOR A WHILE NOW. I'M A REFORMED DRACONEQUUS. SO I THINK YOU'LL JUST NEED TO FIND SOMEPONY ELSE TO... REIGN WITH?
I AM SO VERY DISPLEASED TO HEAR THAT, DARLING.

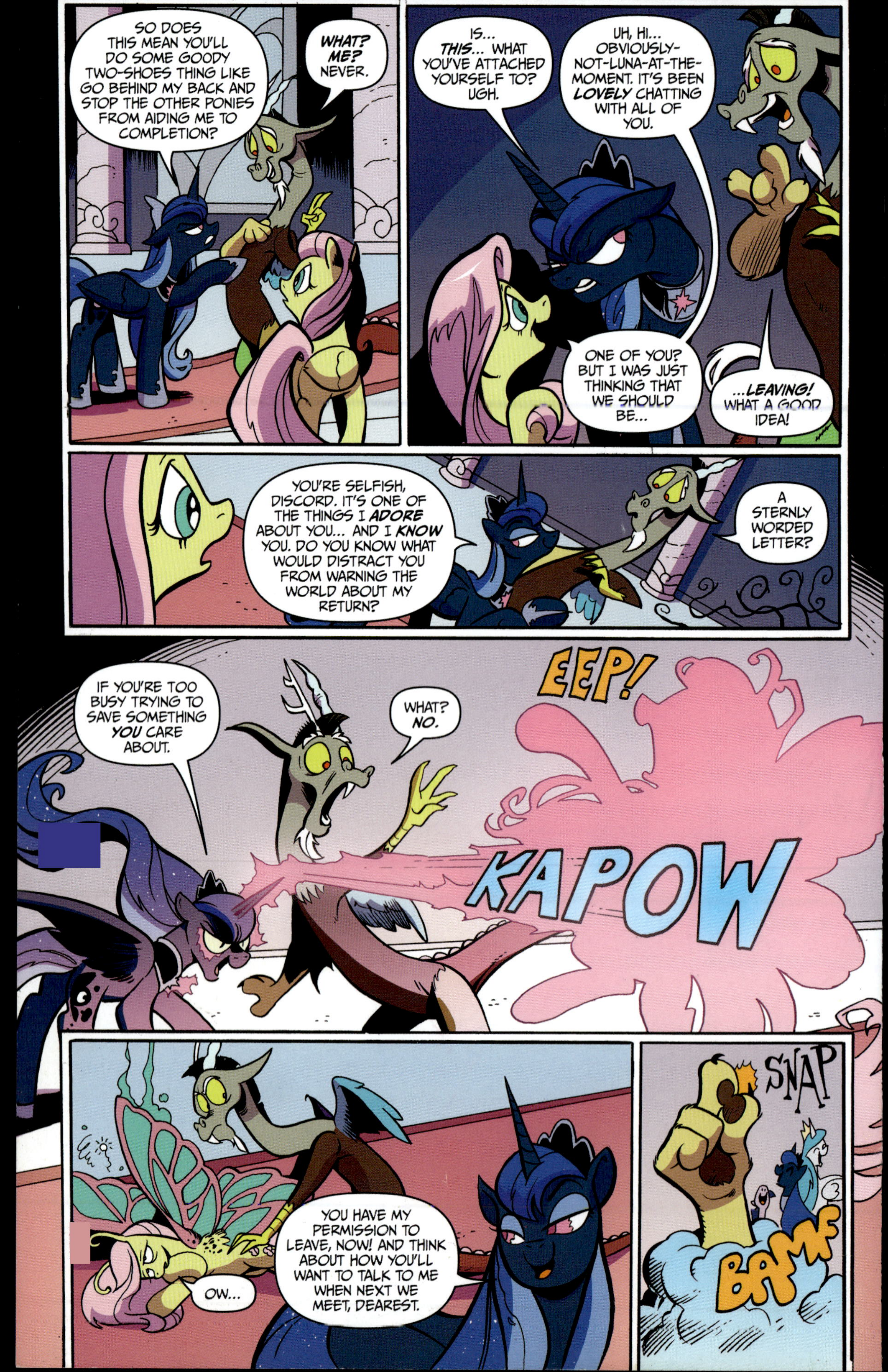
SO DOES THIS MEAN YOU'LL DO SOME GOODY TWO-SHOES THING LIKE GO BEHIND MY BACK AND STOP THE OTHER PONIES FROM AIDING ME TO COMPLETION?
WHAT? ME? NEVER.
IS... THIS... WHAT YOU'VE ATTACHED YOURSELF TO? UGH.
UH, HI... OBVIOUSLY-NOT-LUNA-AT-THE-MOMENT. IT'S BEEN LOVELY CHATTING WITH ALL OF YOU.
ONE OF YOU? BUT I WAS JUST THINKING THAT WE SHOULD BE...
...LEAVING! WHAT A GOOD IDEA!
YOU'RE SELFISH, DISCORD. IT'S ONE OF THE THINGS I ADORE ABOUT YOU... AND I KNOW YOU. DO YOU KNOW WHAT WOULD DISTRACT YOU FROM WARNING THE WORLD ABOUT MY RETURN?
A STERNLY WORDED LETTER?
IF YOU'RE TOO BUSY TRYING TO SAVE SOMETHING YOU CARE ABOUT.
WHAT? NO.
EEP!
KAPOW
YOU HAVE MY PERMISSION TO LEAVE, NOW! AND THINK ABOUT HOW YOU'LL WANT TO TALK TO ME WHEN NEXT WE MEET, DEAREST.
OW...
SNAP
BAMF

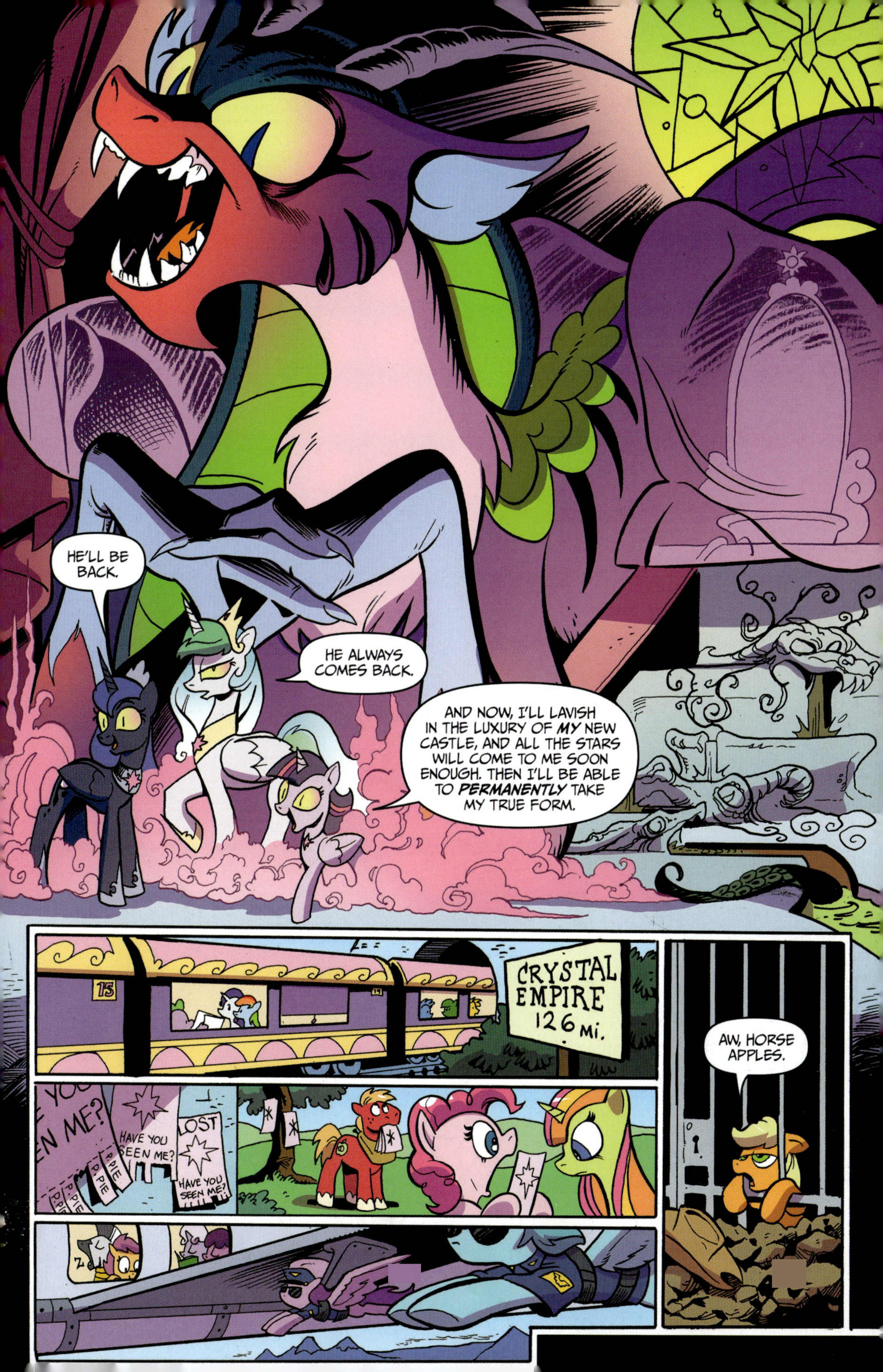
HE'LL BE BACK.
HE ALWAYS COMES BACK.
AND NOW, I'LL LAVISH IN THE LUXURY OF MY NEW CASTLE, AND ALL THE STARS WILL COME TO ME SOON ENOUGH. THEN I'LL BE ABLE TO PERMANENTLY TAKE MY TRUE FORM.
CRYSTAL EMPIRE 126 MI.
HAVE YOU SEEN ME?
LOST
HAVE YOU SEEN ME?
AW, HORSE APPLES.

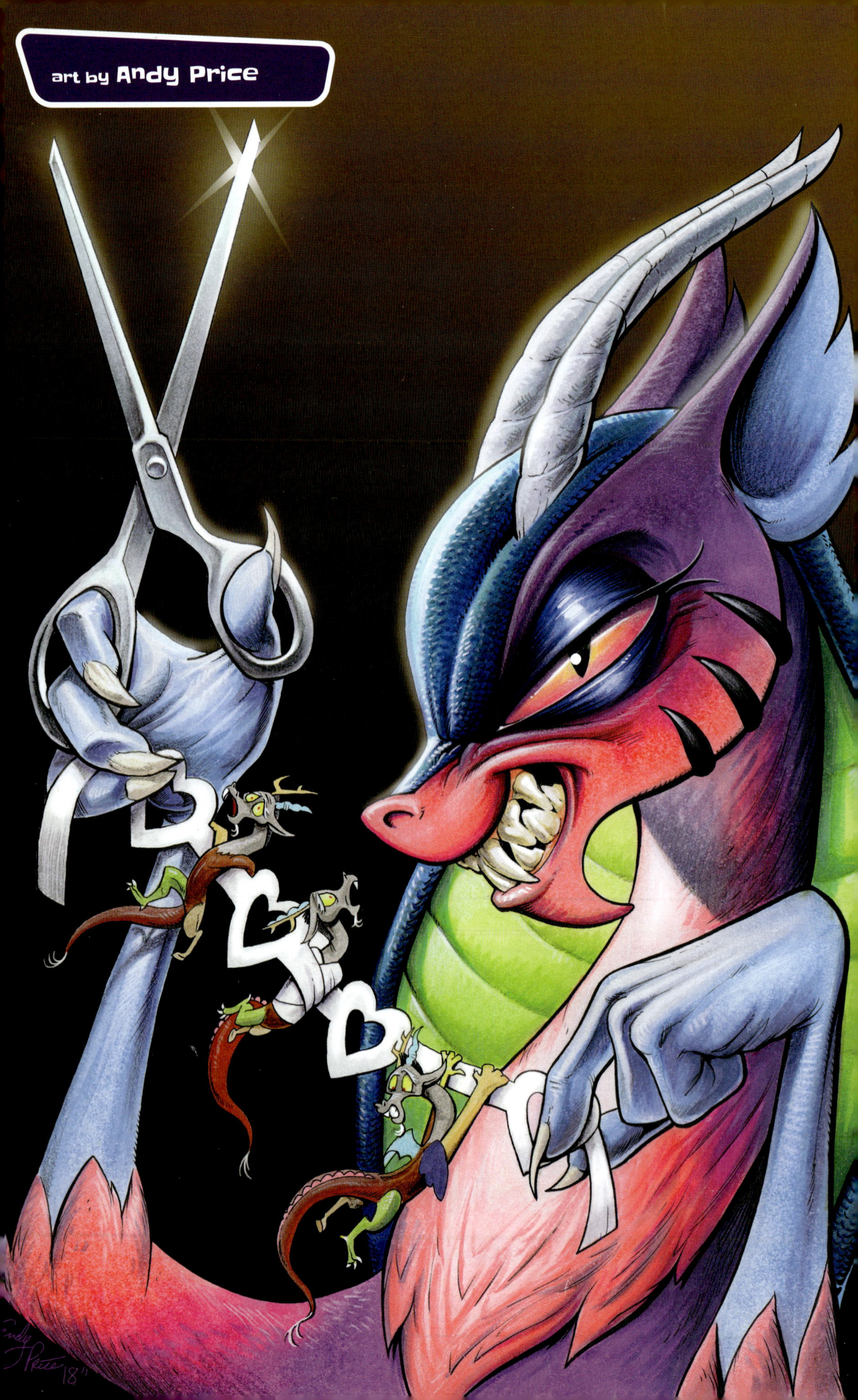

art by Andy Price

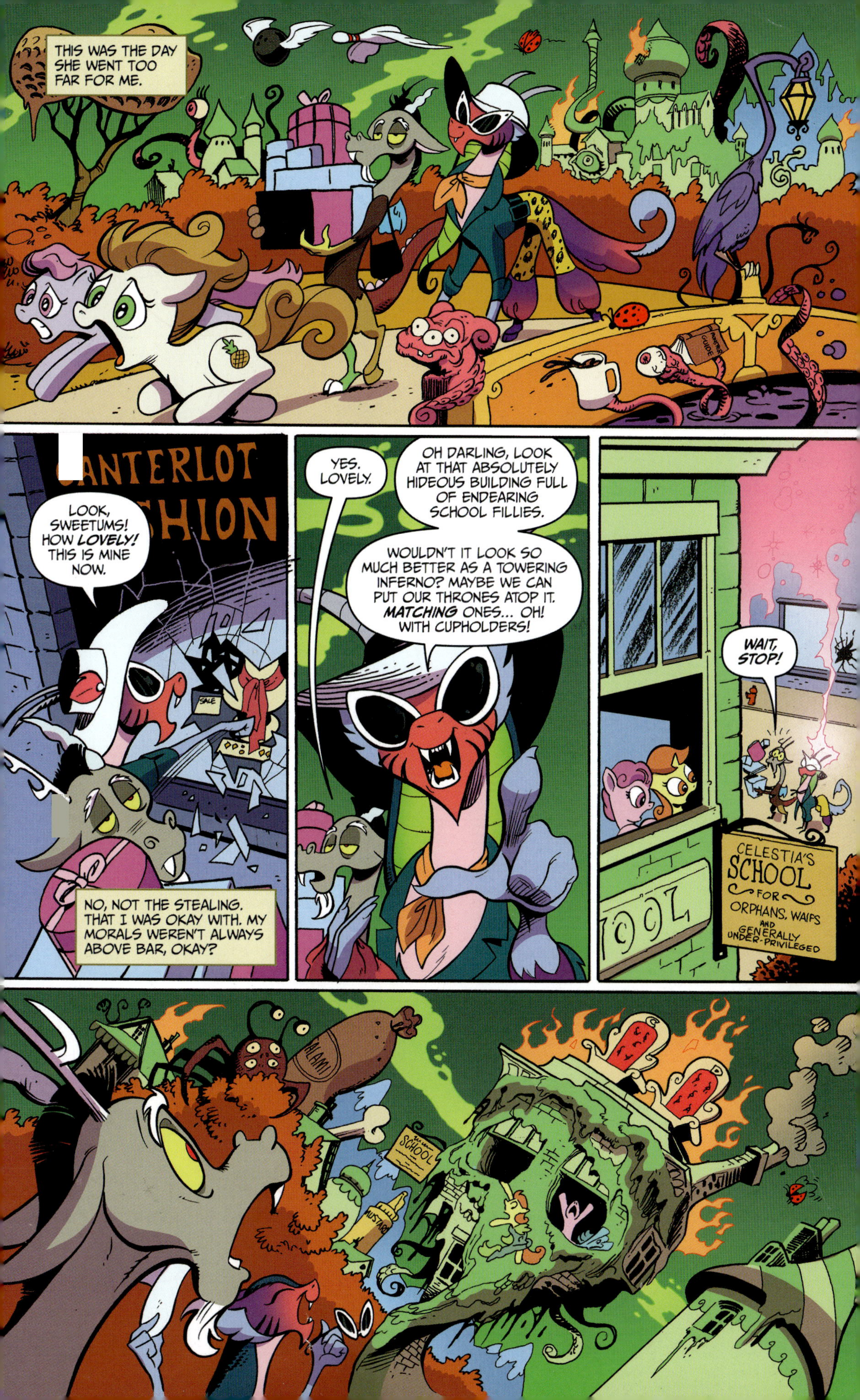
THIS WAS THE DAY SHE WENT TOO FAR FOR ME.
ANTERLOT
SHION
LOOK, SWEETUMS! HOW *LOVELY!* THIS IS MINE NOW.
NO, NOT THE STEALING. THAT I WAS OKAY WITH. MY MORALS WEREN'T ALWAYS ABOVE BAR, OKAY?
OH DARLING, LOOK AT THAT ABSOLUTELY HIDEOUS BUILDING FULL OF ENDEARING SCHOOL FILLIES.
YES. LOVELY.
WOULDN'T IT LOOK SO MUCH BETTER AS A TOWERING INFERNO? MAYBE WE CAN PUT OUR THRONES ATOP IT. ***MATCHING*** ONES... OH! WITH CUPHOLDERS!
WAIT, STOP!
CELESTIA'S SCHOOL FOR ORPHANS, WAIFS AND GENERALLY UNDER-PRIVILEGED
SCHOOL

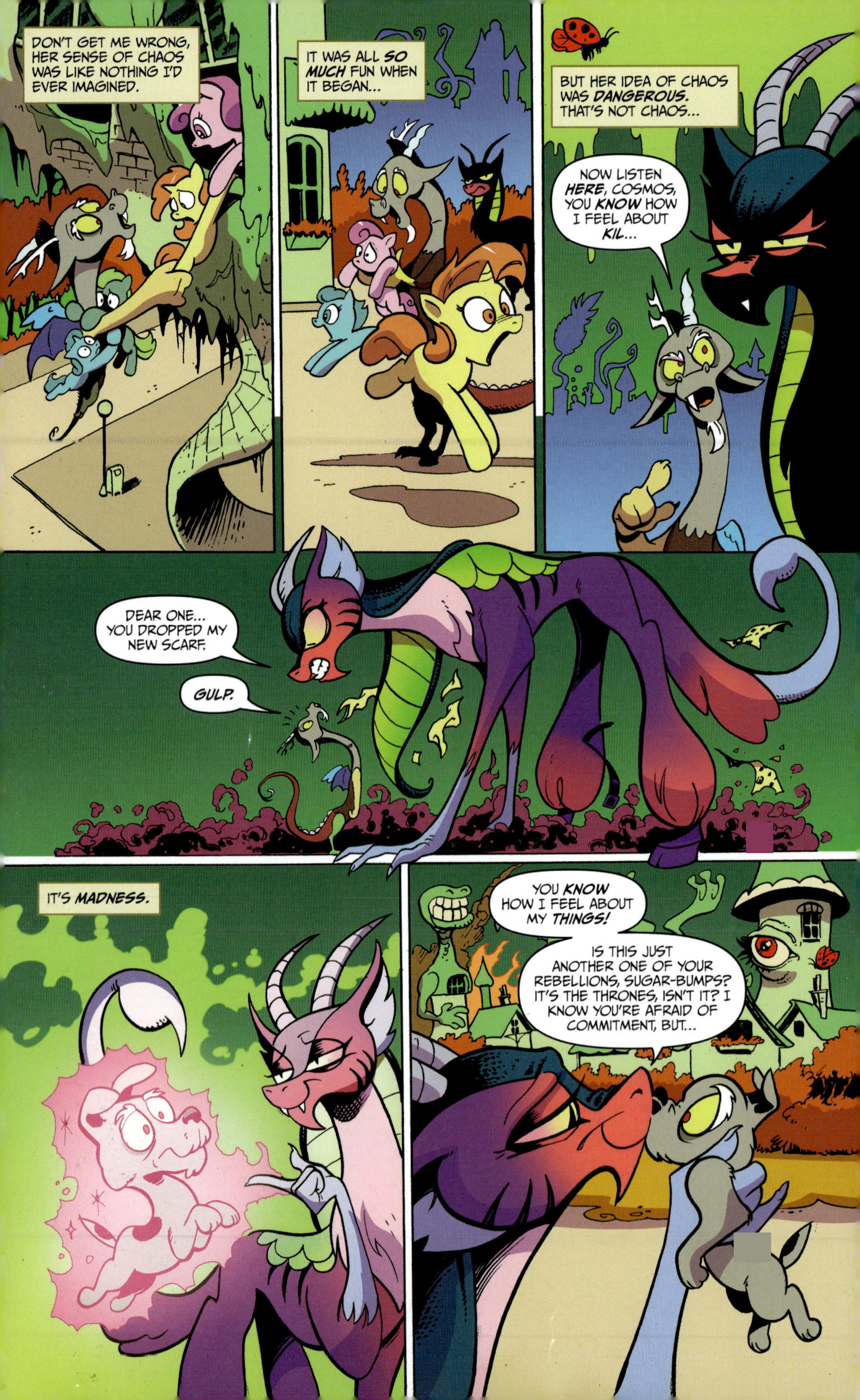
DON'T GET ME WRONG, HER SENSE OF CHAOS WAS LIKE NOTHING I'D EVER IMAGINED.
IT WAS ALL SO MUCH FUN WHEN IT BEGAN...
BUT HER IDEA OF CHAOS WAS DANGEROUS. THAT'S NOT CHAOS...
NOW LISTEN HERE, COSMOS, YOU KNOW HOW I FEEL ABOUT KIL...
DEAR ONE... YOU DROPPED MY NEW SCARF.
GULP.
IT'S MADNESS.
YOU KNOW HOW I FEEL ABOUT MY THINGS!
IS THIS JUST ANOTHER ONE OF YOUR REBELLIONS, SUGAR-BUMPS? IT'S THE THRONES, ISN'T IT? I KNOW YOU'RE AFRAID OF COMMITMENT, BUT...

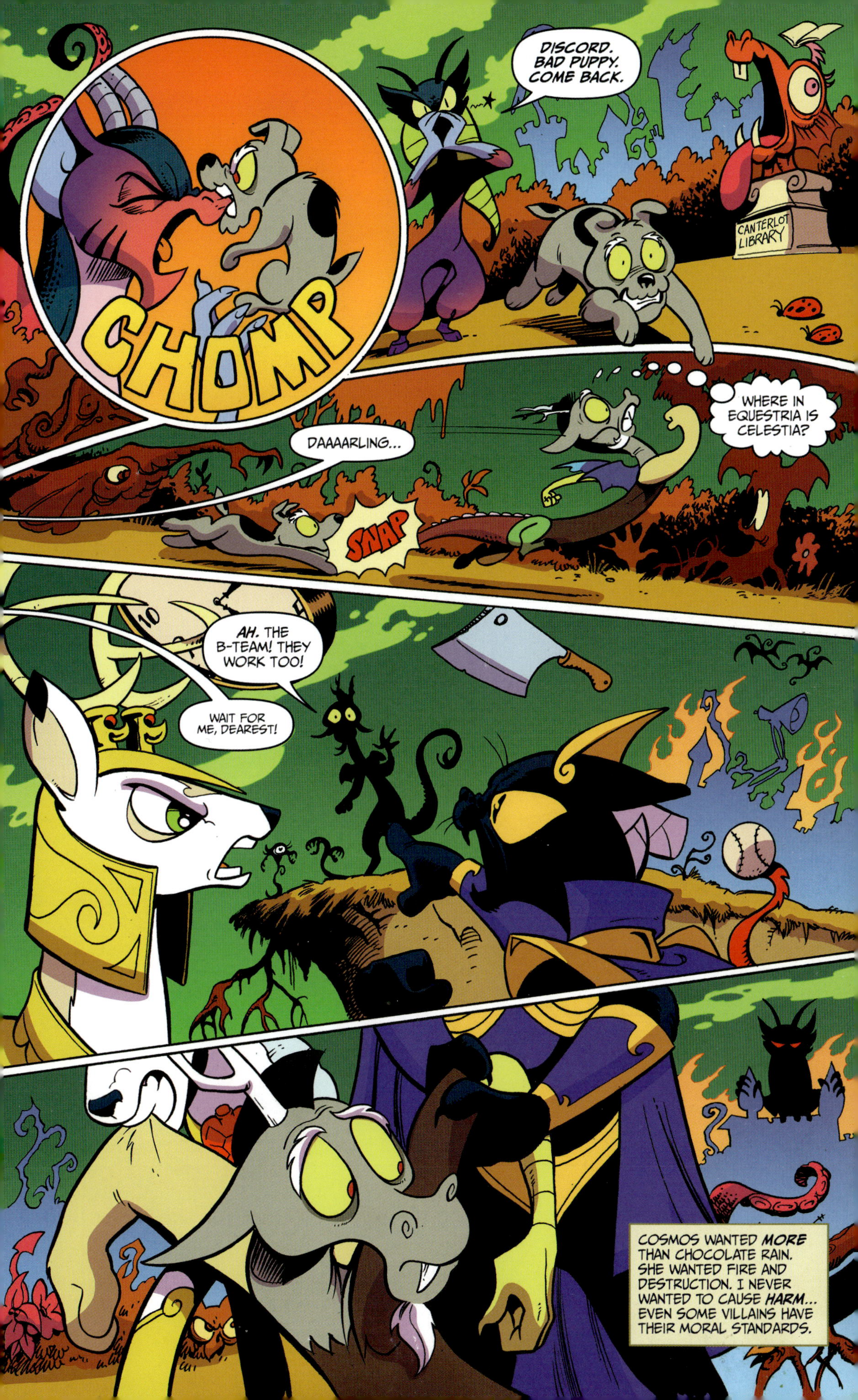
CHOMP
DISCORD. BAD PUPPY. COME BACK.
CANTERLOT LIBRARY
WHERE IN EQUESTRIA IS CELESTIA?
DAAAARLING...
SNAP
AH. THE B-TEAM! THEY WORK TOO!
WAIT FOR ME, DEAREST!
COSMOS WANTED MORE THAN CHOCOLATE RAIN. SHE WANTED FIRE AND DESTRUCTION. I NEVER WANTED TO CAUSE HARM... EVEN SOME VILLAINS HAVE THEIR MORAL STANDARDS.

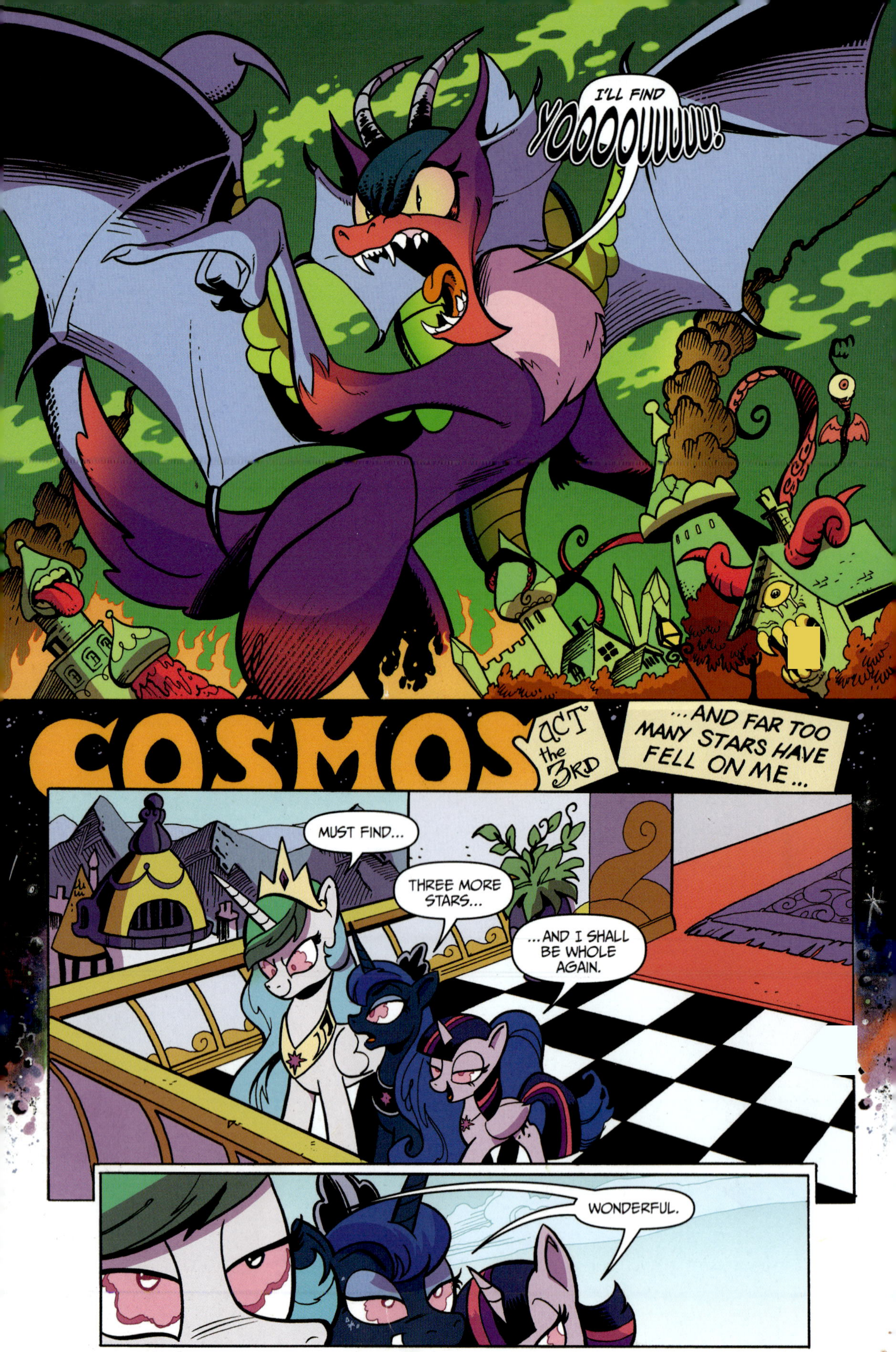
I'LL FIND YOOOOUUUUU!
COSMOS
ACT the 3RD
...AND FAR TOO MANY STARS HAVE FELL ON ME...
MUST FIND...
THREE MORE STARS...
...AND I SHALL BE WHOLE AGAIN.
WONDERFUL.

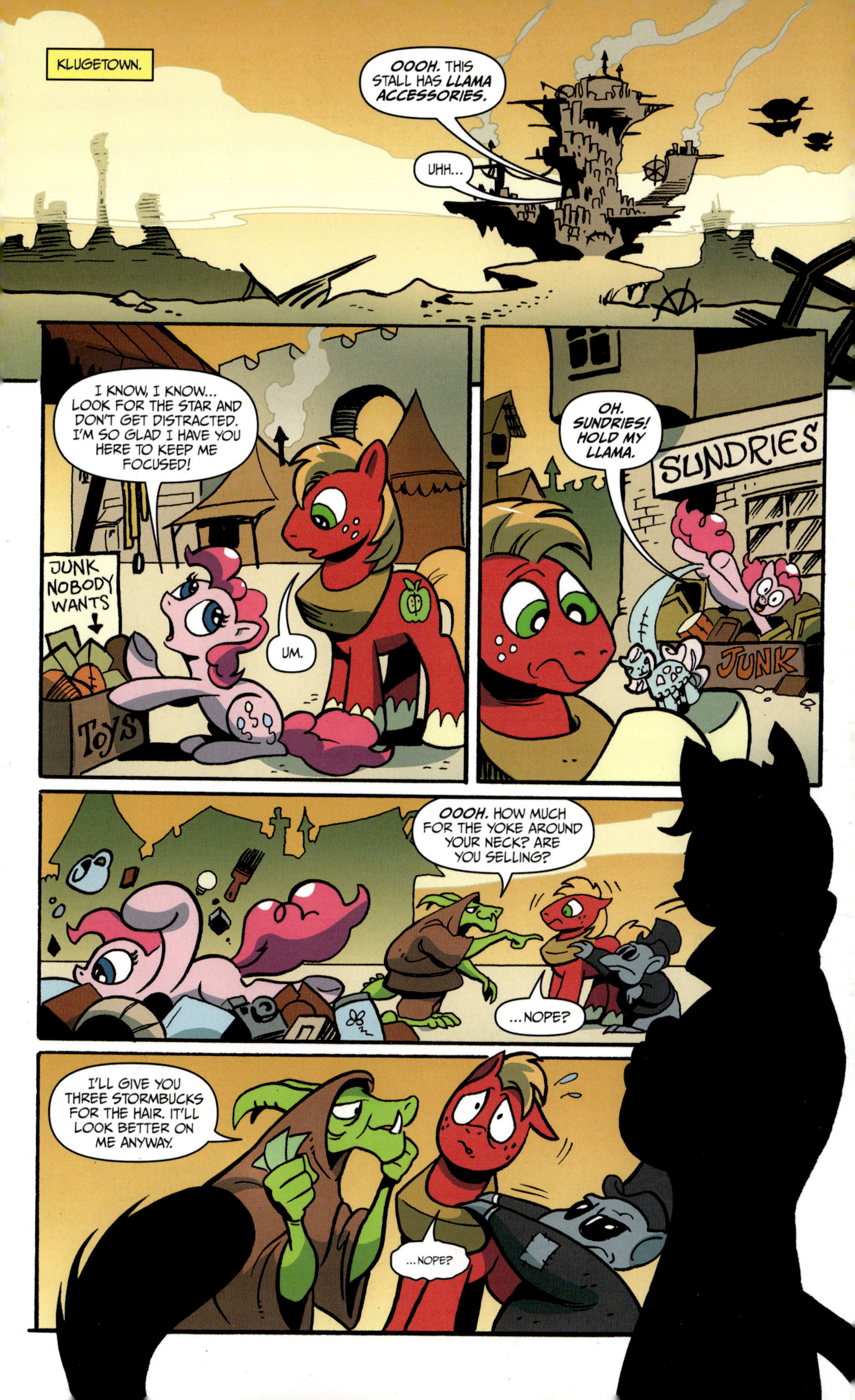
KLUGETOWN.
OOOH. THIS STALL HAS LLAMA ACCESSORIES.
UHH...
I KNOW, I KNOW... LOOK FOR THE STAR AND DON'T GET DISTRACTED. I'M SO GLAD I HAVE YOU HERE TO KEEP ME FOCUSED!
JUNK NOBODY WANTS
UM.
TOYS
OH. SUNDRIES! HOLD MY LLAMA.
SUNDRIES
JUNK
OOOH. HOW MUCH FOR THE YOKE AROUND YOUR NECK? ARE YOU SELLING?
...NOPE?
I'LL GIVE YOU THREE STORMBUCKS FOR THE HAIR. IT'LL LOOK BETTER ON ME ANYWAY.
...NOPE?

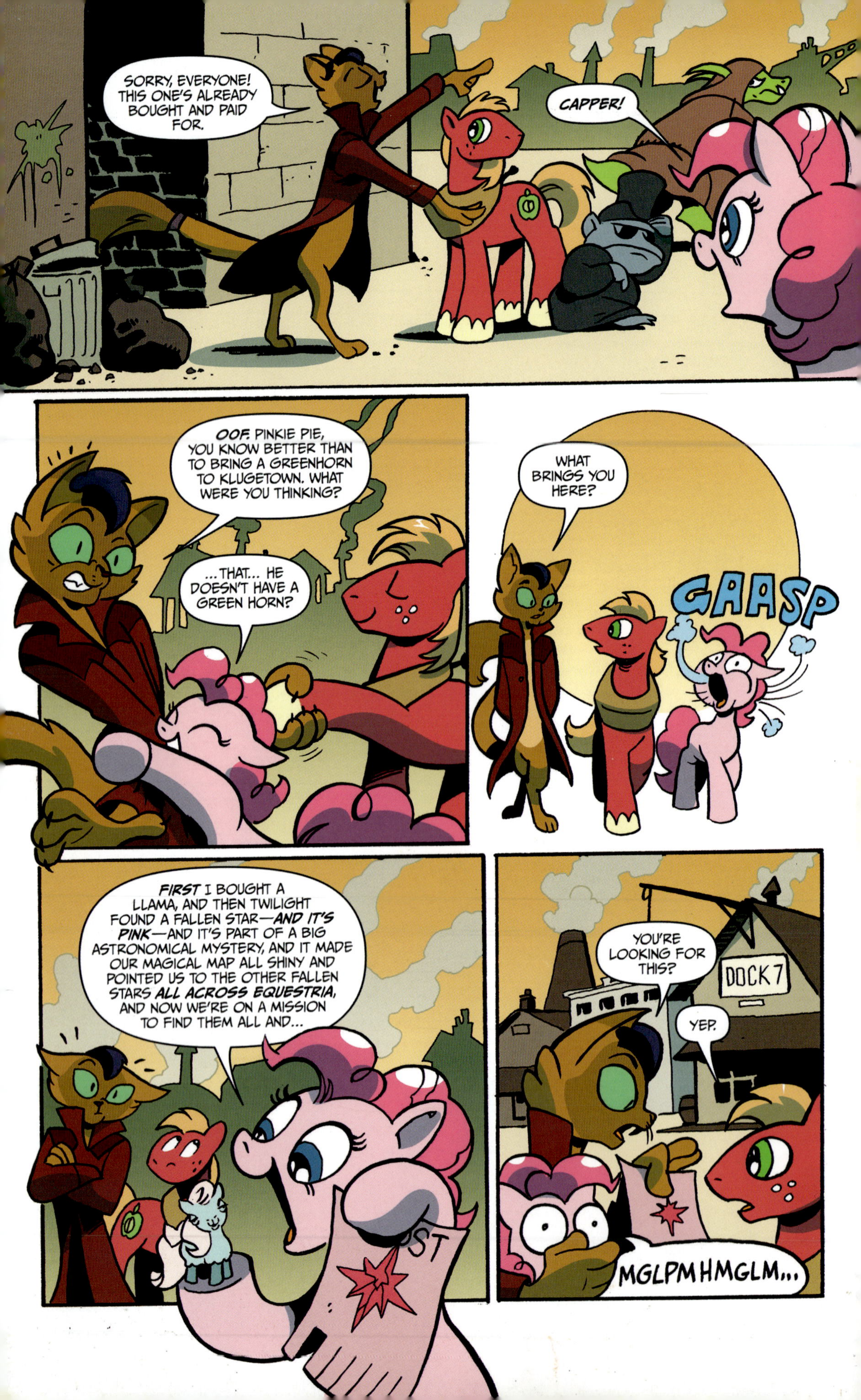
SORRY, EVERYONE! THIS ONE'S ALREADY BOUGHT AND PAID FOR.
CAPPER!
OOF. PINKIE PIE, YOU KNOW BETTER THAN TO BRING A GREENHORN TO KLUGETOWN. WHAT WERE YOU THINKING?
...THAT... HE DOESN'T HAVE A GREEN HORN?
WHAT BRINGS YOU HERE?
GAASP
FIRST I BOUGHT A LLAMA, AND THEN TWILIGHT FOUND A FALLEN STAR—AND IT'S PINK—AND IT'S PART OF A BIG ASTRONOMICAL MYSTERY, AND IT MADE OUR MAGICAL MAP ALL SHINY AND POINTED US TO THE OTHER FALLEN STARS ALL ACROSS EQUESTRIA, AND NOW WE'RE ON A MISSION TO FIND THEM ALL AND...
YOU'RE LOOKING FOR THIS?
DOCK 7
YEP.
MGLPMHMGLM...

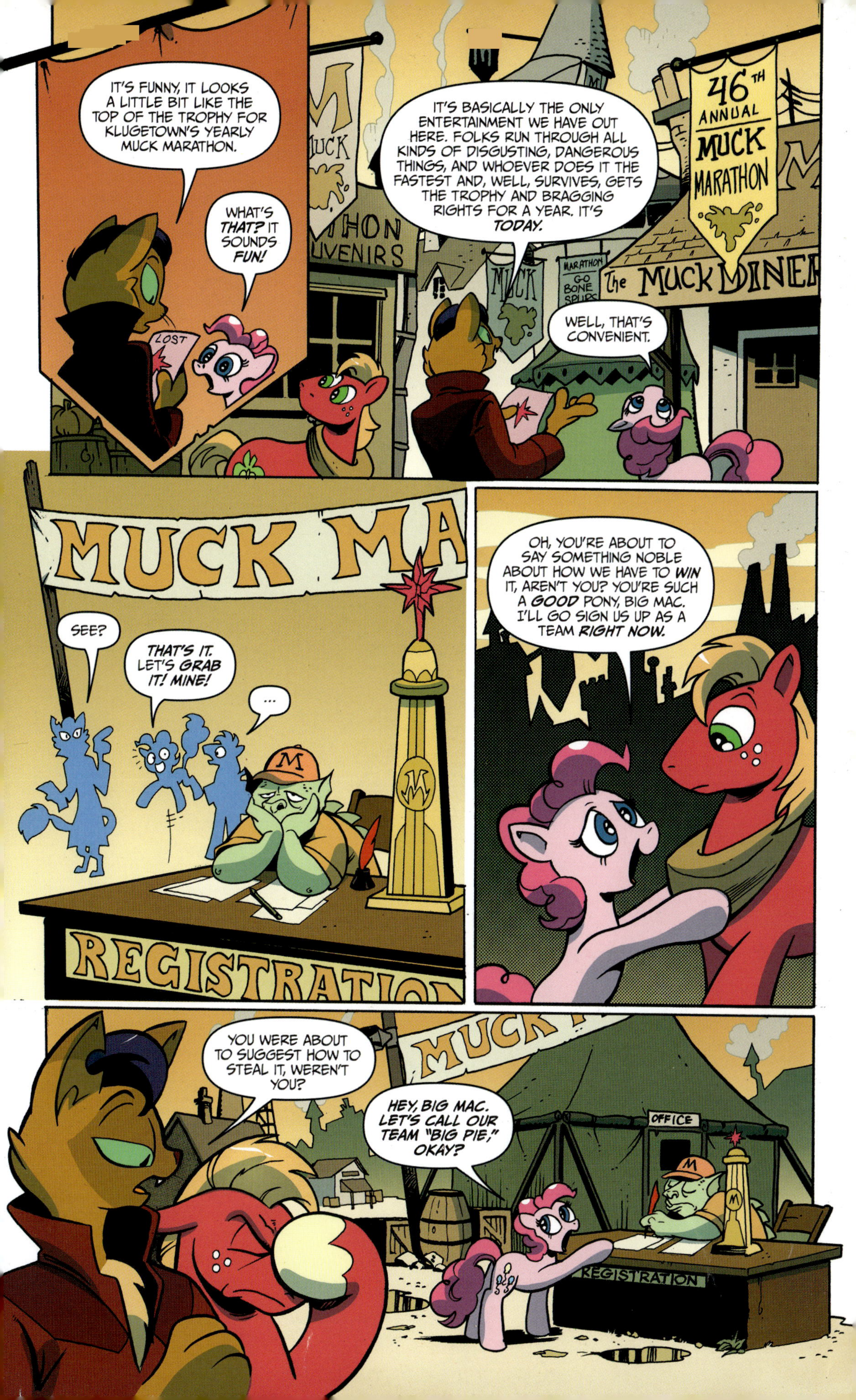
IT'S FUNNY, IT LOOKS A LITTLE BIT LIKE THE TOP OF THE TROPHY FOR KLUGETOWN'S YEARLY MUCK MARATHON.
WHAT'S THAT? IT SOUNDS FUN!
LOST
MUCK
THON
UVENIRS
IT'S BASICALLY THE ONLY ENTERTAINMENT WE HAVE OUT HERE. FOLKS RUN THROUGH ALL KINDS OF DISGUSTING, DANGEROUS THINGS, AND WHOEVER DOES IT THE FASTEST AND, WELL, SURVIVES, GETS THE TROPHY AND BRAGGING RIGHTS FOR A YEAR. IT'S TODAY.
46TH ANNUAL MUCK MARATHON
MUCK
MARATHON GO BONE SPURS
The MUCK DINER
WELL, THAT'S CONVENIENT.
MUCK MA
SEE?
THAT'S IT. LET'S GRAB IT! MINE!
...
REGISTRATION
OH, YOU'RE ABOUT TO SAY SOMETHING NOBLE ABOUT HOW WE HAVE TO WIN IT, AREN'T YOU? YOU'RE SUCH A GOOD PONY, BIG MAC. I'LL GO SIGN US UP AS A TEAM RIGHT NOW.
YOU WERE ABOUT TO SUGGEST HOW TO STEAL IT, WEREN'T YOU?
MUCK
HEY, BIG MAC. LET'S CALL OUR TEAM "BIG PIE," OKAY?
OFFICE
REGISTRATION

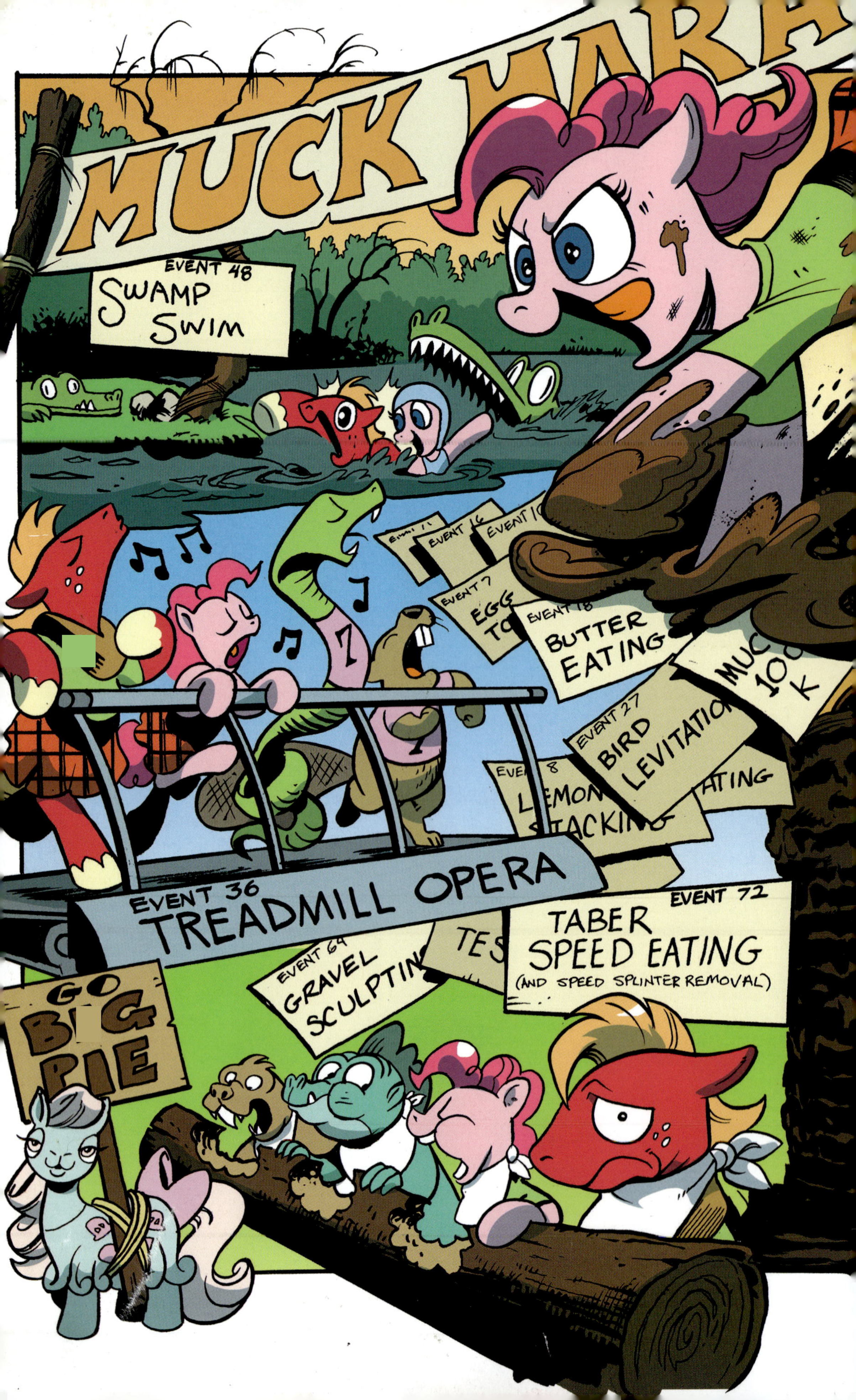
MUCK
EVENT 48
SWAMP SWIM
EVENT 18
BUTTER EATING
EVENT 27
BIRD
EVENT 36
TREADMILL OPERA
EVENT 72
TABER
SPEED EATING
(AND SPEED SPLINTER REMOVAL)
EVENT 64
GRAVEL
GO
PIE

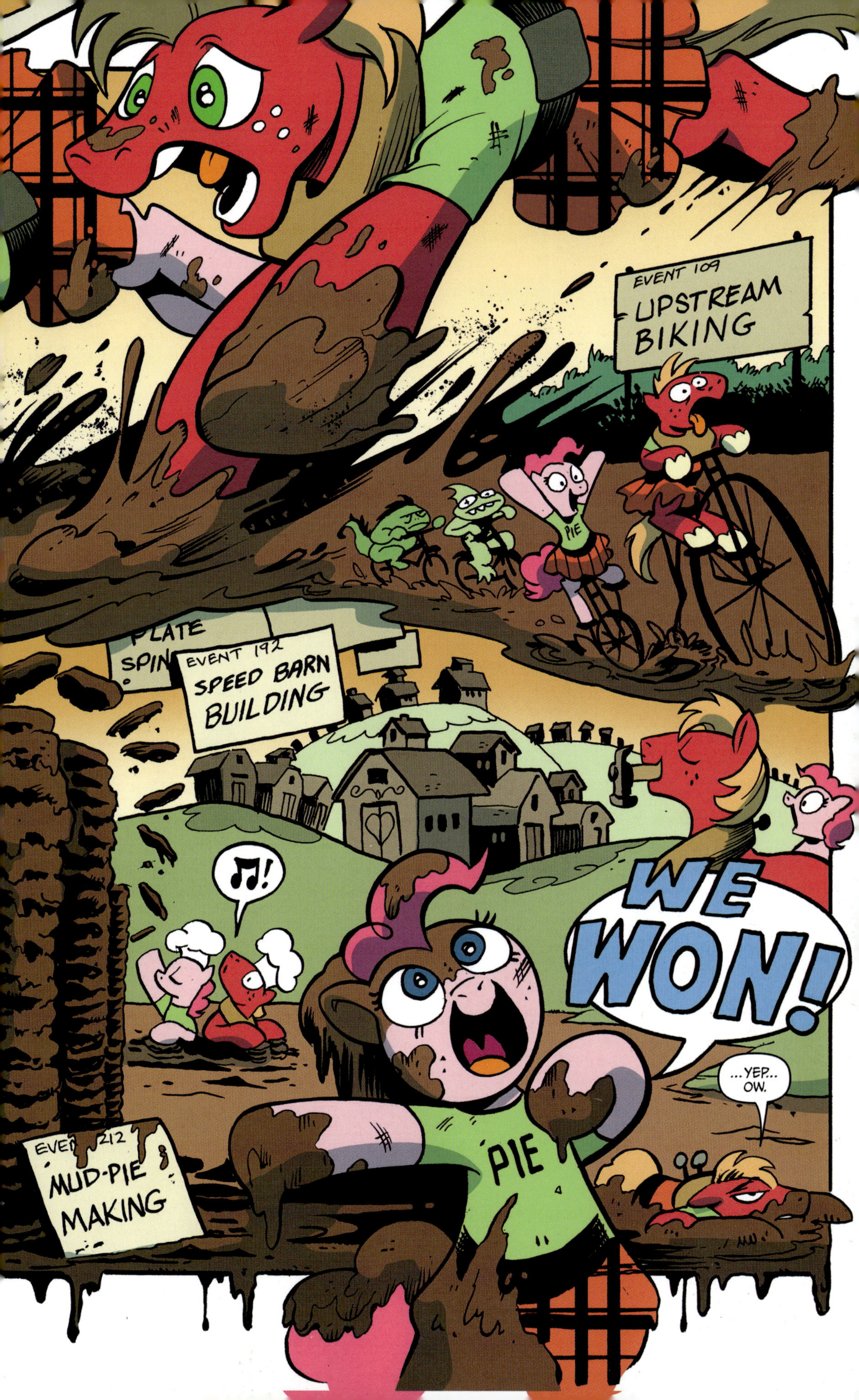
EVENT 109
UPSTREAM BIKING
PIE
PLATE SPIN
EVENT 192
SPEED BARN BUILDING
♫!
WE WON!
...YEP... OW.
EVE 212
MUD-PIE MAKING
PIE

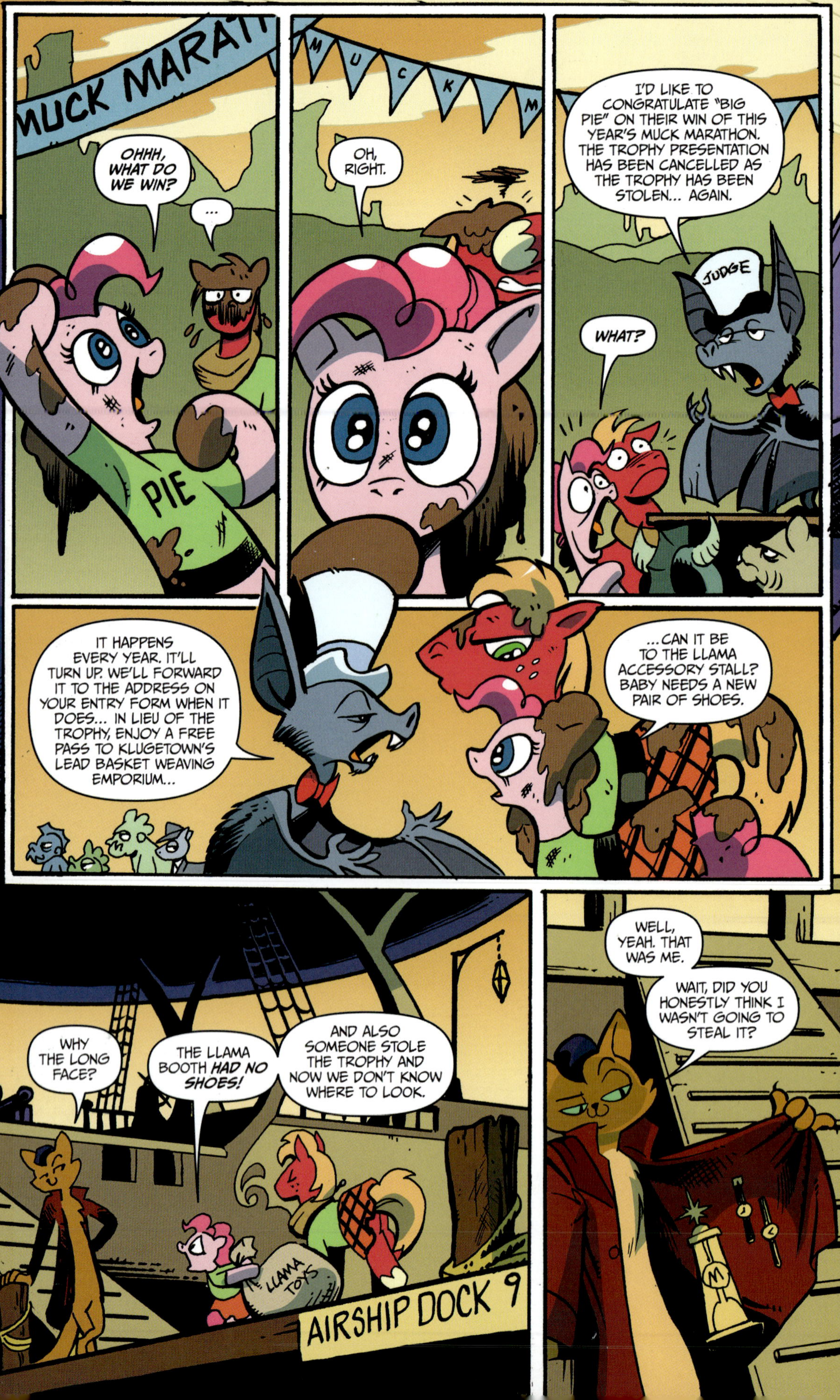
MUCK MARAT
OHHH, WHAT DO WE WIN?
...
MUCK M
OH, RIGHT.
I'D LIKE TO CONGRATULATE "BIG PIE" ON THEIR WIN OF THIS YEAR'S MUCK MARATHON. THE TROPHY PRESENTATION HAS BEEN CANCELLED AS THE TROPHY HAS BEEN STOLEN... AGAIN.
JUDGE
WHAT?
IT HAPPENS EVERY YEAR. IT'LL TURN UP. WE'LL FORWARD IT TO THE ADDRESS ON YOUR ENTRY FORM WHEN IT DOES... IN LIEU OF THE TROPHY, ENJOY A FREE PASS TO KLUGETOWN'S LEAD BASKET WEAVING EMPORIUM...
...CAN IT BE TO THE LLAMA ACCESSORY STALL? BABY NEEDS A NEW PAIR OF SHOES.
WHY THE LONG FACE?
THE LLAMA BOOTH HAD NO SHOES!
AND ALSO SOMEONE STOLE THE TROPHY AND NOW WE DON'T KNOW WHERE TO LOOK.
LLAMA TOYS
AIRSHIP DOCK 9
WELL, YEAH. THAT WAS ME.
WAIT, DID YOU HONESTLY THINK I WASN'T GOING TO STEAL IT?

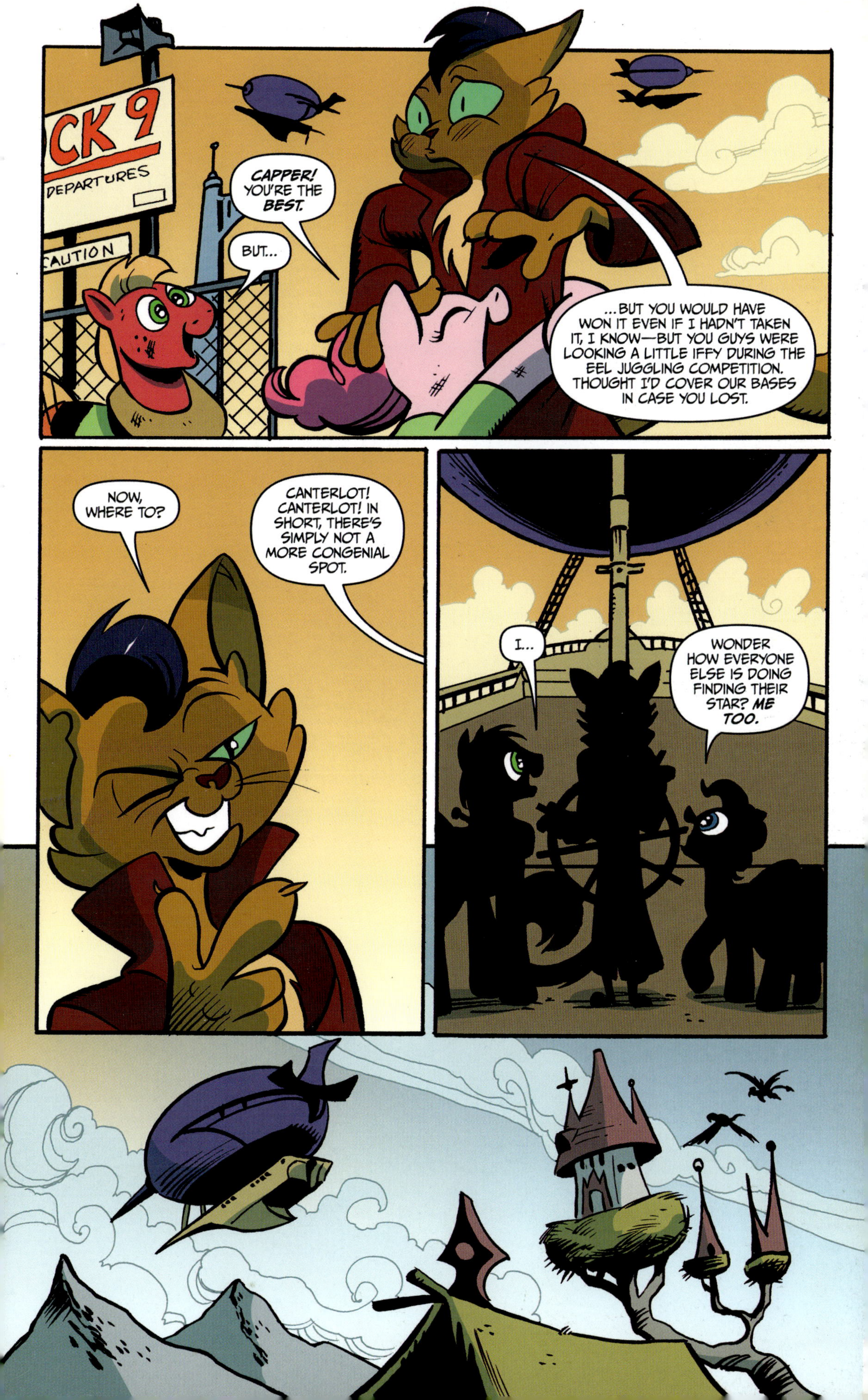
CK 9
DEPARTURES
CAUTION
CAPPER! YOU'RE THE BEST.
BUT...
...BUT YOU WOULD HAVE WON IT EVEN IF I HADN'T TAKEN IT, I KNOW—BUT YOU GUYS WERE LOOKING A LITTLE IFFY DURING THE EEL JUGGLING COMPETITION. THOUGHT I'D COVER OUR BASES IN CASE YOU LOST.
NOW, WHERE TO?
CANTERLOT! CANTERLOT! IN SHORT, THERE'S SIMPLY NOT A MORE CONGENIAL SPOT.
I...
WONDER HOW EVERYONE ELSE IS DOING FINDING THEIR STAR? ME TOO.

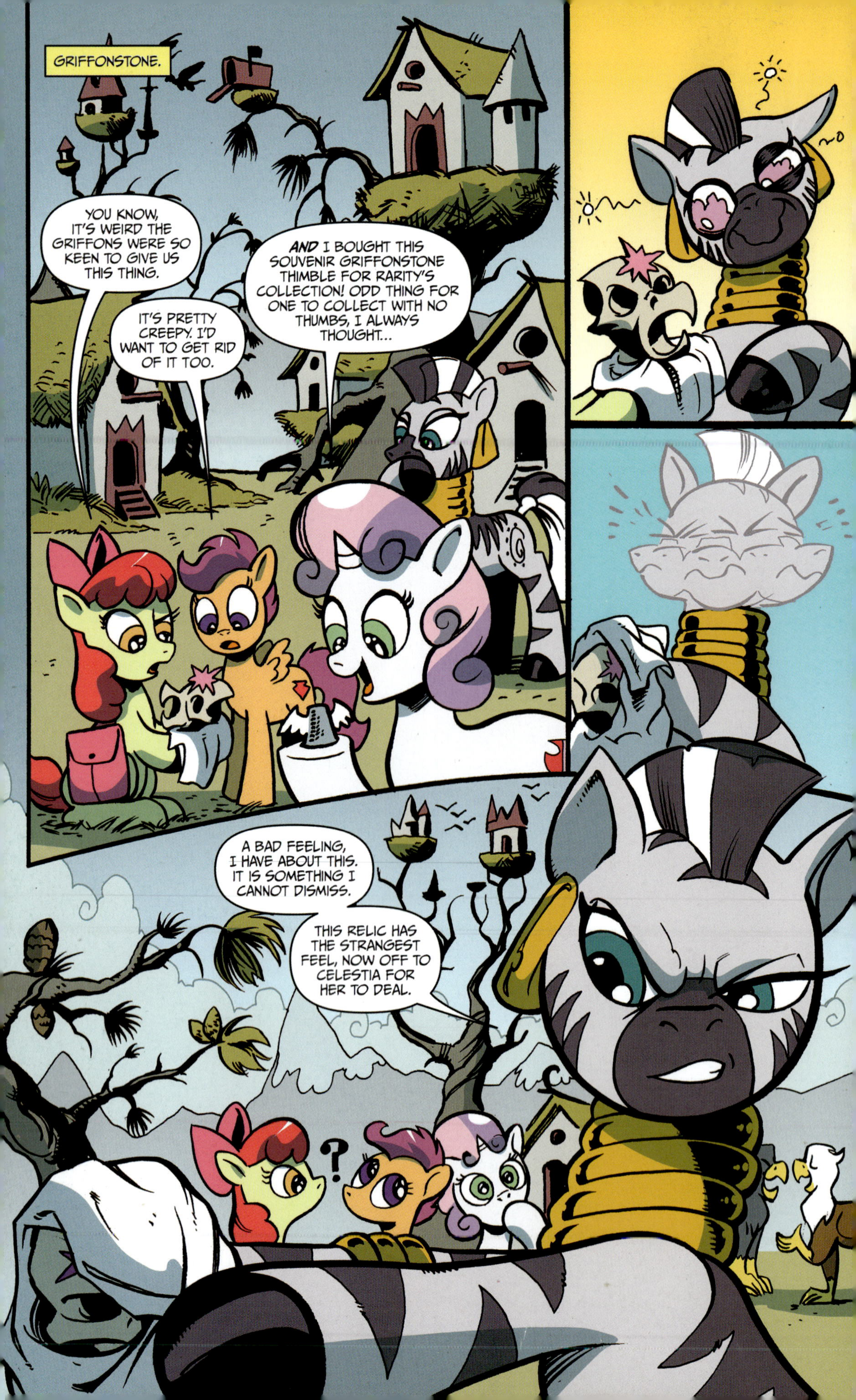
GRIFFONSTONE.
YOU KNOW, IT'S WEIRD THE GRIFFONS WERE SO KEEN TO GIVE US THIS THING.
IT'S PRETTY CREEPY. I'D WANT TO GET RID OF IT TOO.
AND I BOUGHT THIS SOUVENIR GRIFFONSTONE THIMBLE FOR RARITY'S COLLECTION! ODD THING FOR ONE TO COLLECT WITH NO THUMBS, I ALWAYS THOUGHT...
A BAD FEELING, I HAVE ABOUT THIS. IT IS SOMETHING I CANNOT DISMISS.
THIS RELIC HAS THE STRANGEST FEEL, NOW OFF TO CELESTIA FOR HER TO DEAL.
?

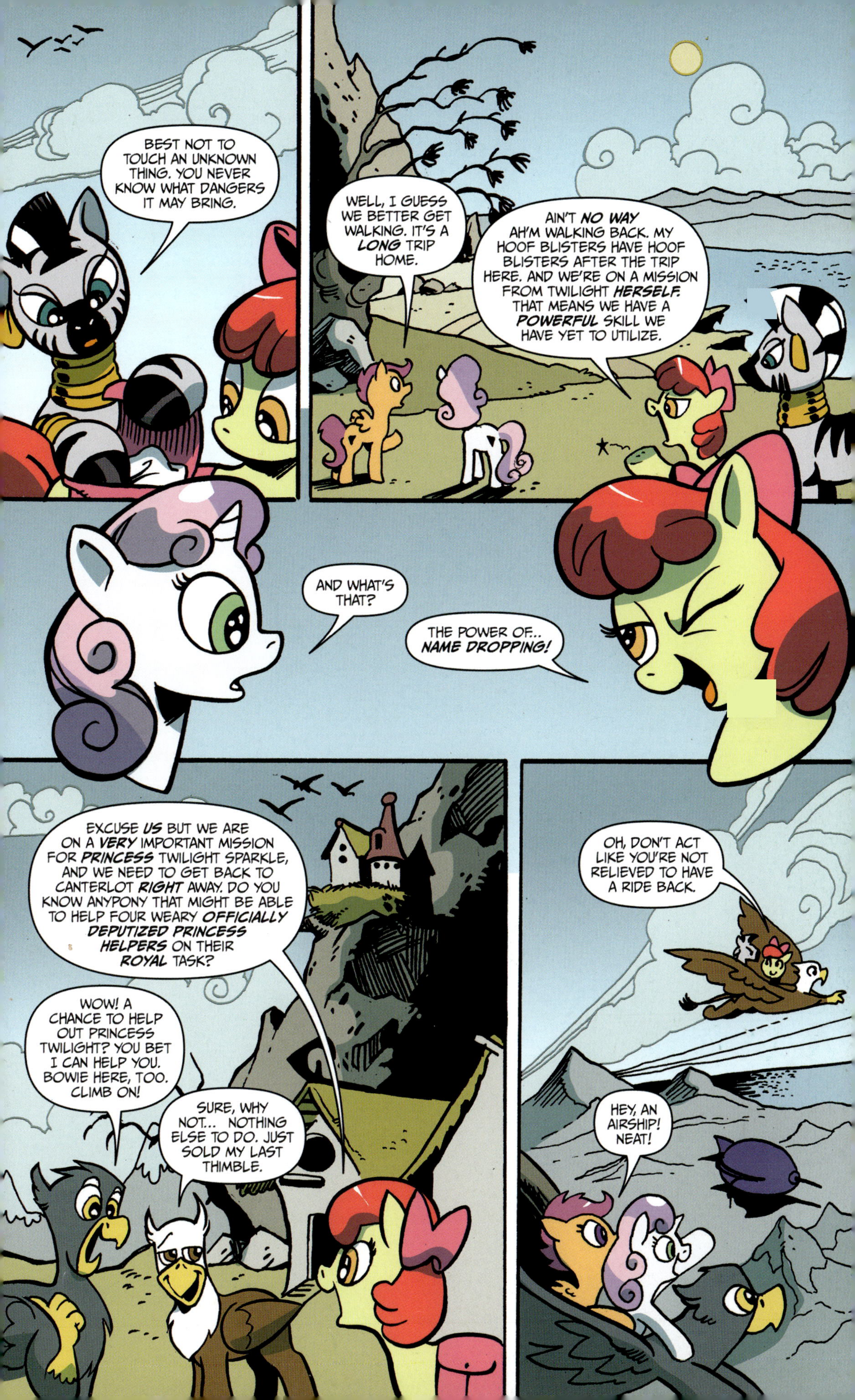
BEST NOT TO TOUCH AN UNKNOWN THING. YOU NEVER KNOW WHAT DANGERS IT MAY BRING.
WELL, I GUESS WE BETTER GET WALKING. IT'S A LONG TRIP HOME.
AIN'T NO WAY AH'M WALKING BACK. MY HOOF BLISTERS HAVE HOOF BLISTERS AFTER THE TRIP HERE. AND WE'RE ON A MISSION FROM TWILIGHT HERSELF. THAT MEANS WE HAVE A POWERFUL SKILL WE HAVE YET TO UTILIZE.
AND WHAT'S THAT?
THE POWER OF... NAME DROPPING!
EXCUSE US BUT WE ARE ON A VERY IMPORTANT MISSION FOR PRINCESS TWILIGHT SPARKLE, AND WE NEED TO GET BACK TO CANTERLOT RIGHT AWAY. DO YOU KNOW ANYPONY THAT MIGHT BE ABLE TO HELP FOUR WEARY OFFICIALLY DEPUTIZED PRINCESS HELPERS ON THEIR ROYAL TASK?
WOW! A CHANCE TO HELP OUT PRINCESS TWILIGHT? YOU BET I CAN HELP YOU. BOWIE HERE, TOO. CLIMB ON!
SURE, WHY NOT... NOTHING ELSE TO DO. JUST SOLD MY LAST THIMBLE.
OH, DON'T ACT LIKE YOU'RE NOT RELIEVED TO HAVE A RIDE BACK.
HEY, AN AIRSHIP! NEAT!

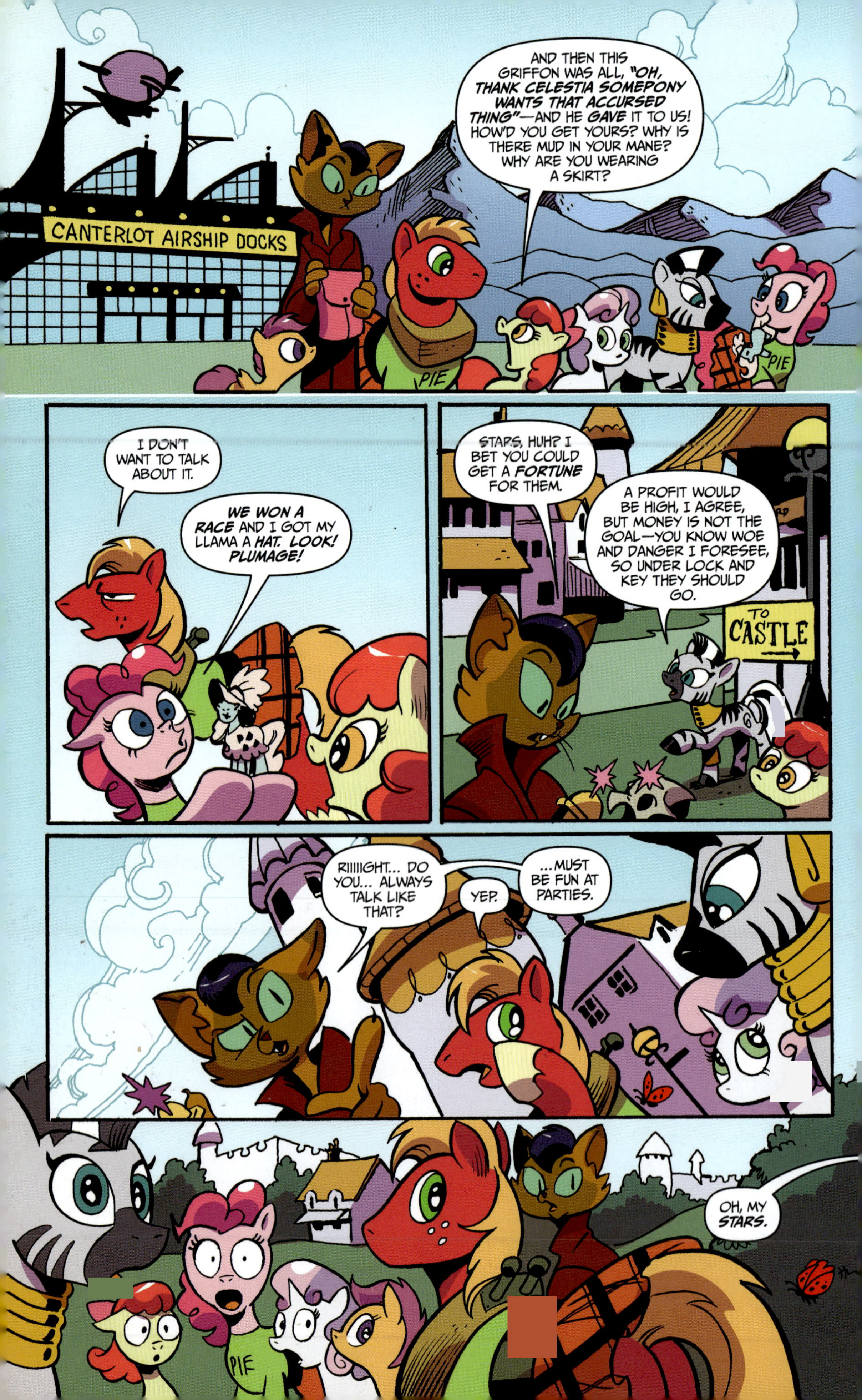

CANTERLOT AIRSHIP DOCKS
AND THEN THIS GRIFFON WAS ALL, "OH, THANK CELESTIA SOMEPONY WANTS THAT ACCURSED THING"—AND HE GAVE IT TO US! HOW'D YOU GET YOURS? WHY IS THERE MUD IN YOUR MANE? WHY ARE YOU WEARING A SKIRT?
PIE
PIE
I DON'T WANT TO TALK ABOUT IT.
WE WON A RACE AND I GOT MY LLAMA A HAT. LOOK! PLUMAGE!
STARS, HUH? I BET YOU COULD GET A FORTUNE FOR THEM.
A PROFIT WOULD BE HIGH, I AGREE, BUT MONEY IS NOT THE GOAL—YOU KNOW WOE AND DANGER I FORESEE, SO UNDER LOCK AND KEY THEY SHOULD GO.
TO CASTLE
RIIIIGHT... DO YOU... ALWAYS TALK LIKE THAT?
YEP.
...MUST BE FUN AT PARTIES.
OH, MY STARS.
PIE

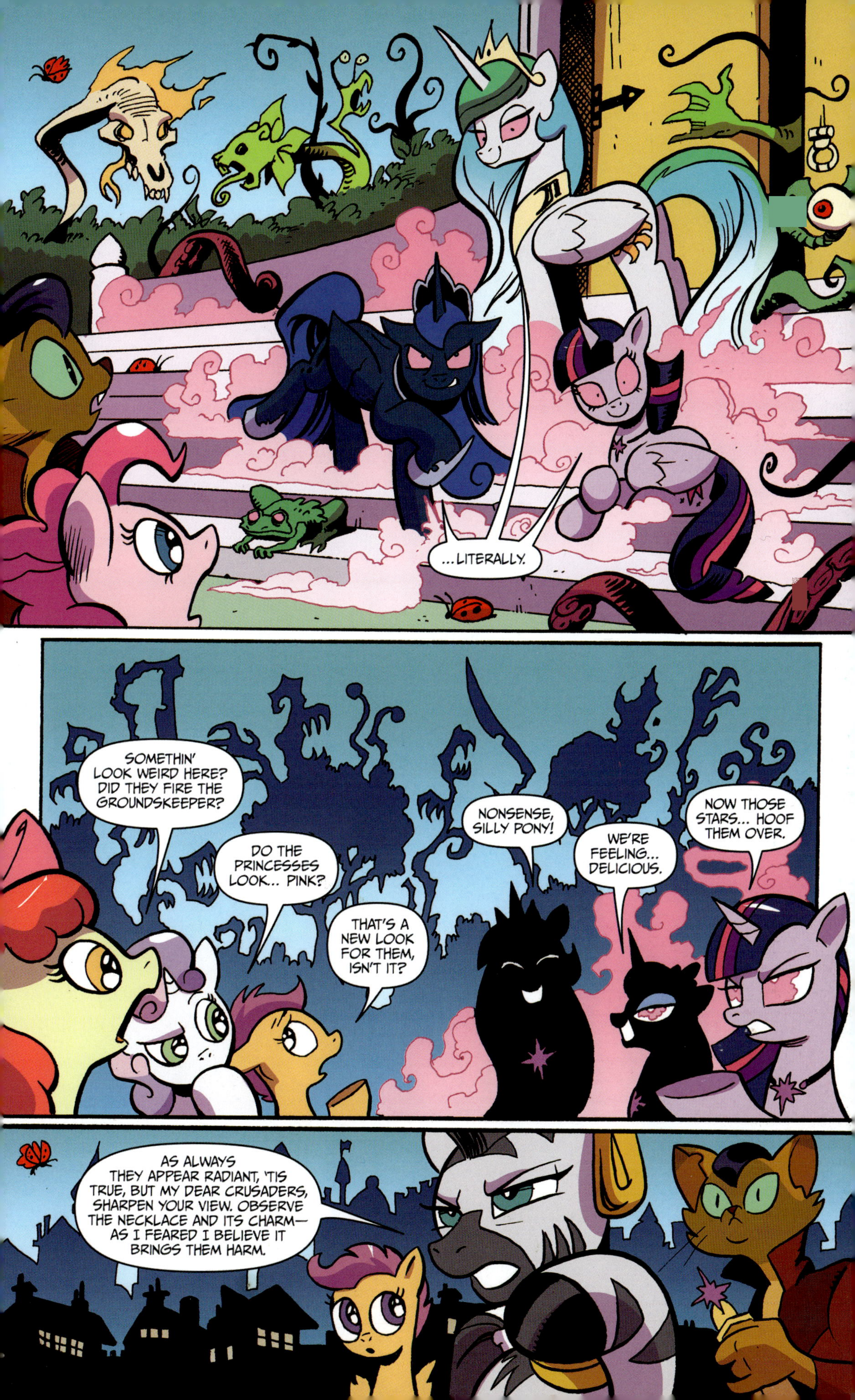
...LITERALLY.
SOMETHIN' LOOK WEIRD HERE? DID THEY FIRE THE GROUNDSKEEPER?
DO THE PRINCESSES LOOK... PINK?
THAT'S A NEW LOOK FOR THEM, ISN'T IT?
NONSENSE, SILLY PONY!
WE'RE FEELING... DELICIOUS.
NOW THOSE STARS... HOOF THEM OVER.
AS ALWAYS THEY APPEAR RADIANT, 'TIS TRUE, BUT MY DEAR CRUSADERS, SHARPEN YOUR VIEW. OBSERVE THE NECKLACE AND ITS CHARM— AS I FEARED I BELIEVE IT BRINGS THEM HARM.

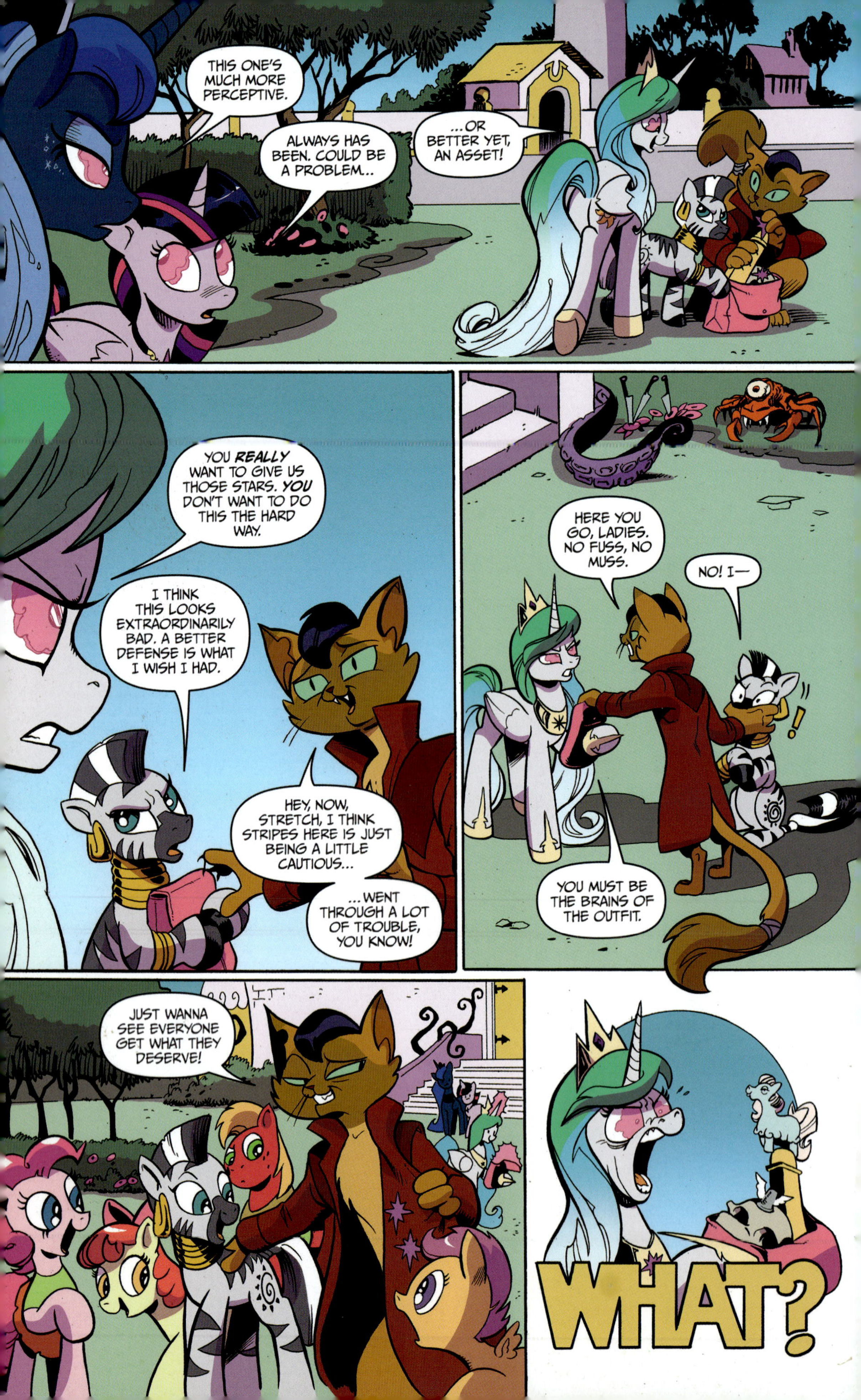
THIS ONE'S MUCH MORE PERCEPTIVE.
ALWAYS HAS BEEN. COULD BE A PROBLEM...
...OR BETTER YET, AN ASSET!
YOU REALLY WANT TO GIVE US THOSE STARS. YOU DON'T WANT TO DO THIS THE HARD WAY.
I THINK THIS LOOKS EXTRAORDINARILY BAD. A BETTER DEFENSE IS WHAT I WISH I HAD.
HEY, NOW, STRETCH, I THINK STRIPES HERE IS JUST BEING A LITTLE CAUTIOUS...
...WENT THROUGH A LOT OF TROUBLE, YOU KNOW!
HERE YOU GO, LADIES. NO FUSS, NO MUSS.
NO! I—
YOU MUST BE THE BRAINS OF THE OUTFIT.
JUST WANNA SEE EVERYONE GET WHAT THEY DESERVE!
WHAT?

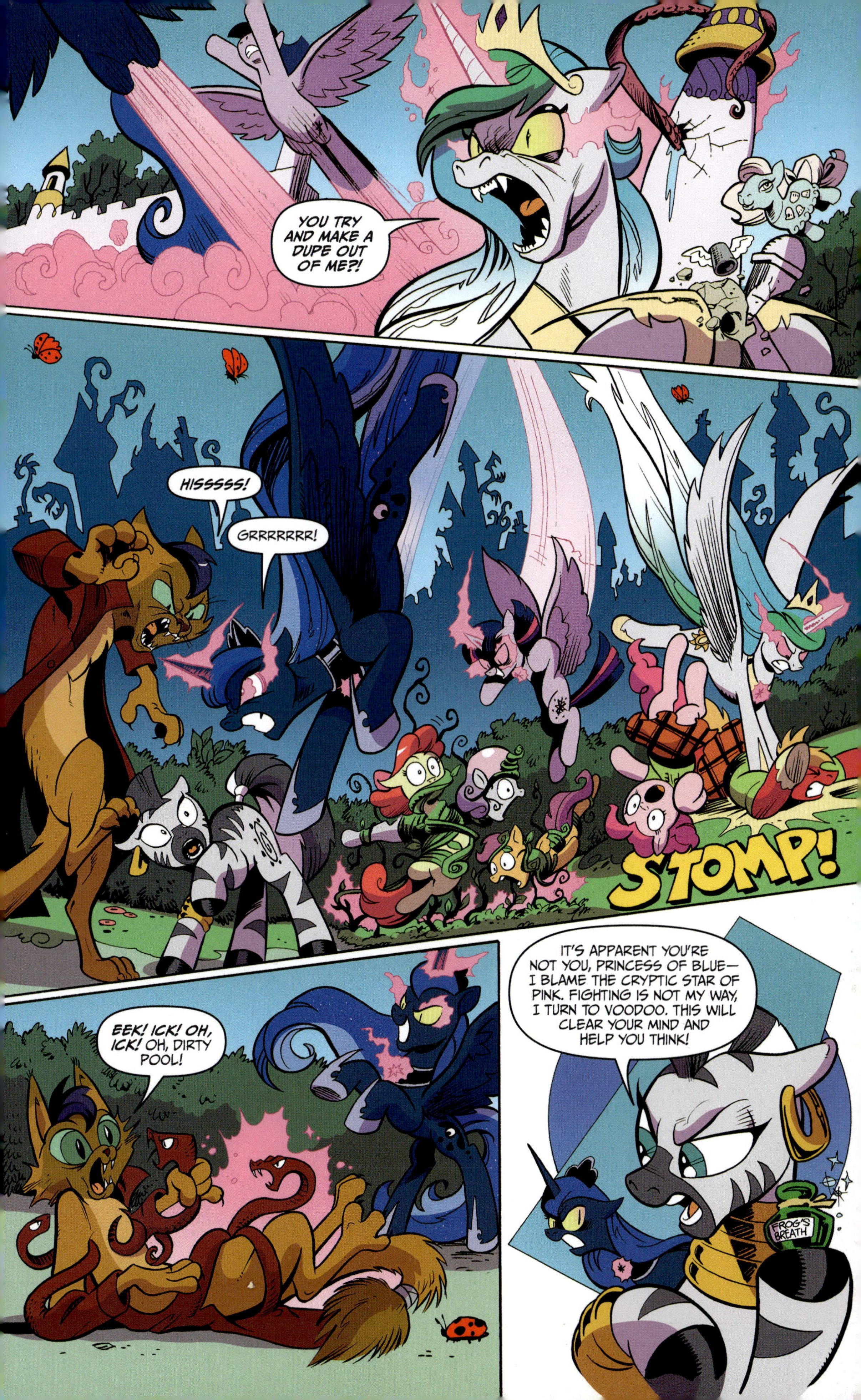
YOU TRY AND MAKE A DUPE OUT OF ME?!
HISSSSS!
GRRRRRRR!
STOMP!
EEK! ICK! OH, ICK! OH, DIRTY POOL!
IT'S APPARENT YOU'RE NOT YOU, PRINCESS OF BLUE— I BLAME THE CRYPTIC STAR OF PINK. FIGHTING IS NOT MY WAY, I TURN TO VOODOO. THIS WILL CLEAR YOUR MIND AND HELP YOU THINK!
FROG'S BREATH

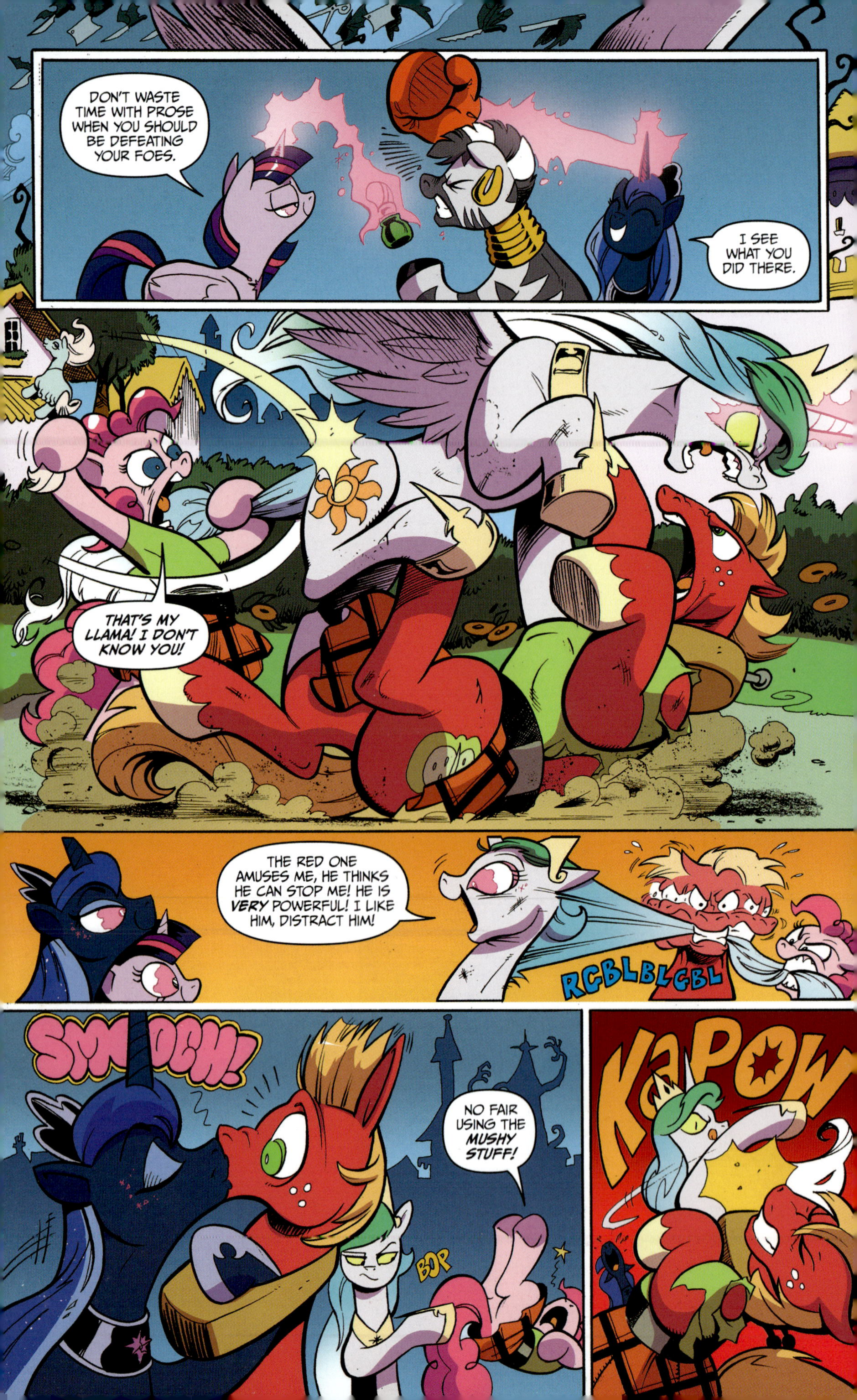
DON'T WASTE TIME WITH PROSE WHEN YOU SHOULD BE DEFEATING YOUR FOES.
I SEE WHAT YOU DID THERE.
THAT'S MY LLAMA! I DON'T KNOW YOU!
THE RED ONE AMUSES ME, HE THINKS HE CAN STOP ME! HE IS VERY POWERFUL! I LIKE HIM, DISTRACT HIM!
RGBLBLGBL
SMOOCH!
NO FAIR USING THE MUSHY STUFF!
BOP
KAPOW

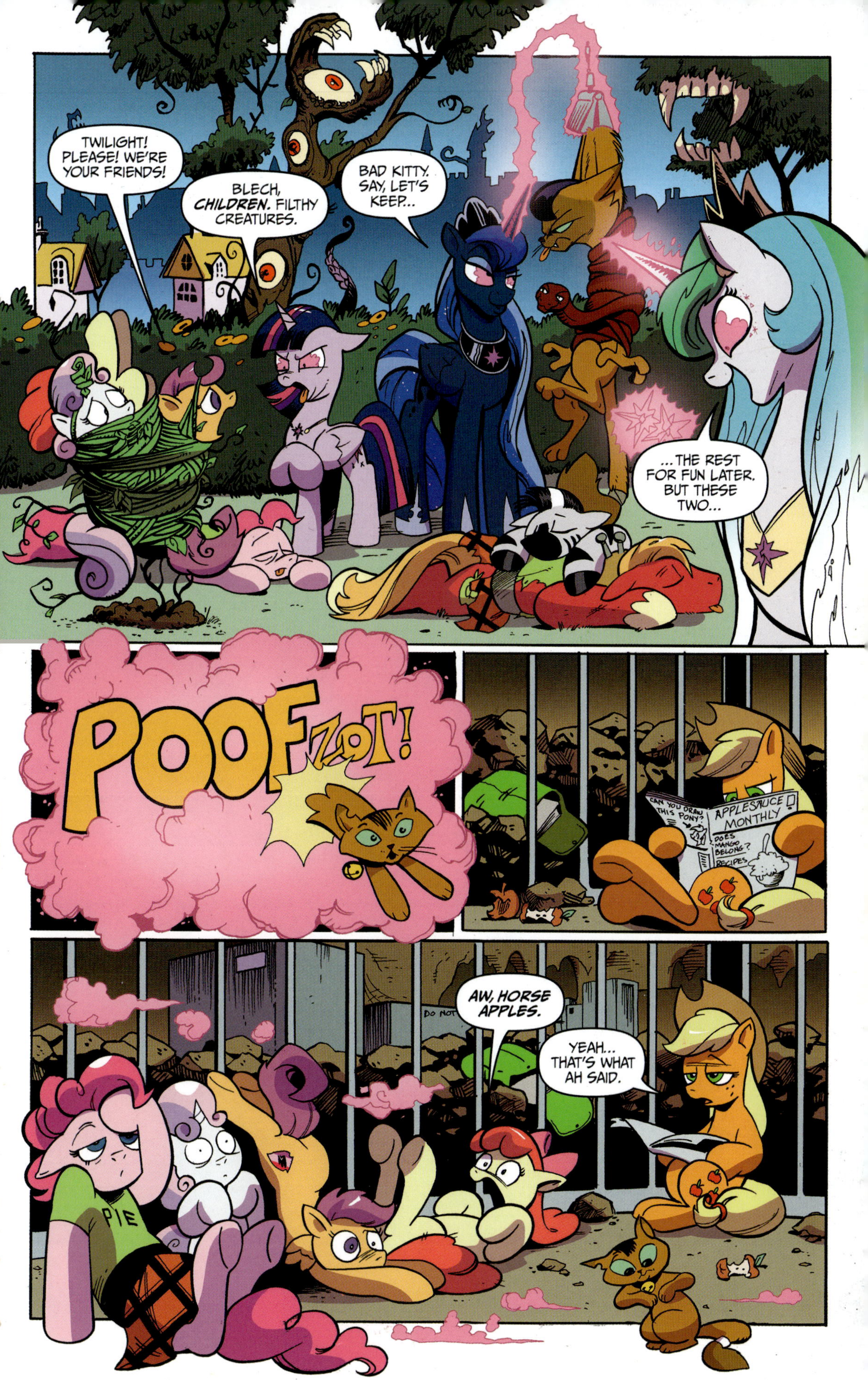

TWILIGHT! PLEASE! WE'RE YOUR FRIENDS!
BLECH, **CHILDREN.** FILTHY CREATURES.
BAD KITTY. SAY, LET'S KEEP...
...THE REST FOR FUN LATER. BUT THESE TWO...
POOF
ZOT!
CAN YOU DRAW THIS PONY?
APPLESAUCE MONTHLY
DOES MANGO BELONG?
RECIPES
DO NOT
AW, HORSE APPLES.
YEAH... THAT'S WHAT AH SAID.
PIE

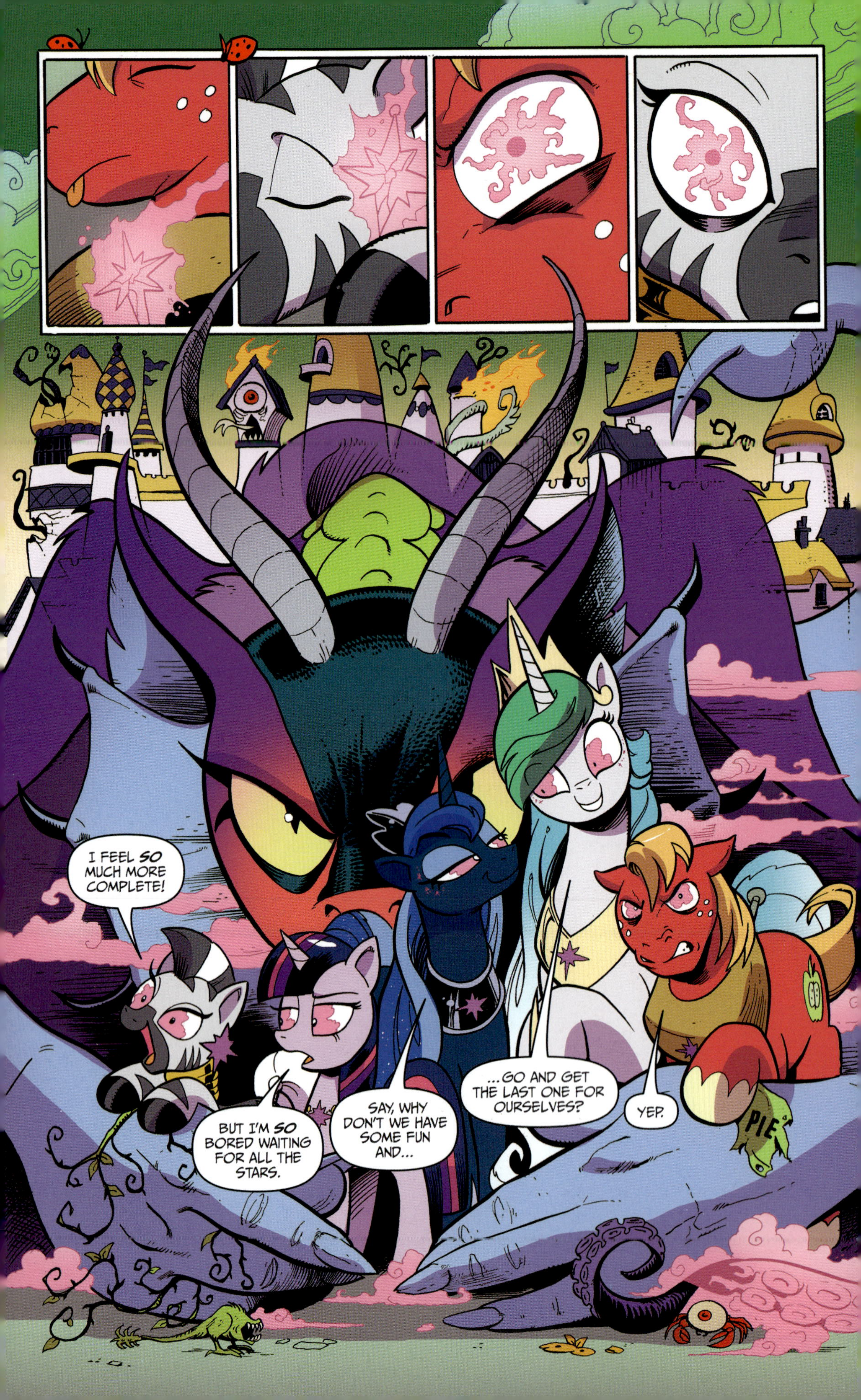
I FEEL SO MUCH MORE COMPLETE!
BUT I'M SO BORED WAITING FOR ALL THE STARS.
SAY, WHY DON'T WE HAVE SOME FUN AND...
...GO AND GET THE LAST ONE FOR OURSELVES?
YEP.
PIE

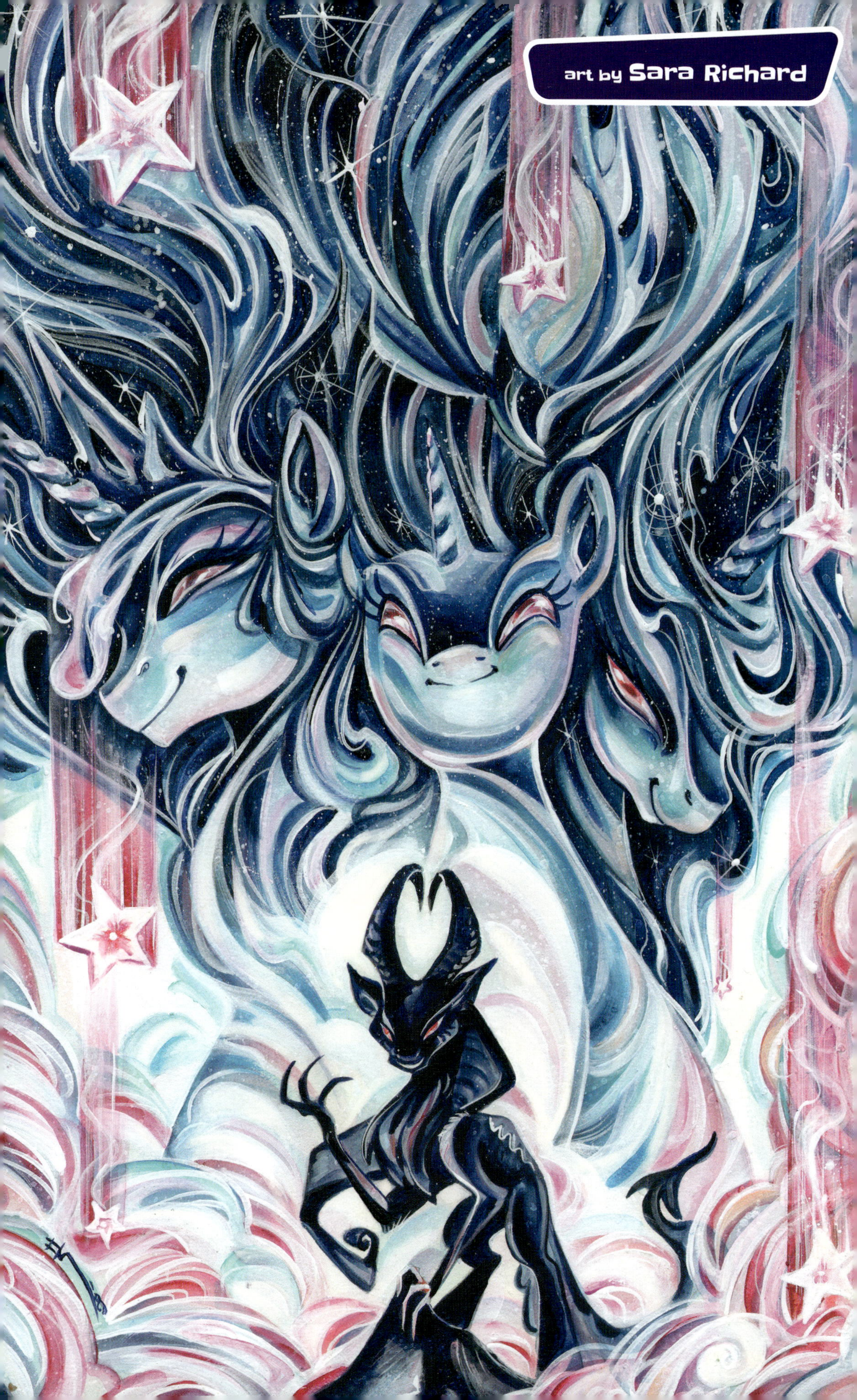

art by Sara Richard

art by Andy Price

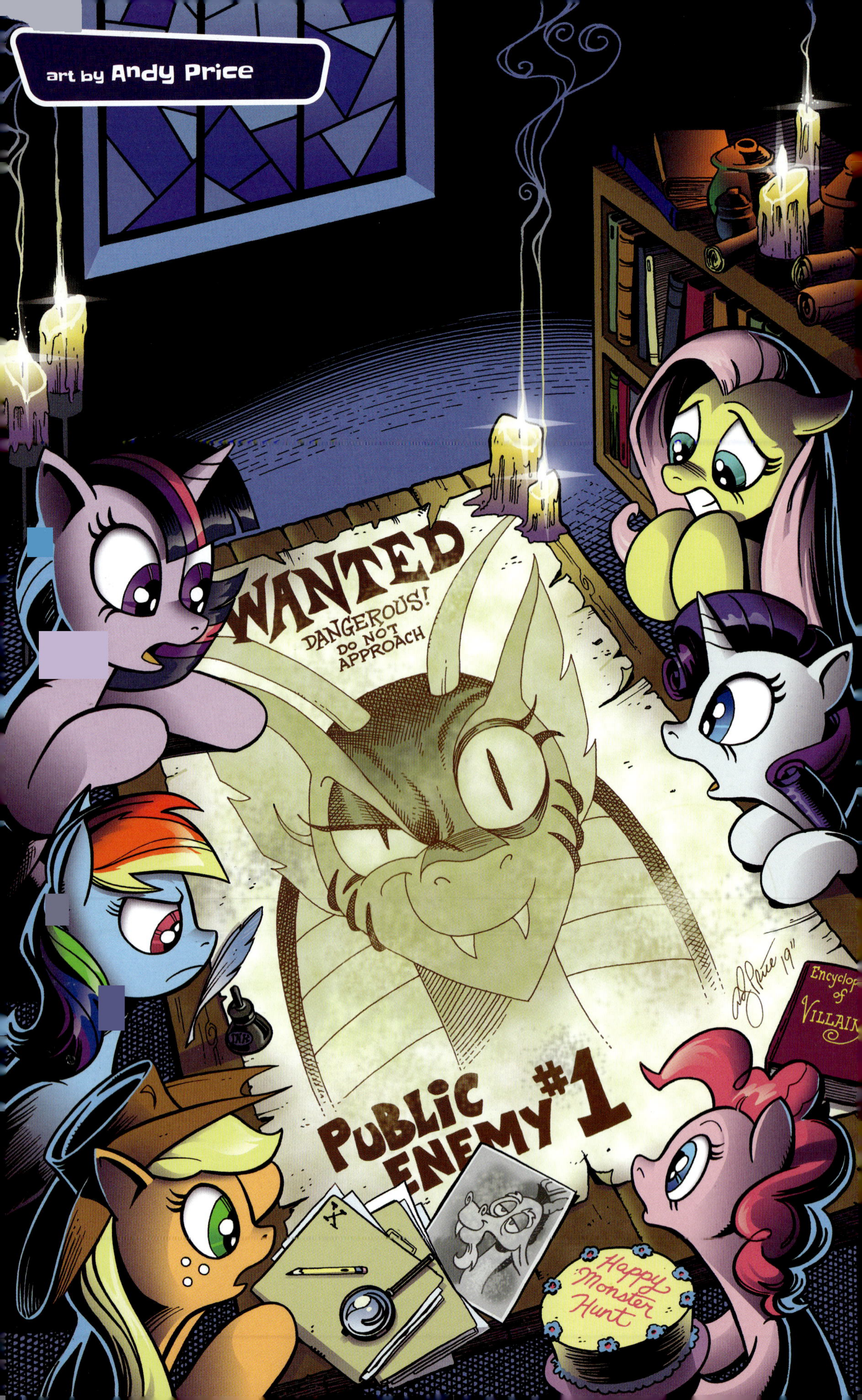
WANTED
DANGEROUS!
DO NOT APPROACH
PUBLIC ENEMY #1
Encyclop of VILLAIN
Happy Monster Hunt

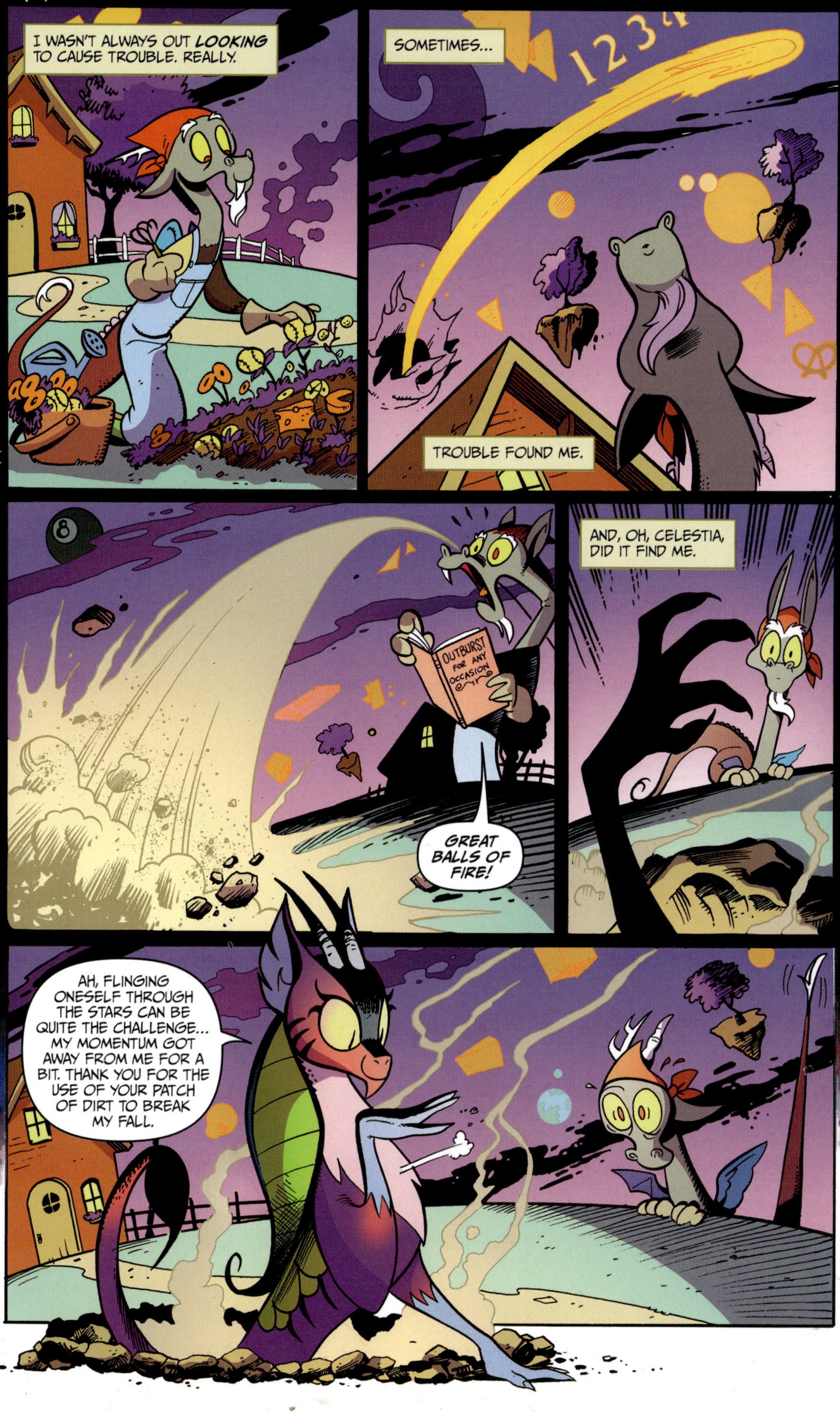
I WASN'T ALWAYS OUT LOOKING TO CAUSE TROUBLE. REALLY.
SOMETIMES...
TROUBLE FOUND ME.
OUTBURST FOR ANY OCCASION
GREAT BALLS OF FIRE!
AND, OH, CELESTIA, DID IT FIND ME.
AH, FLINGING ONESELF THROUGH THE STARS CAN BE QUITE THE CHALLENGE... MY MOMENTUM GOT AWAY FROM ME FOR A BIT. THANK YOU FOR THE USE OF YOUR PATCH OF DIRT TO BREAK MY FALL.

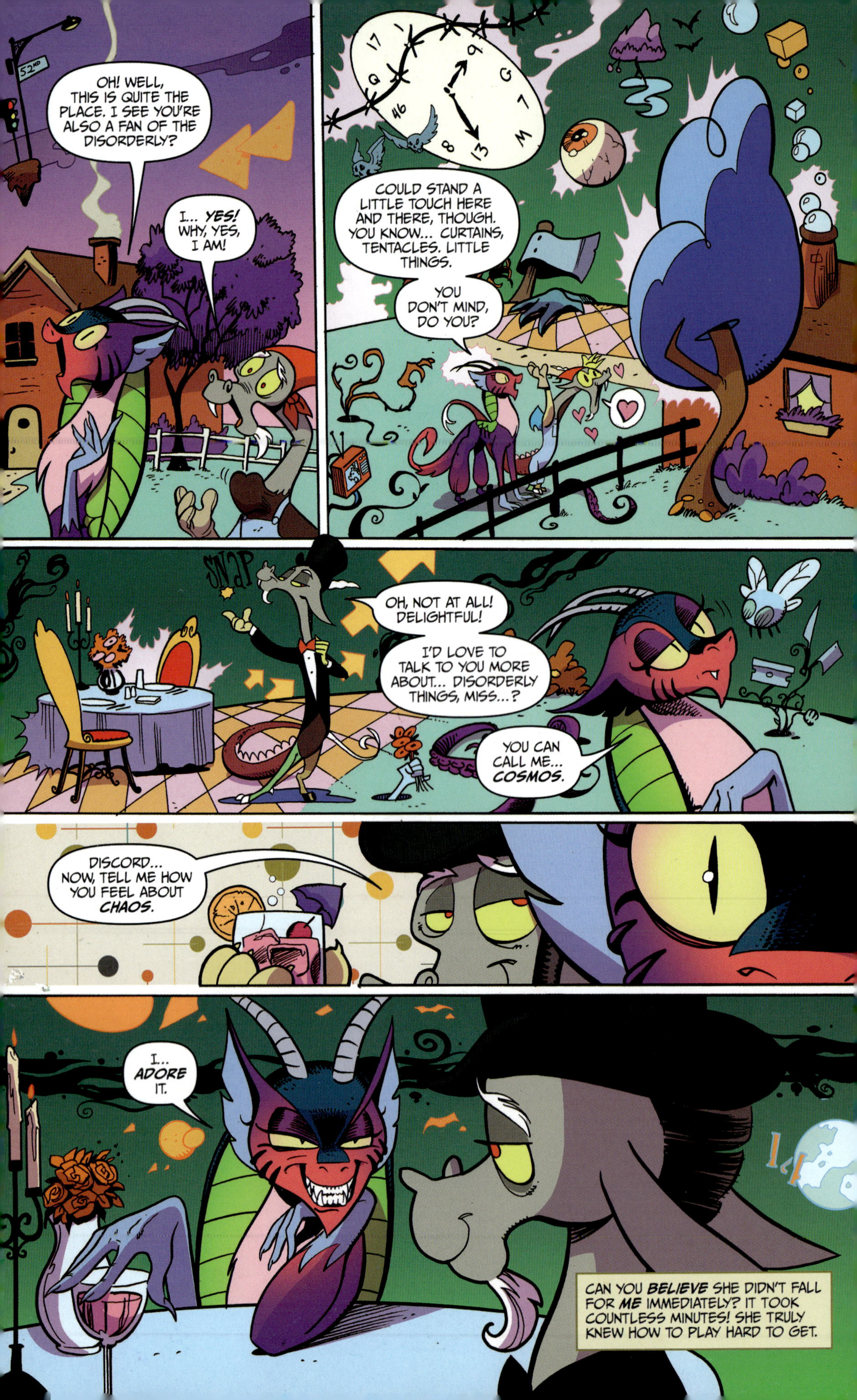
52ND
OH! WELL, THIS IS QUITE THE PLACE. I SEE YOU'RE ALSO A FAN OF THE DISORDERLY?
I... YES! WHY, YES, I AM!
COULD STAND A LITTLE TOUCH HERE AND THERE, THOUGH. YOU KNOW... CURTAINS, TENTACLES. LITTLE THINGS.
YOU DON'T MIND, DO YOU?
SNAP
OH, NOT AT ALL! DELIGHTFUL!
I'D LOVE TO TALK TO YOU MORE ABOUT... DISORDERLY THINGS, MISS...?
YOU CAN CALL ME... COSMOS.
DISCORD... NOW, TELL ME HOW YOU FEEL ABOUT CHAOS.
I... ADORE IT.
CAN YOU BELIEVE SHE DIDN'T FALL FOR ME IMMEDIATELY? IT TOOK COUNTLESS MINUTES! SHE TRULY KNEW HOW TO PLAY HARD TO GET.

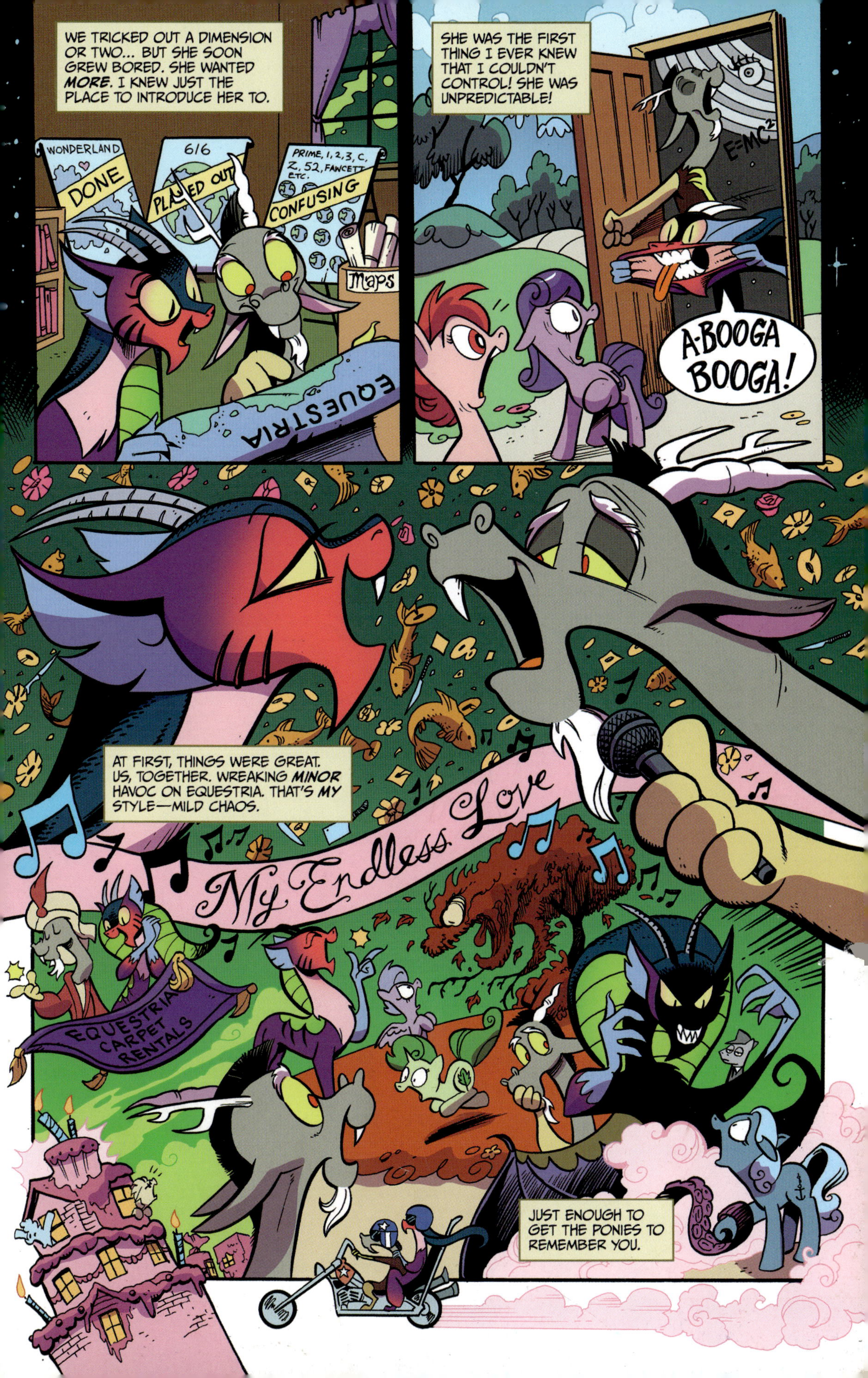
WE TRICKED OUT A DIMENSION OR TWO... BUT SHE SOON GREW BORED. SHE WANTED *MORE*. I KNEW JUST THE PLACE TO INTRODUCE HER TO.
WONDERLAND
DONE
6/6
PLAYED OUT
PRIME, 1, 2, 3, C, Z, 52, FAWCETT ETC.
CONFUSING
MAPS
EQUESTRIA
SHE WAS THE FIRST THING I EVER KNEW THAT I COULDN'T CONTROL! SHE WAS UNPREDICTABLE!
E=MC²
A-BOOGA BOOGA!
AT FIRST, THINGS WERE GREAT. US, TOGETHER. WREAKING *MINOR* HAVOC ON EQUESTRIA. THAT'S *MY* STYLE—MILD CHAOS.
My Endless Love
EQUESTRIA CARPET RENTALS
JUST ENOUGH TO GET THE PONIES TO REMEMBER YOU.

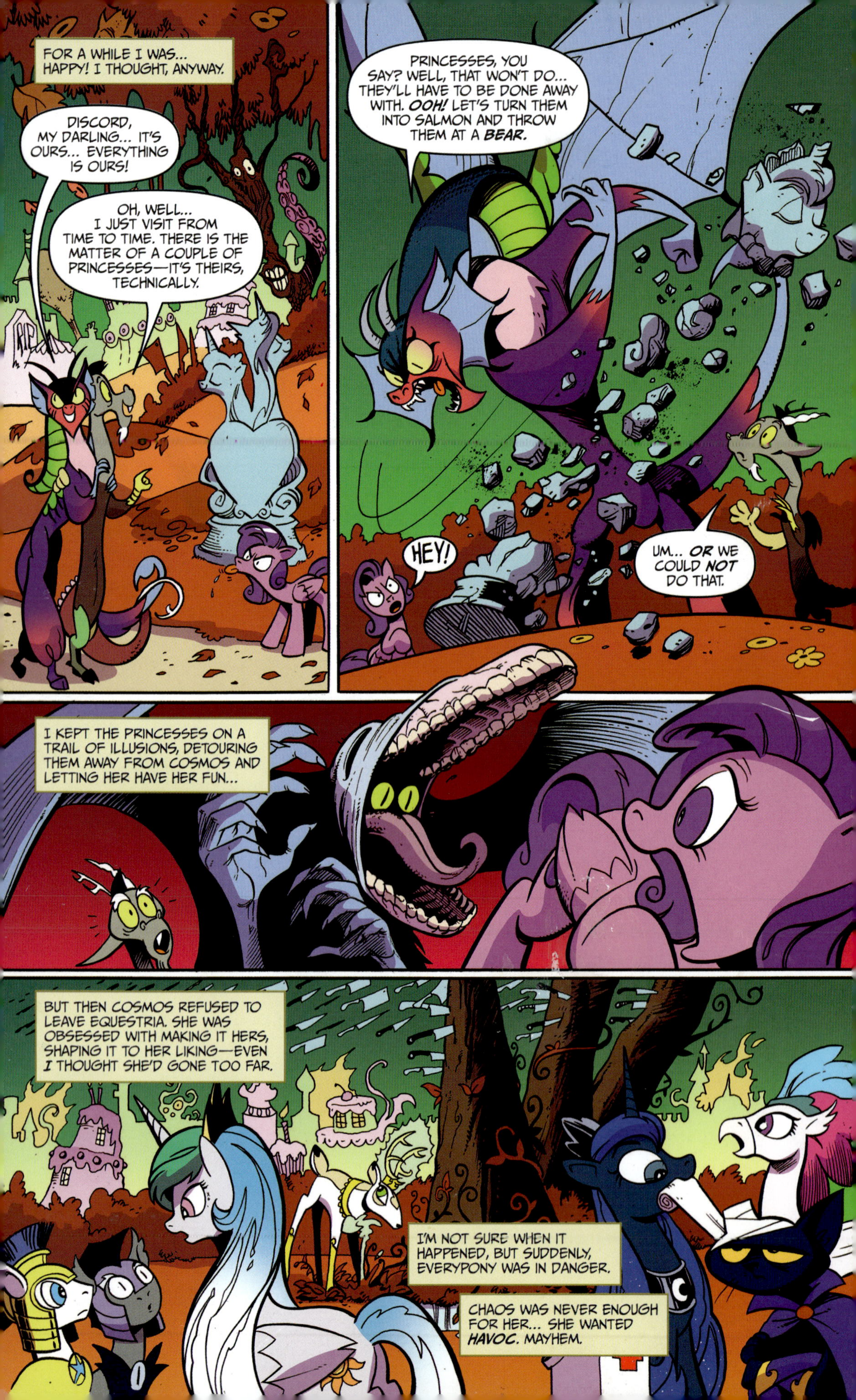

FOR A WHILE I WAS... HAPPY! I THOUGHT, ANYWAY.
DISCORD, MY DARLING... IT'S OURS... EVERYTHING IS OURS!
OH, WELL... I JUST VISIT FROM TIME TO TIME. THERE IS THE MATTER OF A COUPLE OF PRINCESSES—IT'S THEIRS, TECHNICALLY.
PRINCESSES, YOU SAY? WELL, THAT WON'T DO... THEY'LL HAVE TO BE DONE AWAY WITH. OOH! LET'S TURN THEM INTO SALMON AND THROW THEM AT A BEAR.
HEY!
UM... OR WE COULD NOT DO THAT.
I KEPT THE PRINCESSES ON A TRAIL OF ILLUSIONS, DETOURING THEM AWAY FROM COSMOS AND LETTING HER HAVE HER FUN...
BUT THEN COSMOS REFUSED TO LEAVE EQUESTRIA. SHE WAS OBSESSED WITH MAKING IT HERS, SHAPING IT TO HER LIKING—EVEN I THOUGHT SHE'D GONE TOO FAR.
I'M NOT SURE WHEN IT HAPPENED, BUT SUDDENLY, EVERYPONY WAS IN DANGER.
CHAOS WAS NEVER ENOUGH FOR HER... SHE WANTED HAVOC. MAYHEM.

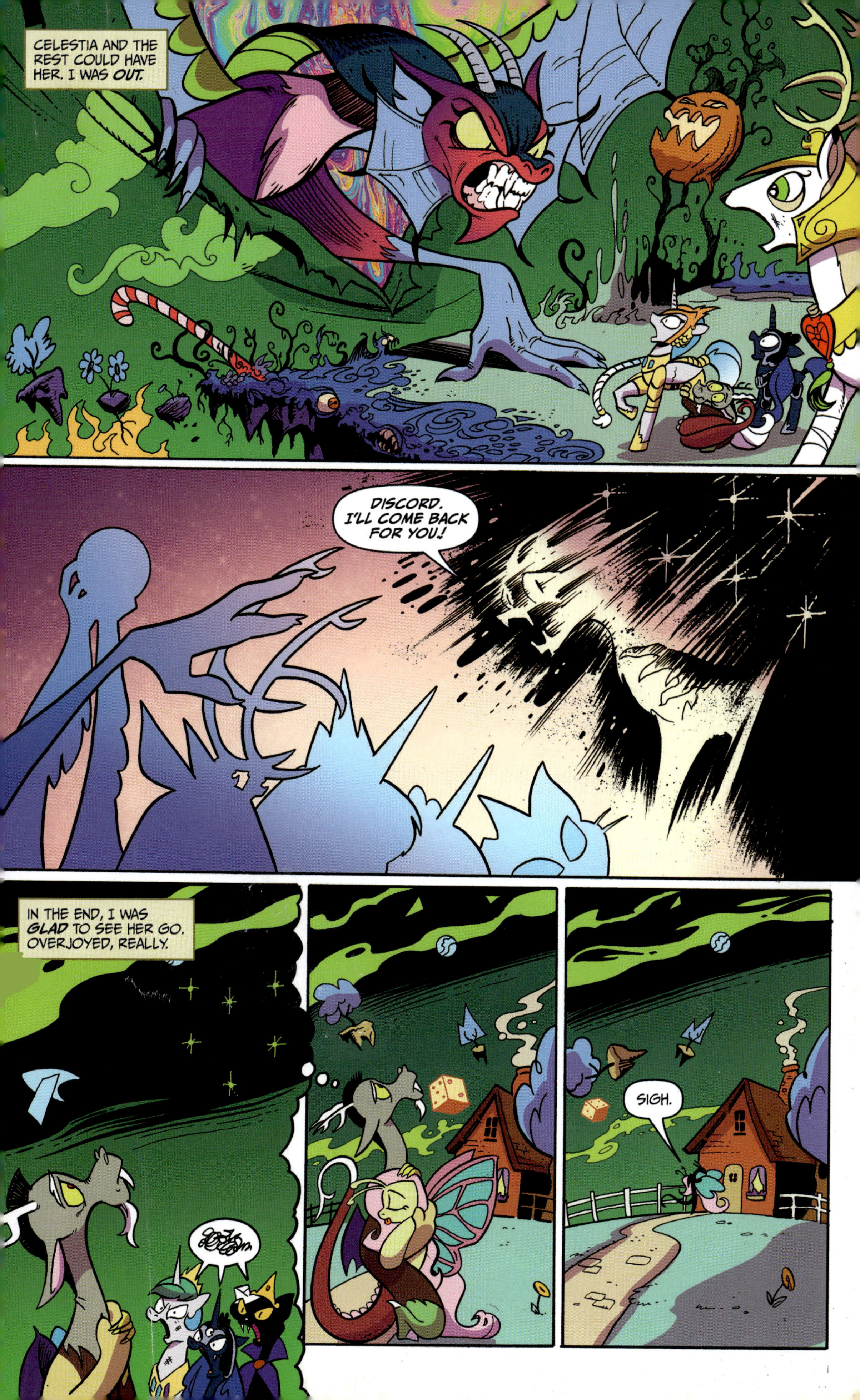
CELESTIA AND THE REST COULD HAVE HER. I WAS *OUT.*
DISCORD. I'LL COME BACK FOR YOU!
IN THE END, I WAS *GLAD* TO SEE HER GO. OVERJOYED, REALLY.
SIGH.

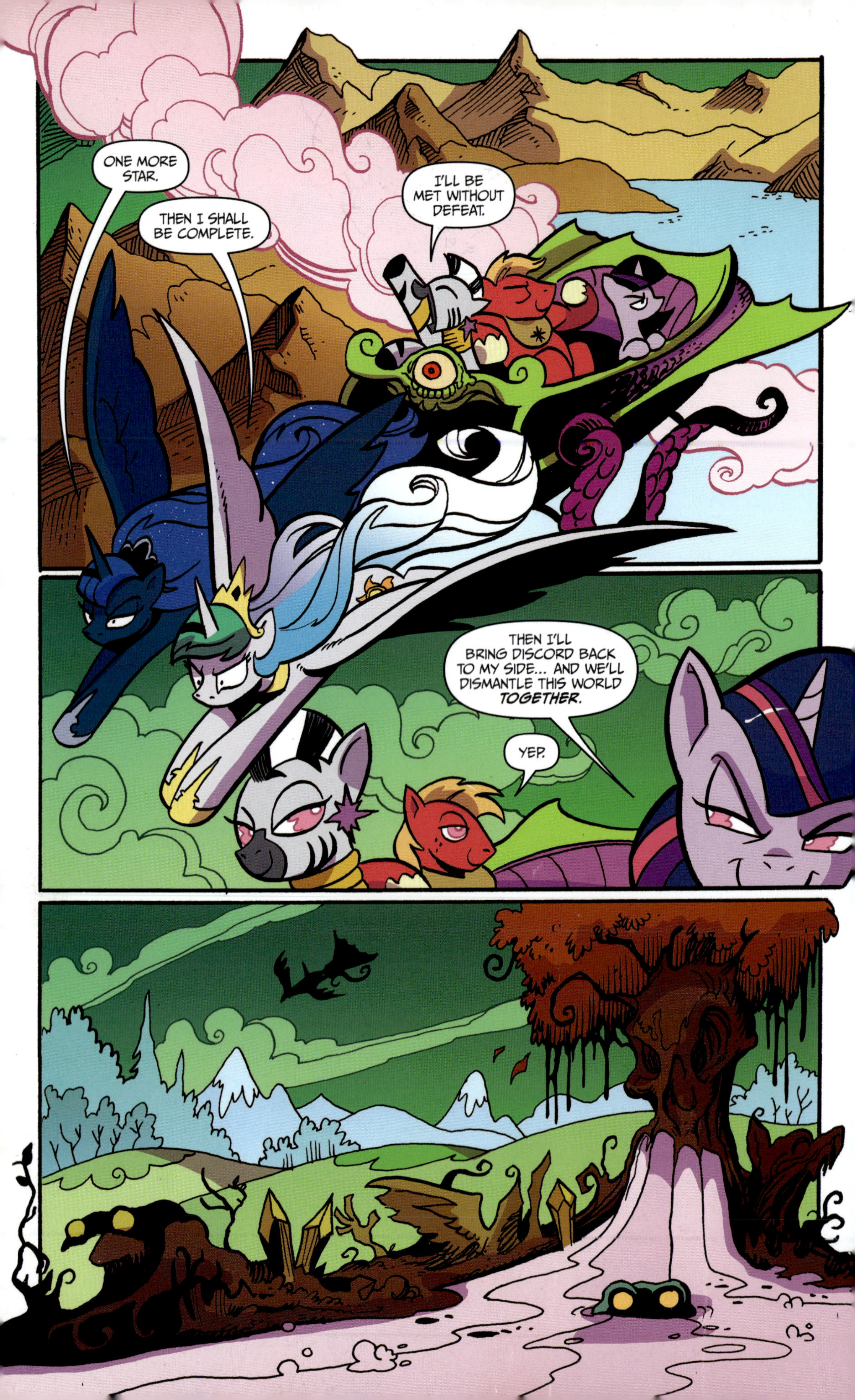
ONE MORE STAR.
THEN I SHALL BE COMPLETE.
I'LL BE MET WITHOUT DEFEAT.
THEN I'LL BRING DISCORD BACK TO MY SIDE... AND WE'LL DISMANTLE THIS WORLD *TOGETHER*.
YEP.

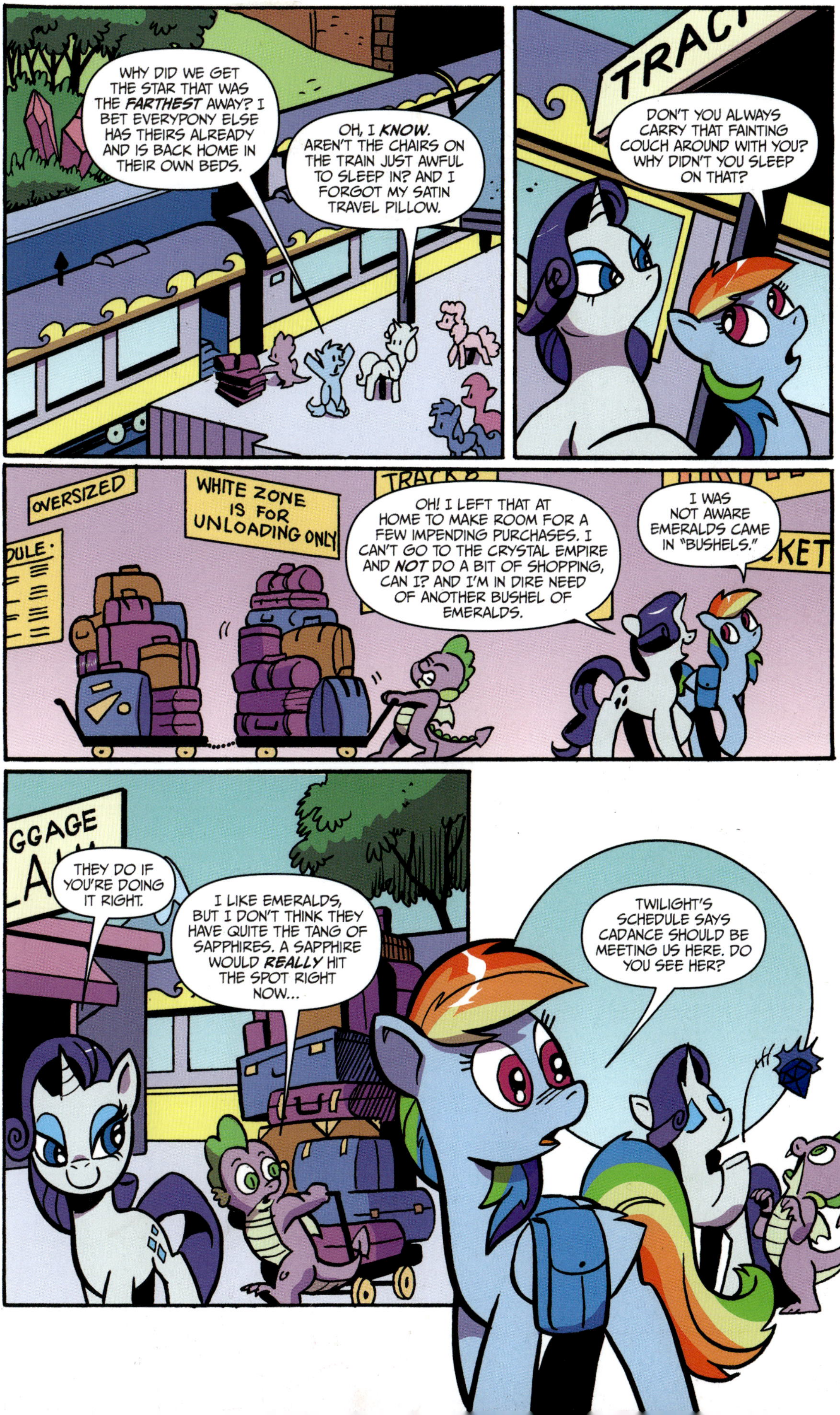
WHY DID WE GET THE STAR THAT WAS THE *FARTHEST* AWAY? I BET EVERYPONY ELSE HAS THEIRS ALREADY AND IS BACK HOME IN THEIR OWN BEDS.
OH, I *KNOW*. AREN'T THE CHAIRS ON THE TRAIN JUST AWFUL TO SLEEP IN? AND I FORGOT MY SATIN TRAVEL PILLOW.
TRAC
DON'T YOU ALWAYS CARRY THAT FAINTING COUCH AROUND WITH YOU? WHY DIDN'T YOU SLEEP ON THAT?
OVERSIZED
WHITE ZONE IS FOR UNLOADING ONLY
DULE
OH! I LEFT THAT AT HOME TO MAKE ROOM FOR A FEW IMPENDING PURCHASES. I CAN'T GO TO THE CRYSTAL EMPIRE AND *NOT* DO A BIT OF SHOPPING, CAN I? AND I'M IN DIRE NEED OF ANOTHER BUSHEL OF EMERALDS.
I WAS NOT AWARE EMERALDS CAME IN "BUSHELS."
CKET
GGAGE
THEY DO IF YOU'RE DOING IT RIGHT.
I LIKE EMERALDS, BUT I DON'T THINK THEY HAVE QUITE THE TANG OF SAPPHIRES. A SAPPHIRE WOULD *REALLY* HIT THE SPOT RIGHT NOW...
TWILIGHT'S SCHEDULE SAYS CADANCE SHOULD BE MEETING US HERE. DO YOU SEE HER?

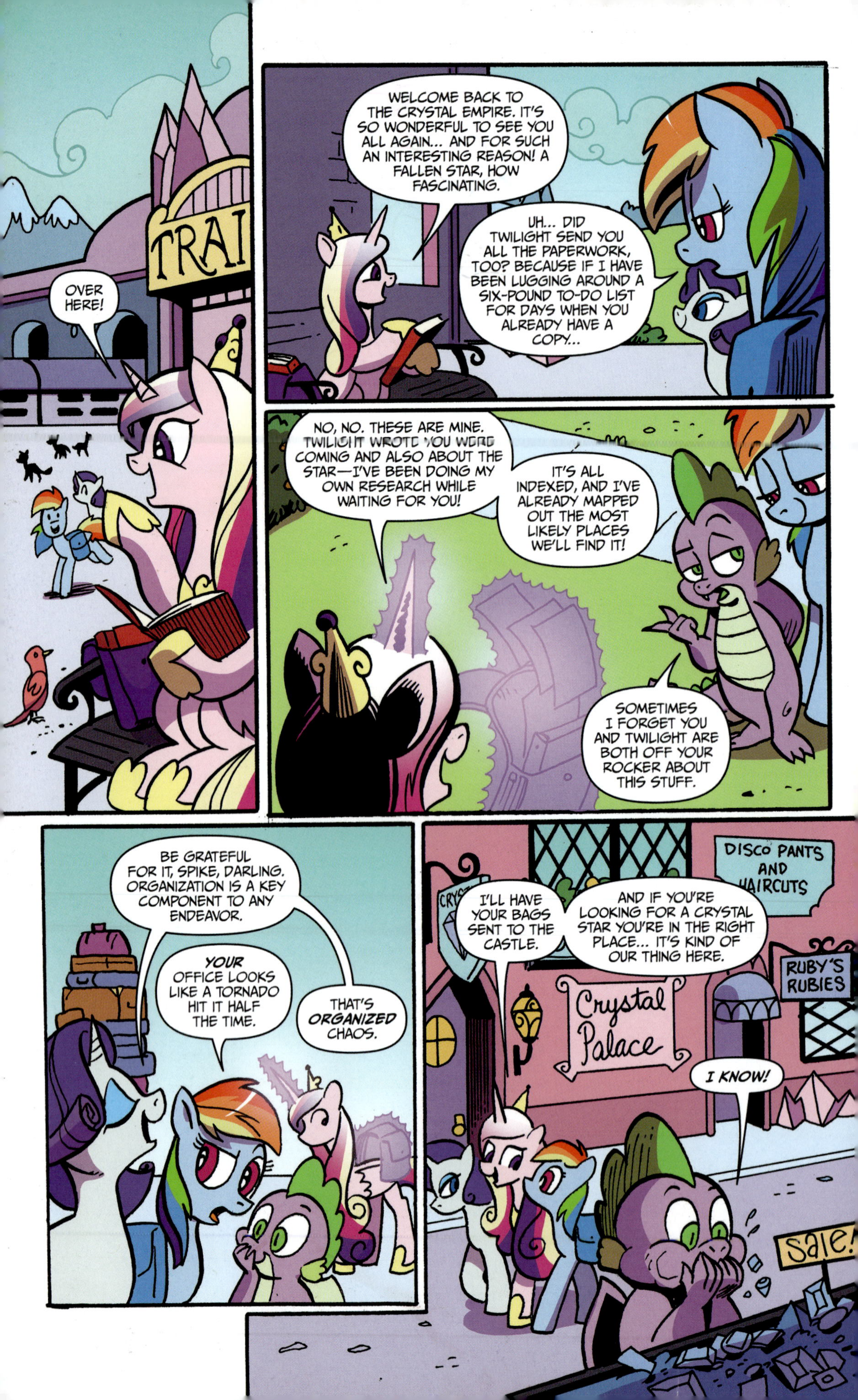
TRAI
OVER HERE!
WELCOME BACK TO THE CRYSTAL EMPIRE. IT'S SO WONDERFUL TO SEE YOU ALL AGAIN... AND FOR SUCH AN INTERESTING REASON! A FALLEN STAR, HOW FASCINATING.
UH... DID TWILIGHT SEND YOU ALL THE PAPERWORK, TOO? BECAUSE IF I HAVE BEEN LUGGING AROUND A SIX-POUND TO-DO LIST FOR DAYS WHEN YOU ALREADY HAVE A COPY...
NO, NO. THESE ARE MINE. TWILIGHT WROTE YOU WERE COMING AND ALSO ABOUT THE STAR—I'VE BEEN DOING MY OWN RESEARCH WHILE WAITING FOR YOU!
IT'S ALL INDEXED, AND I'VE ALREADY MAPPED OUT THE MOST LIKELY PLACES WE'LL FIND IT!
SOMETIMES I FORGET YOU AND TWILIGHT ARE BOTH OFF YOUR ROCKER ABOUT THIS STUFF.
BE GRATEFUL FOR IT, SPIKE, DARLING. ORGANIZATION IS A KEY COMPONENT TO ANY ENDEAVOR.
YOUR OFFICE LOOKS LIKE A TORNADO HIT IT HALF THE TIME.
THAT'S *ORGANIZED* CHAOS.
DISCO PANTS AND HAIRCUTS
I'LL HAVE YOUR BAGS SENT TO THE CASTLE.
AND IF YOU'RE LOOKING FOR A CRYSTAL STAR YOU'RE IN THE RIGHT PLACE... IT'S KIND OF OUR THING HERE.
RUBY'S RUBIES
Crystal Palace
I KNOW!
Sale!

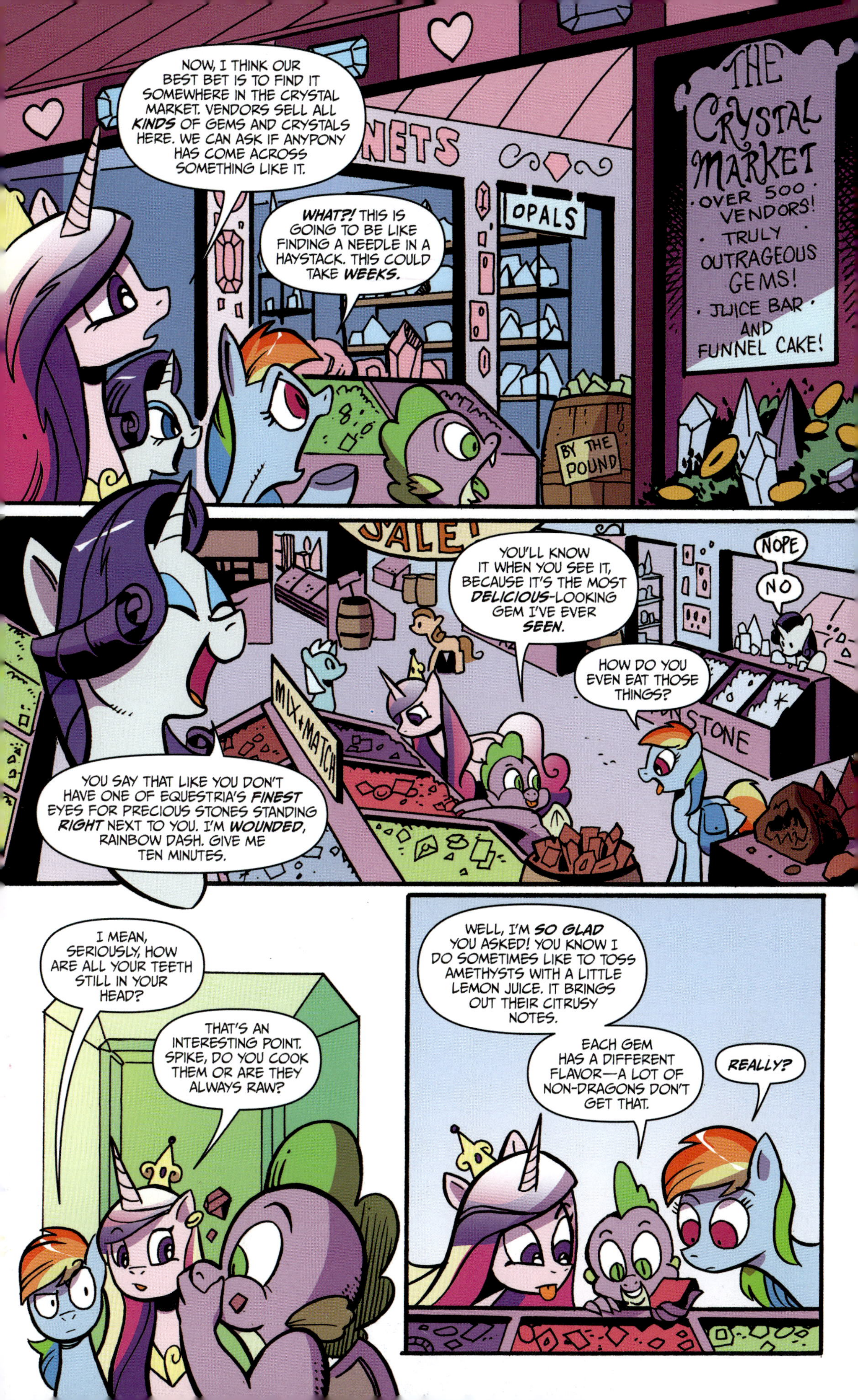
NOW, I THINK OUR BEST BET IS TO FIND IT SOMEWHERE IN THE CRYSTAL MARKET. VENDORS SELL ALL KINDS OF GEMS AND CRYSTALS HERE. WE CAN ASK IF ANYPONY HAS COME ACROSS SOMETHING LIKE IT.
THE CRYSTAL MARKET
· OVER 500 VENDORS! · TRULY OUTRAGEOUS GEMS! · JUICE BAR AND FUNNEL CAKE!
OPALS
WHAT?! THIS IS GOING TO BE LIKE FINDING A NEEDLE IN A HAYSTACK. THIS COULD TAKE WEEKS.
BY THE POUND
YOU SAY THAT LIKE YOU DON'T HAVE ONE OF EQUESTRIA'S FINEST EYES FOR PRECIOUS STONES STANDING RIGHT NEXT TO YOU. I'M WOUNDED, RAINBOW DASH. GIVE ME TEN MINUTES.
MIX + MATCH
YOU'LL KNOW IT WHEN YOU SEE IT, BECAUSE IT'S THE MOST DELICIOUS-LOOKING GEM I'VE EVER SEEN.
HOW DO YOU EVEN EAT THOSE THINGS?
NOPE
NO
I MEAN, SERIOUSLY, HOW ARE ALL YOUR TEETH STILL IN YOUR HEAD?
THAT'S AN INTERESTING POINT. SPIKE, DO YOU COOK THEM OR ARE THEY ALWAYS RAW?
WELL, I'M SO GLAD YOU ASKED! YOU KNOW I DO SOMETIMES LIKE TO TOSS AMETHYSTS WITH A LITTLE LEMON JUICE. IT BRINGS OUT THEIR CITRUSY NOTES.
EACH GEM HAS A DIFFERENT FLAVOR—A LOT OF NON-DRAGONS DON'T GET THAT.
REALLY?

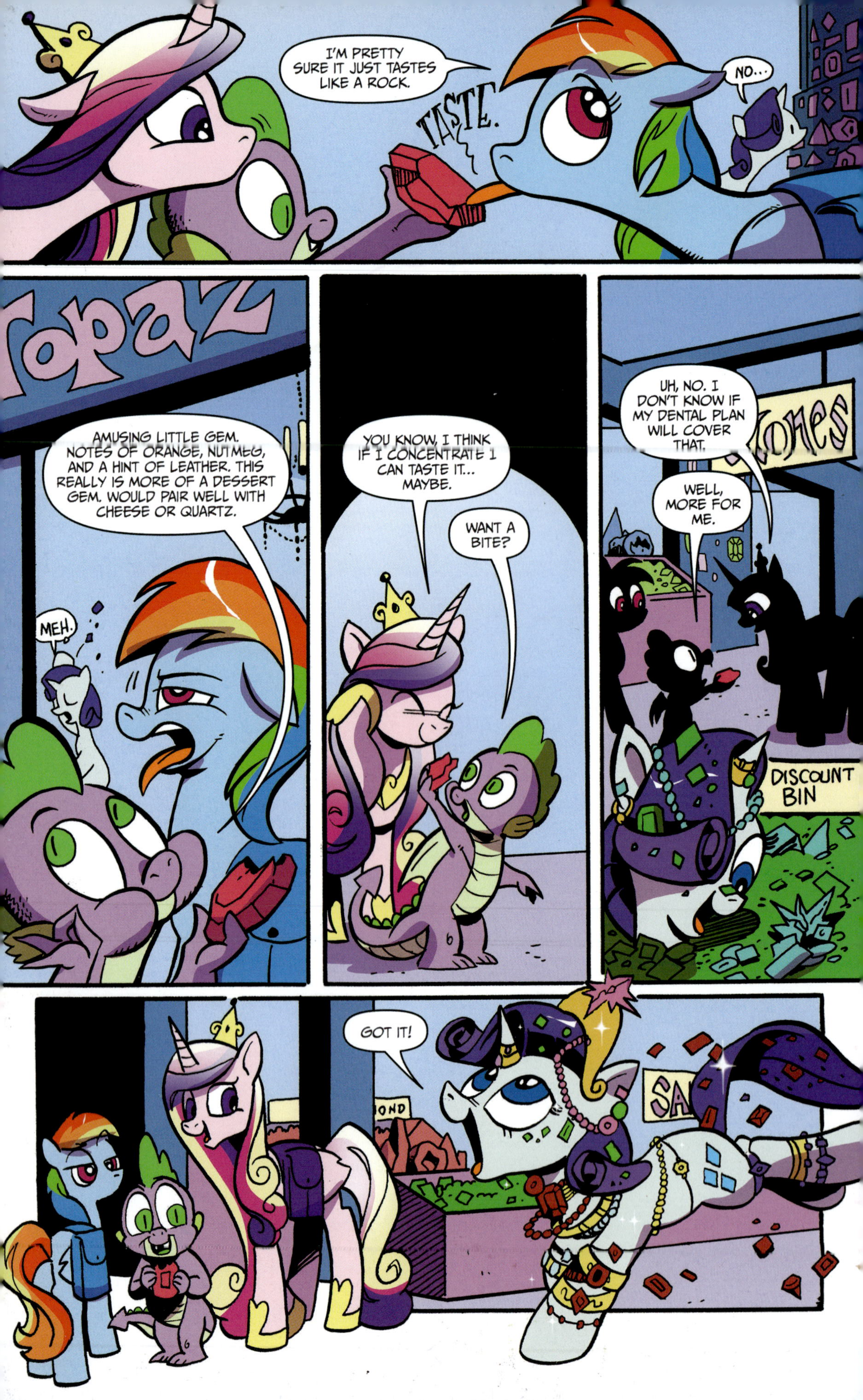
I'M PRETTY SURE IT JUST TASTES LIKE A ROCK.
TASTE.
NO...
Topaz
AMUSING LITTLE GEM. NOTES OF ORANGE, NUTMEG, AND A HINT OF LEATHER. THIS REALLY IS MORE OF A DESSERT GEM. WOULD PAIR WELL WITH CHEESE OR QUARTZ.
MEH.
YOU KNOW, I THINK IF I CONCENTRATE I CAN TASTE IT... MAYBE.
WANT A BITE?
UH, NO. I DON'T KNOW IF MY DENTAL PLAN WILL COVER THAT.
WELL, MORE FOR ME.
DISCOUNT BIN
GOT IT!

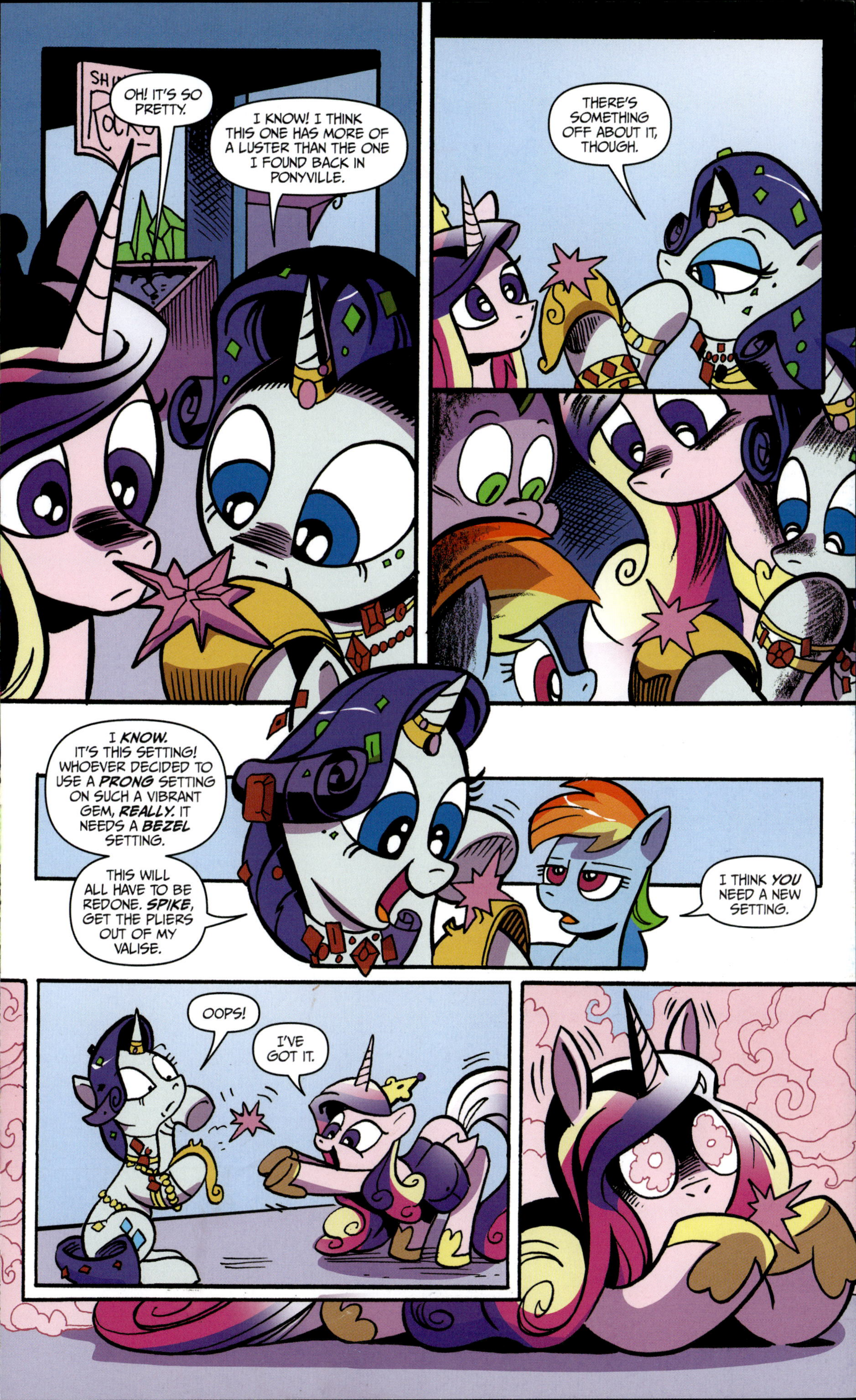
SHI
ROCK
OH! IT'S SO PRETTY.
I KNOW! I THINK THIS ONE HAS MORE OF A LUSTER THAN THE ONE I FOUND BACK IN PONYVILLE.
THERE'S SOMETHING OFF ABOUT IT, THOUGH.
I *KNOW.* IT'S THIS SETTING! WHOEVER DECIDED TO USE A ***PRONG*** SETTING ON SUCH A VIBRANT GEM, ***REALLY.*** IT NEEDS A ***BEZEL*** SETTING.
THIS WILL ALL HAVE TO BE REDONE. ***SPIKE,*** GET THE PLIERS OUT OF MY VALISE.
I THINK *YOU* NEED A NEW SETTING.
OOPS!
I'VE GOT IT.

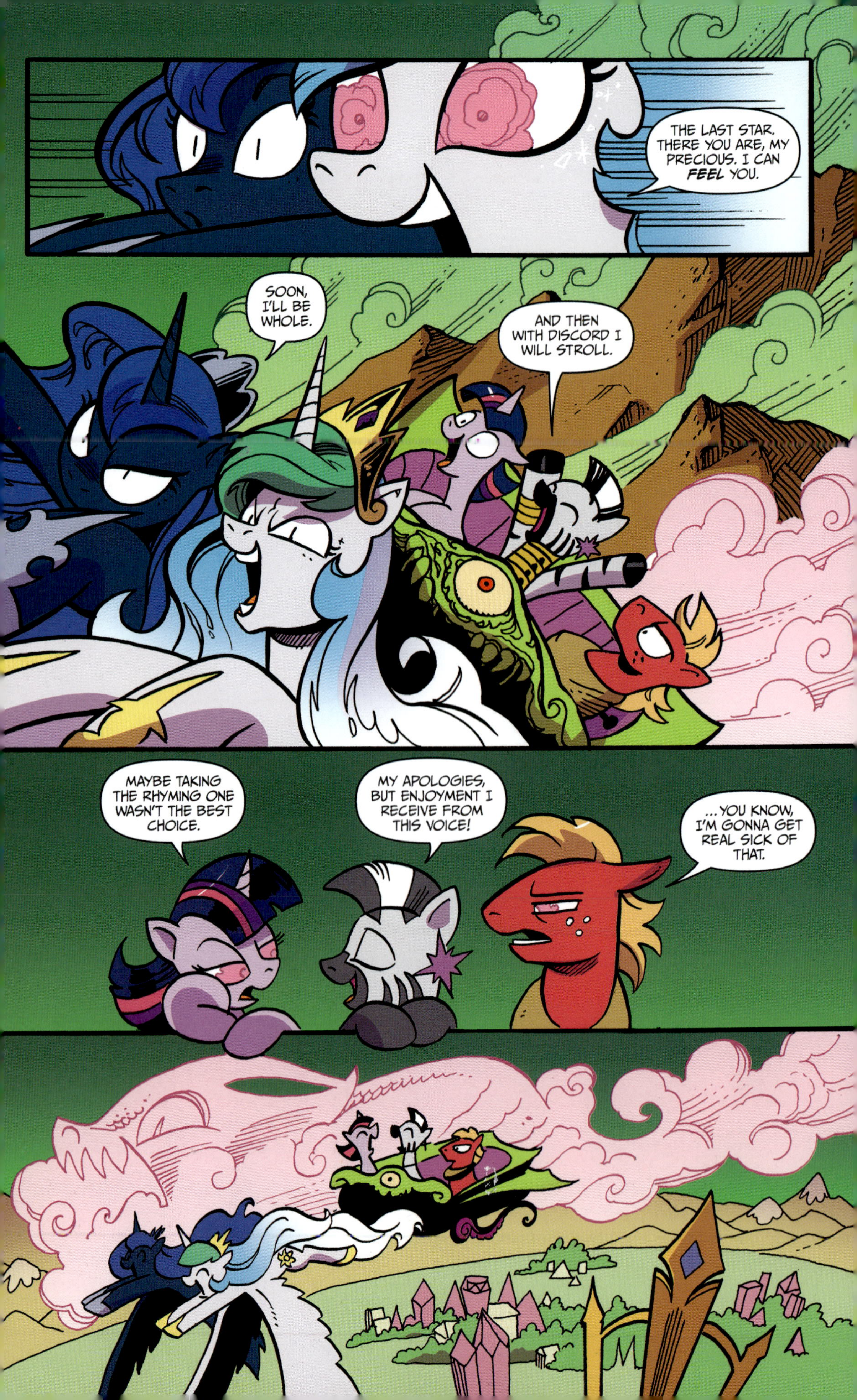
THE LAST STAR. THERE YOU ARE, MY PRECIOUS. I CAN FEEL YOU.
SOON, I'LL BE WHOLE.
AND THEN WITH DISCORD I WILL STROLL.
MAYBE TAKING THE RHYMING ONE WASN'T THE BEST CHOICE.
MY APOLOGIES, BUT ENJOYMENT I RECEIVE FROM THIS VOICE!
...YOU KNOW, I'M GONNA GET REAL SICK OF THAT.

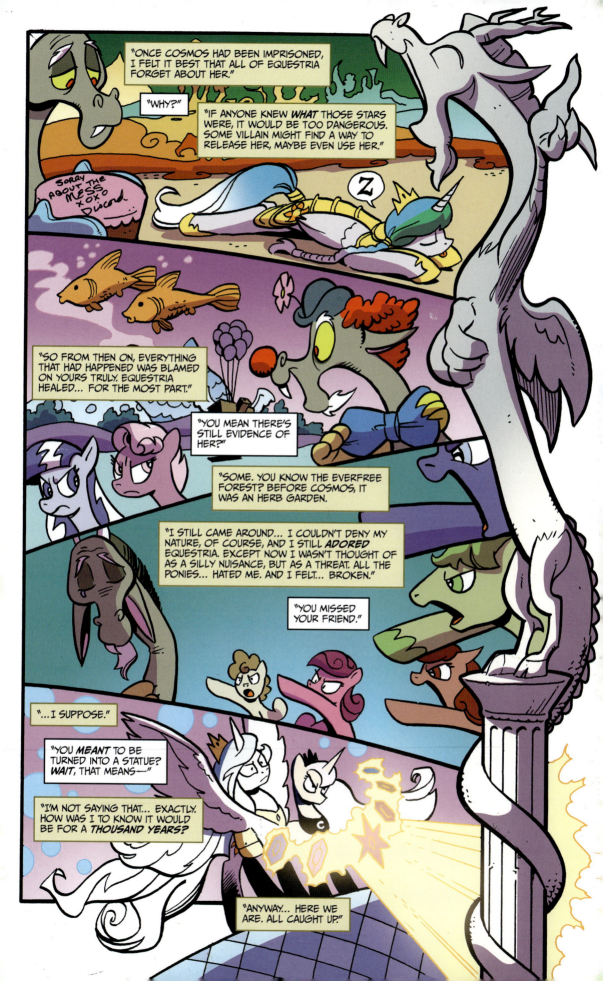

"ONCE COSMOS HAD BEEN IMPRISONED, I FELT IT BEST THAT ALL OF EQUESTRIA FORGET ABOUT HER."

"WHY?"

"IF ANYONE KNEW *WHAT* THOSE STARS WERE, IT WOULD BE TOO DANGEROUS. SOME VILLAIN MIGHT FIND A WAY TO RELEASE HER, MAYBE EVEN USE HER."

SORRY THE MESS XOXO Discord

Z

"SO FROM THEN ON, EVERYTHING THAT HAD HAPPENED WAS BLAMED ON YOURS TRULY. EQUESTRIA HEALED... FOR THE MOST PART."

"YOU MEAN THERE'S STILL EVIDENCE OF HER?"

"SOME. YOU KNOW THE EVERFREE FOREST? BEFORE COSMOS, IT WAS AN HERB GARDEN.

"I STILL CAME AROUND... I COULDN'T DENY MY NATURE, OF COURSE, AND I STILL *ADORED* EQUESTRIA. EXCEPT NOW I WASN'T THOUGHT OF AS A SILLY NUISANCE, BUT AS A THREAT. ALL THE PONIES... HATED ME. AND I FELT... BROKEN."

"YOU MISSED YOUR FRIEND."

"...I SUPPOSE."

"YOU *MEANT* TO BE TURNED INTO A STATUE? *WAIT*, THAT MEANS—"

"I'M NOT SAYING THAT... EXACTLY. HOW WAS I TO KNOW IT WOULD BE FOR A *THOUSAND YEARS*?"

"ANYWAY... HERE WE ARE. ALL CAUGHT UP."

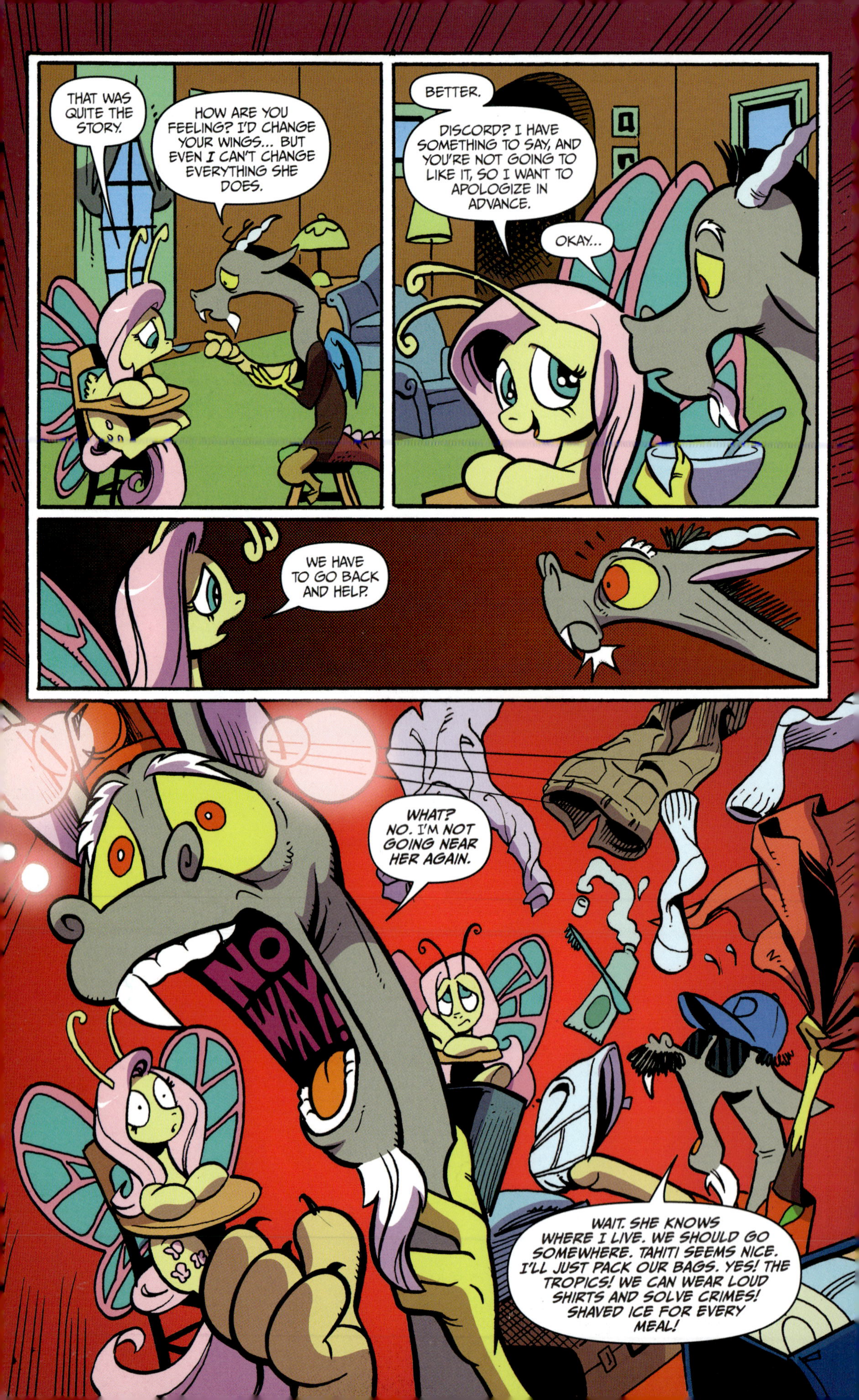

THAT WAS QUITE THE STORY.
HOW ARE YOU FEELING? I'D CHANGE YOUR WINGS... BUT EVEN *I* CAN'T CHANGE EVERYTHING SHE DOES.
BETTER.
DISCORD? I HAVE SOMETHING TO SAY, AND YOU'RE NOT GOING TO LIKE IT, SO I WANT TO APOLOGIZE IN ADVANCE.
OKAY...
WE HAVE TO GO BACK AND HELP.
WHAT? NO. I'M NOT GOING NEAR HER AGAIN.
NO WAY!
WAIT. SHE KNOWS WHERE I LIVE. WE SHOULD GO SOMEWHERE. TAHITI SEEMS NICE. I'LL JUST PACK OUR BAGS. YES! THE TROPICS! WE CAN WEAR LOUD SHIRTS AND SOLVE CRIMES! SHAVED ICE FOR EVERY MEAL!

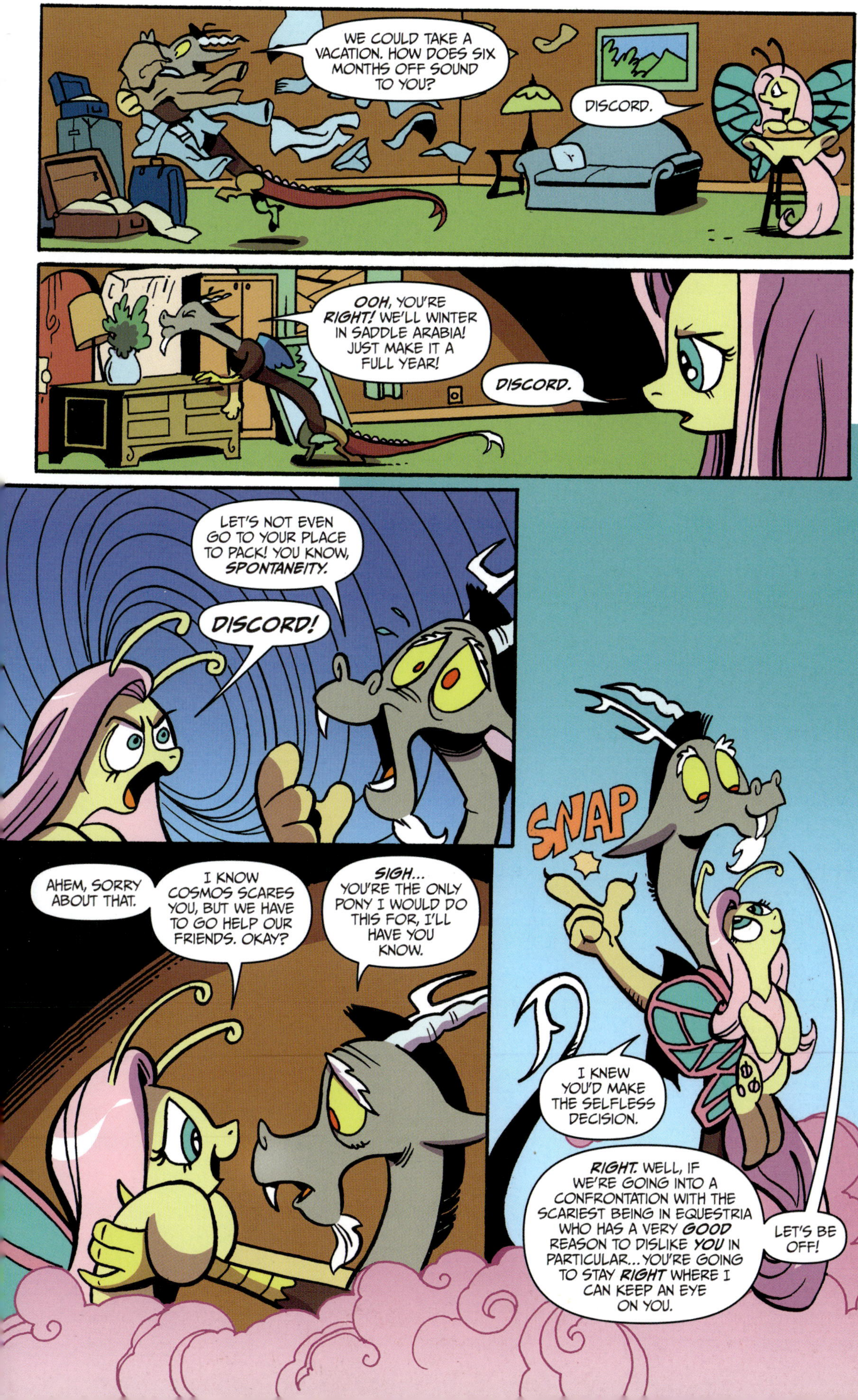

WE COULD TAKE A VACATION. HOW DOES SIX MONTHS OFF SOUND TO YOU?
DISCORD.
OOH, YOU'RE RIGHT! WE'LL WINTER IN SADDLE ARABIA! JUST MAKE IT A FULL YEAR!
DISCORD.
LET'S NOT EVEN GO TO YOUR PLACE TO PACK! YOU KNOW, SPONTANEITY.
DISCORD!
AHEM, SORRY ABOUT THAT.
I KNOW COSMOS SCARES YOU, BUT WE HAVE TO GO HELP OUR FRIENDS. OKAY?
SIGH... YOU'RE THE ONLY PONY I WOULD DO THIS FOR, I'LL HAVE YOU KNOW.
SNAP
I KNEW YOU'D MAKE THE SELFLESS DECISION.
RIGHT. WELL, IF WE'RE GOING INTO A CONFRONTATION WITH THE SCARIEST BEING IN EQUESTRIA WHO HAS A VERY GOOD REASON TO DISLIKE YOU IN PARTICULAR... YOU'RE GOING TO STAY RIGHT WHERE I CAN KEEP AN EYE ON YOU.
LET'S BE OFF!

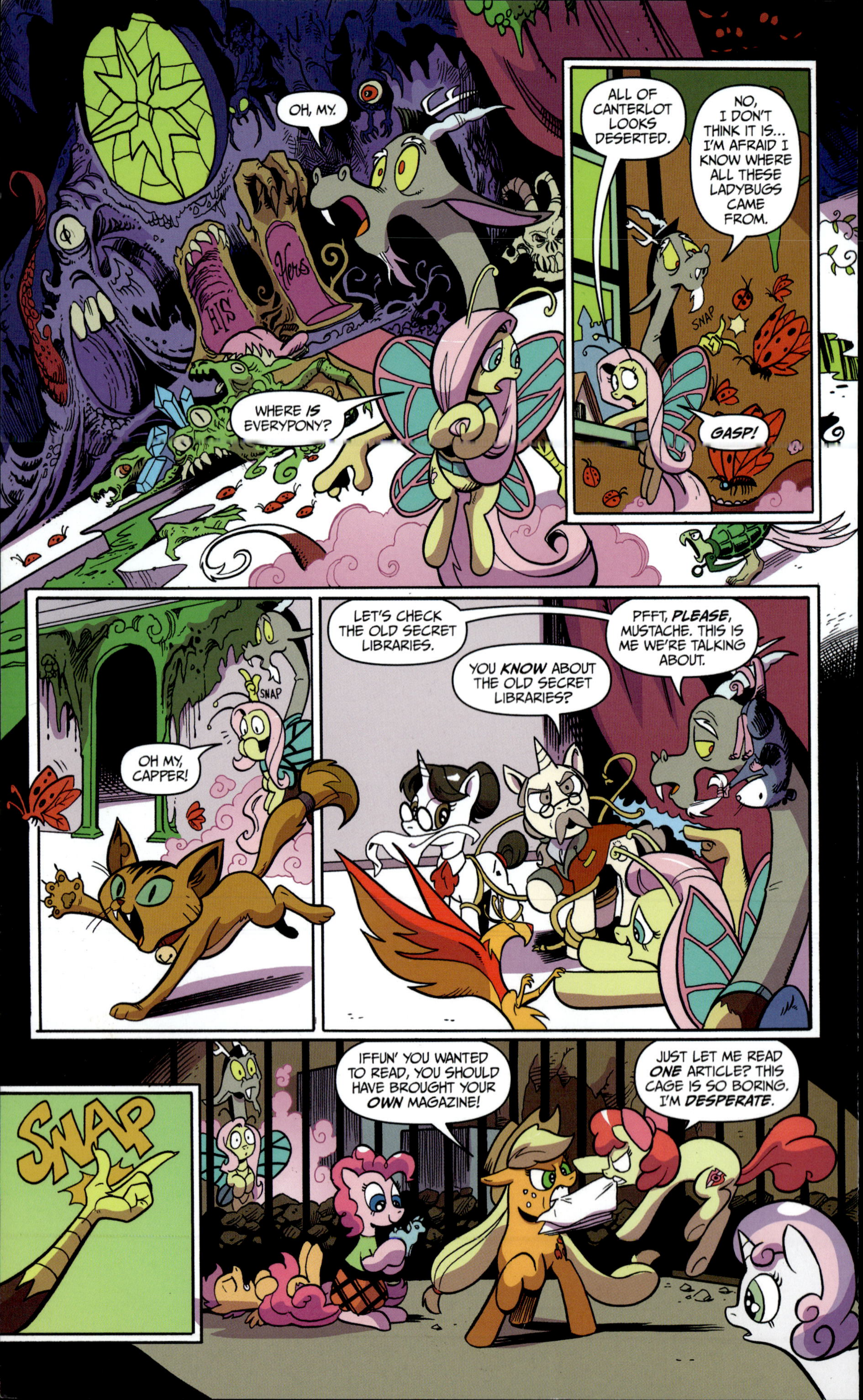
OH, MY.
HIS
Hers
WHERE IS EVERYPONY?
ALL OF CANTERLOT LOOKS DESERTED.
NO, I DON'T THINK IT IS... I'M AFRAID I KNOW WHERE ALL THESE LADYBUGS CAME FROM.
SNAP
GASP!
SNAP
OH MY, CAPPER!
LET'S CHECK THE OLD SECRET LIBRARIES.
YOU KNOW ABOUT THE OLD SECRET LIBRARIES?
PFFT, PLEASE, MUSTACHE. THIS IS ME WE'RE TALKING ABOUT.
SNAP
IFFUN' YOU WANTED TO READ, YOU SHOULD HAVE BROUGHT YOUR OWN MAGAZINE!
JUST LET ME READ ONE ARTICLE? THIS CAGE IS SO BORING. I'M DESPERATE.

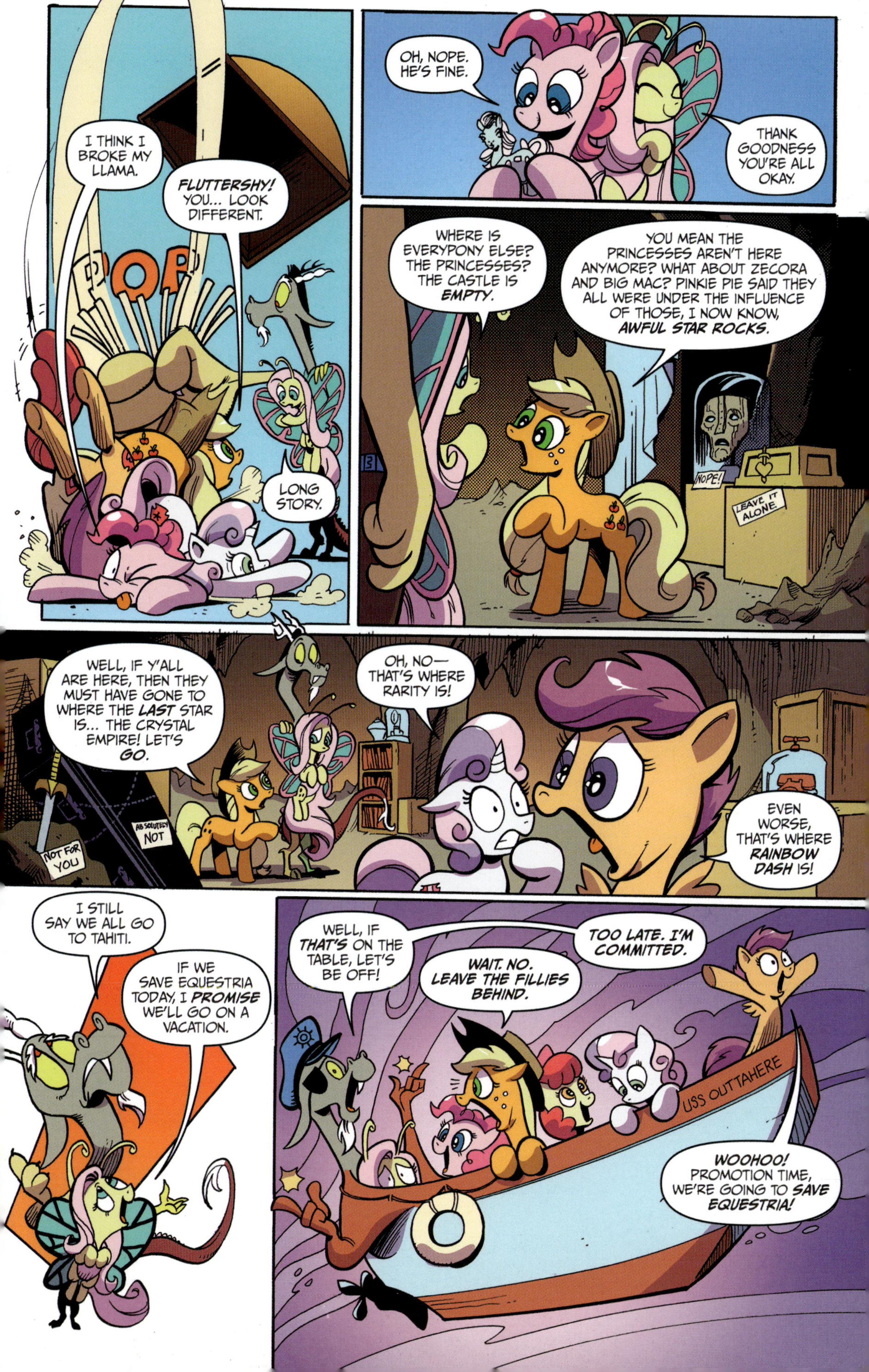

POP
I THINK I BROKE MY LLAMA.
FLUTTERSHY! YOU... LOOK DIFFERENT.
LONG STORY.
OH, NOPE. HE'S FINE.
THANK GOODNESS YOU'RE ALL OKAY.
WHERE IS EVERYPONY ELSE? THE PRINCESSES? THE CASTLE IS EMPTY.
YOU MEAN THE PRINCESSES AREN'T HERE ANYMORE? WHAT ABOUT ZECORA AND BIG MAC? PINKIE PIE SAID THEY ALL WERE UNDER THE INFLUENCE OF THOSE, I NOW KNOW, AWFUL STAR ROCKS.
NOPE!
LEAVE IT ALONE.
WELL, IF Y'ALL ARE HERE, THEN THEY MUST HAVE GONE TO WHERE THE LAST STAR IS... THE CRYSTAL EMPIRE! LET'S GO.
NOT FOR YOU
ABSOLUTELY NOT
OH, NO— THAT'S WHERE RARITY IS!
EVEN WORSE, THAT'S WHERE RAINBOW DASH IS!
I STILL SAY WE ALL GO TO TAHITI.
IF WE SAVE EQUESTRIA TODAY, I PROMISE WE'LL GO ON A VACATION.
WELL, IF THAT'S ON THE TABLE, LET'S BE OFF!
TOO LATE. I'M COMMITTED.
WAIT. NO. LEAVE THE FILLIES BEHIND.
USS OUTTAHERE
WOOHOO! PROMOTION TIME, WE'RE GOING TO SAVE EQUESTRIA!

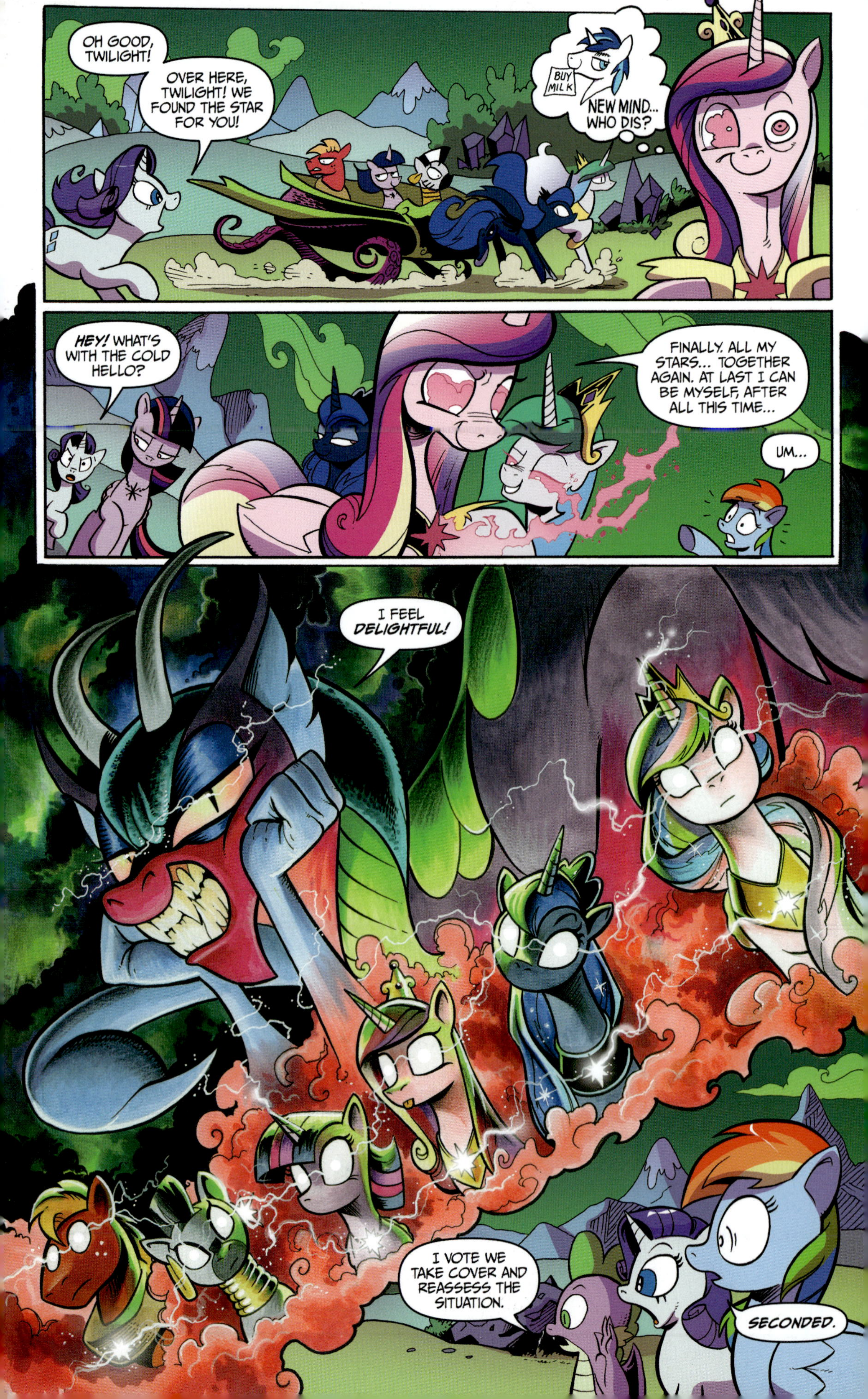
OH GOOD, TWILIGHT!
OVER HERE, TWILIGHT! WE FOUND THE STAR FOR YOU!
BUY MILK
NEW MIND... WHO DIS?
HEY! WHAT'S WITH THE COLD HELLO?
FINALLY. ALL MY STARS... TOGETHER AGAIN. AT LAST I CAN BE MYSELF, AFTER ALL THIS TIME...
UM...
I FEEL DELIGHTFUL!
I VOTE WE TAKE COVER AND REASSESS THE SITUATION.
SECONDED.

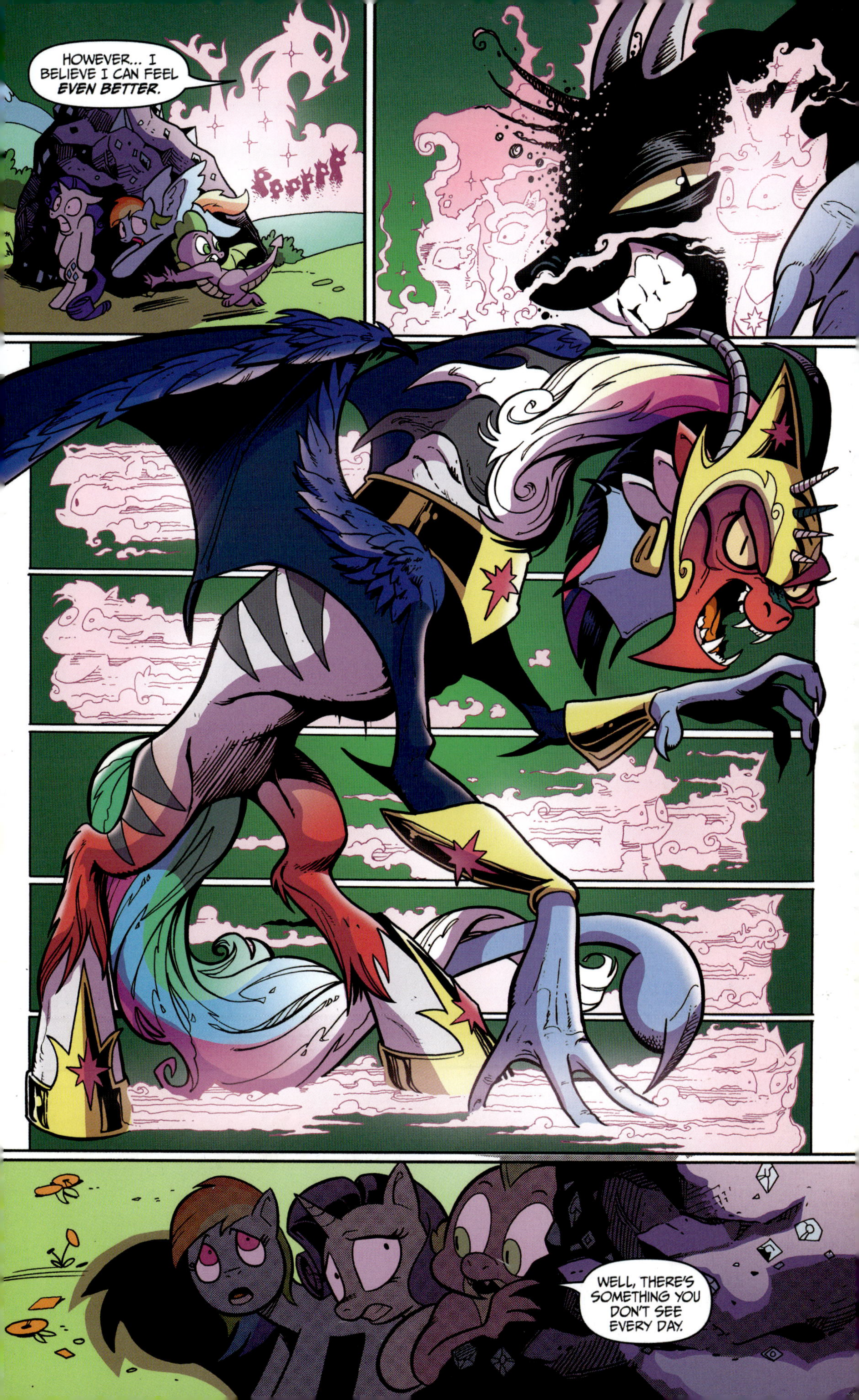
HOWEVER... I BELIEVE I CAN FEEL *EVEN BETTER.*
PPPPPF
WELL, THERE'S SOMETHING YOU DON'T SEE EVERY DAY.

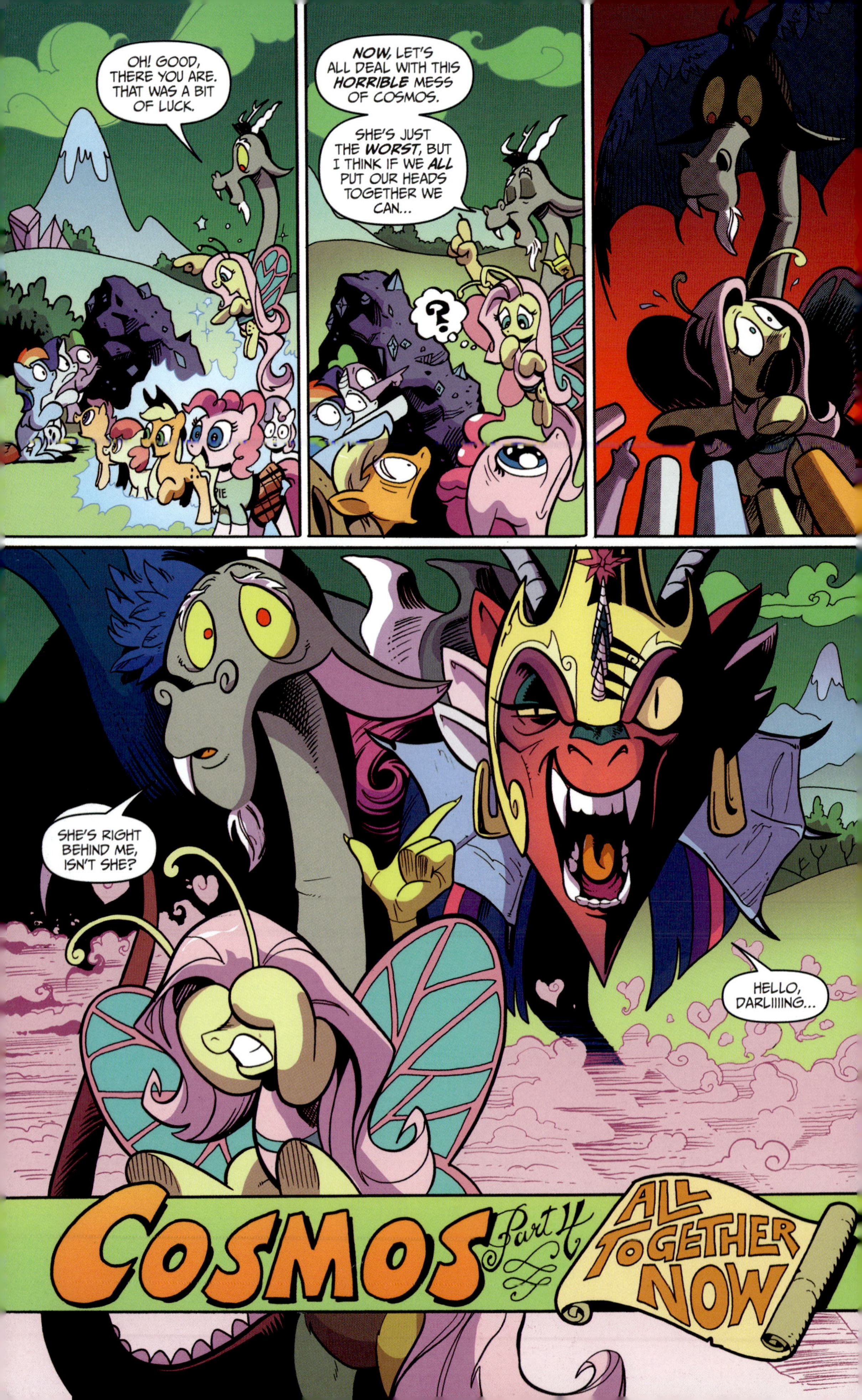
OH! GOOD, THERE YOU ARE. THAT WAS A BIT OF LUCK.
NOW, LET'S ALL DEAL WITH THIS HORRIBLE MESS OF COSMOS.
SHE'S JUST THE WORST, BUT I THINK IF WE ALL PUT OUR HEADS TOGETHER WE CAN...
?
SHE'S RIGHT BEHIND ME, ISN'T SHE?
HELLO, DARLIIIING...
COSMOS Part 4
ALL TOGETHER NOW

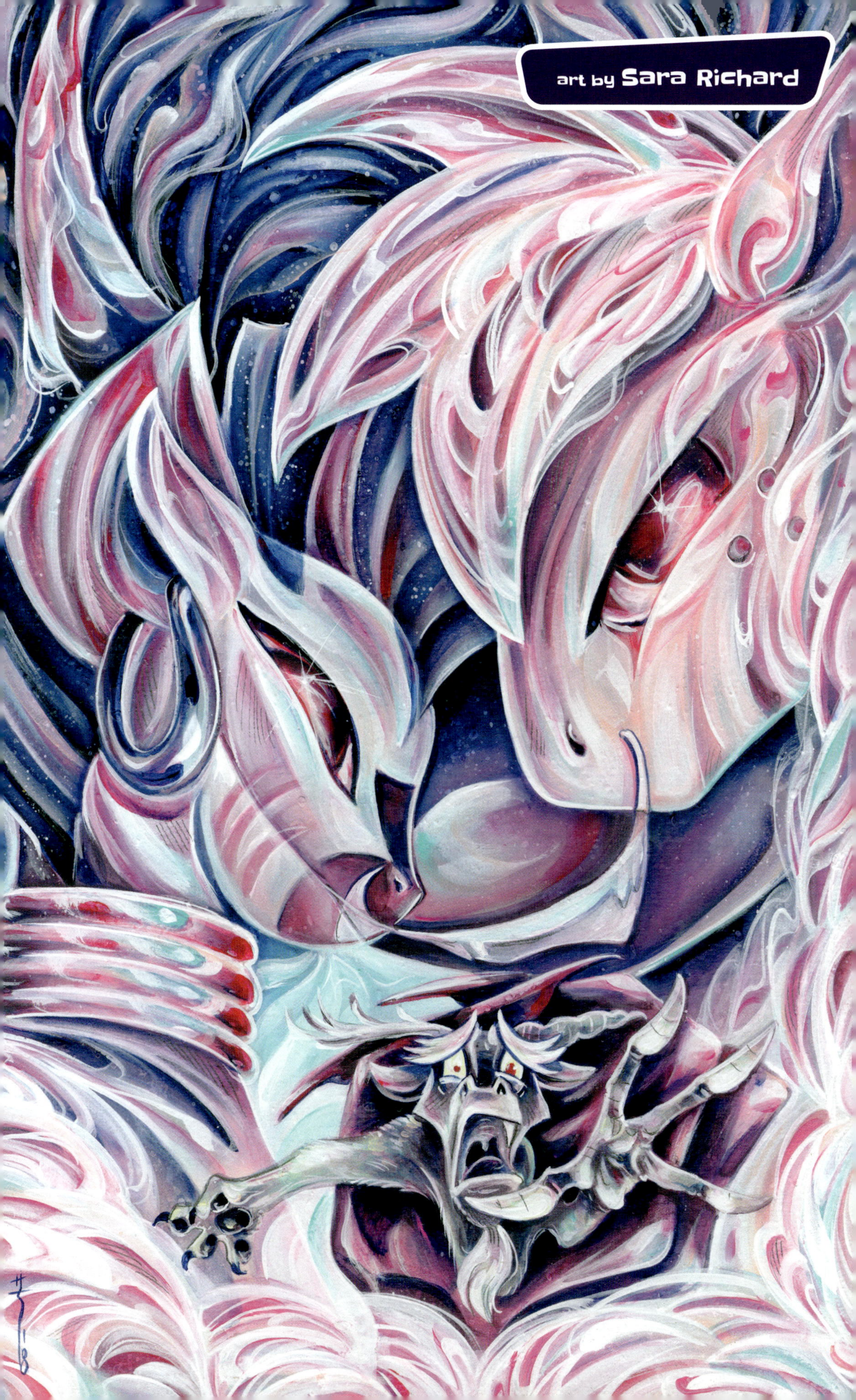

art by Andy Price

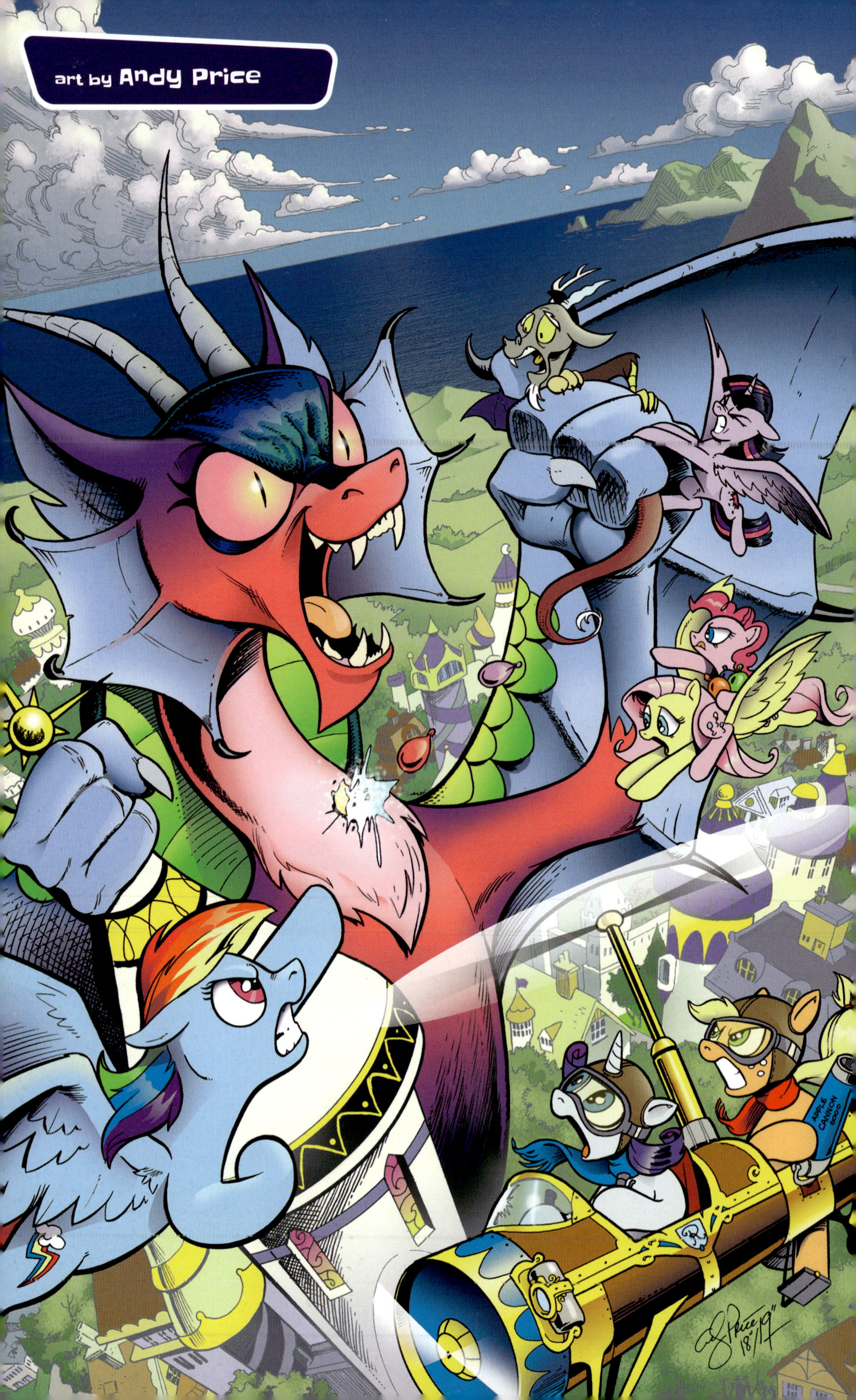
APPLE
CANNON
6000

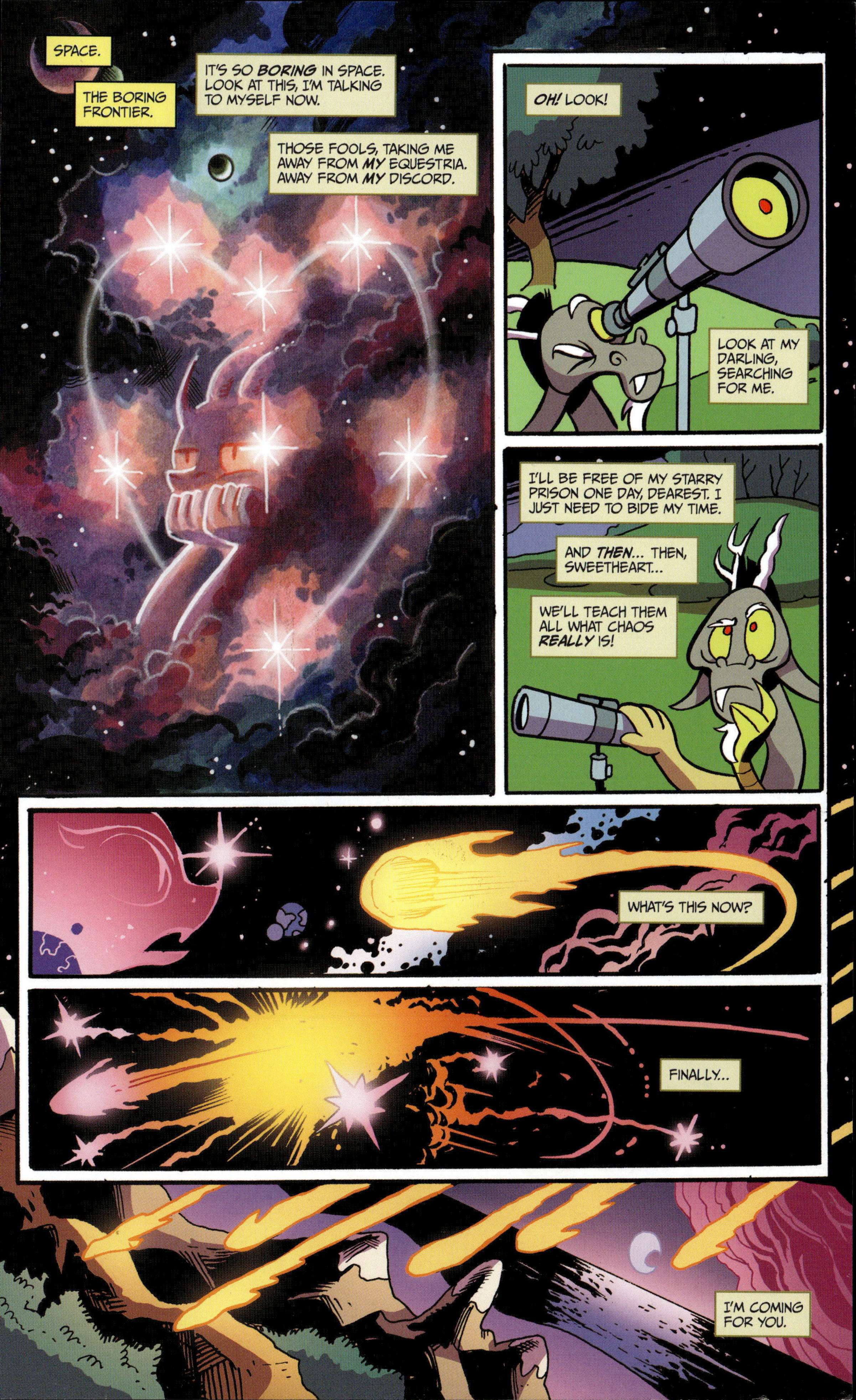
SPACE.
THE BORING FRONTIER.
IT'S SO BORING IN SPACE. LOOK AT THIS, I'M TALKING TO MYSELF NOW.
THOSE FOOLS, TAKING ME AWAY FROM MY EQUESTRIA. AWAY FROM MY DISCORD.
OH! LOOK!
LOOK AT MY DARLING, SEARCHING FOR ME.
I'LL BE FREE OF MY STARRY PRISON ONE DAY, DEAREST. I JUST NEED TO BIDE MY TIME.
AND THEN... THEN, SWEETHEART...
WE'LL TEACH THEM ALL WHAT CHAOS REALLY IS!
WHAT'S THIS NOW?
FINALLY...
I'M COMING FOR YOU.

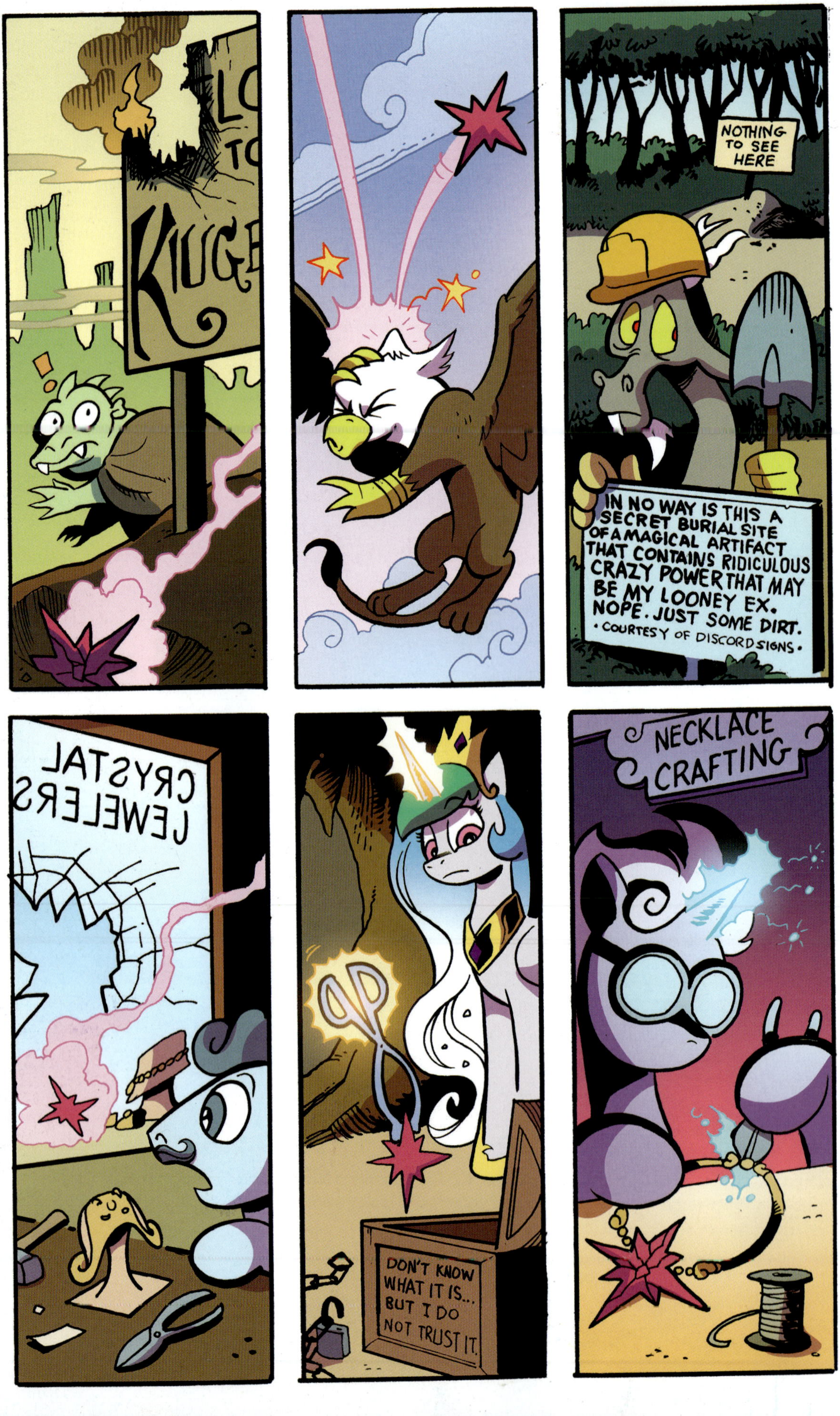
NOTHING TO SEE HERE
IN NO WAY IS THIS A SECRET BURIAL SITE OF A MAGICAL ARTIFACT THAT CONTAINS RIDICULOUS CRAZY POWER THAT MAY BE MY LOONEY EX. NOPE. JUST SOME DIRT.
• COURTESY OF DISCORD SIGNS •
CRYSTAL JEWELERS
DON'T KNOW WHAT IT IS... BUT I DO NOT TRUST IT.
NECKLACE CRAFTING

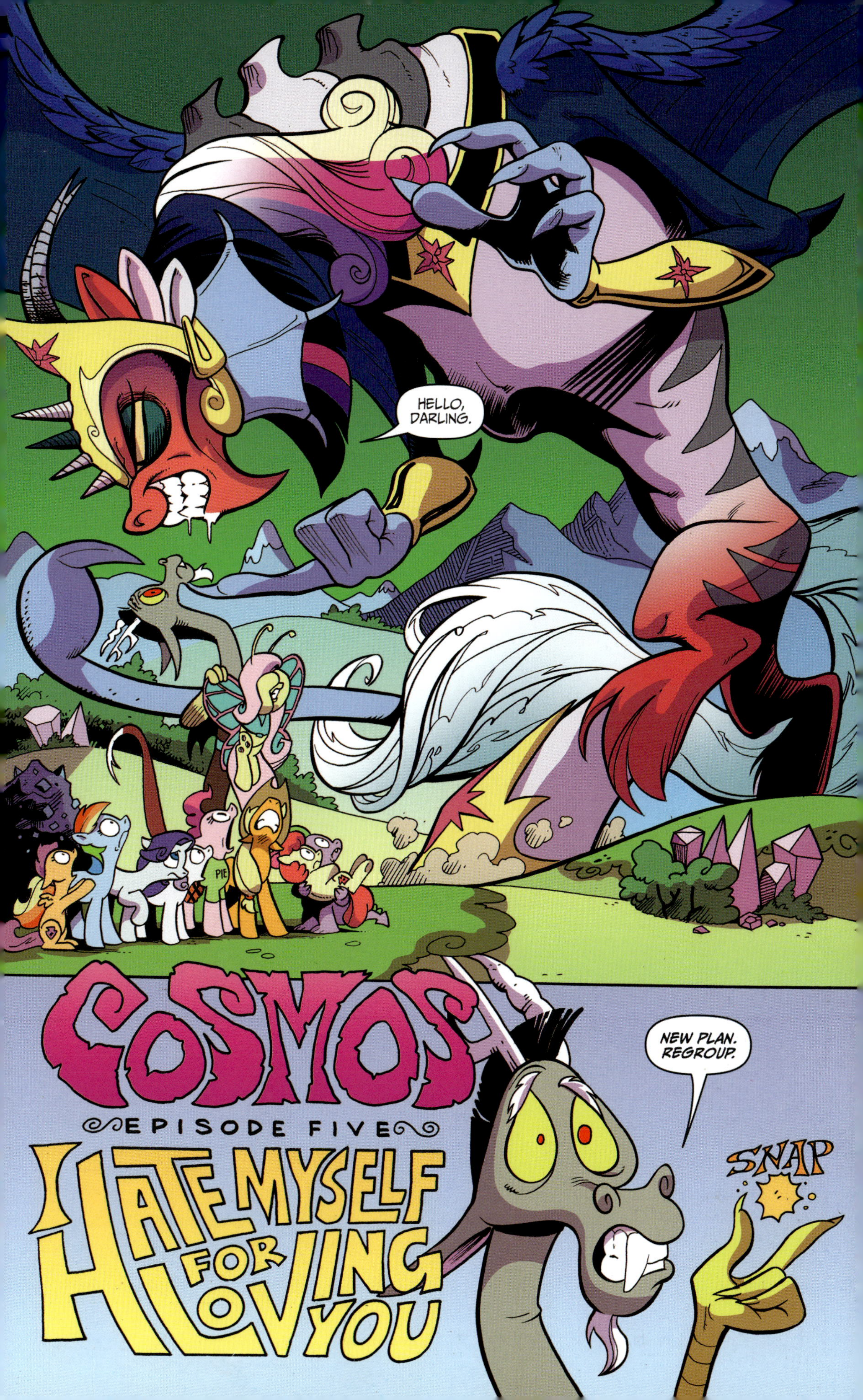
HELLO, DARLING.
COSMOS
EPISODE FIVE
HATE MYSELF FOR LOVING YOU
NEW PLAN. REGROUP.
SNAP

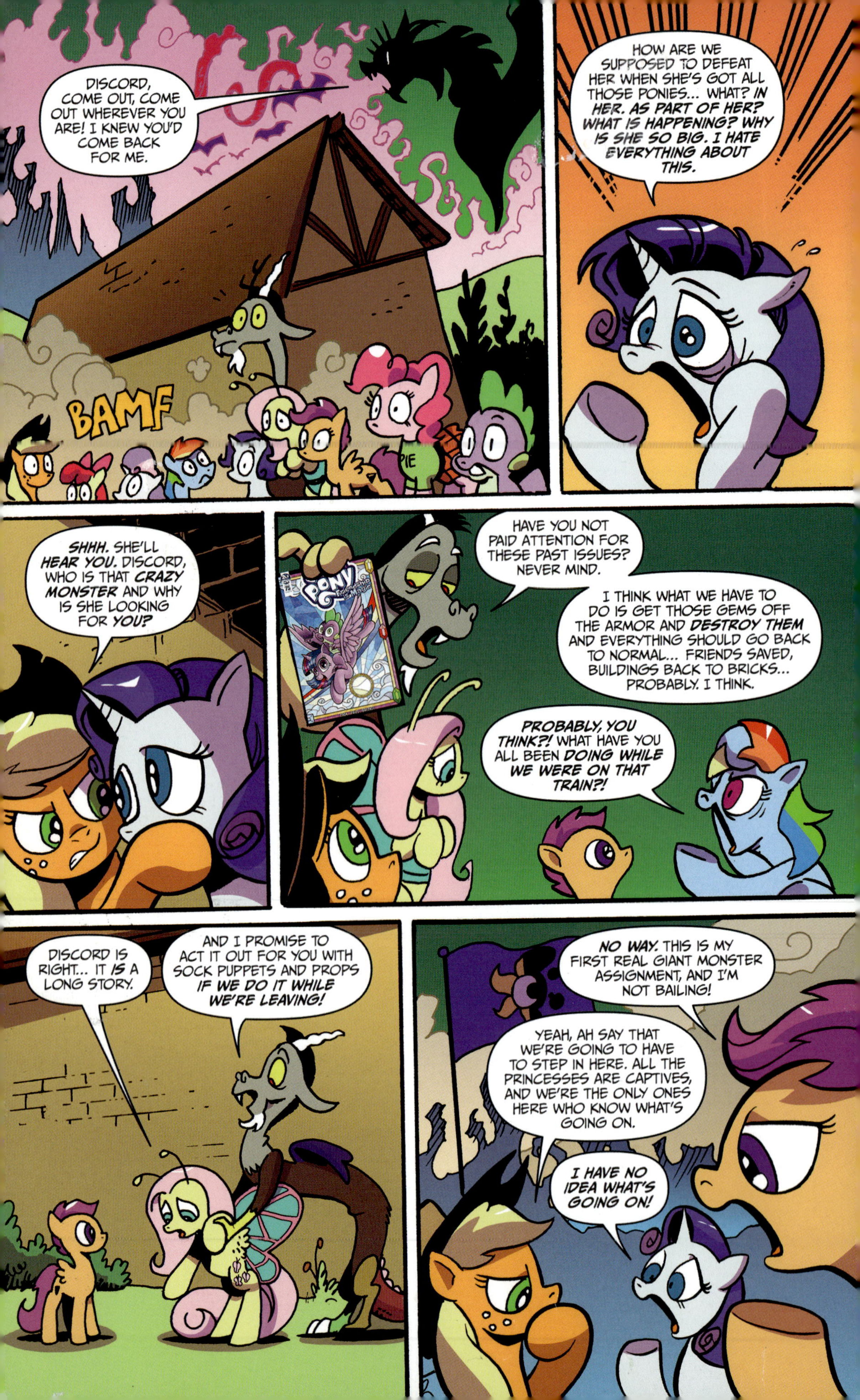
DISCORD, COME OUT, COME OUT WHEREVER YOU ARE! I KNEW YOU'D COME BACK FOR ME.
BAMF
PIE
HOW ARE WE SUPPOSED TO DEFEAT HER WHEN SHE'S GOT ALL THOSE PONIES... WHAT? IN HER. AS PART OF HER? WHAT IS HAPPENING? WHY IS SHE SO BIG. I HATE EVERYTHING ABOUT THIS.
SHHH. SHE'LL HEAR YOU. DISCORD, WHO IS THAT CRAZY MONSTER AND WHY IS SHE LOOKING FOR YOU?
HAVE YOU NOT PAID ATTENTION FOR THESE PAST ISSUES? NEVER MIND.
I THINK WHAT WE HAVE TO DO IS GET THOSE GEMS OFF THE ARMOR AND DESTROY THEM AND EVERYTHING SHOULD GO BACK TO NORMAL... FRIENDS SAVED, BUILDINGS BACK TO BRICKS... PROBABLY. I THINK.
PROBABLY, YOU THINK?! WHAT HAVE YOU ALL BEEN DOING WHILE WE WERE ON THAT TRAIN?!
DISCORD IS RIGHT... IT IS A LONG STORY.
AND I PROMISE TO ACT IT OUT FOR YOU WITH SOCK PUPPETS AND PROPS IF WE DO IT WHILE WE'RE LEAVING!
NO WAY. THIS IS MY FIRST REAL GIANT MONSTER ASSIGNMENT, AND I'M NOT BAILING!
YEAH, AH SAY THAT WE'RE GOING TO HAVE TO STEP IN HERE. ALL THE PRINCESSES ARE CAPTIVES, AND WE'RE THE ONLY ONES HERE WHO KNOW WHAT'S GOING ON.
I HAVE NO IDEA WHAT'S GOING ON!

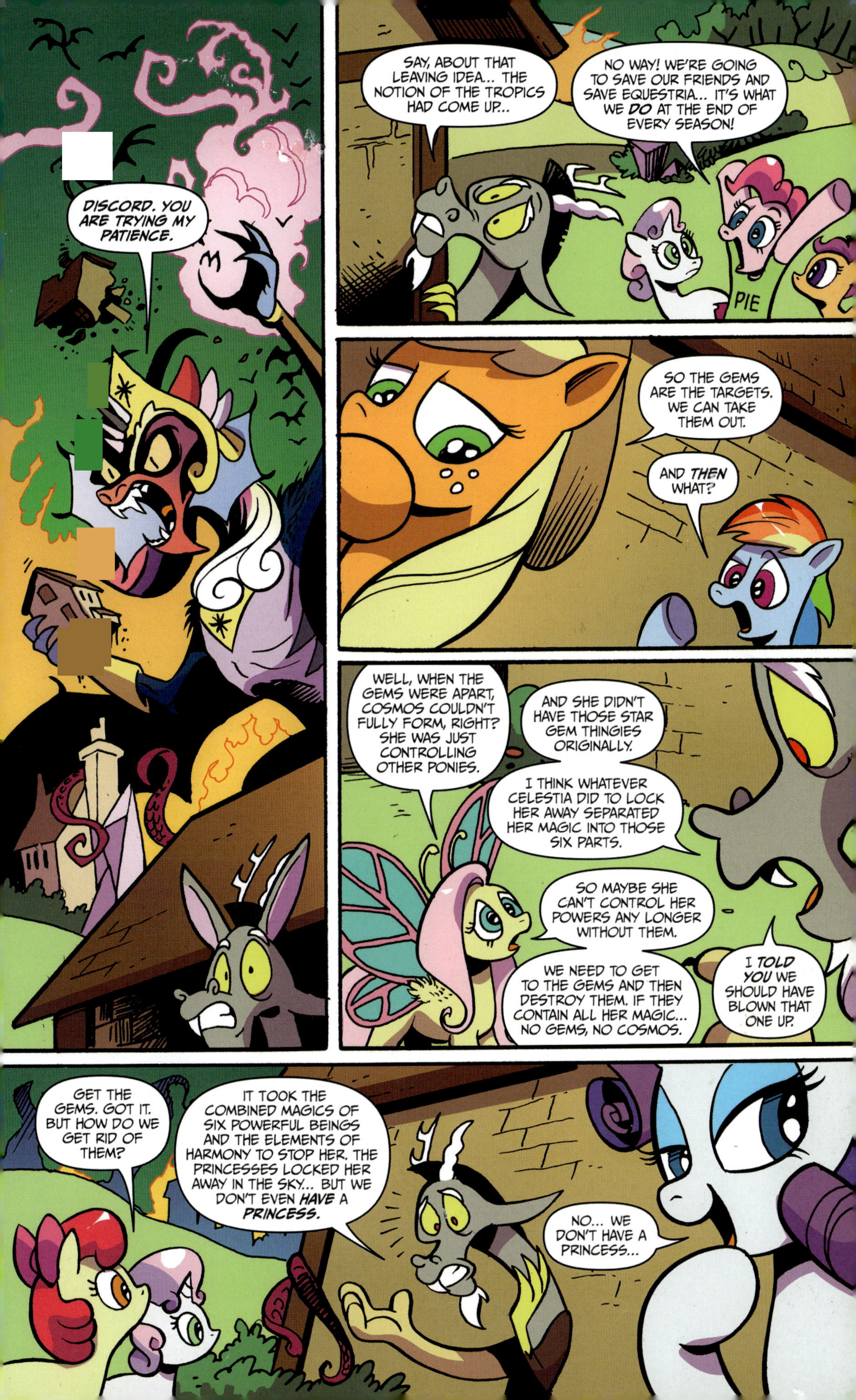
DISCORD. YOU ARE TRYING MY PATIENCE.
SAY, ABOUT THAT LEAVING IDEA... THE NOTION OF THE TROPICS HAD COME UP...
NO WAY! WE'RE GOING TO SAVE OUR FRIENDS AND SAVE EQUESTRIA... IT'S WHAT WE DO AT THE END OF EVERY SEASON!
PIE
SO THE GEMS ARE THE TARGETS. WE CAN TAKE THEM OUT.
AND THEN WHAT?
WELL, WHEN THE GEMS WERE APART, COSMOS COULDN'T FULLY FORM, RIGHT? SHE WAS JUST CONTROLLING OTHER PONIES.
AND SHE DIDN'T HAVE THOSE STAR GEM THINGIES ORIGINALLY.
I THINK WHATEVER CELESTIA DID TO LOCK HER AWAY SEPARATED HER MAGIC INTO THOSE SIX PARTS.
SO MAYBE SHE CAN'T CONTROL HER POWERS ANY LONGER WITHOUT THEM.
WE NEED TO GET TO THE GEMS AND THEN DESTROY THEM. IF THEY CONTAIN ALL HER MAGIC... NO GEMS, NO COSMOS.
I TOLD YOU WE SHOULD HAVE BLOWN THAT ONE UP.
GET THE GEMS. GOT IT. BUT HOW DO WE GET RID OF THEM?
IT TOOK THE COMBINED MAGICS OF SIX POWERFUL BEINGS AND THE ELEMENTS OF HARMONY TO STOP HER. THE PRINCESSES LOCKED HER AWAY IN THE SKY... BUT WE DON'T EVEN HAVE A PRINCESS.
NO... WE DON'T HAVE A PRINCESS...

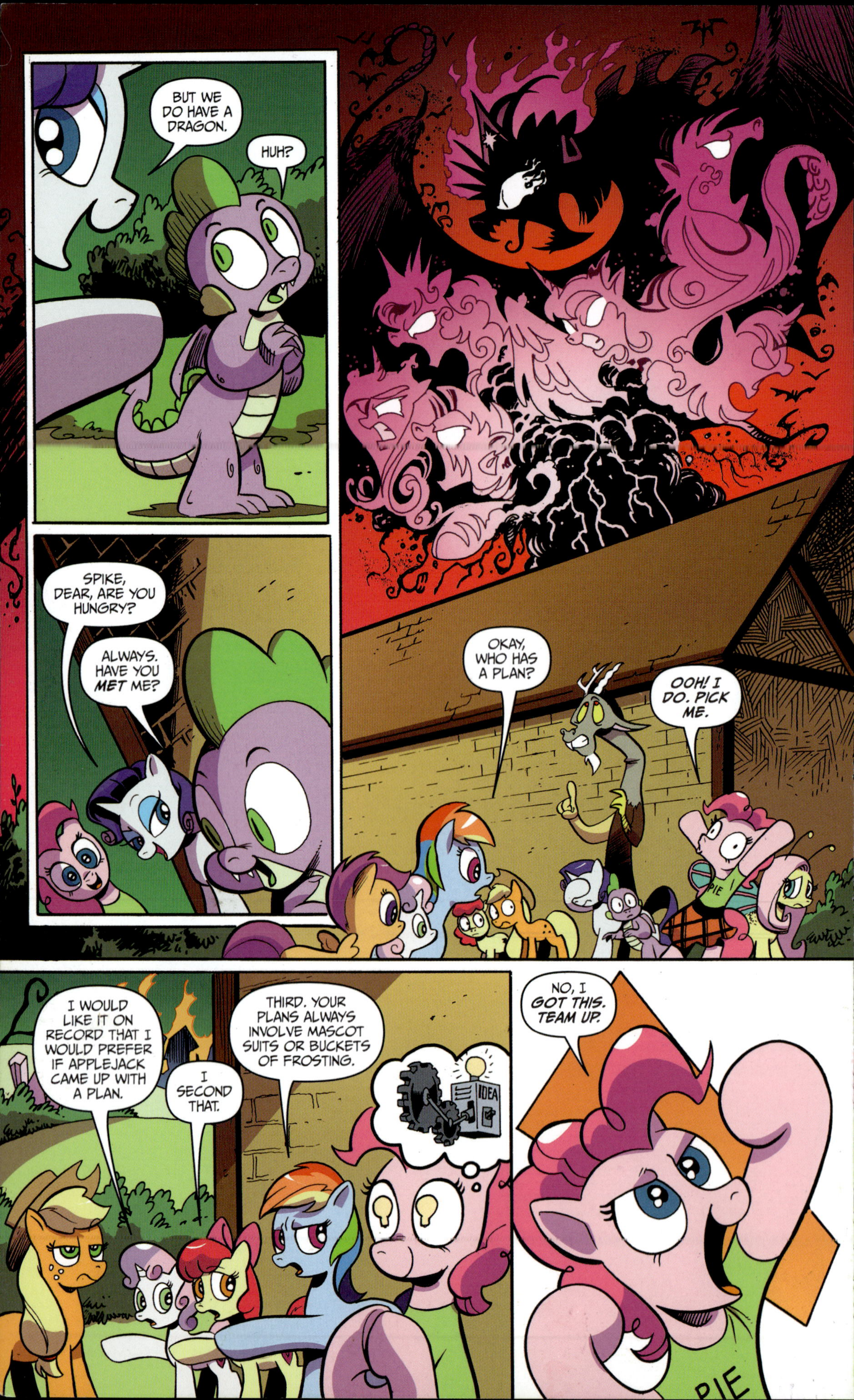

BUT WE DO HAVE A DRAGON.
HUH?
SPIKE, DEAR, ARE YOU HUNGRY?
ALWAYS. HAVE YOU *MET* ME?
OKAY, WHO HAS A PLAN?
OOH! I DO. PICK ME.
PIE
I WOULD LIKE IT ON RECORD THAT I WOULD PREFER IF APPLEJACK CAME UP WITH A PLAN.
I SECOND THAT.
THIRD. YOUR PLANS ALWAYS INVOLVE MASCOT SUITS OR BUCKETS OF FROSTING.
IDEA
NO, I *GOT THIS. TEAM UP.*
PIE

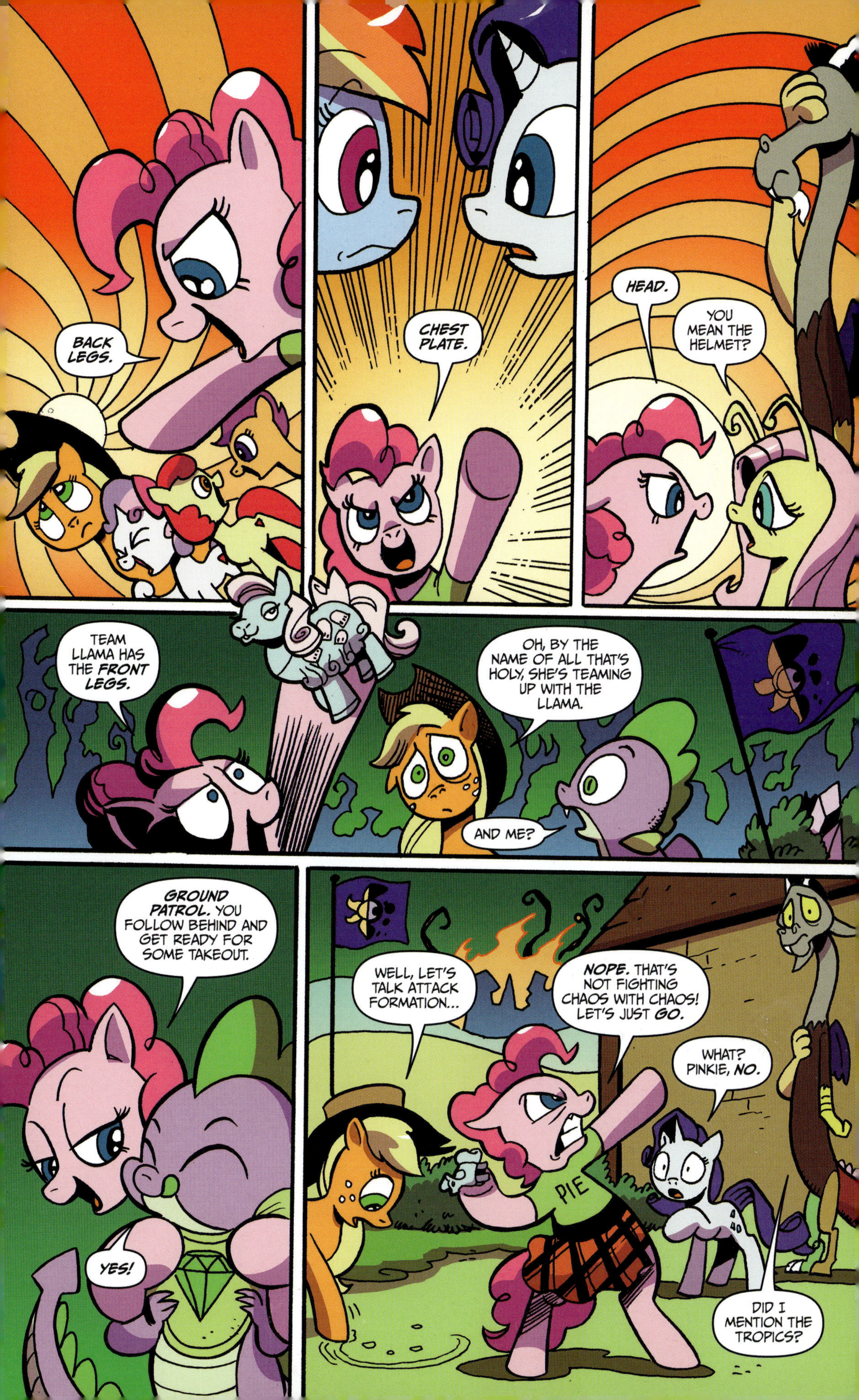
BACK LEGS.
CHEST PLATE.
HEAD.
YOU MEAN THE HELMET?
TEAM LLAMA HAS THE FRONT LEGS.
OH, BY THE NAME OF ALL THAT'S HOLY, SHE'S TEAMING UP WITH THE LLAMA.
AND ME?
GROUND PATROL. YOU FOLLOW BEHIND AND GET READY FOR SOME TAKEOUT.
YES!
WELL, LET'S TALK ATTACK FORMATION...
NOPE. THAT'S NOT FIGHTING CHAOS WITH CHAOS! LET'S JUST GO.
WHAT? PINKIE, NO.
DID I MENTION THE TROPICS?
PIE

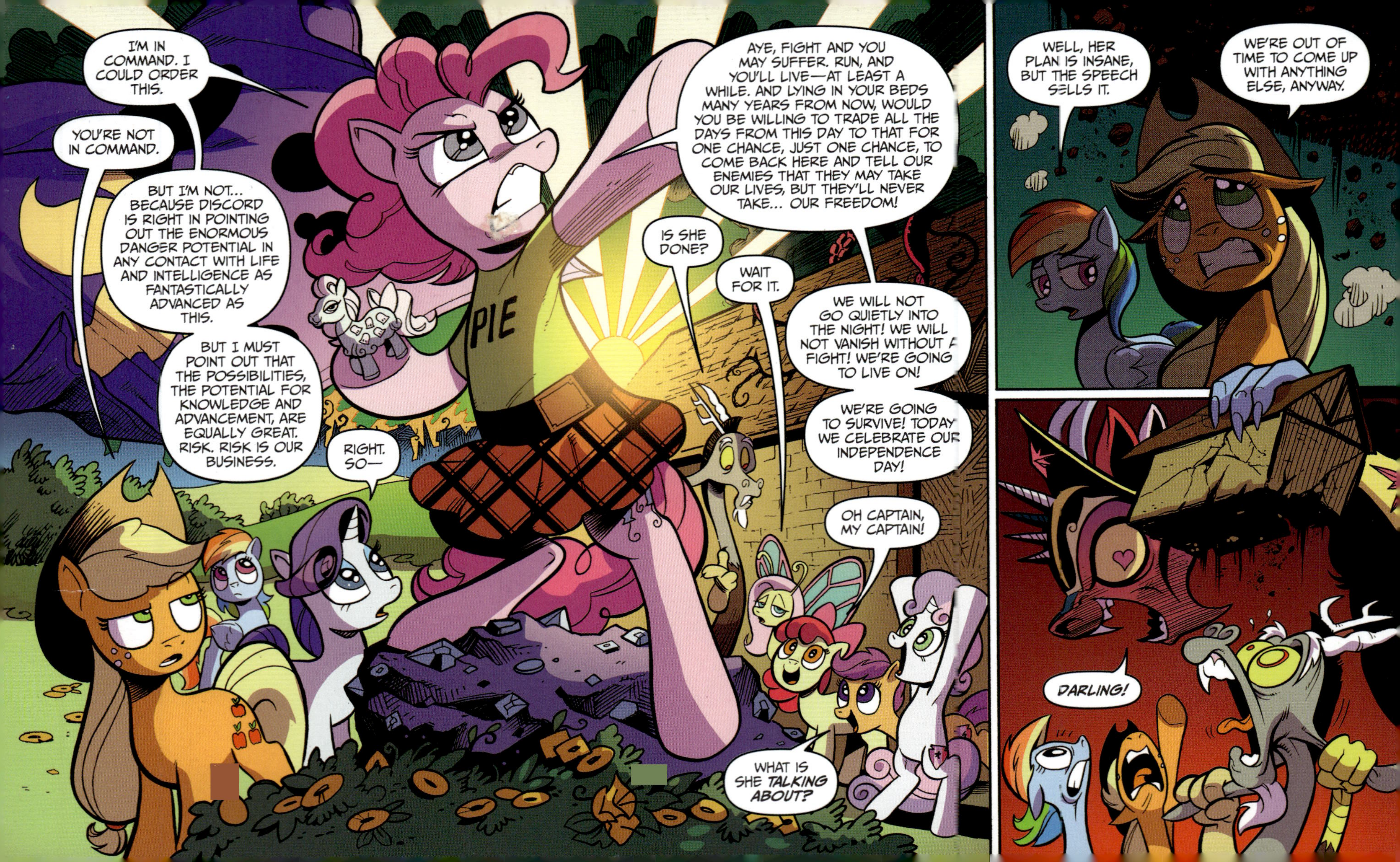
I'M IN COMMAND. I COULD ORDER THIS.
YOU'RE NOT IN COMMAND.
BUT I'M NOT... BECAUSE DISCORD IS RIGHT IN POINTING OUT THE ENORMOUS DANGER POTENTIAL IN ANY CONTACT WITH LIFE AND INTELLIGENCE AS FANTASTICALLY ADVANCED AS THIS.
BUT I MUST POINT OUT THAT THE POSSIBILITIES, THE POTENTIAL FOR KNOWLEDGE AND ADVANCEMENT, ARE EQUALLY GREAT. RISK. RISK IS OUR BUSINESS.
RIGHT. SO—
AYE, FIGHT AND YOU MAY SUFFER. RUN, AND YOU'LL LIVE—AT LEAST A WHILE. AND LYING IN YOUR BEDS MANY YEARS FROM NOW, WOULD YOU BE WILLING TO TRADE ALL THE DAYS FROM THIS DAY TO THAT FOR ONE CHANCE, JUST ONE CHANCE, TO COME BACK HERE AND TELL OUR ENEMIES THAT THEY MAY TAKE OUR LIVES, BUT THEY'LL NEVER TAKE... OUR FREEDOM!
PIE
IS SHE DONE?
WAIT FOR IT.
WE WILL NOT GO QUIETLY INTO THE NIGHT! WE WILL NOT VANISH WITHOUT A FIGHT! WE'RE GOING TO LIVE ON!
WE'RE GOING TO SURVIVE! TODAY WE CELEBRATE OUR INDEPENDENCE DAY!
OH CAPTAIN, MY CAPTAIN!
WHAT IS SHE TALKING ABOUT?
WELL, HER PLAN IS INSANE, BUT THE SPEECH SELLS IT.
WE'RE OUT OF TIME TO COME UP WITH ANYTHING ELSE, ANYWAY.
DARLING!

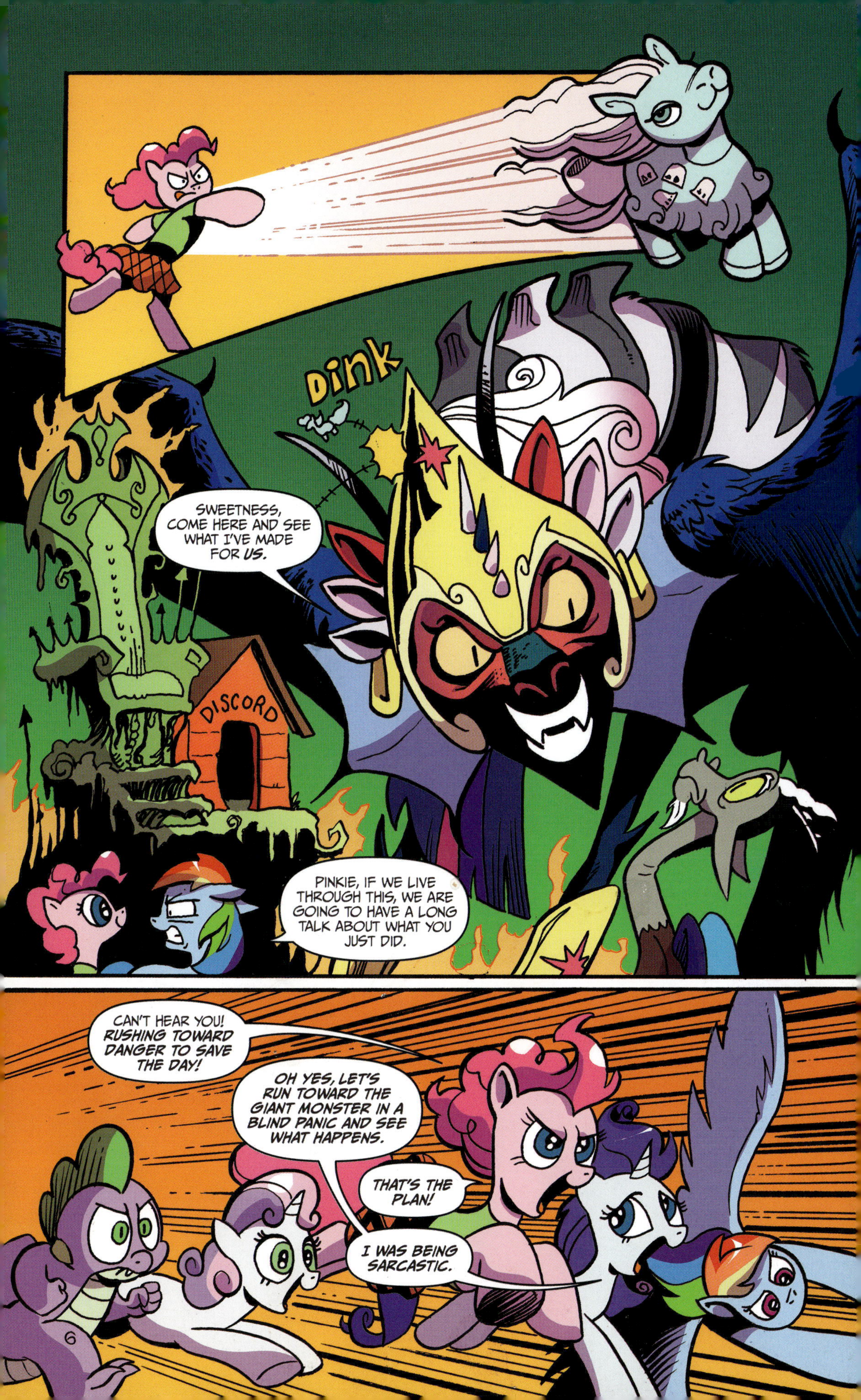
DINK
SWEETNESS, COME HERE AND SEE WHAT I'VE MADE FOR *US*.
DISCORD
PINKIE, IF WE LIVE THROUGH THIS, WE ARE GOING TO HAVE A LONG TALK ABOUT WHAT YOU JUST DID.
CAN'T HEAR YOU! *RUSHING TOWARD DANGER TO SAVE THE DAY!*
OH YES, LET'S RUN TOWARD THE GIANT MONSTER IN A BLIND PANIC AND SEE WHAT HAPPENS.
THAT'S THE PLAN!
I WAS BEING SARCASTIC.

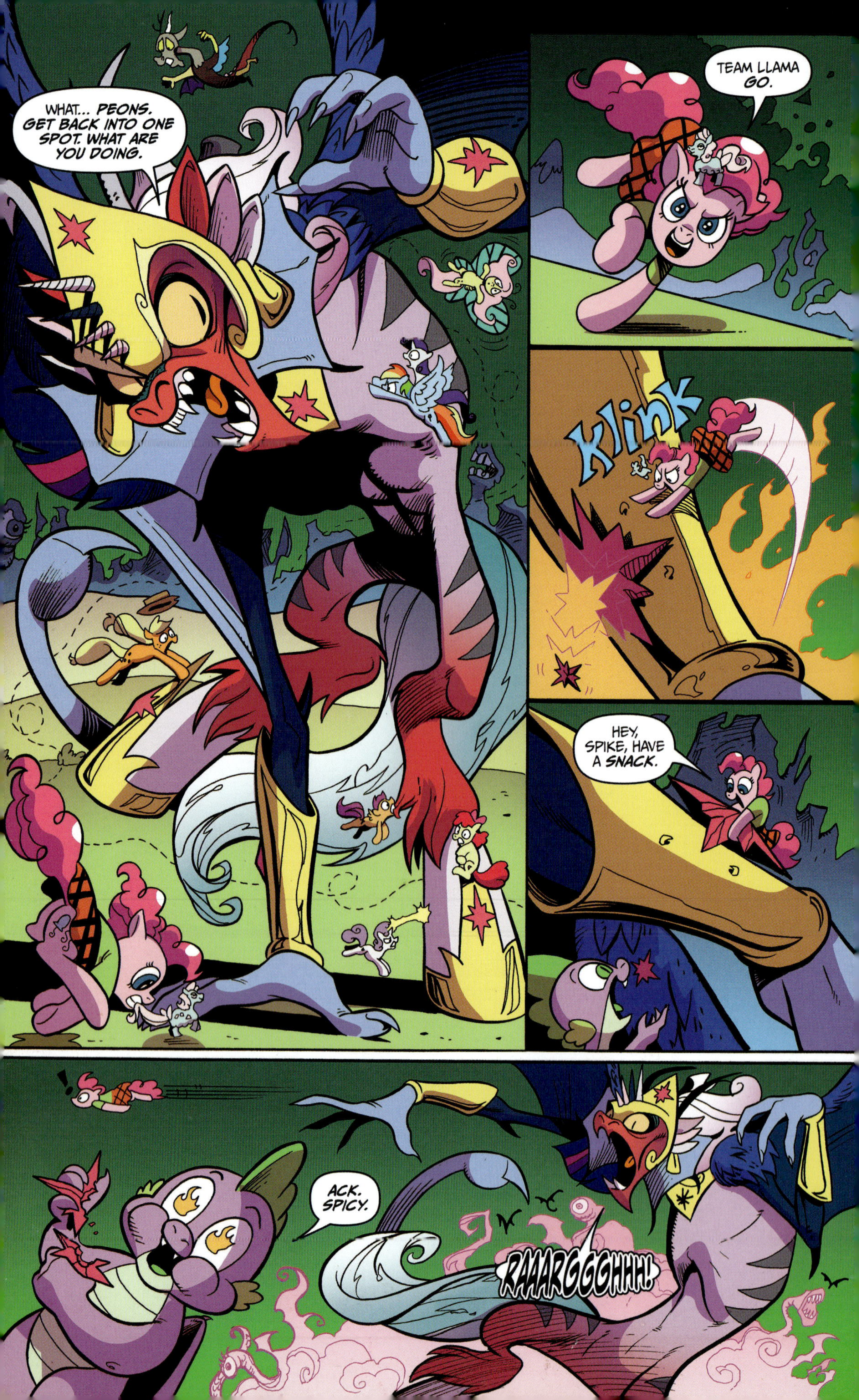
WHAT... PEONS. GET BACK INTO ONE SPOT. WHAT ARE YOU DOING.
TEAM LLAMA GO.
KLINK
HEY, SPIKE, HAVE A SNACK.
!
ACK. SPICY.
RAAARGGGHHH!

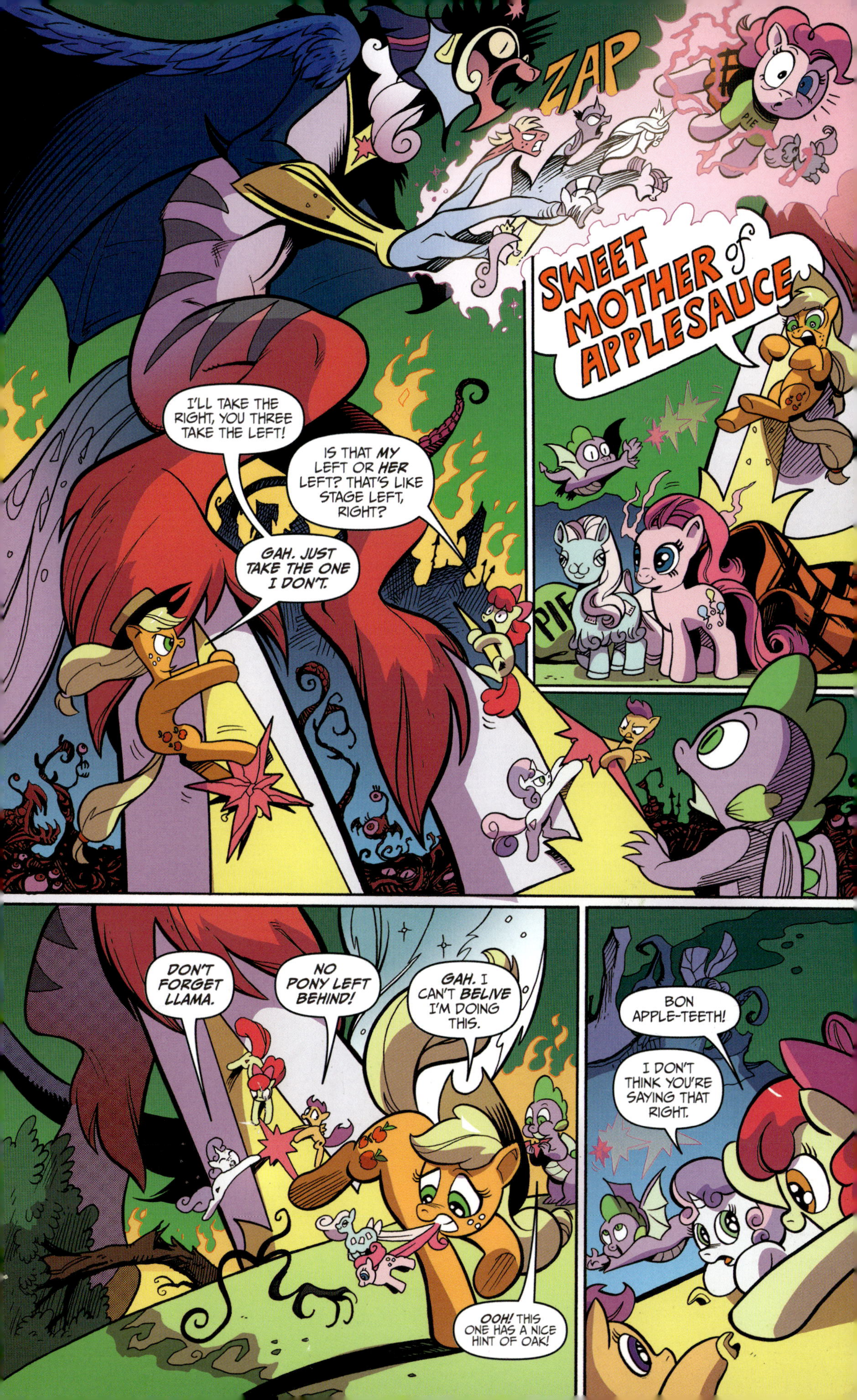
ZAP
SWEET MOTHER of APPLESAUCE
I'LL TAKE THE RIGHT, YOU THREE TAKE THE LEFT!
IS THAT MY LEFT OR HER LEFT? THAT'S LIKE STAGE LEFT, RIGHT?
GAH. JUST TAKE THE ONE I DON'T.
PIE
DON'T FORGET LLAMA.
NO PONY LEFT BEHIND!
GAH. I CAN'T BELIVE I'M DOING THIS.
OOH! THIS ONE HAS A NICE HINT OF OAK!
BON APPLE-TEETH!
I DON'T THINK YOU'RE SAYING THAT RIGHT.

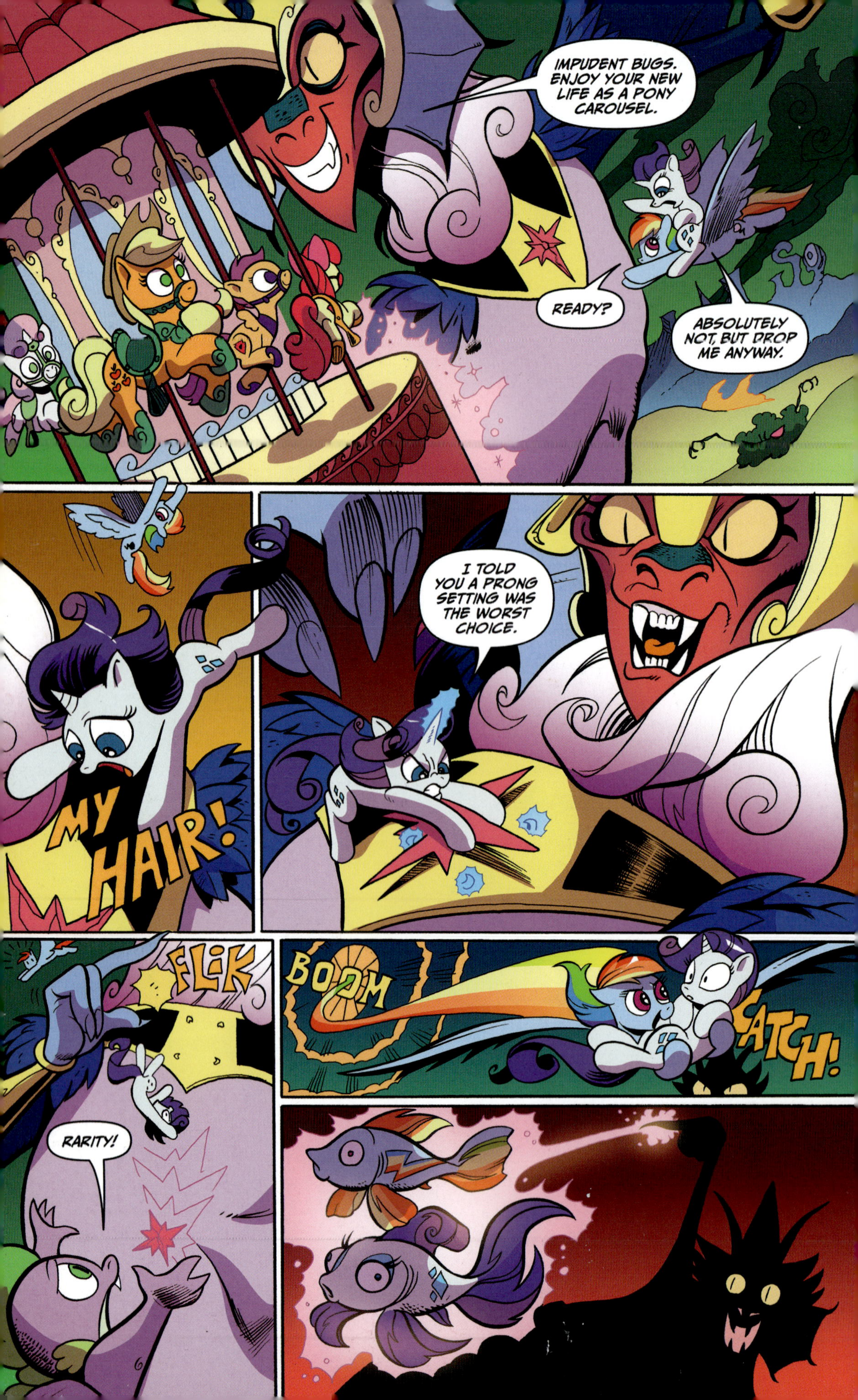
IMPUDENT BUGS. ENJOY YOUR NEW LIFE AS A PONY CAROUSEL.
READY?
ABSOLUTELY NOT, BUT DROP ME ANYWAY.
MY HAIR!
I TOLD YOU A PRONG SETTING WAS THE WORST CHOICE.
FLIK
RARITY!
BOOM
CATCH!

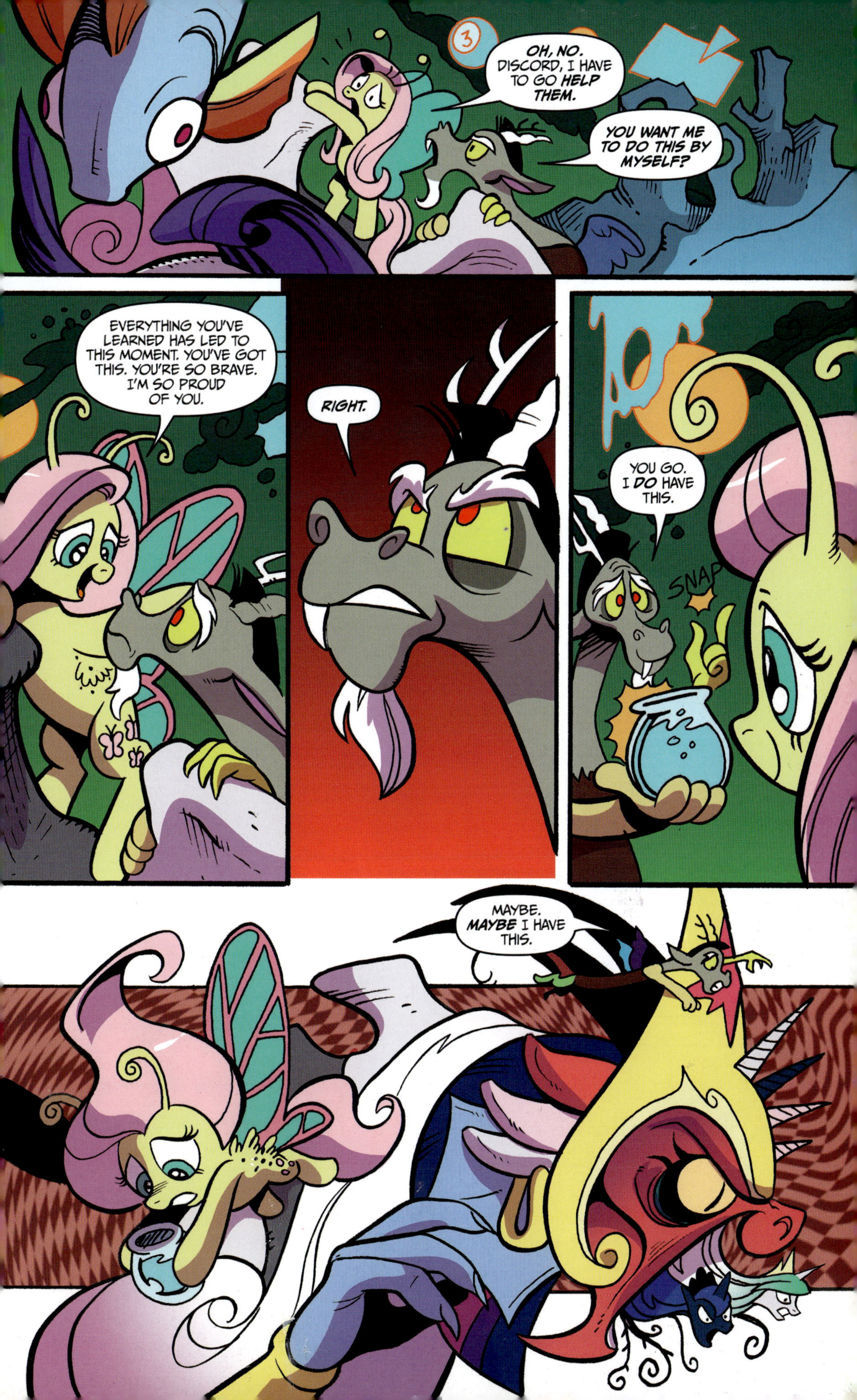

3
OH, NO. DISCORD, I HAVE TO GO HELP THEM.
YOU WANT ME TO DO THIS BY MYSELF?
EVERYTHING YOU'VE LEARNED HAS LED TO THIS MOMENT. YOU'VE GOT THIS. YOU'RE SO BRAVE. I'M SO PROUD OF YOU.
RIGHT.
YOU GO. I DO HAVE THIS.
SNAP
MAYBE. MAYBE I HAVE THIS.

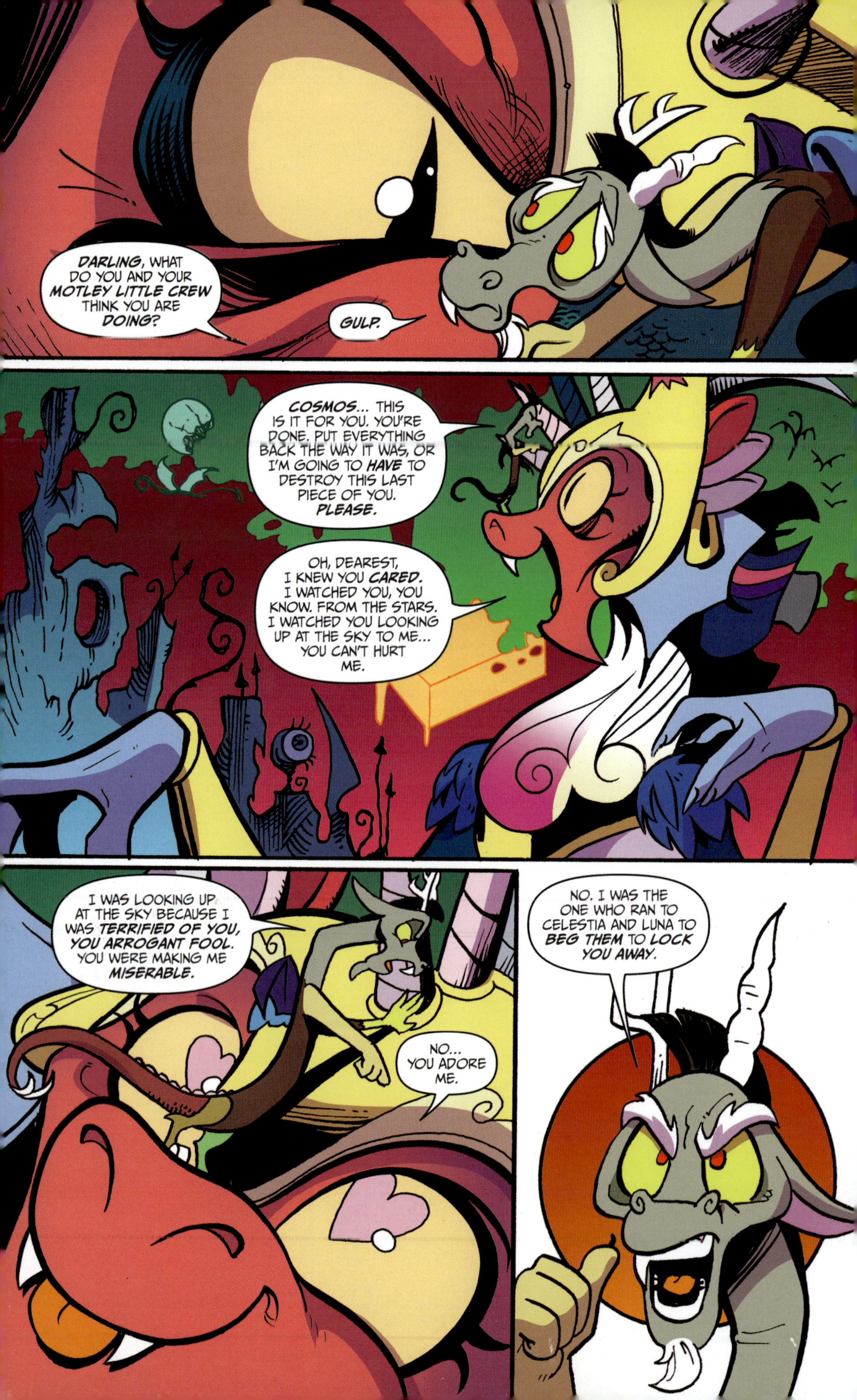
DARLING, WHAT DO YOU AND YOUR MOTLEY LITTLE CREW THINK YOU ARE DOING?
GULP.
COSMOS... THIS IS IT FOR YOU. YOU'RE DONE. PUT EVERYTHING BACK THE WAY IT WAS, OR I'M GOING TO HAVE TO DESTROY THIS LAST PIECE OF YOU. PLEASE.
OH, DEAREST, I KNEW YOU CARED. I WATCHED YOU, YOU KNOW. FROM THE STARS. I WATCHED YOU LOOKING UP AT THE SKY TO ME... YOU CAN'T HURT ME.
I WAS LOOKING UP AT THE SKY BECAUSE I WAS TERRIFIED OF YOU, YOU ARROGANT FOOL. YOU WERE MAKING ME MISERABLE.
NO... YOU ADORE ME.
NO. I WAS THE ONE WHO RAN TO CELESTIA AND LUNA TO BEG THEM TO LOCK YOU AWAY.

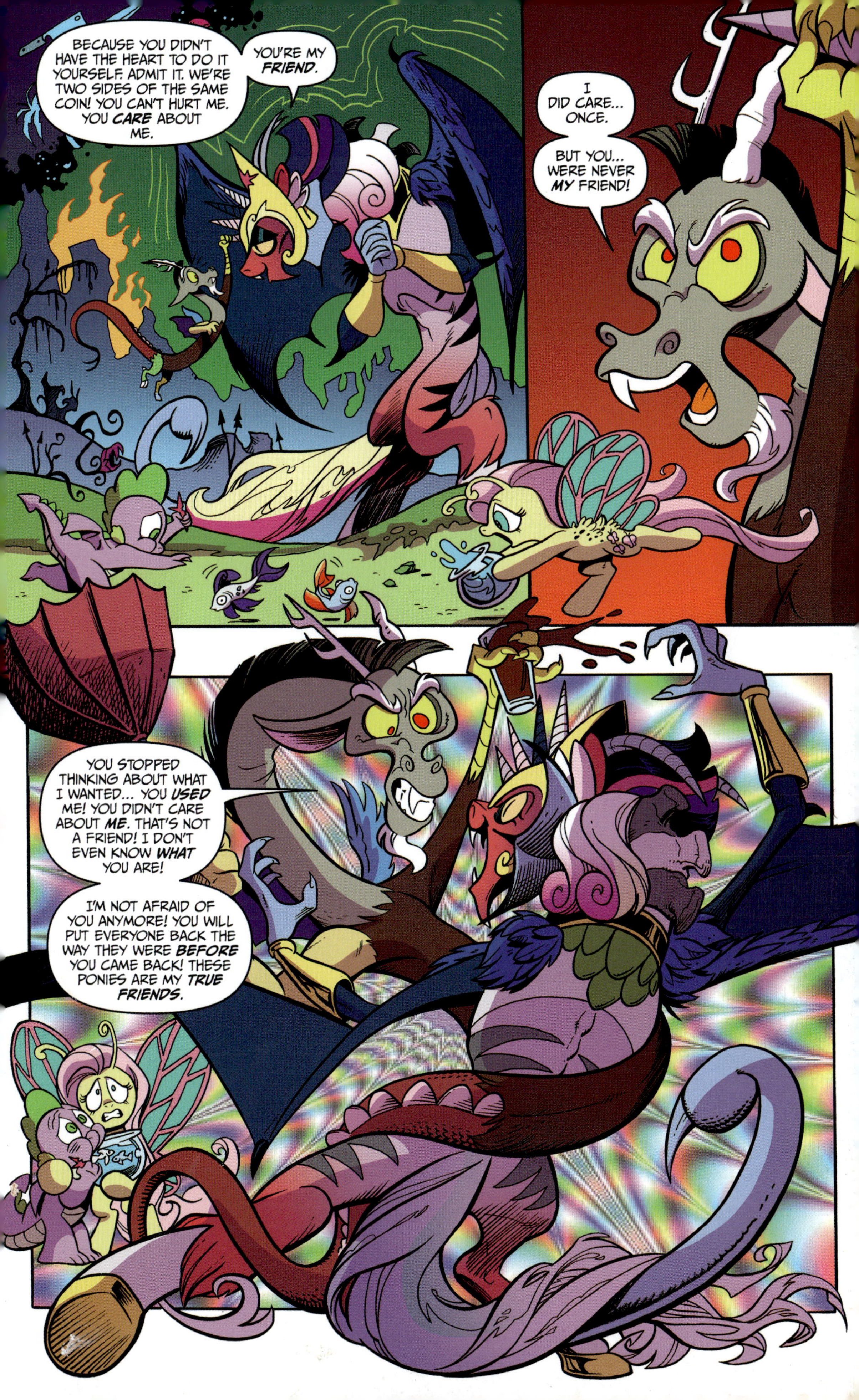
BECAUSE YOU DIDN'T HAVE THE HEART TO DO IT YOURSELF. ADMIT IT. WE'RE TWO SIDES OF THE SAME COIN! YOU CAN'T HURT ME. YOU *CARE* ABOUT ME.
YOU'RE MY *FRIEND*.
I DID CARE... ONCE.
BUT YOU... WERE NEVER *MY* FRIEND!
YOU STOPPED THINKING ABOUT WHAT I WANTED... YOU *USED* ME! YOU DIDN'T CARE ABOUT *ME*. THAT'S NOT A FRIEND! I DON'T EVEN KNOW *WHAT* YOU ARE!
I'M NOT AFRAID OF YOU ANYMORE! YOU WILL PUT EVERYONE BACK THE WAY THEY WERE *BEFORE* YOU CAME BACK! THESE PONIES ARE MY *TRUE FRIENDS*.

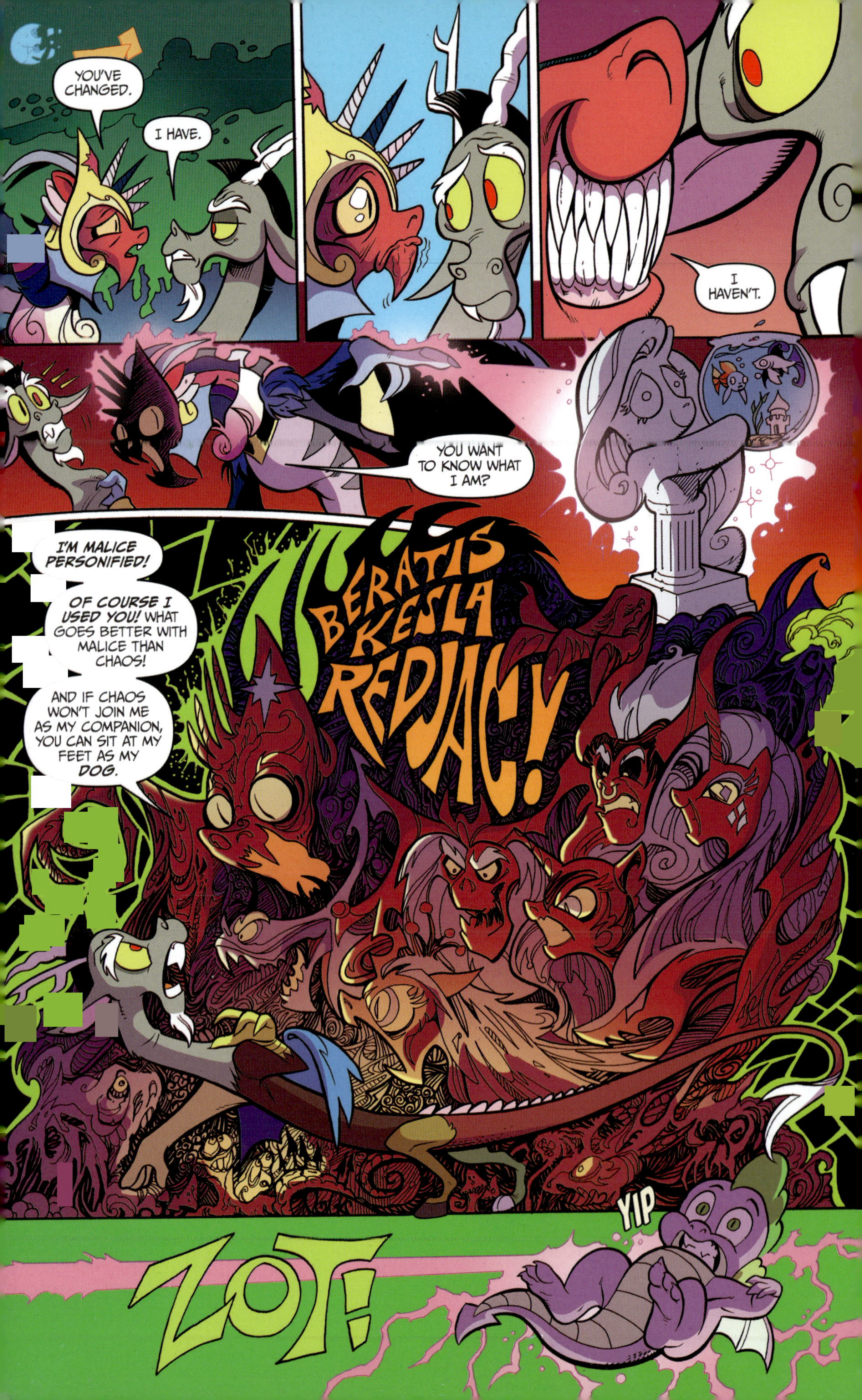

YOU'VE CHANGED.
I HAVE.
I HAVEN'T.
YOU WANT TO KNOW WHAT I AM?
BERATIS KESLA REDJAC!
I'M MALICE PERSONIFIED!
OF COURSE I USED YOU! WHAT GOES BETTER WITH MALICE THAN CHAOS!
AND IF CHAOS WON'T JOIN ME AS MY COMPANION, YOU CAN SIT AT MY FEET AS MY DOG.
YIP
ZOT!

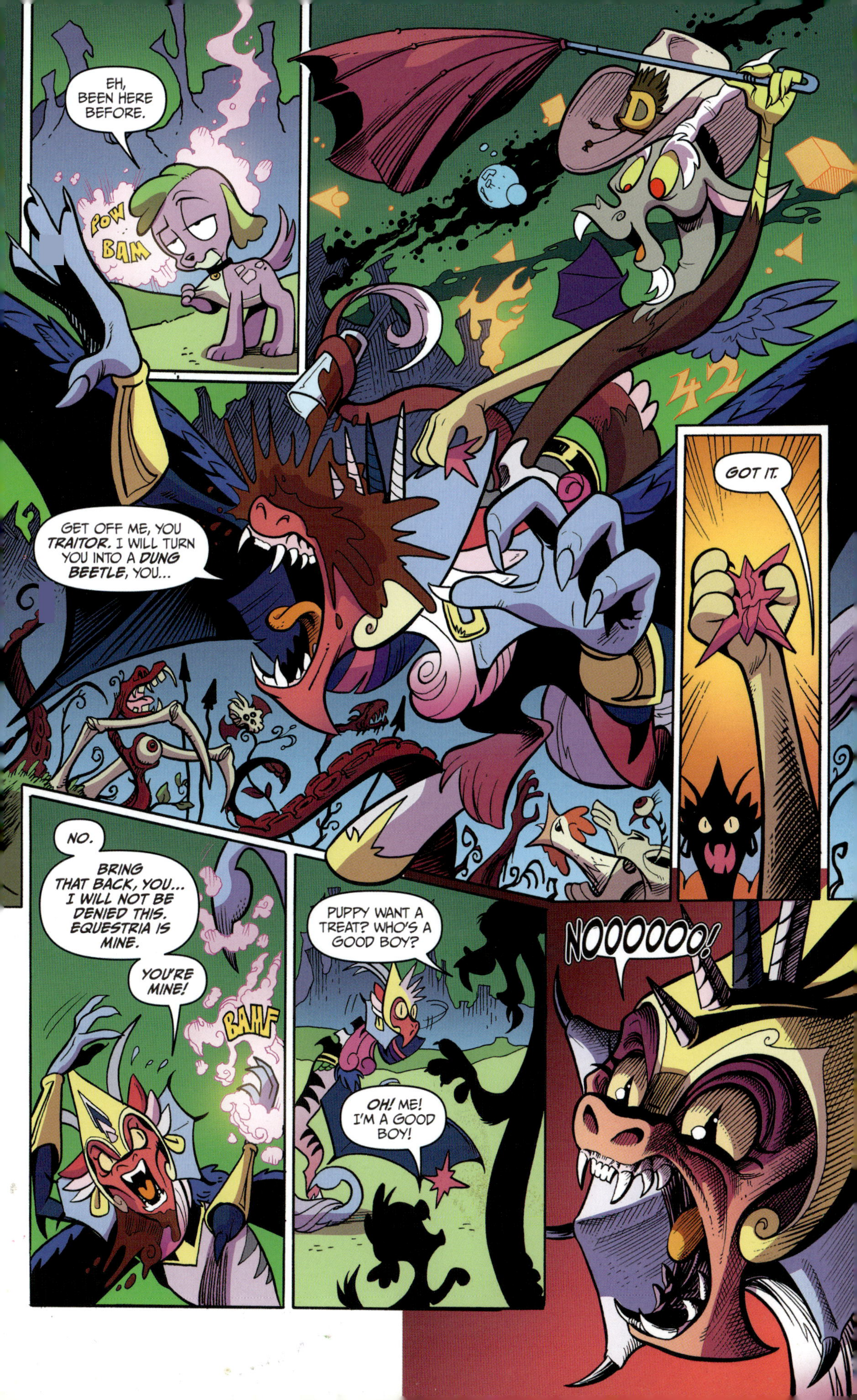
EH, BEEN HERE BEFORE.
POW
BAM
42
GET OFF ME, YOU TRAITOR. I WILL TURN YOU INTO A DUNG BEETLE, YOU...
GOT IT.
NO.
BRING THAT BACK, YOU... I WILL NOT BE DENIED THIS. EQUESTRIA IS MINE.
YOU'RE MINE!
BAHF
PUPPY WANT A TREAT? WHO'S A GOOD BOY?
OH! ME! I'M A GOOD BOY!
NOOOOOO!

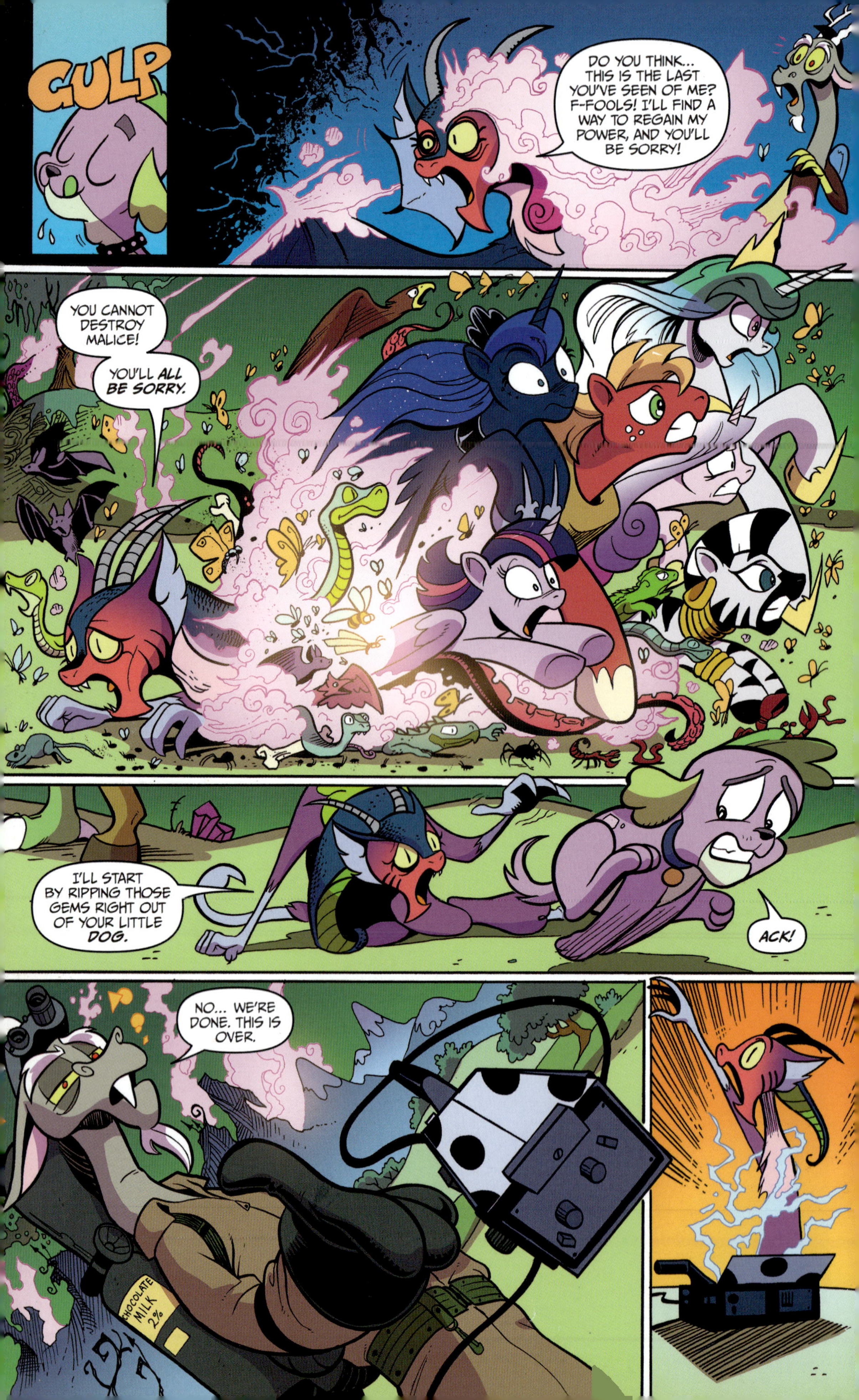
GULP
DO YOU THINK... THIS IS THE LAST YOU'VE SEEN OF ME? F-FOOLS! I'LL FIND A WAY TO REGAIN MY POWER, AND YOU'LL BE SORRY!
YOU CANNOT DESTROY MALICE!
YOU'LL ALL BE SORRY.
I'LL START BY RIPPING THOSE GEMS RIGHT OUT OF YOUR LITTLE DOG.
ACK!
NO... WE'RE DONE. THIS IS OVER.
CHOCOLATE MILK 2%

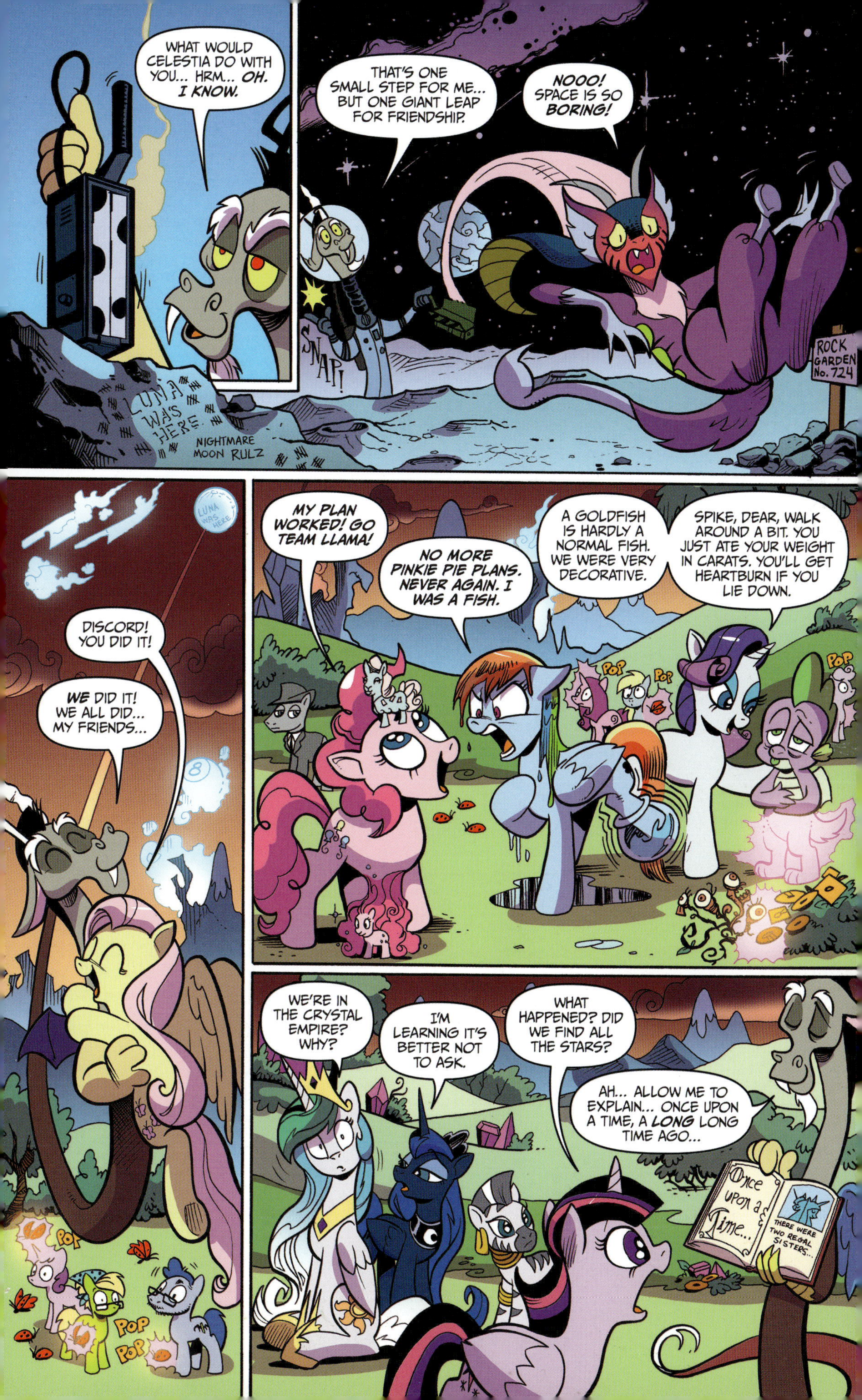

WHAT WOULD CELESTIA DO WITH YOU... HRM... OH. I KNOW.
LUNA WAS HERE
NIGHTMARE MOON RULZ
THAT'S ONE SMALL STEP FOR ME... BUT ONE GIANT LEAP FOR FRIENDSHIP.
NOOO! SPACE IS SO BORING!
SNAP!
ROCK GARDEN No. 724
LUNA WAS HERE
DISCORD! YOU DID IT!
WE DID IT! WE ALL DID... MY FRIENDS...
POP
POP
POP
MY PLAN WORKED! GO TEAM LLAMA!
NO MORE PINKIE PIE PLANS. NEVER AGAIN. I WAS A FISH.
A GOLDFISH IS HARDLY A NORMAL FISH. WE WERE VERY DECORATIVE.
SPIKE, DEAR, WALK AROUND A BIT. YOU JUST ATE YOUR WEIGHT IN CARATS. YOU'LL GET HEARTBURN IF YOU LIE DOWN.
POP
POP
POP
WE'RE IN THE CRYSTAL EMPIRE? WHY?
I'M LEARNING IT'S BETTER NOT TO ASK.
WHAT HAPPENED? DID WE FIND ALL THE STARS?
AH... ALLOW ME TO EXPLAIN... ONCE UPON A TIME, A LONG LONG TIME AGO...
Once upon a Time...
THERE WERE TWO REGAL SISTERS...

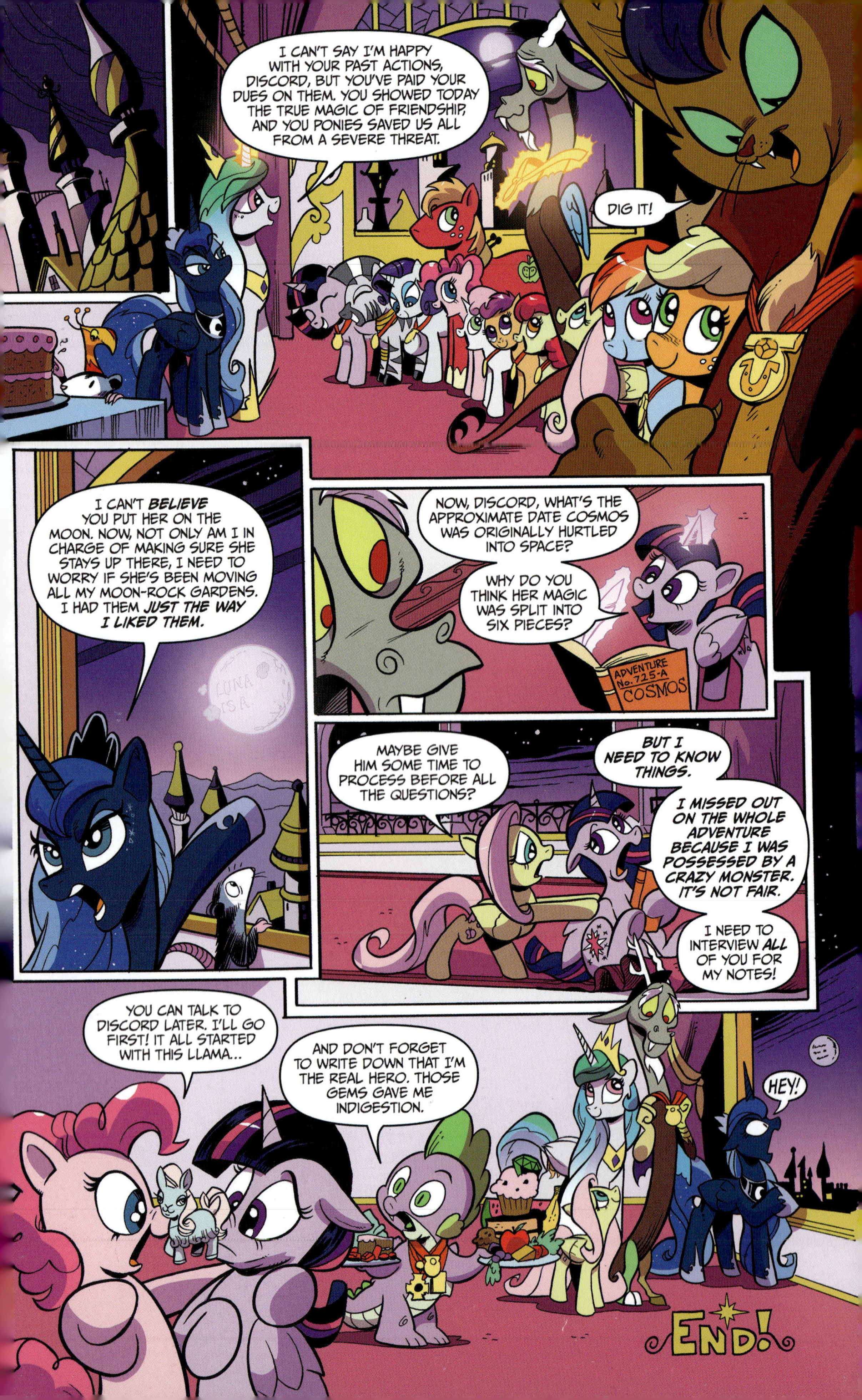
I CAN'T SAY I'M HAPPY WITH YOUR PAST ACTIONS, DISCORD, BUT YOU'VE PAID YOUR DUES ON THEM. YOU SHOWED TODAY THE TRUE MAGIC OF FRIENDSHIP, AND YOU PONIES SAVED US ALL FROM A SEVERE THREAT.
DIG IT!
I CAN'T *BELIEVE* YOU PUT HER ON THE MOON. NOW, NOT ONLY AM I IN CHARGE OF MAKING SURE SHE STAYS UP THERE, I NEED TO WORRY IF SHE'S BEEN MOVING ALL MY MOON-ROCK GARDENS. I HAD THEM *JUST THE WAY I LIKED THEM.*
NOW, DISCORD, WHAT'S THE APPROXIMATE DATE COSMOS WAS ORIGINALLY HURTLED INTO SPACE?
WHY DO YOU THINK HER MAGIC WAS SPLIT INTO SIX PIECES?
ADVENTURE No. 725-A COSMOS
MAYBE GIVE HIM SOME TIME TO PROCESS BEFORE ALL THE QUESTIONS?
BUT I NEED TO KNOW THINGS.
I MISSED OUT ON THE WHOLE ADVENTURE BECAUSE I WAS POSSESSED BY A CRAZY MONSTER. IT'S NOT FAIR.
I NEED TO INTERVIEW *ALL* OF YOU FOR MY NOTES!
YOU CAN TALK TO DISCORD LATER. I'LL GO FIRST! IT ALL STARTED WITH THIS LLAMA...
AND DON'T FORGET TO WRITE DOWN THAT I'M THE REAL HERO. THOSE GEMS GAVE ME INDIGESTION.
HEY!
END!

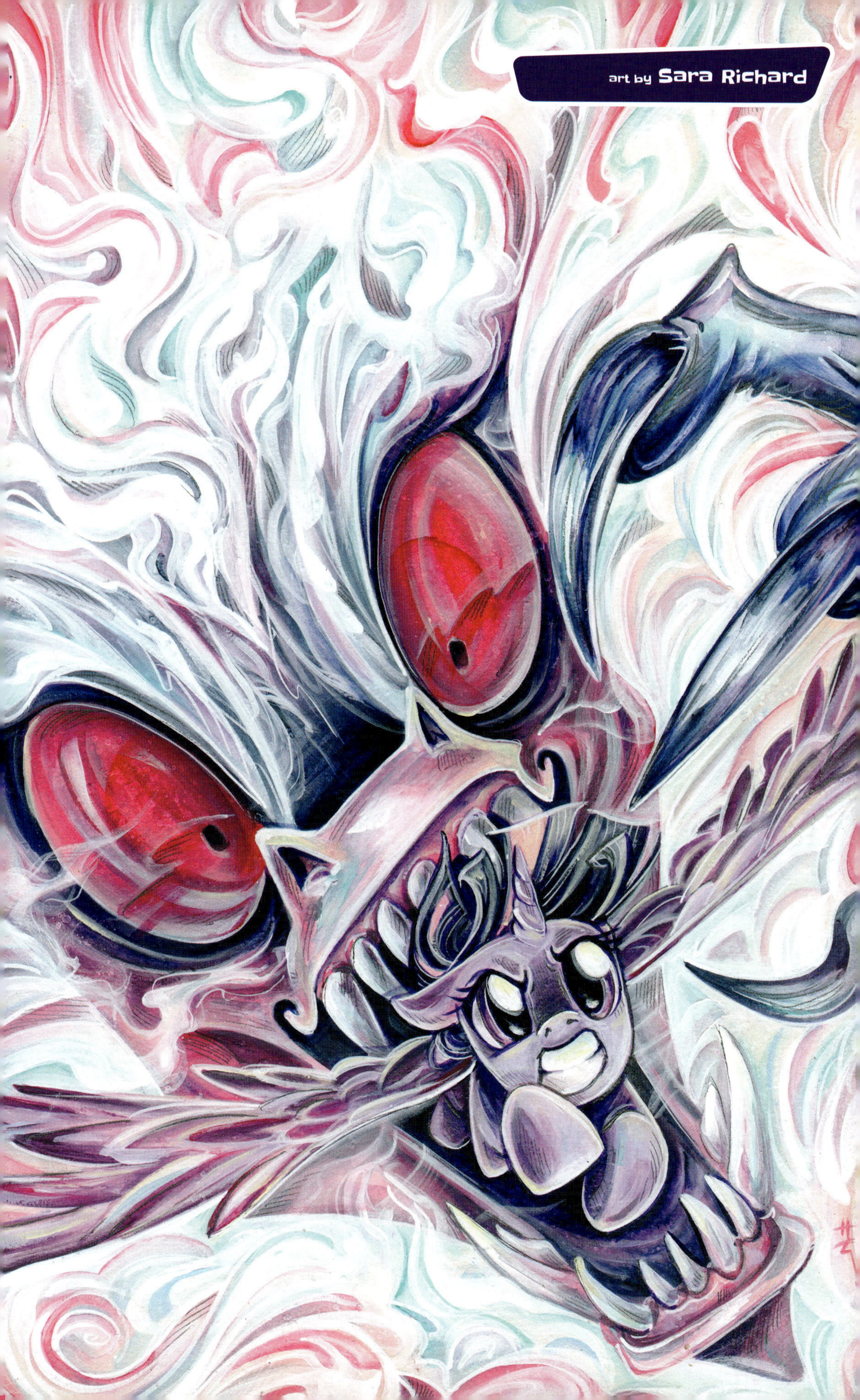

art by Sara Richard

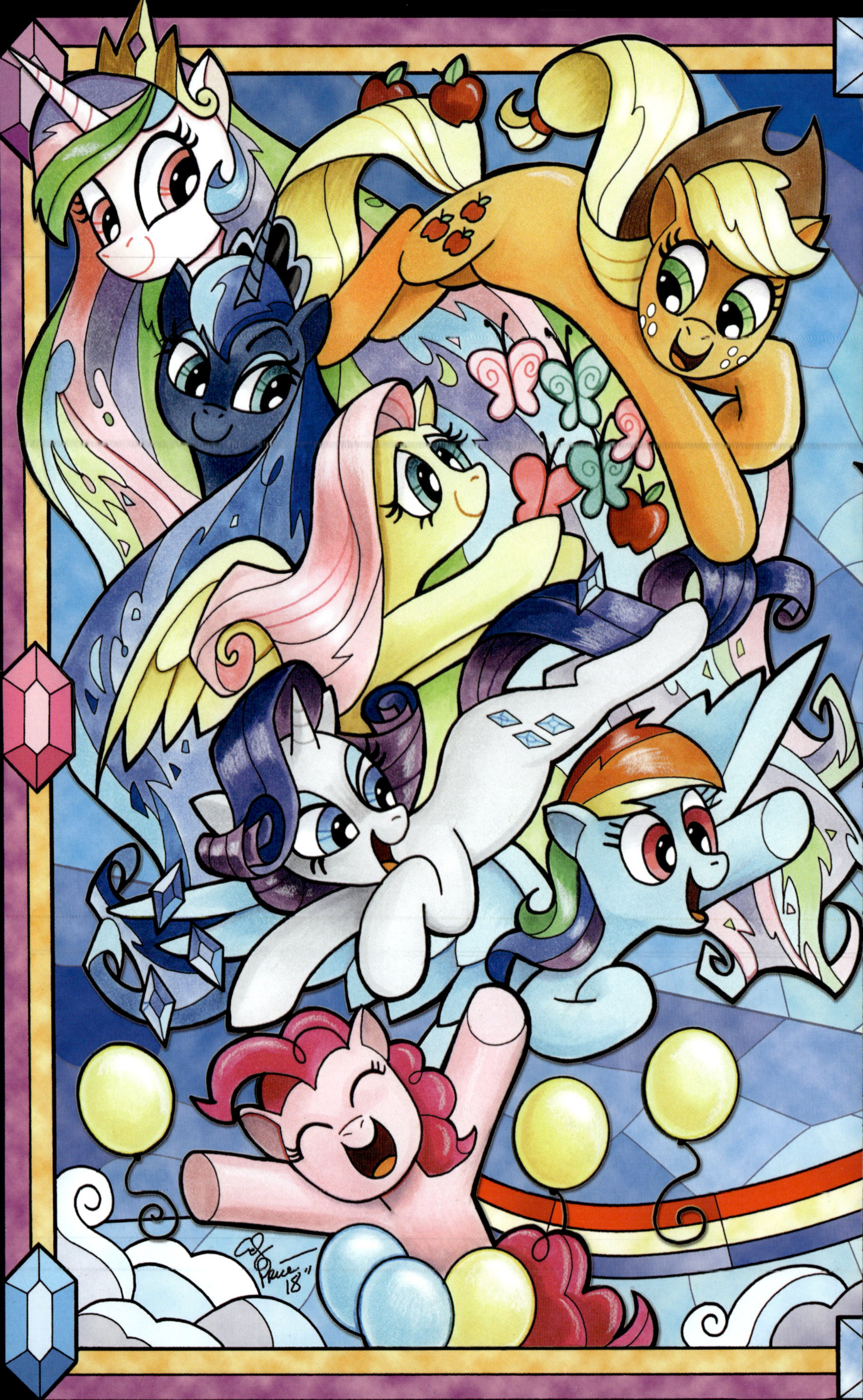

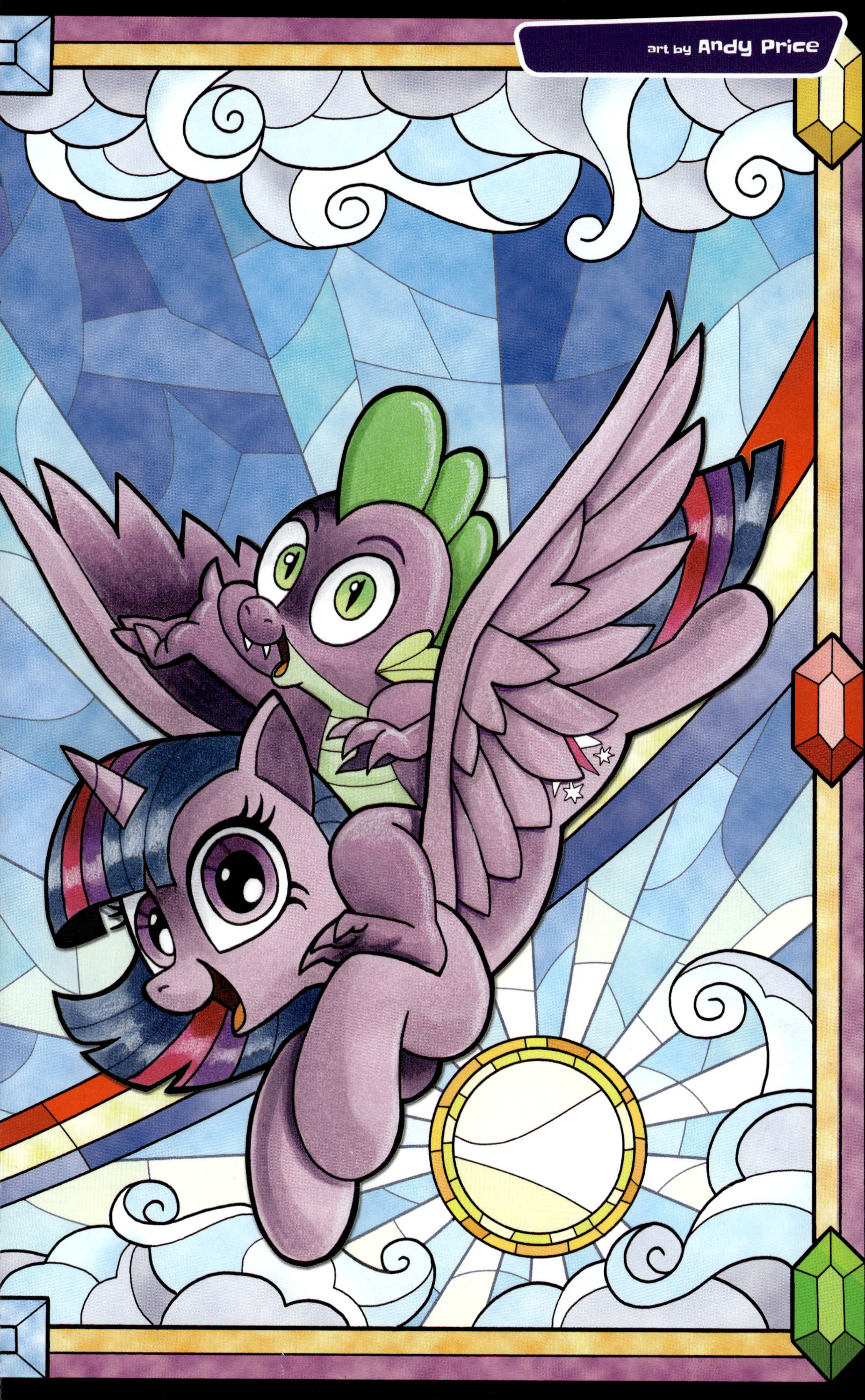
art by Andy Price

art by Lanna Souvanny

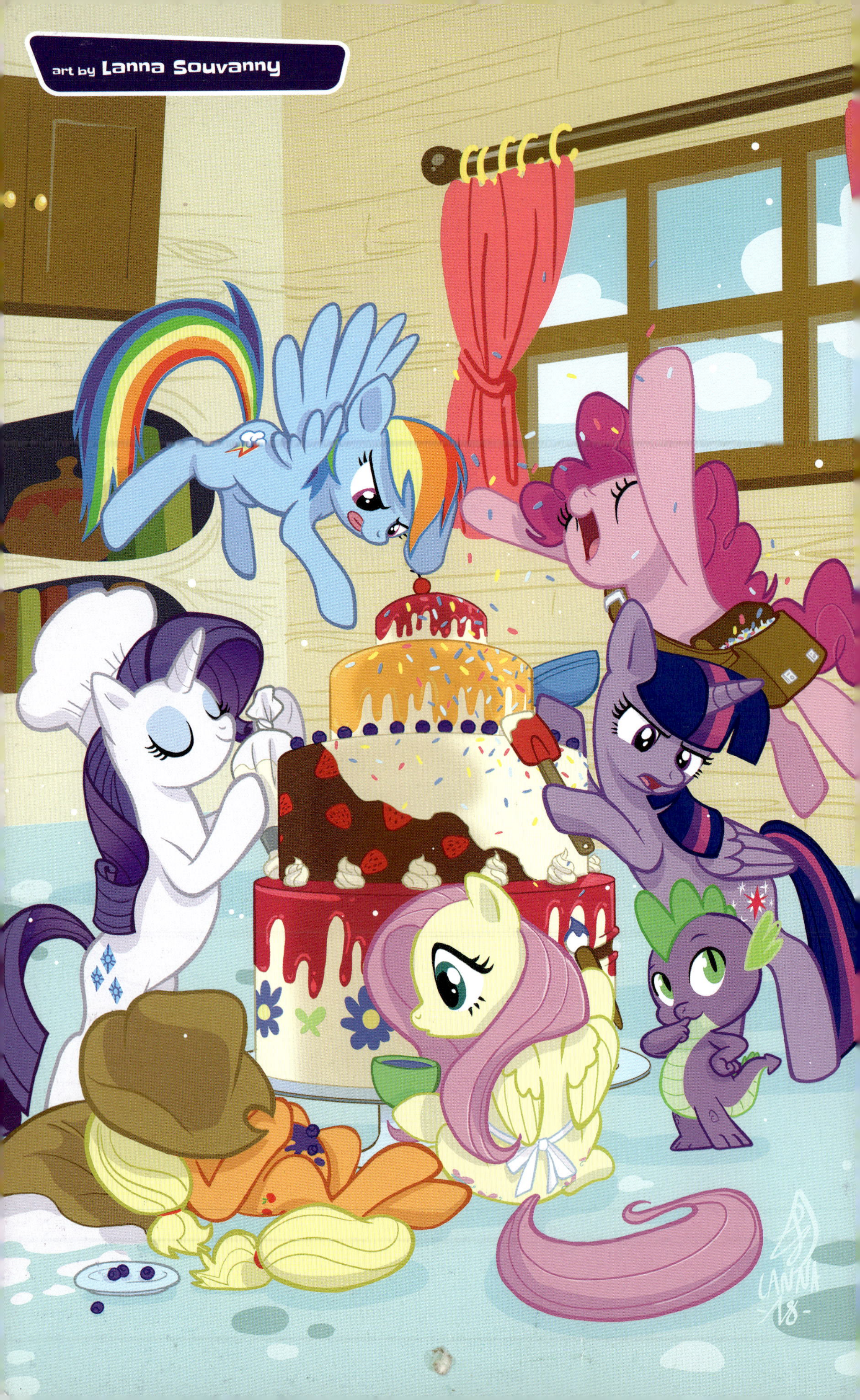
LANNA
-18-

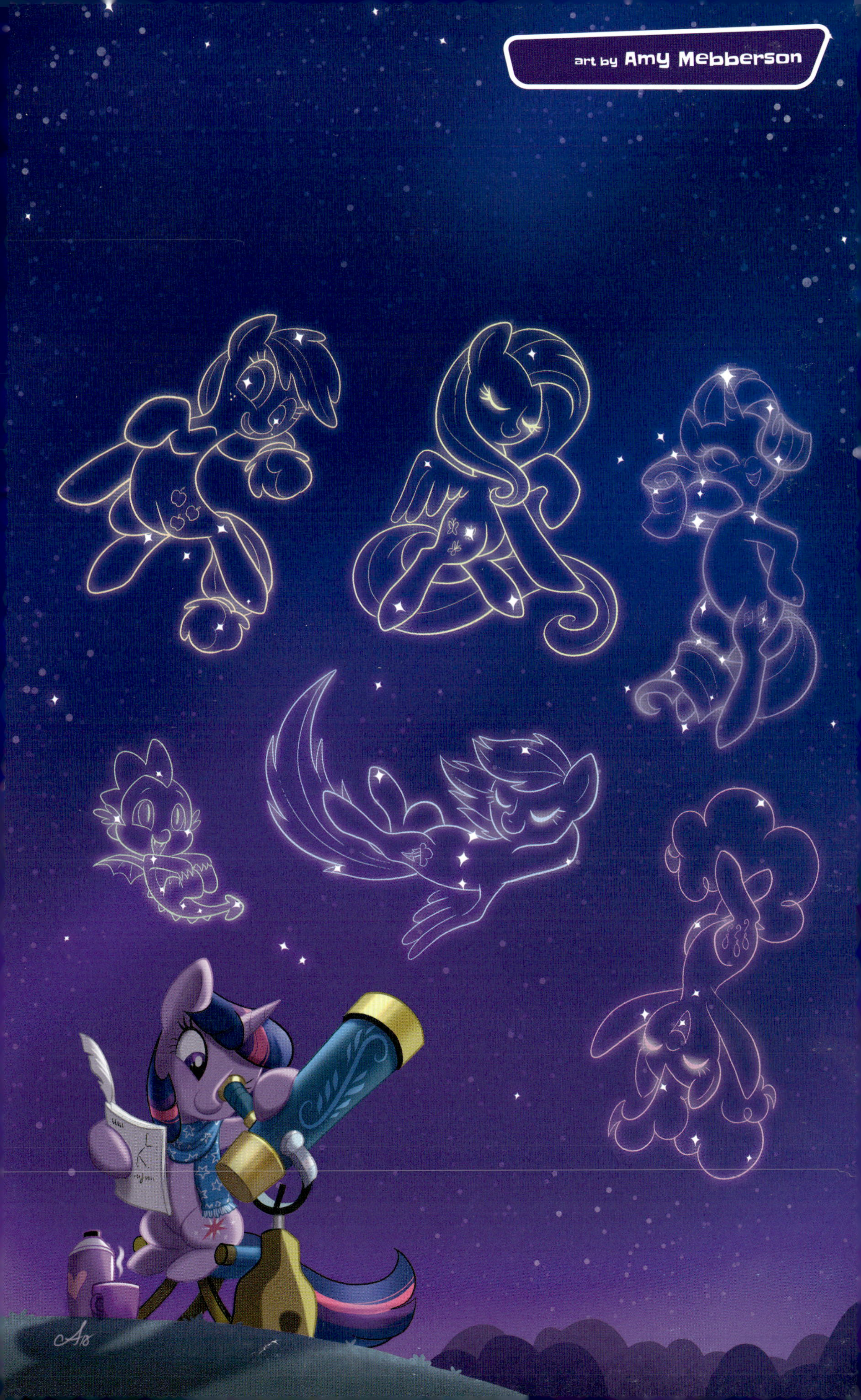
Ale

art by Amy Mebberson

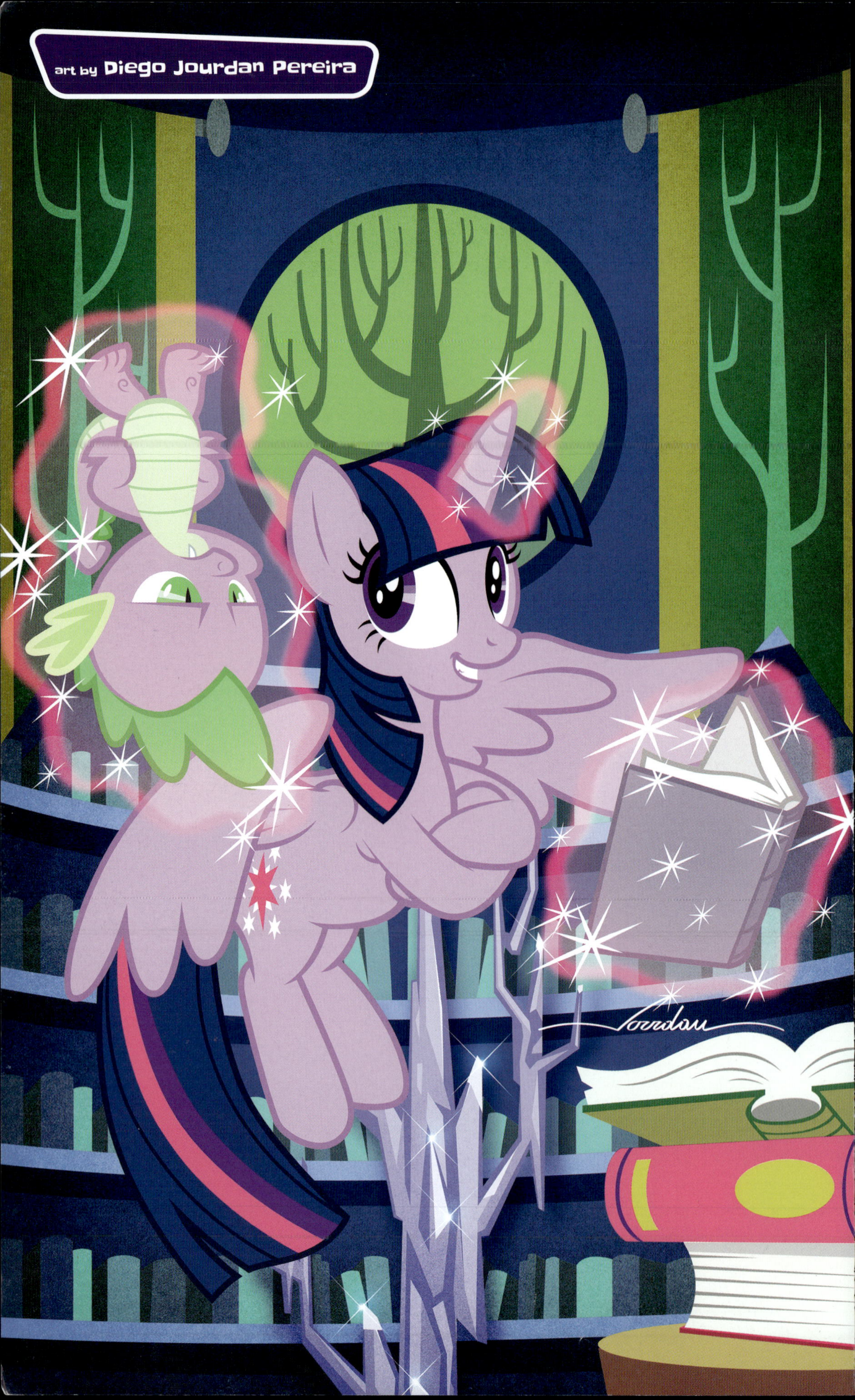
art by Diego Jourdan Pereira

art by Philip Murphy

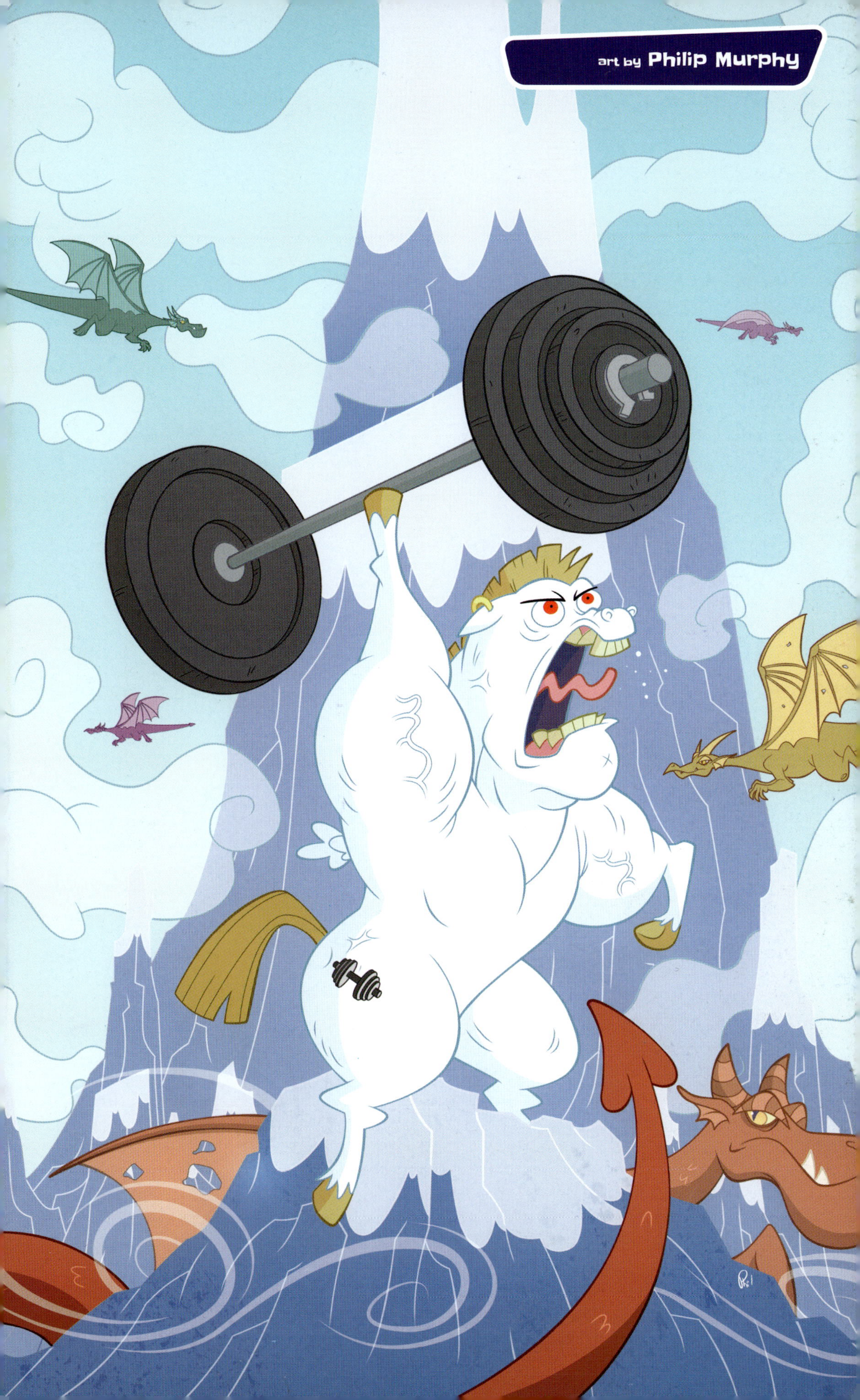

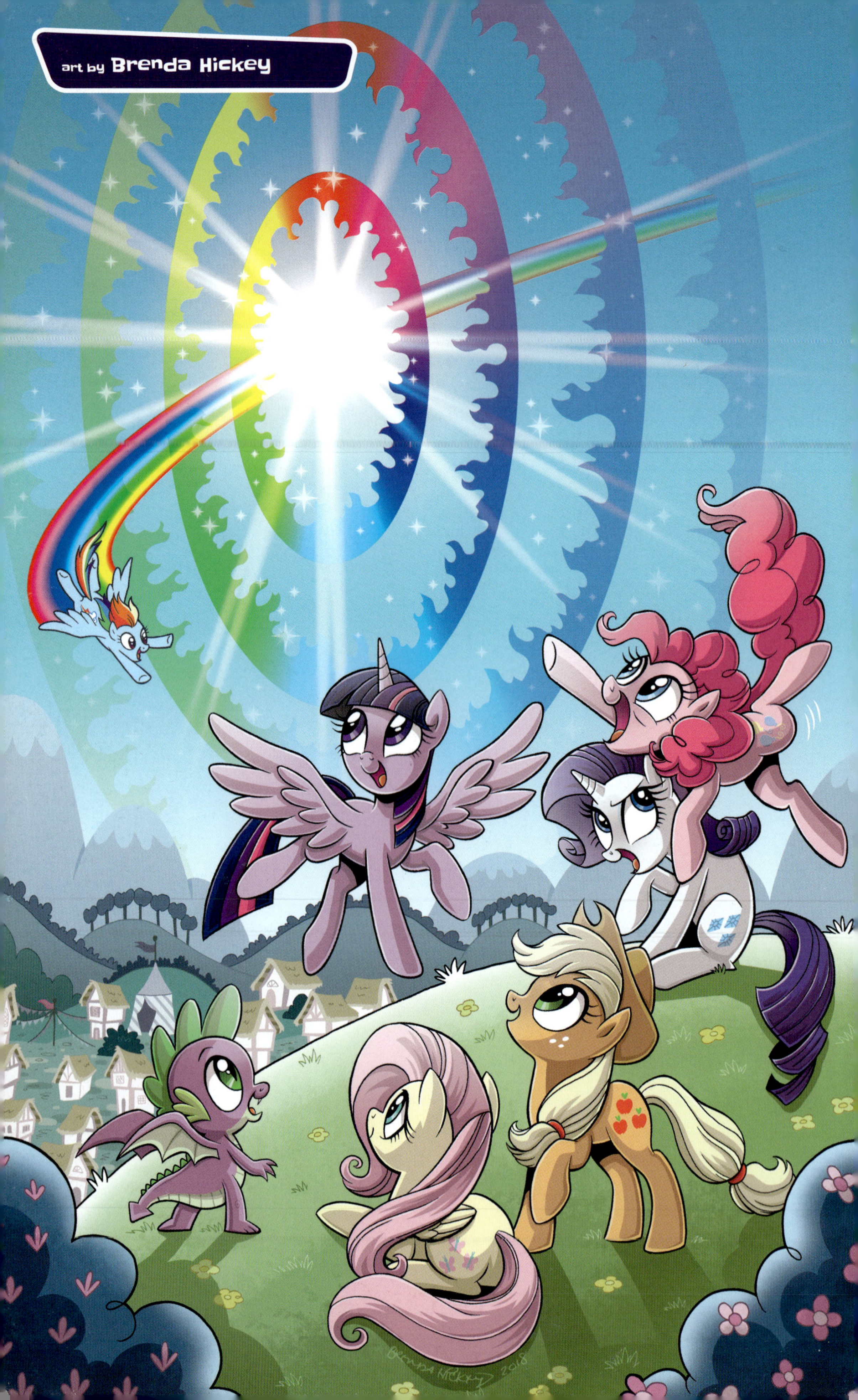
Brenda Hickey 2018

art by Brenda Hickey

art by Andy Price

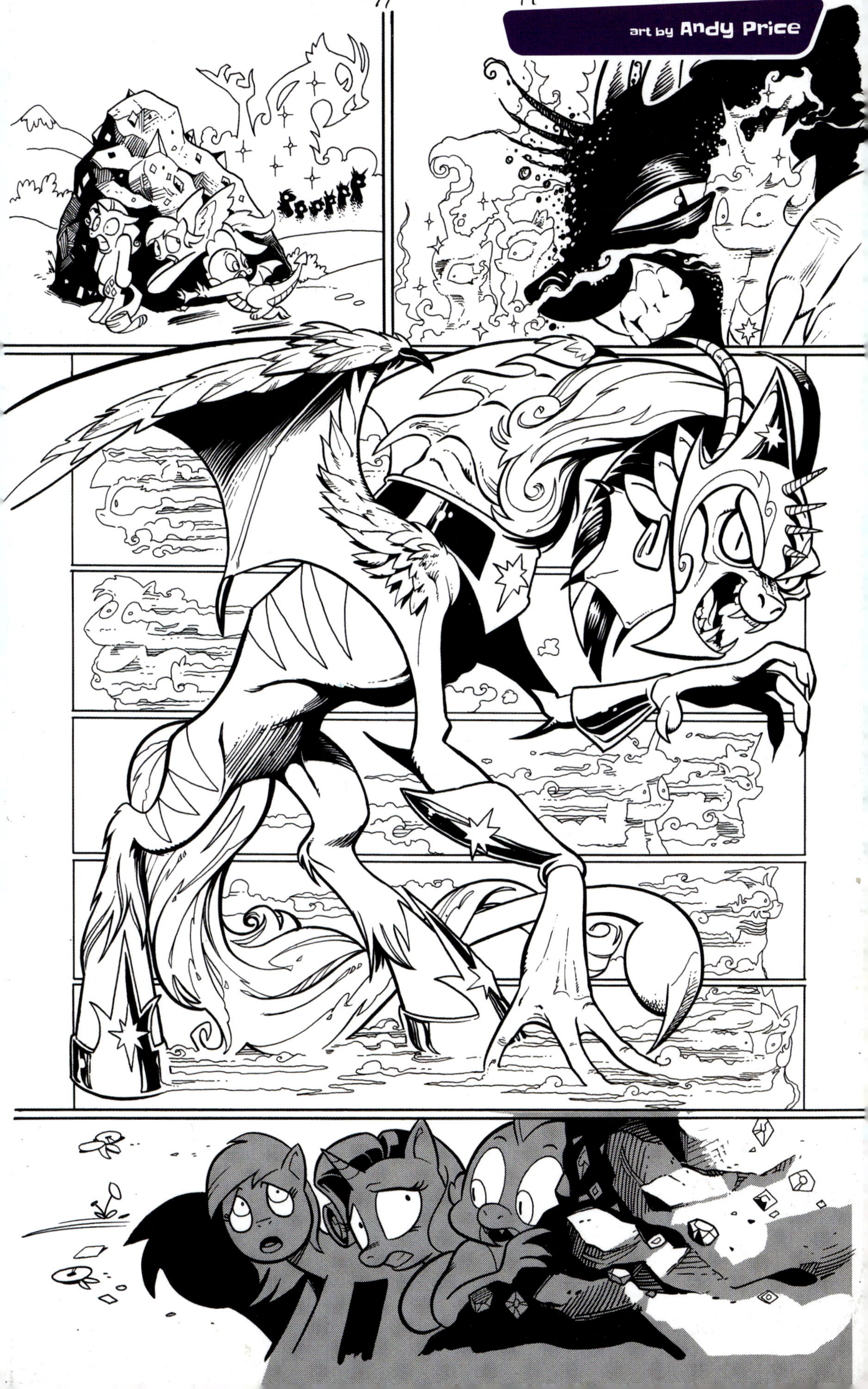

MLP 76 8

art by Andy Price

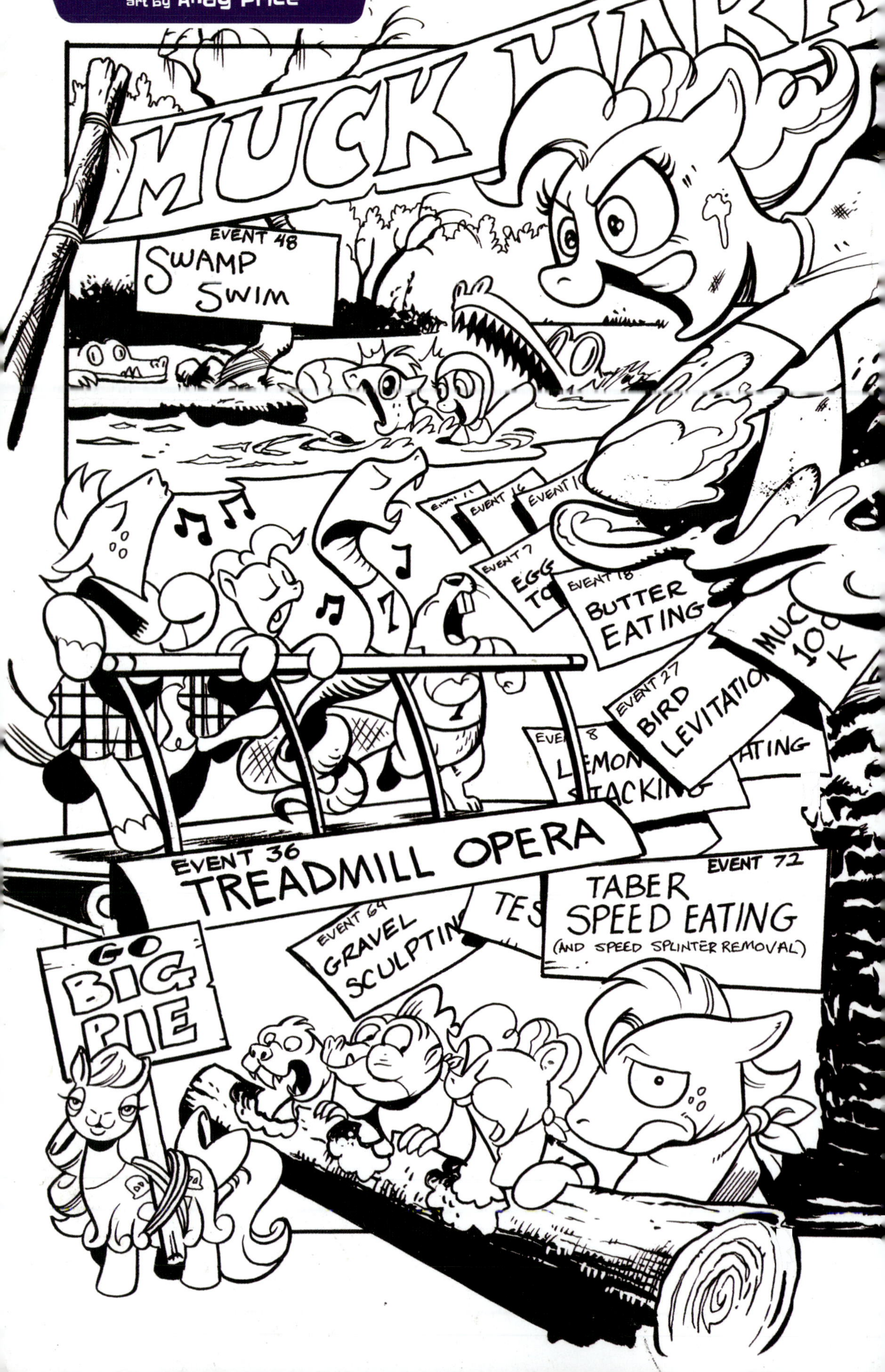

MUCK MARA
EVENT 48
SWAMP SWIM
EVENT 7
EGG
EVENT 18
BUTTER EATING
EVENT 27
BIRD LEVITATIO
EVENT 36
TREADMILL OPERA
EVENT 72
TABER SPEED EATING
(AND SPEED SPLINTER REMOVAL)
EVENT 64
GRAVEL SCULPTIN
GO BIG PIE

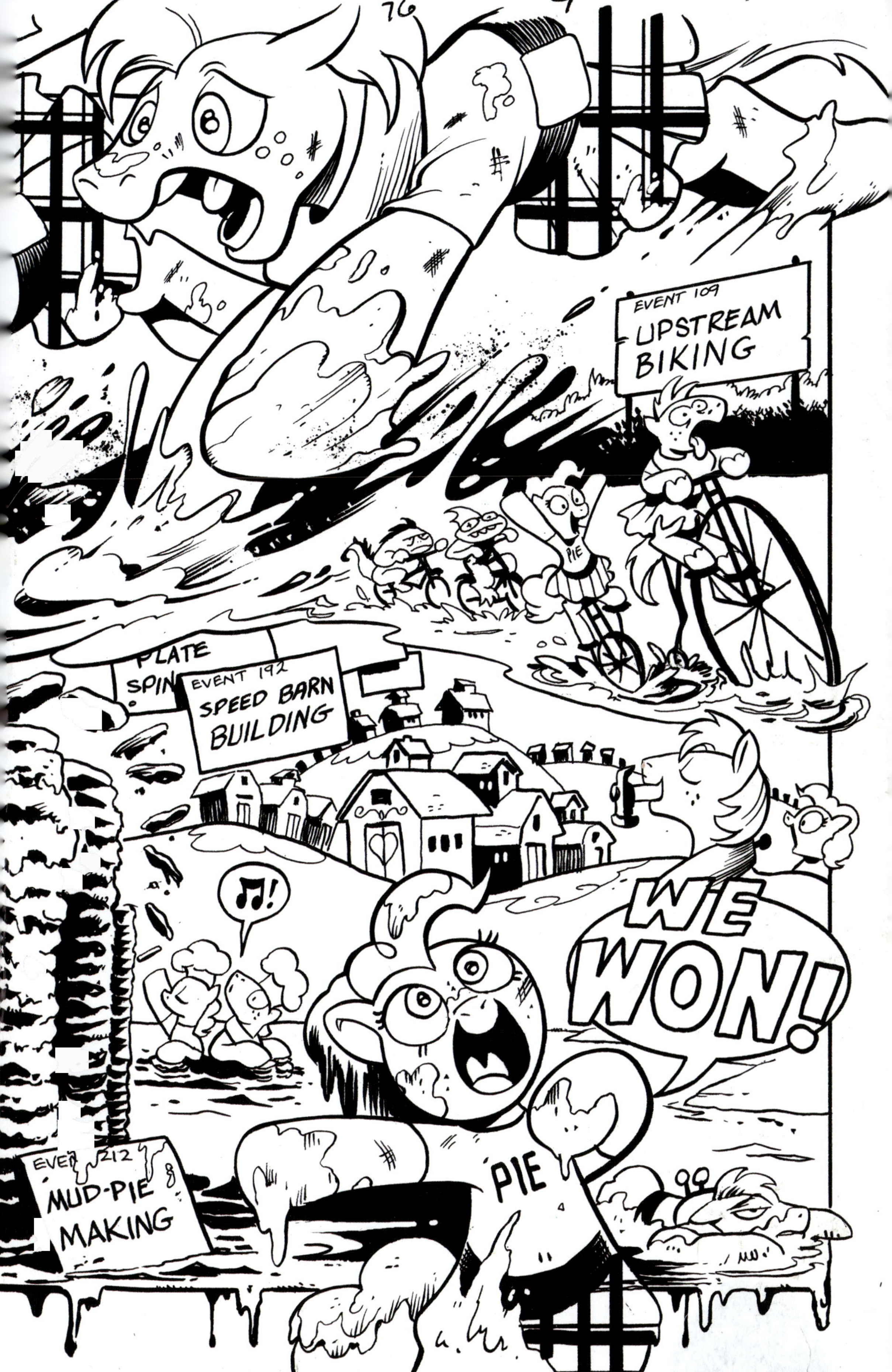
EVENT 109
UPSTREAM BIKING
PIE
PLATE SPIN
EVENT 192
SPEED BARN BUILDING
♫!
WE WON!
EVENT 212
MUD-PIE MAKING
PIE

my LITTLE PONY
Friendship is Magic

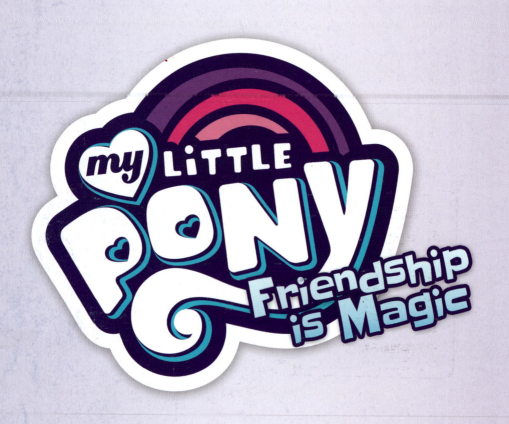